Books by
DANIELLE STEEL

Kaleidoscope	Remembrance
Fine Things	Palomino
Wanderlust	Love
Secrets .	The Ring
Family Album	Loving
Full Circle	To Love Again
Changes	Summer's End
Thurston House	Season of Passion
Crossings	The Promise
Once in a Lifetime	Now and Forever
A Perfect Stranger	Passion's Promise

A
PERFECT
STRANGER

Danielle Steel

A DELL BOOK

Published by
Dell Publishing Co., Inc.
1 Dag Hammarskjold Plaza
New York, New York 10017

Dell ® TM 681510, Dell Publishing Co., Inc.

ISBN: 0-440-16872-4

Printed in the United States of America

One Previous Edition
New Edition
-August 1985

10 9 8

WFH

To Nicholas,

*May you find what you want in life,
know it when you see it, and
have the good luck to get it—
and keep it!!!*

With all my love,

D.S.

A
PERFECT
STRANGER

CHAPTER 1

The garage door opened eerily, its mouth yawning expectantly, a large dark toad about to gobble an unsuspecting fly. From across the street a little boy watched it, fascinated. He loved watching the door open like that, knowing that the beautiful sports car would be around the corner in an instant. He waited, counting . . . five . . . six . . . seven. . . . Unknown to the man who had pressed the remote-control device on his dashboard, the little boy watched him come home every night. It was a favorite ritual and the boy was disappointed when the man in the black Porsche came home late or not at all. The boy stood there, in the shadows, counting . . . eleven . . . twelve . . . and then he saw it, a sleek black shadow speeding around the bend, and then in a smooth maneuver sliding into the garage. The unseen child stared hungrily at the beautiful black car for one more moment and then slowly went home, with visions of the black Porsche still dancing in his eyes.

Inside the garage Alexander Hale turned off the motor, and then sat there for a moment staring into the familiar darkness of his garage. For the hundredth time that day his mind drifted once again to Rachel. For the hundredth time he pushed the thought of her away from his mind. He sighed softly, picked up his briefcase, and got out of the car. A moment later the electronic device would automatically close the garage door. He let himself into the house through a back door in his garden and he stood in the downstairs hall of the pretty little Victorian town house, staring into the emptiness of the once cozy kitchen. There were copper pots hanging from a wrought-iron rack near the stove, but the cleaning lady hadn't shined them in ages, and there was no one else to give a damn. The plants, which hung thickly in front of the windows, were looking dry and lifeless, and he noticed, as he switched on the lights in the kitchen, that some of them had already died. He turned away then, glancing only briefly into the small wood-paneled dining room across the hall, and then walked slowly upstairs.

Now when he came home, he always used the garden entrance. It was less depressing than coming in through the main hall. Whenever he came through the front door in the evening, he somehow still expected her to be there. He expected to see her with the luscious pile of thick blond hair knotted on top of her head and the deceptively prim suits she wore to court. Rachel . . . dazzling lawyer . . . noble friend . . . intriguing female . . . until she hurt him . . . until she left . . . until their divorce, exactly two years before, to the day.

He had wondered on his way home from the office if he would always remember the day so exactly. Would some part of him call out in remembered pain on a given morning in October, for the rest of time? Would he always be reminded? It was strange really how both of their anniversaries had fallen on the same day. The anniversary of their marriage, and that of their divorce. Coincidence, Rachel had called it matter-of-factly. Ironic, he had said. How awful, his mother had said when she called him the night the papers came and found him blind drunk and laughing because he didn't want to cry.

Rachel. The thought of her still disturbed him. He knew it shouldn't after two years, but it did. . . . The golden hair and the eyes the color of the Atlantic Ocean just before a storm, dark gray, tinged with blue and green. The first time he had seen her had been as the attorney for the opposition in a case that had settled out of court. It had been a mighty battle though, and Joan of Arc couldn't have pleaded the case with more enthusiasm and flair. Alexander had watched her throughout the proceedings, fascinated and amused, and more attracted to her than he had been to any woman in his life. He had invited her to dinner that night, and she had insisted on paying her half of the check. She didn't "corrupt professional relationships," she had told him with an arch little smile that half made him want to slap her, and half made him want to tear off her clothes. She had been so goddamn beautiful, and so goddamn smart.

The memory of her made him knit his brows as he

walked past the empty living room. She had taken all the living room furniture with her to New York. She had left the rest of their furniture to Alex, but the big double parlor on the main floor of the pretty little Victorian house they had bought together had been stripped bare. Sometimes he wondered if he hadn't bought new furniture just so he could remember, so he could resent her, each time he walked past the empty living room to the front door. But now, as he walked upstairs, he didn't see the emptiness around him. His mind was a million miles away, thinking back to the days before she left him, thinking about what they had and had not shared. They had shared hope and wit and laughter and their professions, their bed, this house, and very little else.

Alex had wanted children, to fill the bedrooms on the top floor with noise and laughter. Rachel had wanted to go into politics or get a job with an important law firm in New York. The politics she had mentioned vaguely when she met him. It would have been natural for her. Her father was a powerful man in Washington and had once been governor of their home state. It was something else she had in common with Alex, whose sister was a congresswoman in New York. Rachel always admired her greatly, and she and Alex's sister, Kay, had rapidly become fast friends. But it wasn't politics that took Rachel away from Alex. It was the other half of her dream, the law firm in New York. In the end it had taken her two years to pick up stakes and leave him. He ran the finger of his mind over the wound now. It no longer smarted as it once had. But at first it had hurt him more than anything in his life.

She was beautiful, brilliant, successful, dynamic,

amusing . . . but there had always been something missing, something tender and gentle and kind. Those were not words one used to describe Rachel. And she had wanted more out of life than just loving Alexander, more than just being an attorney in San Francisco and someone's wife. She had been exactly twenty-nine years old when they met, and she had never been married. She'd been too busy for that, she told him, too busy chasing her life's goals. She had promised herself when she left law school that by the time she was thirty she would have made it "big." What does that mean? he had asked her. A hundred thousand a year was the answer, and she didn't even blink. For an instant he had laughed at her. Until he saw the look in her eyes. She meant it. And she'd get it. Her whole life was geared to that kind of success. Success measured by that kind of yardstick, dollar bills and important cases, no matter who was destroyed in the process. Before she left for New York, Rachel had walked over half of San Francisco, and even Alex had finally let himself see what she was. She was cold and ruthless and ambitious and she stopped at nothing to reach her goals.

Four months after they were married, a spot opened up in one of the most prestigious law firms in town. At first Alex was impressed that she was even being considered. She was, after all, a fairly young woman, and a young attorney, but it didn't take long to figure out that she was willing to use every ugly maneuver she could to get the job. And she did, and she got it. For two years Alex tried to forget what he'd seen her pull to get the job. He told himself that she only used tactics like that in business, and then the final crunch came. She was made a full partner and offered a spot in the firm's New York office. This time it was more than a hundred-thousand-dollar-a-year job. And Rachel Hale was only thirty-one. Alexander watched with horror and fascination as she wrestled with the choice. The choice was simple, and as far as Alex was concerned, it shouldn't have been a choice at all. New York or San Francisco. Alexander or not. In the end, she told him gently, it was just too good an opportunity to pass up. "But it didn't have to change their relationship." She could still fly home to San Francisco almost every weekend, or of course if Alex wanted to . . . he could give up his own law practice and come East with her.

"And do what? Prepare your briefs?" He had stared at her in hurt and fury. "So where does that leave me, Rachel?" He had stared at her after she had announced her decision to take the job in New York. He had wanted it to be different, wanted her to tell him that she wouldn't take it, that he mattered more. But that hadn't been Rachel's style, any more than it would have been Alex's sister's. Once he was willing to face it, he realized that he had known one other woman like Rachel before. His sister, Kay, had pushed her way to what she wanted, storming over obstacles and devouring or destroying those who inadvertently crossed her path. The only difference was that Kay did it in politics and Rachel in law.

It was easier to understand, and respect, a woman like his mother. Charlotte Brandon had somehow successfully managed both children and a career. For twenty-five years she had been one of the country's best-selling authors, yet she had managed Alex and his sister, stayed close to them, loved them, and given them her all. When her husband had died when Alex was a baby, she took a part-time job doing research for a newspaper column, and eventually ghostwrote it completely, while, in whatever spare time she had, she sat up until the wee hours writing her first book. The rest was history, chronicled on the book jackets of the nineteen books she had written and sold in the millions over the years. Her career had been an accident created by need. But whatever her reasons, she had always somehow managed to treat what had happened as a special gift, as something she could share and enjoy with her children, not as something she loved more than she loved them. Charlotte Brandon was truly a remarkable woman, but her daughter was different, angry, jealous, compulsive, she had none of her mother's gentleness or warmth or ability to give. And in time Alex learned that neither did his wife.

When Rachel left for New York, she had insisted that she didn't want to divorce him. For a while she had even tried to commute, but with their separate work loads at opposite ends of the country, their weekends together became less and less frequent. It was hopeless, as she eventually admitted to Alex, and for two endless weeks he had actually considered closing his own lucrative practice and moving to New York. Hell, what did it mean to him? Maybe it wasn't worth hanging on to, if it meant losing his wife. At four o'clock one morning he made the decision: He would close his practice and go. Exhausted, but feeling hopeful, he reached for the phone to call her. It was seven in the morning in New York. But it wasn't Rachel who answered. It was a man with a deep honey-smooth voice. "Mrs. Hale?" He sounded blank for a moment. "Oh, Miss Patterson." Rachel Patterson. Alex hadn't realized that she had begun her new life in New York under her old name. But he hadn't realized either that along with the new job she had begun a whole new way of life. There was very little she could say to him that morning, and he listened to her voice at the other end with tears in his eyes. She called him back later from her office.

"What can I say, Alex? I'm sorry . . ." Sorry? For leaving? For having an affair? What was she sorry for? Or was she just sorry for him, poor pathetic bastard that he was, sitting alone out in San Francisco.

"Is there any point trying to work it out?" He had been willing to try, but at least this time she was honest.

"No, Alex, I'm afraid not." They had talked for a few more minutes, and then finally hung up the phone. There was nothing left to say, except to their own attorneys. The following week Alex filed for divorce. It all went smoothly. "Perfectly civilized," as Rachel had said. There had been no problems at all, yet it had shaken Alex to the very roots of his being.

And for an entire year he had felt as though someone near and dear to him had died.

Possibly it was himself he mourned. He felt as though part of him had been put away in crates and boxes, like the living room furniture that had been shipped to New York. He functioned perfectly normally: he ate; he slept; he went on dates; he swam; he played tennis, racquetball, squash; he went to parties; he traveled; and his law practice boomed. But some essential part of him was missing. And he knew it, even if no one else did. He had had nothing, except his body, to give to a woman in more than two years.

As he walked upstairs to his study the silence in the house became suddenly unbearable and all he wanted was to run. Lately it was something that happened to him often, that overpowering urge to get out, to get away from the emptiness and the silence. It was only now after two years without her that the numbness was wearing off. It was as though the bandages were finally peeling away, and what was left beneath was lonely and raw.

Alex changed into jeans, sneakers, and an old parka, and thumped rapidly back downstairs, one long, powerful hand lightly touching the banister, his dark hair slightly rumpled, his blue eyes intense as he slammed the door behind him and turned right until he reached Divisadero, where he began running slowly up the steep hill to Broadway, where at last he stopped and turned to look at the breathtaking view. Beneath him the bay shone like satin in the twilight, the hills were veiled in mist, and the lights of Marin sparkled like diamonds and rubies and emeralds just across the bay.

When he reached the stately mansions on Broadway, he turned right and began to walk toward the Presidio, glancing alternately at the huge impressive houses and the tranquil beauty of the bay. The houses themselves were among the finest in San Francisco. These were the two or three most expensive residential blocks in the city, boasting brick palaces and Tudor mansions, remarkable gardens, breathtaking views, and towering trees. One saw not a soul walking and heard not a sound from the neat row of houses, though one could easily imagine the tinkle of crystal, the ring of fine silver, the liveried servants, and gentlemen and ladies in dinner jackets and dresses of satin or silk. Alex always smiled to himself at the images he painted. Somehow they made him less lonely than what he imagined as he drifted past the smaller houses on the less impressive streets he frequently walked. There he always envisioned men with their arms around their women, with smiling children and puppies playing in the kitchen, or stretched out in front of warm, crackling fires. In the big houses there was nothing that he wanted. That was a world he did not aspire to, though he had often been in houses like those. What Alex wanted for himself was something very different, something that he and Rachel had never had.

It was difficult to imagine being in love anymore, caring deeply about someone, difficult to imagine looking into someone's eyes and wanting to explode with joy. There had been none of that for Alex in so long that he had almost forgotten what it could feel like, and sometimes he wasn't even sure that he wanted that anymore. He was tired of the bustling career women, more interested in their salaries and how quickly they'd get their next promotion than in getting married and having kids. He wanted an old-fashioned woman, a miracle, a rarity, a gem. And there were none. There had been nothing but expensive fakes in Alex's life for almost two years. And what he wanted was the real thing, a perfect, flawless, remarkable diamond, and he doubted very seriously that there were any around. But one thing he did know and that was that he wasn't going to settle for anything less than his dream. And he didn't want another woman like Rachel. That much he knew too.

He put her out of his thoughts again now and he stood there, looking at the view from the Baker Street stairs. They were carved steeply into the hillside joining Broadway to Vallejo Street below, and he enjoyed the view and the cool breeze as he decided to go no further and sit down on the top step. As he unraveled his long legs in front of him, he smiled at the city he had adopted. Maybe he'd never find the right woman. Maybe he'd never marry again. So what? He had a good life, a nice house, a law practice that was both enjoyable and successful. Maybe he didn't need more than that. Maybe he had no right to ask for more.

He let his gaze take in the pastel-colored houses of the marina, the little gingerbread Victorians in Cow Hollow, not unlike his own, the rounded Grecian splendor of the Palace of Fine Arts well below him, and then, as his eyes left the dome Maybeck had created half a century earlier, he found himself looking down at the rooftops below him, and then suddenly there she was. A woman sitting huddled at the bottom of the steps, almost as though she were carved there, a statue like those on the Palace of Fine Arts, only this one far more delicate, with her head bowed and her profile silhouetted by the light across the street. He found himself sitting very still and staring, as though she were a sculpture, a statue, a work of art that someone had abandoned there, a handsome marble in the form of a woman, so skillfully fashioned that it seemed almost real.

She did not move and he watched her for almost five minutes, and then, sitting up very straight, she took a long, deep breath of the fresh night air, and exhaled it slowly as though she had had a very hard day. There was a cloud of pale fur coat around her, and Alex could see her face and her features come clear in the dark. There was something unusual about her that made him want to see more. He found himself sitting there, unable to look away. It was the oddest feeling Alex could remember, sitting there, staring down at her in the dim light from the street-lamps, feeling pulled by her. Who was she? What was she doing there? Her presence seemed to touch him to the very core of his being as he sat very still, want-ing to know more.

Her skin looked very white in the darkness, and her hair was shiny and dark, swept softly into a knot at the nape of her neck. Her hair gave the impression of being very long, and held in place perhaps by only one or two well-placed pins. For a moment he had an insane desire to run down the steps toward her, to touch her, and to take her in his arms and loosen the dark hair. And almost as though she sensed what he was thinking, she looked up suddenly from her rev-erie, as though pulled back from a very great distance by a firm hand. She turned toward him, and started, her face turned up toward where he sat. And what he saw as he looked down at her was the most beautiful face he had ever seen. A face, as he had first sus-pected, with the perfect proportions of a work of art, tiny, delicate features, a flawless face filled with enormous dark eyes and a gently curving mouth. But her eyes were what captivated him as they looked at him—unseeing eyes that seemed to fill her entire face, eyes that seemed to be filled with immeasurable sor-row, and in the lamplight now he could see two shin-ing rivers of tears on the white marble cheeks. For one endless instant their eyes met, and Alex felt as though every ounce of his being reached out to the unknown beauty with the big eyes and dark hair. She looked so vulnerable and so lost as she sat there, and then, as though embarrassed by what she had let him see even briefly, she quickly bowed her head. For an instant Alex didn't move, and then suddenly he felt pulled toward her again, as though he had to go to her. He watched her, trying to decide what to do, and in an instant she stood up, enveloped in fur. It was a lynx coat that drifted about her like a cloud. Her eyes flew to Alex's again, but this time for only an instant, and then, as though she had been only an apparition, she seemed to walk into a hedge and disappear.

For a long moment Alex stared at where she had been, rooted to the spot where he sat. It had all happened so quickly. Then suddenly he stood and ran quickly down the steps toward where she had sat. He saw a narrow pathway leading to a heavy door. He could only guess at a garden beyond it, and there was no way of knowing to which house it belonged. It could have been any one of several. So the mystery ended there. For an impotent moment Alex found himself wanting to knock on the door she had entered. Perhaps she was sitting in the hidden garden behind the locked door. There was an instant of desperation, knowing that he would never see her again. And then, feeling foolish, he reminded himself that she was only a stranger. He stared at the door for a long pensive moment, and then turned slowly and walked back up the stairs.

CHAPTER 2

Even as Alex put the key in his front door, he was
haunted by the face of the crying woman. Who was
she? Why had she been crying? From which house
had she come? He sat on the narrow circular staircase
in his front hallway staring into the empty living room
and watching the moonlight reflected on the bare
wood floor. He had never seen a woman so lovely.
It was a face that could easily haunt one for a lifetime
and he realized as he sat there without moving that, if
not for a lifetime, he would certainly remember her
for a very long time. He didn't even hear the phone
when it rang a few minutes later. He was still lost in
thought, pondering the vision he had seen. But when
he finally heard the phone, he ran to the first landing
with a few quick bounds and into his den in time to
dig the phone out from beneath a stack of papers on
his desk.

"Hello, Alex." Instantly there was a moment of silent
tension. It was his sister, Kay.

"What's up?" Which meant what did she want. She never called anyone unless she wanted or needed something.

"Nothing special. Where were you? I've been calling for the last half hour. The girl working late in your office told me you were going straight home." She was always like that. She wanted what she wanted when she wanted it, whether it suited anyone else or not.

"I was out for a walk."

"At this hour?" She sounded suspicious. "Why? Something wrong?" He sighed softly to himself. For years now his sister had exhausted him. There was so little give, so little softness to her. She was all angles—cold and hard and sharp. She reminded him sometimes of a very sharp crystal object one would put on a desk. Pretty to look at, but not something one would ever want to pick up or touch. And it had been obvious for years that her husband felt the same way.

"No, nothing's wrong, Kay." But he also had to admit that for a woman as indifferent as she was to other people's feelings, she had an uncanny knack for sensing when he was down or out of sorts. "I just needed some air. I had a long day." And then, attempting to soften the conversation and turn her attention slightly away from him, "Don't you ever go for a walk, Kay?"

"In New York? You must be crazy. You could die here just from breathing."

"Not to mention mugging and rape." He smiled gently into the phone and he could sense her smile too. Kay Willard wasn't a woman who smiled often. She was too intense, too hurried, too harassed, and too seldom amused. "To what do I owe the honor of this phone call?" He sat back in his chair and looked at the view as he waited patiently for an answer.

For a long time Kay would call about Rachel. Kay had stayed in touch with her ex-sister-in-law for obvious reasons. The old governor was someone she wanted to keep in her court. And if she could have talked Alex into going back to Rachel, the old man would have loved it. Provided, of course, that she could have convinced Rachel of how desperately unhappy Alex was without her and how much it would mean to him if she'd only give it another try. And Kay wasn't above that kind of pushing. She had already tried to maneuver a meeting between them several times when Alex had come to New York. But even if Rachel had been willing, of which Kay was never entirely sure, it had become clear over the years that Alex was not. "So, Congresswoman Willard?"

"Nothing special. I just wondered when you were coming to New York."

"Why?"

"Don't be so blunt, for chrissake. I just thought I'd have a few people over for dinner."

"Like who?" Alex saw her coming and he grinned. She was amazing, his sister the steamroller. You had to say one thing for her, she never quit.

"All right, Alex, don't get so defensive."

"Who's defensive? I just wanted to know whom you want to have with me to dinner. What's wrong with that? Unless of course there happens to be someone on your guest list who might just make us all a little uncomfortable. Should I guess initials, Kay, would that make it easier?"

She had to laugh in spite of herself. "All right, all right, I get the message. But for chrissake, Alex, I ran into her the other day on a plane back from D.C. and she looks just great."

"She should. On her salary so would you."

"Thank you, dear."

"Anytime."

"Did you know that she's been asked to run for councilwoman?"

"No." There was a long silence. "But I'm not really surprised. Are you?"

"No." And then his sister sighed loudly. "Sometimes I wonder if you realize what you gave up there."

"I certainly do, and I'm grateful every day of my life. I don't want to be married to a politician, Kay. That's an honor that should be reserved only for men like George."

"What the hell does that mean?"

"He's so busy with his practice, I'm sure he doesn't even notice when you're in Washington for three weeks. Me, I'd notice." And he didn't tell her that her daughter noticed too. He knew because he talked to Amanda at great length whenever he went to New York. He took her out to lunch, or dinner, or for long walks. He knew his niece better than her own parents. Sometimes he thought Kay didn't give a damn. "By the way, how's Amanda?"

"All right, I guess."

"What do you mean, 'you guess'?" The criticism in his tone was easy to read. "Haven't you seen her?"

"Jesus Christ, I just got off the fucking plane from D.C. What do you want from me, Alex?"

"Not much. What you do is none of my business. What you do to her is something else."

"That's none of your business either."

"Isn't it? Then whose business is it, Kay? George's?

Does he notice that you never spend ten minutes with your daughter? He certainly doesn't."

"She's sixteen years old, for chrissake, she doesn't need a baby-sitter anymore, Alex."

"No, but she needs a mother and a father desperately—every young girl does.

"I can't help that. I'm in politics. You know how demanding that is."

"Yeah." He shook his head slowly, and that was what she wanted to wish on him. A life with Rachel "Patterson," a life that would relegate him to being the First Man. "Anything else?" He didn't want to talk to her anymore. He'd had enough of listening to her in just five minutes.

"I'm running for the Senate next year."

"Congratulations." His voice was flat.

"Don't get too excited."

"I'm not. I was thinking about Mandy, and what that might mean for her."

"If I win, it'll mean she's a senator's daughter, that's what." Kay sounded suddenly vicious and Alex wanted to slap her face.

"Do you think she really cares about that, Kay?"

"Probably not. The kid has her head so high in the clouds, she probably wouldn't give a shit if I ran for President." For a moment Kay sounded sad and Alex shook his head.

"That's not what matters, Kay. We're all proud of you, we love you, but there's more than that. . . ." How could he tell her? How could he explain? She cared about nothing except her career, her work.

"I don't think any of you understand what this means to me, Alex, how hard I've worked for it, how far I've come. It's been killing, and I've made it, and all you do is bitch about what kind of mother I am. And our dear mother is worse. And George is too busy cutting people open to remember if I'm congresswoman or mayor. It's a little discouraging, kiddo, to say the least."

"I'm sure it is. But sometimes people get hurt by careers like yours."

"That's to be expected."

"Is it? Is that what it's all about?"

"Maybe." She sounded tired. "I don't have all the answers. I wish I did. And what about you? What's happening in your life these days?"

"Nothing much. Work."

"Are you happy?"

"Sometimes."

"You ought to go back to Rachel."

"At least you get to the point quickly. I don't want to, Kay. Besides, what makes you think she'd want me?"

"She said she'd like to see you."

"Oh, Christ." He sighed into the phone. "You never give up, do you? Why don't you just marry her father and leave me in peace? That would get you the same results, wouldn't it?"

This time Kay laughed. "Maybe."

"Do you really expect me to run my love life to further your career?" The very idea amused him, but underneath the outrageousness of it, he knew there was a grain of truth. "I think what I love best about you, big sister, is your unlimited nerve."

"It gets me where I want to go, little brother."

"I'm sure it does, but not this time, love."

"No little dinner with Rachel?"

"Nope. But if you see her again, give her my best."

Something in his guts tugged again at the mention of her name. He didn't love her anymore, but now and then just hearing about her still hurt.

"I'll do that. And think about it. I can always throw something together when you're in New York."

"With any luck at all you'll be in Washington and too busy to see me."

"Could be. When are you coming East?"

"Probably in a couple of weeks. I've got a client to see in New York. I'm cocounsel for him on a fairly big case out here."

"I'm impressed."

"Are you?" His eyes narrowed as he glanced out at the view. "Why? Will it sound good in your campaign material? I think Mother's readers will get you more votes than I will, don't you?" There was a touch of irony in his voice. "Unless of course I have the good sense to remarry Rachel."

"Just don't get into any trouble."

"Have I ever?" He sounded amused.

"No, but if I run for the Senate, it'll be a tight race. I'm running against that morality maniac, and if anyone even remotely related to me does something unsavory, I'll be up shit creek."

"Be sure you tell Mother." He said it in jest but she responded immediately with a serious voice.

"I already have."

"Are you kidding?" He laughed at the very thought of his elegant, long-legged, couture-clad, white-haired mother doing anything unsuitable that might jeopardize Kay's bid for a seat in the Senate, or anywhere else.

"I am not kidding, I mean it. I can't afford any problems right now. No nonsense, no scandal."

"What a shame."

"What does that mean?"

"I don't know . . . I was thinking of having an affair with this ex-hooker who just got out of jail."

"Very funny. I'm serious."

"Unfortunately I think you are. Anyway, you can give me my list of instructions when I come to New York. I'll try to behave myself until then."

"Do that, and let me know when you're going to be here."

"Why? So you can arrange a blind date with Rachel? I'm afraid, Congresswoman Willard, that even for the sake of your career I wouldn't do that."

"You're a fool."

"Maybe so." But he didn't think so anymore. He didn't think so at all, and after the phone call with Kay ended, he found himself staring out the window and thinking not of Rachel, but of the woman he had seen on the steps. With his eyes closed, he could still see her, the perfectly carved profile, the huge eyes, and the delicate mouth. He had never seen a woman so beautiful or so haunting. And he sat there at his desk, with his eyes closed, thinking of her, and then with a sigh, he shook his head and opened his eyes again and stood up. It was ridiculous to be dreaming of a total stranger. And then feeling foolish, he laughed softly and brushed her from his mind. There was no point falling in love with a perfect stranger. But he found, as he went downstairs to make something for dinner, that he had to remind himself of that again and again.

CHAPTER 3

Sunlight flooded into the room and shimmered on the beige silk bedspread and identically upholstered chairs. It was a large handsome room with long French windows that looked out over the bay. From the boudoir, which adjoined the bedroom, one could see the Golden Gate Bridge. There was a white marble fireplace in each room, and there were carefully selected French paintings, and a priceless Chinese vase stood in a corner in a Louis XV inlaid vitrine. In front of the windows was a handsome Louis XV desk, which would have dwarfed any room except this one. It was beautiful and enormous and sterile and cold. Next to the boudoir, there was also a small wood-paneled room filled with books in English and Spanish and French. The books were the soul of her existence, and it was here that Raphaella stood quietly for a moment looking out at the bay. It was nine o'clock in the morning and she was wearing a perfectly sculptured black suit molded to her form, showing off her

graceful perfection subtly yet with immense style. The
suit had been made for her in Paris, like most of her
clothes, except those she bought in Spain. She rarely
bought clothes in San Francisco. She almost never
went out. In San Francisco she was an invisible person, a name people rarely mentioned and never saw.
For most of them it would have been difficult to asso-
ciate a face with the name of Mrs. John Henry Phillips, and certainly not this face. It would have been
difficult to imagine this perfect snow-white beauty
with the huge black eyes. When she had married John
Henry, one reporter had written that she looked like a
fairy-tale princess, and had then gone on to explain
that in many ways she was. But the eyes that gazed
out at the bay on an October morning were not those
of a fairy-tale princess, they were those of a very
lonely young woman, locked in a very lonely world.

"Your breakfast is ready, Mrs. Phillips." A maid in a
crisp white uniform stood in the doorway, her announcement more like a command, Raphaella thought,
but she always felt that way about John Henry's servants. She had felt that way, too, in her father's house
in Paris and her grandfather's house in Spain. It always seemed to her that it was the servants who
gave the orders, when to get up, when to get
ready, when to eat lunch, when to eat dinner.
"Madam is served" announced dinner in her father's
house in Paris. But what if Madam didn't want to be
served? What if Madam only wanted a sandwich, sitting on the floor in front of the fire? Or a dish of ice
cream for breakfast instead of toast and poached
eggs? The very idea made her smile as she walked
back to her bedroom and looked around. Everything
was ready. Her bags were stacked neatly in the cor-

ner—they were all glove soft in a chocolate-colored suede—and there was a large tote bag in which Raphaella could carry some gifts for her mother and aunt and cousins, her jewelry, and something to read on the plane.

As she looked at her luggage she felt no thrill of pleasure to be going on a trip. She almost never felt a thrill of pleasure anymore. There was none left in her life. There was an endless strip of highway, heading toward a destination both unseen and unknown, and about which Raphaella no longer cared. She knew that each day would be just like the day before. Each day she would do exactly what she had for almost seven years, except for the four weeks in the summer when she went to Spain, and the few days before that when she went to Paris to see her father. And there were occasional trips to join her Spanish relatives for a few days in New York. It seemed years now since she had last been there, since she had left Europe, since she had become John Henry's wife. It was all so different now than it had been at first.

It had all happened like a fairy tale. Or a merger. There was a little bit of both in the tale. The marriage of the Banque Malle in Paris, Milan, Madrid, and Barcelona to the Phillips Bank of California and New York. Both empires consisted of investment banks of major international proportions. And her father's first gargantuan business deal with John Henry had won them, jointly, the cover of *Time*. It was also what had brought her father and John Henry together so often that spring, and as their plans began to prosper, so had John Henry's suit with Antoine's only child.

Raphaella had never met anyone like John Henry. He was tall, handsome, impressive, powerful, yet gentle, kind, and soft spoken, with a constant glimmer of laughter in his eyes. There was mischief there too sometimes, and in time, Raphaella had learned how much he liked to tease and play. He was a man of extraordinary imagination and creativity, a man of great wit, a man of great eloquence, great style. He had everything that she or any other girl could ever want.

The only thing that John Henry Phillips had lacked was youth. And in the beginning even that was difficult to believe as one looked into the lean, handsome face or watched the powerful arms when he played tennis or swam. He had a long, beautiful body that men half his age would have envied.

His age had, at first, discouraged him from pursuing Raphaella, yet as time went on, and the frequency of his trips to Paris increased, he found her more charming, more open, more delightful on each occasion. And despite the rigidity of his ideas about his daughter, Antoine de Mornay-Malle did not resist the prospect of seeing his old friend marry his only child. He himself was aware of his daughter's beauty, her gentleness and openness, and her innocent charm. And he was also aware of what a rare catch John Henry Phillips would be for any woman, despite the difference of years. He was also not blind to what it would mean to the future of his bank, a consideration that had weighed with him at least once before. His own marriage had been based on affection, and good business sense as well.

The aging Marquis de Quadral, his wife's father, had been the reigning financial genius of Madrid, but his sons had not inherited his passion for the world of finance and had, for the most part, gone into other

fields. For years the elderly marquis had had an eye
out for someone to succeed him in the banks he had
founded over the years. What happened instead was
that he met Antoine, and eventually, after a great deal
of fancy footwork, the Banque Malle joined forces on
numerous deals with the Banco Quadral. The union
rapidly quadrupled Antoine's power and fortune, de-
lighted the marquis, and brought along with it the
marquis's daughter, Alejandra, Marquesa de Santos y
Quadral. Antoine had been instantly taken with the
flaxen-haired, blue-eyed Spanish beauty, and at the
time he had been thinking for a while that it was time
he married and produced an heir. At thirty-five he
had been too busy building his family's banking business into an empire, but now other considerations had
begun to weigh with him as well. Alejandra was the
perfect solution to the problem, and a very handsome
solution at that. At nineteen she was a startling
beauty, with the most devastatingly exquisite face Antoine had ever seen. It was he who looked like the
Spaniard beside her, with his black hair and dark
eyes. And together they made an extraordinary pair.

Seven months after they met, their wedding was the
main event of the social season, after which they
honeymooned for a month in the South of France. Immediately thereafter they dutifully appeared at the
marquis's country estate, Santa Eugenia, on the Coast
of Spain. The estate was palatial, and it was here that
Antoine began to understand what marriage to Alejandra would mean. He was a member of the family
now, yet another son of the elderly marquis. He was
expected to make frequent appearances at Santa Eugenia, and come as often as possible to Madrid. It was
certainly what Alejandra planned to do, and when it

was time to return to Paris, she implored her husband
to let her stay at Santa Eugenia for a few more weeks.
And when at last she returned to him in Paris, six
weeks later than she had promised, Antoine fully understood what was going to happen after that. Alejandra was going to spend most of her time as she always
had, surrounded by her family, on their estates in
Spain. She had spent all of the war years sequestered
there and now, even after the war, and married, she
wanted to continue to live in those familiar surroundings.

Predictably, on their first anniversary, Alejandra
gave birth to their first child, a son named Julien, and
Antoine was well pleased. He had an heir for his own
empire now, and he and the marquis strolled quietly
for hours on the grounds of Santa Eugenia when the
child was a month old, discussing all of Antoine's future plans for the banks and his son. He had his
father-in-law's full endorsement, and in the year since
he had married Alejandra, both the Banque Malle and
the Banco Quadral had grown.

Alejandra remained at Santa Eugenia for the summer with her brothers and sisters, their children, cousins, nieces, and friends. And when Antoine returned to
Paris, Alejandra had already conceived again. This
time Alejandra suffered a miscarriage, and the next
time she delivered twins, born prematurely and dead
at birth. There was then a brief hiatus when she spent
six months resting, with her family, in Madrid. When
she returned to Paris to her husband, she conceived
yet again. This fourth pregnancy yielded Raphaella,
two years younger than Julien. There were then two
more miscarriages and another stillbirth, after which
the ravishingly beautiful Alejandra announced that it

was the climate in Paris that did not agree with her
and that her sisters felt she would be healthier in
Spain. Having seen her inevitable return to Spain
coming throughout their marriage, Antoine quietly ac-
quiesced. It was the way of women of her country,
and it was a battle that he never could have won.

From then on he was content to see her at Santa
Eugenia, or in Madrid, surrounded by female cousins,
sisters, and duennas, perfectly content to be always in
the company of her relatives, assorted women friends,
and a handful of their unmarried brothers, who
squired them to concerts, operas, and plays. Alejandra
was still one of Spain's great beauties, and in Spain
she led an exceedingly pleasant life of indolence and
opulence, with which she was well pleased. It was no
great problem for Antoine to fly back and forth to
Spain, when he could get away from the bank, which
he did less and less. In time he induced her to let the
children come back to Paris to attend school, on the
condition of course that they flew to Santa Eugenia
for every possible vacation and for four months in the
summer. And now and then she consented to visit him
in Paris, despite what she constantly referred to as the
detrimental effects of the French weather on her
health. After the last stillbirth there were no more babies, in fact after that there was only a platonic affection between Alejandra and her husband, which she
knew from her sisters was perfectly normal.

Antoine was perfectly content to leave things as
they were, and when the marquis died, the marriage
paid off. No one was surprised at the arrangement.
Alejandra and Antoine had jointly inherited the Banco
Quadral. Her brothers were amply compensated, but
to Antoine went the empire he so desperately wanted

to add to his own. Now it was of his son that he thought as he continued to build it, but Antoine's only son was not destined to be his heir. At sixteen Julien de Mornay-Malle died in an accident, in Buenos Aires, playing polo, leaving his mother stunned, his father bereft, and Raphaella Antoine's only child.

And it was Rahpaella who consoled her father, who flew with him to Buenos Aires to bring the boy's body back to France. It was she who held her father's hand during those endless hours and as they watched the casket being lowered solemnly onto the runway at Orly. Alejandra flew back to Paris separately, surrounded by sisters, cousins, one of her brothers, and several close friends, but always surrounded, protected, as she had lived her entire life. And hours after the funeral they urged her to go back to Spain with them, and acquiescing tearfully, she allowed them to take her away. Alejandra had a veritable army to protect her, and Antoine had no one, only a fourteen-year-old child.

But later the tragedy provided a strange bond between them. It was something they never spoke of, but it was always there. The tragedy also provided a strange bond between her father and John Henry, as the two men discovered that they had shared a similar loss, the deaths of their only sons. John Henry's boy had died in a plane crash. At twenty-one the young man had been flying his own plane. John Henry's wife had also died, five years later. But it was the loss of their sons that for each had been an intolerable blow. Antoine had had Raphaella to console him, but John Henry had no other children, and after his wife died, he had never married again.

At the start of their business association, each time

John Henry came to Paris, Raphaella was in Spain. He began to tease Antoine about his imaginary daughter. It became a standing joke between them until a day when the butler ushered John Henry into Antoine's study, but instead of Antoine, he found himself staring into the dark eyes of a ravishingly beautiful young girl who looked at him tremulously, like a frightened doe. She gazed up almost in terror at the sight of a strange man in the room. She had been going over some papers for school and checking through some reference books her father kept there, and her long black hair poured over her shoulders in straight streams of black silk punctured by cascades of soft curls. For a moment he had stood there, silent, awed. And then quickly he had recovered, and the warm light in his eyes reached out to her, reassuring her that he was a friend. But during her months of study in Paris she saw few people, and in Spain she was so well guarded and protected that it was rare for her to be alone anywhere with a strange man. She had no idea what to say to him at first, but after a few moments of easy banter she met the twinkle in his eyes and laughed. It was half an hour later when Antoine found them, apologizing profusely for a delay at the bank. On the way home in the car he had wondered if John Henry had finally met her, and he had to admit to himself later that he had hoped they had.

Raphaella had withdrawn a few moments after her father's arrival, her cheeks blushing to a delicate pink on the perfect creamy skin.

"My God, Antoine, she's a beauty." He looked at his French friend with an odd expression, and Antoine smiled.

"So you like my imaginary daughter, do you? She

wasn't too impossibly shy? Her mother has convinced her that all men who attempt to talk to a young girl alone are murderers or at least rapists. Sometimes I worry about that look of terror in her eyes."

"What do you expect? All her life she has been totally protected. It's hardly surprising after all, then, if she's shy."

"No, but she's almost eighteen now, and it's going to be a real problem for her, unless she spends the rest of her life in Spain. In Paris she ought to be able to at least talk to a man without half a dozen women standing in the room, most, if not all, of them related to her." He said it in a tone of amusement, but there was also something very serious in his eyes. He was looking long and hard at John Henry, sizing up the expression he still saw lingering in the American's eyes. "She is lovely, isn't she? It's immodest of me to say it about my own daughter, but . . ." He spread his hands helplessly and smiled.

And this time John Henry met his smile fully. "Lovely isn't quite the right word." And then in an almost boyish way he asked a question that brought a smile to Antoine's eyes. "Will she dine with us this evening?"

"If you don't mind very much. I thought we'd dine here, and then we can stop in at my club. Matthieu de Bourgeon will be there this evening, and I've been promising him for months that I'd introduce you the next time you're here."

"That sounds fine." But it wasn't Matthieu de Bourgeon that John Henry was thinking of when he smiled.

He had managed to draw Raphaella out successfully that evening and yet again two days later when he had come to the house for tea. He had come especially to see her and brought her two books he had told her about at dinner two days before. She had blushed again and fallen once more into silence, but this time he was able to tease her back into chatting with him, and by the end of the afternoon they were almost friends. Over the next six months she came to regard him as a personage almost as revered and cherished as her father, and it was in the light of an uncle of sorts that she explained him to her mother when she went to Spain.

It was during that trip that John Henry appeared at Santa Eugenia with her father. They stayed for only one brief weekend, during which John Henry successfully charmed Alejandra and the armies of others staying at Santa Eugenia that spring. It was then that Alejandra understood John Henry's intentions, but Raphaella didn't come to learn of them until the summer. It was the first week of her vacation, and she was due to fly to Madrid in a few days. In the meantime she was enjoying the last of her days in Paris, and when John Henry arrived, she urged him to come out with her for a walk along the Seine. They talked about the street artists and the children, and her face lit up when she told him about all of her cousins in Spain. She seemed to have a passion for the children, and she looked infinitely beautiful as she looked up at him with her huge dark eyes.

"And how many do you want when you grow up, Raphaella?" He always said her name so deliberately. It pleased her. For an American it was a difficult name.

"I am grown up."

"Are you? At eighteen?" He looked at her in amusement, and there was something odd in his eyes that she didn't understand. Something tired and old and wise and sad, as though for an instant he had thought of his son. They had talked about him too. And she had told him about her brother.

"Yes, I am grown up. I'm going to the Sorbonne in the fall." They had smiled at each other, and he had had to fight himself to keep from kissing her then and there.

All the while, as they walked, he was wondering how he was going to ask her, and if he had gone totally mad for wanting to ask her at all. "Raphaella, have you ever thought about going to college in the States?" They were walking slowly along the Seine, dodging children, and she was gently pulling the petals off a flower. But she looked up at him and shook her head.

"I don't think I could."

"Why not? Your English is excellent."

She shook her head slowly and when she looked up at him again, her eyes were sad. "My mother would never let me. It's just . . . it's just too different from her way of life. And it's so far."

"But is that what you want? Your father's life is different from hers too. Would you be happy with that life in Spain?"

"I don't think so." She said it matter-of-factly. "But I don't think I have much choice. I think Papa always meant to take Julien into the bank with him, and it was understood that I'd go to Spain with my mother." The thought of her surrounded by duennas for the rest of her life appalled him. Even as her friend he wanted more for her than that. He wanted to see her free and alive and laughing and independent, but not buried at Santa Eugenia like her mother. It wasn't right for this girl. He felt it in his soul.

"I don't think you should have to do that, if that's not what you want to do."

She smiled up at him with resignation mingled with wisdom in her eighteen-year-old eyes. "There are duties in life, Mr. Phillips."

"Not at your age, little one. Not yet. Some duties, yes. Like school. And listening to your parents to a certain extent, but you don't have to take on a whole way of life if you don't want it."

"What else, then? I don't know anything else."

"That's no excuse. Are you happy at Santa Eugenia?"

"Sometimes. And sometimes not. Sometimes I find all those women very boring. My mother loves it though. She even goes on trips with them. They travel in great bunches, they go to Rio and Buenos Aires and Uruguay and New York, and even when she comes to Paris, she brings them with her. They always remind me of girls in boarding school, they seem so—so"—the huge eyes looked up at him apologetically—"so silly. Don't they?" She looked at him and he nodded.

"Maybe a little. Raphaella. . . ." But as he said it she stopped walking suddenly and swung around to face him, ingenuous, totally unaware of her beauty; her long graceful body leaned toward him and she looked into his eyes with such trust that he was afraid to say more.

"Yes?"

And then he couldn't stop it anymore. He couldn't. He had to. . . . "Raphaella, darling. I love you." The words were the merest whisper in the soft Paris air, and his lined handsome face hovered next to hers for a

moment before he kissed her. His lips were gentle and
soft, his tongue probing her mouth as though his hunger for her knew no bounds, but her mouth was
pressed hard against his now too, her arms around his
neck, pressing her body into his, and then just as gently he pulled away from her, not wanting her to sense
the urgency that had sprung up in his loins. "Raphaella . . . I've wanted to kiss you for so long." He
kissed her again, more gently this time, and she smiled
with a womanly pleasure he had never seen before in
her face.

"So have I." She hung her head then, like a schoolgirl. "I've had a crush on you since we first met." And
then she smiled up at him bravely. "You're so beautiful." And this time she kissed him. She took his hand
then, as though to lead him further down the Seine,
but he shook his head and took her hand in his.

"We have something to talk about first. Do you
want to sit down?" He motioned to a bench and she
followed him.

She looked at him questioningly and saw something
in his eyes that puzzled her. "Is something wrong?"
Slowly he grinned. "No. But if you think I just
brought you out here this afternoon to 'spoon,' as they
said in my day, you're mistaken, little one. There's
something I want to ask you, and I've been afraid to
all day."

"What is it?" But suddenly her heart was pounding
and her voice was very soft.

He looked at her for an endless moment, his face
close to hers and her hand held tightly in his own.
"Will you marry me, Raphaella?" He heard her sharp
intake of breath, and then closed his eyes and kissed
her again, and when he pulled slowly away, there

were tears in her eyes and she was smiling as he had never seen her smile before and slowly, the smile broadening, she nodded.

"Yes . . . I will. . . ."

The wedding of Raphaella de Mornay-Malle y de Santos y Quadral and John Henry Phillips IV was of a magnitude seldom seen. It took place in Paris and there was a luncheon for two hundred on the day of the civil ceremony, a dinner for a hundred fifty family members and "intimate friends" that night, and a crowd of more than six hundred at Notre-Dame for the wedding the next day. Antoine had taken over the entire Polo Club and everyone agreed that both the wedding and the reception were the most beautiful they had ever seen. Remarkably they had also managed to strike up a bargain with the press so that if Raphaella and John Henry would pose for photographs for half an hour, and answer whatever questions arose, they would be left in peace after that.

The wedding stories were featured in *Vogue, Women's Wear Daily,* and the following week's *Time.* Throughout the press interviews Raphaella had clutched John Henry's hand almost desperately, and her eyes seemed larger and darker than ever before in the snow-white face.

It was then that he vowed to keep her shielded in the future from the prying eyes of the press. He didn't want her having to cope with anything that made her uncomfortable or unhappy. He was well aware of how carefully protected she had been during her early years. The problem was that John Henry was a man who attracted the attention of the press with alarming frequency, and when he took a bride forty-four years his junior, then his wife became an object of fascination too. Fortunes of the magnitude of John Henry's were almost unheard of, and an eighteen-year-old girl, born of a marquesa and an illustrious French banker was almost too good to be true. It was all very much like a fairy tale, and no fairy tale was complete without a fairy princess. But thanks to John Henry's efforts she remained sheltered. Together they maintained an anonymity no one would have thought possible over the years. Raphaella even managed to attend two years of school at the University of California in Berkeley and it went very smoothly. No one had any idea who she was during the entire two years. She even refused to be driven to Berkeley by the chauffeur, and John Henry bought her a little car that she drove to school.

It was exciting, too, to be among the students and to have a secret and a man she adored. Because she did love John Henry, and he was gentle and loving in every way. He felt as though he had been given a gift so precious, he barely dared to touch it, so grateful was he for the new life he shared with this ravishingly beautiful, delicate young girl. In many ways she was childlike, and she trusted him with her entire soul. It was perhaps because of that that it was such a bitter disappointment to him when he discovered that he had become sterile presumably from a severe kidney infection he'd had ten years before. He knew how desperately she had wanted children and he felt the burden of guilt for depriving her of something she wanted so much. She insisted, when he told her, that it didn't matter, that she had all the children at Santa Eugenia whom she could spoil and amuse and love.

She loved to tell them stories and buy them presents. She kept endless lists of their birthdays and was always going downtown to send some fabulous new toy off to Spain.

But even his failure to father children could not sever the bond that held them together over the years. It was a marriage in which she worshiped him and he adored her, and if the difference in their ages caused comment among others, it never bothered either of them. They played tennis together almost every morning, sometimes John Henry ran in the Presidio or along the beach and Raphaella ran along beside him, like a puppy dog at his heels, laughing and teasing and sometimes just walking along in silence afterward, holding his hand. Her life was filled with John Henry, her studies, and her letters to her family in Paris and Spain. She led a very protected, old-fashioned existence, and she was a happy woman, truly more of a happy girl, until she was twenty-five.

Two days before John Henry's sixty-ninth birthday he was to fly to Chicago to close a major deal. He had been talking about retiring for several years now, but like her father, there was no real end in sight. He had too much passion for the world of high finance, for the running of banks, the acquiring of new corporations, and the buying and selling of huge blocks of stock. He loved putting together mammoth real-estate deals like the first one he had done with her father. Retirement just wasn't for him. But when he left for Chicago he had a headache, and despite the pills Raphaella had pressed on him that morning, the headache had grown steadily worse.

In terror his assistant had chartered a plane and flown back with him from Chicago that evening, arriving with John Henry barely conscious. Raphaella looked down into the pale gray face as they brought him off the plane on a stretcher. He was in so much pain, he could barely speak to her, yet he pressed her hand several times on their way to the hospital in the ambulance, and as she looked at him in terror and despair, fighting back the tears that had clogged her throat, she suddenly noticed something odd about his mouth. An hour later his face looked strangely distorted, and shortly thereafter he fell into a coma from which he did not rouse for several days. John Henry Phillips had had a stroke, it was explained on the news that evening. It was his office that had prepared the press release, keeping Raphaella, as always, from the prying eyes of the news.

John Henry stayed in the hospital for almost four months and had two more smaller strokes before he left. When they brought him home, he had permanently lost the use of his right arm and leg, the youthful handsome face sagged pitifully on one side, and the aura of strength and power was gone. John Henry Phillips was suddenly an old man. He was broken in body and spirit from that moment, yet for another seven years his life had dwindled on.

He never left his home again. The nurse wheeled him into the garden for some sunshine and Raphaella sat with him for hours at a time, but his mind wasn't always clear anymore, and his life, once so vital, so busy, so full, had changed radically. There was nothing more than a shell of the man left. And it was this shell that Raphaella lived with, faithfully, devotedly, lovingly, reading to him, talking to him, comforting him. As the nurses who tended him around the clock cared for the broken body, she attempted to console the spirit. But his spirit was broken, and at times she wondered if hers was as well. It had been seven years since the first series of strokes. There had been two more strokes since, which had reduced him still further, until he was unable to do much more than sit in his wheelchair, and most of the time he stared into space, thinking back to what was no more. He was still able to speak, though with difficulty, but much of the time he seemed to have nothing more to say. It was a cruel joke that a man who had been so alive should be rendered so small and so useless. When Antoine had flown over from Paris to see him, he had left John Henry's room with tears streaming unashamedly down his cheeks, and his words to his daughter had been quite clear. She was to stand by this man who had loved her and whom she had loved and married, until he died. There was to be no nonsense, no whimpering, no shrinking from her duties, no complaining. Her duty was clear. And so it had remained, and Raphaella had not shrunk or whispered or complained for seven long years.

Her only respite from the grim reality of her existence was when she traveled to Spain in the summers. She only went for two weeks now, instead of four. But John Henry absolutely insisted that she go. It tortured him to realize that the girl he had married was as much a prisoner of his infirmities as he was himself. It was one thing to keep her from the prying eyes of the world while amusing her himself night and day. It was quite another to lock her in the house with him, as his body decayed slowly around his soul. If he could have found the means, he would have killed himself, he said often to his doctor, if only to set both of them free. He had mentioned it once to Antoine, who had been outraged at the very idea.

"The girl adores you!" he thundered and his voice reverberated against the walls of his friend's sick room. "You owe it to her not to do anything crazy like that!"

"Not like this." The words had been garbled but comprehensible. "It's a crime to do this to her. I have no right." He had choked on his own tears.

"You have no right to deprive her of you. She loves you. She loved you for seven years before this happened. That doesn't change overnight. It doesn't change because you are ill. What if she were ill? Would you love her any less?"

John Henry painfully shook his head. "She should be married to a young man, she should have children."

"She needs you, John. She belongs with you. She has grown up with you. She'll be lost without you. How can you think of leaving her a moment sooner than you must? You could have years left!" He had meant to be encouraging, but John Henry had faced him with despair. Years . . . and by then how old would Raphaella be? Thirty-five? Forty? Forty-two? She would be so totally unprepared to start looking for a new life. These were the thoughts that rambled agonizingly through his mind, that left him filled with silence and his eyes glazed with anguish and grief, not so much for himself, but for her. He insisted that she go away as often as possible, but she felt guilty for leaving him, and going away wasn't even a relief. Always John Henry was on her mind.

But John Henry repeatedly urged her to break out

of her prison. Whenever he learned from Raphaella
that her mother was going to New York for a few
days, on her way to Buenos Aires or Mexico City, or
wherever else, with the usual crowd of sisters and
cousins, he was quick to urge Raphaella to join them.
Whether it was for two days or ten, he always wanted
her to join them, to get out into the world if only for a
moment, and he knew that in that crowd she would
always be safe, well protected, heavily escorted. The
only moments in which she was alone were on the
flights to Europe or New York. His chauffeur always
put her on the plane in San Francisco, and there was
always a rented limousine waiting for her at the other
end. The life of a princess was still Raphaella's, but
the fairy tale had considerably changed. Her eyes
were larger and quieter than ever now, she would sit
silent and pensive for hours, looking into the fire, or
staring out at the bay. The sound of her laughter was
barely more than a memory, and when it rang out for
a moment, it somehow seemed like a mistake.

Even when she joined her family for their few-day
visits to New York or wherever, it was as though she
weren't really there. In the years since John Henry's
illness Raphaella had increasingly withdrawn, until
she was scarcely different from John Henry. Her life
seemed as much over as his. The only difference was
that hers had never really begun. It was only in Santa
Eugenia that she seemed to come alive again, with a
child on her lap, and another teetering on her knees,
three or four more clustered around, as she told them
wonderful tales that kept them staring at her in rap-
ture and awe. It was with the children that she forgot
the pain of what had happened, and her own loneli-

ness, and her overwhelming sense of loss. With the
grown-ups she was always reticent and quiet, as
though there were nothing left to say and joining in
their merriment seemed obscene. For Raphaella it was
like a funeral that had gone on for half a lifetime, or
more precisely for seven years. But she knew only too
well how much he suffered and how much guilt he
felt for his invalid state over the last year. So when
she was with him, there was only tenderness and com-
passion in her voice, a gentle tone, and a still gentler
hand. But what he saw in her eyes cut him to the very
core of his being. It was not so much that he was
dying, but that he had killed a very young girl and
left in her place this sad, lonely young woman with
the exquisite face and the huge, haunted eyes. This
was the woman he had created. This was what he had
done to the girl he had once loved.

As Raphaella walked swiftly down the thickly car-
peted steps onto the next landing, she glanced quickly
down the hall and saw the staff already dusting the
long antique tables that stretched down the endless
halls. The house they lived in was one that John Henry's grandfather had built when he first came to San
Francisco after the Civil War. It had survived the
earthquake in 1906 and was now one of the most important architectural landmarks in San Francisco, with
its sweeping lines and five stories perched next to the
Presidio and looking out at the bay. It was unusual
also because it had some of the finest stained-glass
skylights in the city, and because it was still in the
hands of the family that had originally owned it,
which was very rare. But it was not a house in which
Raphaella could be happy now. It seemed more like a

museum or a mausoleum to her than a home. It seemed cold and unfriendly, as did the staff, all of whom John Henry had had when she arrived. And she had never had the chance to redecorate any of the rooms. The house stood now, as it had then. For fourteen years it had been her home, and yet each time she left it, she felt like an orphan with her suitcase.

"More coffee, Mrs. Phillips?" The elderly woman who had been the downstairs maid for thirty-six years gazed into Raphaella's face as she did each morning. Raphaella had seen that face five days a week for the last fourteen years, and still the woman was a stranger to her, and always would be. Her name was Marie.

But this time Raphaella shook her head. "Not this morning. I'm in a hurry, thank you." She glanced at the plain gold watch on her wrist, put down her napkin, and stood up. The flowered Spode dishes had belonged to John Henry's first wife. There were a lot of things like that in the house. Everything seemed to be someone else's. "The first Mrs. Phillips," as the servants put it, or John Henry's mother's, or grandmother's. . . . Sometimes she felt that if a stranger were to walk through the house inquiring about artifacts and paintings and even small unimportant objects, there was not a single thing about which someone would say, "Oh, that's Raphaella's." Nothing was Raphaella's, except her clothes and her books, and the huge collection of letters from the children in Spain, which she kept in boxes.

Raphaella's heels clicked briefly across the black and white marble floor of the pantry. She picked up a phone there and buzzed softly on an inside line. A moment later it was picked up on the third floor by the morning nurse.

"Good morning. Is Mr. Phillips awake yet?"

"Yes, but he's not quite ready." Ready. Ready for what? Raphaella felt an odd tug in her soul as she stood there. How could she resent him for what wasn't his fault? And yet how could this have happened to her? For those first seven years it had been so wonderful, so perfect . . . so . . .

"I'd like to come up for a moment, before I leave."

"Oh, dear, you're leaving this morning?"

Raphaella glanced at her watch again. "In half an hour."

"All right. Then give us fifteen or twenty minutes. You can stop in for a few minutes on your way out." Poor John Henry. Ten minutes, and then nothing. There would be no one to visit him while she was gone. She would only be gone for four or five days, but still she wondered if maybe she shouldn't leave him. What if something happened? What if the nurses didn't pay attention to what they were doing? She always felt that way when she left him. Troubled, tormented, guilty, as though she had no right to a few days of her own. And then John Henry would persuade her to go, emerging from his reverie long enough to force her away from this nightmare that they had shared for so long. It wasn't even a nightmare anymore. It was just an emptiness, a limbo, a comatose state, while their lives continued to drone on.

She took the elevator to the second floor and then walked to her bedroom after telling the nurse that she would be in to see her husband in fifteen minutes. She looked long and hard in the mirror then, smoothed the silky black hair, and ran a hand over the tight, heavy knot of it at the nape of her neck. She took a hat out of her closet. It was a beautiful creation she had

bought in Paris the year before when hats returned to
the world of high style. As she put it on carefully, tilt-
ing it to just the right angle, she wondered for a moment why she had bothered to buy it at all. Who
would notice her beautiful hat? It had a whisper of
black veiling that lent further mystery to her large al-
mond-shaped eyes, and with the contrast of the black
hat and her hair and the little veil, the creamy white of
her skin seemed to stand out even more than before.
She carefully applied a thin gloss of bright lipstick
and clipped pearls on her ears. She ran a hand over
her suit, straightened her stockings, and looked in her
handbag to ascertain that the cash she always carried
on trips was concealed in a side pocket of the black
lizard bag her mother had sent her from Spain. She
looked, when she stood in front of the mirror, like a
woman of incredible elegance, beauty, and style. This
was a woman who dined at Maxim's and went to the
races at Longchamp. This was a woman who partied
in Venice and Rome and Vienna and New York. This
was a woman who went to the theater in London.
This wasn't the face or the body or the look of a girl
who had slipped into womanhood unnoticed and who
was now married to a crippled and dying seventy-six-
year-old man. As she saw herself, and the truth, all too
clearly, Raphaella picked up her bag and her clothes
and grinned ruefully to herself, knowing more than
ever how appearances can lie.

She shrugged to herself as she left her bedroom,
tossing a long, handsome, dark mink coat over one arm
as she made her way once more to the stairs. The elevator had been put in for John Henry, and most of the
time she still preferred to walk. She did so now, up to
the third floor, where a suite had long since been set

up for her husband, with three rooms adjoining it, for each of the nurses who cared for him in shifts. They were three matronly women, content with their quarters, their patient, and the job. They were handsomely paid for their services, and like the woman who had served Raphaella breakfast, they had somehow managed to remain unobtrusive and faceless over the years. Frequently she found herself missing the passionate and often impossible servants of Santa Eugenia. They were servile for the most part, yet often rebellious and childlike, having served her mother's family sometimes for generations, or at least for many years. They were warlike and childlike and loving and giving. They were filled with laughter and outrage and devotion for the people they worked for not like these cool professionals who worked for John Henry.

Raphaella knocked softly on the door to her husband's suite of rooms, and a face appeared rapidly at the door. "Good morning, Mrs. Phillips We're all ready." Are *we*? Raphaella nodded and stepped inside, down a short hall into a bedroom, which like her own room downstairs had both a boudoir and a small library. Now John Henry was tucked into his bed, staring across the room at the fire already burning behind the grate. She advanced toward him slowly, and he seemed not to hear her, until at last she sat down in a chair next to his bed and took his hand.

"John Henry. . . ." After her fourteen years in San Francisco her accent was still evident when she said his name, but her English was perfect now, and had been for many years. "John Henry. . . ." He turned his eyes slowly toward her without moving his head, and then slowly he moved himself so that he could look at her, and the lined, tired face contorted into a half-smile.

"Hello, little one." His speech was slurred but she could understand him, and the agony of the smile now rendered crooked since the stroke always tore at her heart. "You look very pretty." And then after another pause, "My mother had a hat like that a long time ago."

"I think on me it is very silly, but . . ." She shrugged, suddenly looking very French as she smiled a hesitant little smile. But it was her mouth that smiled now. Her eyes seldom did. And his never did anymore, except on rare occasions when he looked at her.

"You're going today?" He looked worried, and again she wondered if she should cancel her trip.

"Yes. But, darling, do you want me to stay?"

He shook his head and smiled again. "No. Never. I wish you would go away more often. It does you good. You're meeting . . ." He looked vague for a moment, searching his memory for something obviously no longer there.

"My mother, my aunt, and two of my cousins."

He nodded and closed his eyes. "Then I know you'll be safe."

"I'm always safe." He nodded again, as though he were very tired, and she stood up, bent to kiss his cheek, and then ever so gently let go of his hand. She thought for a moment that he was going to fall asleep, but suddenly he opened his eyes as she stood staring down at his face.

"Be careful, Raphaella."

"I promise. And I'll call you."

"You don't have to. Why don't you forget about all this and have some fun." With whom? Her mother? Her aunt? A sigh fought its way through her, but she didn't let it escape.

"I'll be back very soon, and everyone here knows where I'll be if you need me."

"I don't need you. . . ." He grinned for a moment. "Not like that. Not enough to spoil your fun."

"You never have." She whispered the words to him and bent to kiss him again. "I'll miss you."

This time he shook his head and turned away from her. "Don't."

"Darling. . . ." She had to leave him to go to the airport but somehow she didn't feel right leaving him like this. She never did. Was it right to leave him? Should she stay?

"John Henry. . . ." She touched his hand and he turned to face her again. "I must go now."

"It's all right, little one. It's all right." The look in his eyes absolved her, and this time he took her firm young hand in his gnarled, worn fingers that had once seemed so gentle and so young. "Have a good trip." He tried to fill the words with every ounce of meaning he could give them, and he shook his head when he saw her eyes fill with tears. He knew what she was thinking.

"Just go, I'll be fine."

"You promise?" Her eyes were bright with tears, and his smile was very gentle as he kissed her hand.

"I promise. Now be a good girl and go, and have a good time. Promise me you'll buy yourself something outrageous and absolutely beautiful in New York."

"Like what?"

"A fur coat or a wonderful piece of jewelry." He

looked wistful for a moment. "Something you would have liked me to buy you." And then he looked into her eyes and smiled.

She shook her head as the tears rolled down her cheeks. It only made her look more beautiful, and the little black veil added further mystery to her eyes. "I'm never as generous as you are, John Henry."

"Then try harder." He tried to bellow it at her, and this time they both laughed. "Promise?"

"All right, I promise. But not another fur."

"Then something that sparkles."

"I'll see." But where would she wear it? At home in San Francisco, sitting by the fire? The futility of it all almost overwhelmed her as she smiled at him from the doorway and waved at him.

CHAPTER 4

At the airport the chauffeur slid the car to the curb at the section marked DEPARTING FLIGHTS and showed the policeman his special pass. John Henry's drivers had gotten special passes from the governor's office, and they were renewed every year. It allowed them to park where they wanted to, and now it would allow the chauffeur to leave the limousine at the curb while he took Raphaella inside to put her on the plane. The airline was always warned that she was coming, and she was always allowed to board the plane before everyone else.

Now, as they walked sedately down the huge bustling hallway, the chauffeur carrying her tote bag, strangers glanced at the startlingly beautiful woman in the mink coat and the veil. The hat added an aura of drama and there were gaunt hollows beneath the perfectly carved ivory cheekbones that framed her splendid dark eyes.

"Tom, would you wait here for me for a minute, please?" She had touched his arm gently to stop him as he marched dutifully along the airport corridor beside her, bent on getting her to the plane as quickly as he could. Mr. Phillips didn't like her lingering in airports, not that reporters or photographers had bothered them for years. Raphaella had been so totally kept away from public attention that even the reporters no longer knew who she was.

She left the chauffeur standing near a pillar and walked rapidly into the bookstore, glancing around as the driver took up his post against the wall, holding her large leather tote bag tightly in one hand. From where he stood, he could admire her striking beauty as she wandered between the shelves of magazines and books and candy, looking very different from the other travelers wandering past in parkas and car coats and old jeans. Here and there you'd see an attractive woman, or maybe a well-dressed man, but nothing to compare with Mrs. Phillips. Tom watched her take a hardcover book off a shelf, walk to the cash register, and reach into her bag.

It was then that Alex Hale came hurrying through the airport, his briefcase in his hand, and a suit bag draped over the other arm. He was distracted. It was early, but he still had to call his office before he got on the plane. He stopped at a bank of telephones just outside the bookshop, put down his bags, and dug into his trouser pocket for a dime. He dialed his office number quickly and inserted the extra coins the operator requested as his receptionist picked up the phone. He had several last-minute messages to leave for his partners, there was a memo he wanted to explain to his secretary before leaving, and he was anxious to know if the call he was expecting from London had come, and just as he asked the last question he happened to turn around and with amusement he saw a copy of his mother's latest book changing hands at the counter of the bookstore. A woman was buying it, wearing a mink coat and a black hat with a veil. He stared at her with fascination as the secretary on the other end put him on hold while she took another call. And it was then that Raphaella began to walk toward him, her eyes only slightly concealed by the veil, and the book carried in her gloved hand. As she passed near him he was suddenly aware of the lure of her perfume, and then suddenly it dawned on him that this was not the first time he had seen those eyes.

"Oh, my God." The words were a whisper as he stood there staring. It was the woman on the steps. Suddenly there she was, disappearing into the crowd at the airport, with his mother's latest book in her hand. For an insane moment he wanted to shout "Wait!" but he was trapped on hold and couldn't move until the secretary returned with the answer to his question. His eyes desperately combed the constantly moving crowd. In a moment, despite his attempts not to lose sight of her, she had passed beyond him and once again disappeared. The secretary came back on the line a moment later, only to give him an unsatisfactory answer to his question and tell him that she had to return to another call. "And for this I waited on the phone all this time, Barbara?" For the first time in a long time, the receptionist noted, he sounded angry, but she only had time to mutter "Sorry" and then had to answer two more calls.

And then, as though he could still find her if he hurried, he found himself rushing through the crowd, looking for the fur coat and the black hat with the veil. But it was obvious within a few moments that she was nowhere in sight. But what the hell difference did it make anyway? Who was she? No one. A stranger.

He chided himself for the romanticism that made him chase some mystery woman halfway through an airport. It was like looking for the white rabbit in *Alice in Wonderland,* only in this case he was looking for a beautiful woman with dark eyes, wearing a mink coat and a black hat with a veil and of course carrying *Lovers and Lies* by Charlotte Brandon. "Cool it," he told himself softly as he passed through the crowd to the airport desk, where people were already lining up for their seat assignments and boarding passes. There seemed to be mobs ahead of him, and when at last he got to the counter, the only seats they had left were in the last two rows of the plane.

"Why not just put me in the bathroom while you're at it?" He looked ruefully at the young man at the counter, who only smiled.

"Believe me, whoever gets here after you will be, and after that we'll be sticking them in the cargo hold. This one is filled to the gills."

"That ought to be pleasant."

The airline's representative smiled disarmingly and held out both hands. "Can we help it if we're popular?" And then they both laughed. Suddenly Alex found himself looking around for her again, and once more to no avail. For an insane moment he wanted to ask the man waiting on him at the counter if he had seen her, but he recognized that that temptation was more than a little mad.

The airline rep handed him his ticket, and a moment later he took his place on line at the gate. He had enough on his mind as he stood there: the client he was planning to see in New York; his mother; his sister; and Amanda, his niece. Still, the woman in the mink coat once more began to haunt him, just as she had the night he had seen her crying on the stairs. Or was he totally crazy and it wasn't the same woman at all? He grinned to himself, his fantasies even bought his mother's books. Maybe it was all very psychotic and he was finally losing his mind. But the prospect seemed to amuse him as the line moved slowly forward and he pulled his boarding pass out of his pocket. Once more he pushed his thoughts ahead to what he had to do in New York.

Raphaella took her seat quickly as Tom stowed the tote bag under her seat and the stewardess quietly took the beautifully cut dark mink coat. All of the personnel on board had been warned that morning that they would be carrying a VIP on the trip to New York, but she would be traveling in coach instead of first class, which was apparently her standard choice. For years she had insisted to John Henry that it was much more "discreet." No one would expect to find the wife of one of the richest men in the world lost among the housewives and secretaries and salesmen and babies in the coach section. When they preboarded her as they always did, she settled quickly into the next to the last row, where she always sat. It was discreet almost to the point of being invisible. Raphaella also knew that the airline's personnel would make every effort not to place any other passengers in the seat beside her, so that it was almost certain that she would sit alone for the entire flight. She thanked Tom for his help and she watched him leave the plane just as the first passengers came on board.

CHAPTER 5

Alex stood with the throng of others, inching his way along the narrow gangway to the door of the plane, where one by one they were funneled into the mammoth aircraft, their boarding passes checked and taken, their seats pointed out by the flock of smiling stewardesses who stood ready to greet them. The passengers in first class had already been seated, and they sat hidden in their private world, two curtains drawn to protect them from any curious gaze. In the main body of the plane the masses were already settling in, shoving too big pieces of hand baggage into the aisle or stuffing briefcases and packages into the overhead racks, so that the stewardesses were rapidly obliged to cruise up and down, urging passengers to put everything except hats and coats beneath their seats. It was an old litany for Alex, who searched for his seat mechanically, knowing already where it was. He had already surrendered his suit bag to a stewardess at the entrance, and his briefcase he would slide beneath his seat after selecting one or two files that he wanted to read during the first part of the trip. It was of this that he was thinking as he made his way toward the rear of the plane, attempting not to bump other passengers or their children as he moved along. For an instant he had thought again about the woman, but it was futile to wonder about her here. She had been nowhere in the crowd that had waited to board the aircraft, so he knew that she would not be on this plane.

He reached the seat they had assigned him and quietly stowed his briefcase underneath it, preparing to sit down. He noticed with only mild annoyance that there was already a small piece of luggage stowed under one of the seats beside him, and he realized with dismay that he would not be sitting alone for the flight.

He hoped it would be someone with as much work to do as he had. He didn't want to be bothered with conversation on the trip. He settled himself quickly, pulled the briefcase back out from under his seat, extricated the two files he wanted, glad that his seatmate had momentarily disappeared. It was several moments later when he felt a stir beside him and he instinctively shifted his gaze from the page he was reading to the floor. And as he did so he found himself staring down at a pair of very graceful and expensive black lizard shoes. Gucci, he registered without thinking, the little gold clips embedded in the throat of the shoe. He then noticed, all in a split second, that the ankles were even more attractive than the shoes. Feeling faintly like a schoolboy, he found himself looking slowly up the long elegant legs to the hem of the black skirt, and then up the interminable expanse of fine French suit to the face looking down at him, her head cocked slightly to one side. She looked as though she were going to ask him a question, and as though she were perfectly aware that he had just looked her over from her shoes to the top of her head. But as he looked up to see her a look of total astonishment overtook Alex and, without thinking, he stood up beside her and said, "My God, it's you."

She looked equally startled as he said it and only stared at him, wondering what he had meant and who he was. He seemed to think he knew her, and for a terrified instant she wondered if it was someone who had long ago seen her photograph somewhere or read of her in the press. Perhaps he was even a member of the press, and for a long moment she had the urge to turn and run away. But on the plane she would be his prisoner for hours. Anxious, she began to back away from him, her eyes wide and frightened, her handbag clutched beneath her arm. She was going to find the stewardess and insist that this time she had to be moved to first class. Or perhaps it was not too late for them to deplane her. She could make the next flight to New York. "I . . . no. . . ." She murmured softly as she turned away, but before she could take one step from him, she felt his hand on her arm. He had seen the terror in her eyes and was horrified at what he'd done.

"No, don't."

She turned to face him then, not quite sure she did it. All her instincts were still telling her to flee. "Who are you?"

"Alex Hale. I just . . . it's that . . ." He smiled gently at her, pained at what he saw in the beautiful woman's eyes. They were eyes filled with sorrow and terror. Perhaps injured too, but that he did not know yet. All he knew was that he didn't want her to run away, not again. "I saw you buy that in the airport." He glanced toward the book that still lay on her seat, and to Raphaella it was a non sequitur that made no sense at all. "And I—I saw you once on the steps, at Broderick and Broadway about a week ago. You were—" How could he tell her now that she had been crying? It would only make her run from him again. But his words seemed to jar her, and she looked at him long and hard this time. She seemed to be remembering, and slowly a faint blush overtook her face.

"I—" She nodded and looked away. Perhaps he was not a paparazzo. Perhaps he was only a madman or a fool. But she didn't want to travel five hours sitting beside him, wondering why he had held her arm or said "My God, it's you." But while she stared at him, immobile, wondering, as his eyes held her tightly, standing where she was, the final announcement to take their seats came over the loudspeaker in the airplane, and he moved slowly around her, to clear the way for her to her seat.

"Why don't you sit down?" He stood, looking very strong and tall and handsome, and as though unable to escape him, she silently walked past him and took her seat. She had put the hat in the overhead rack before Alex had found his seat, and now her hair shone like black silk as she bowed her head and turned away. She seemed to be looking out the window, so Alex said nothing further to her and sat down in his own seat, leaving a vacant seat between them.

He felt his heart hammering inside him. She was as beautiful as he had at first thought the night he saw her sitting on the steps, surrounded by the cloud of lynx, her haunting black eyes looking up toward him and the rivers of tears pouring silently down her face. This was the same woman sitting only inches away from him, and every fiber of his being wanted to reach out to her, to touch her, to take her in his arms. It was madness and he knew it. She was a perfect stranger. And then he smiled to himself. The words were apt. She seemed perfect in every way. As he gazed at her neck, her hands, the way she sat, all he could see was her perfection, and when he saw her profile for an instant, he could not tear his eyes away from her face. And then, aware of how uncomfortable it made her, he suddenly grabbed the two files and stared into them blindly, hoping to make her think that he had forgotten his fascination with her and had turned his mind to something else. It wasn't until after takeoff that he saw her glance toward him, and from the corner of his eye he saw her stare at him long and hard.

Unable to play the game any longer then, he turned toward her, his eyes gentle on her, his smile hesitant but warm. "I'm sorry if I frightened you before. It's just . . . I don't usually do things like this." The smile broadened, but she didn't smile in return. "I—I don't know how to explain it." For a moment he felt like a true crazy trying to explain it all to her as she sat there staring, with no expression on her face other than the look in her eyes that had so touched him when he had first seen it. "When I saw you that night on the steps, when you"—he decided to go ahead and say it—"when you were crying, I felt so helpless when you looked up at me, and then you disappeared. Just like that. You just vanished. And for days it bothered me. I keep thinking of the way you looked, with the tears running down your face." As he spoke to her he thought he saw something soften in her eyes, but there was no trace of anything different in her face. He smiled again and shrugged softly. "Maybe I just can't resist damsels in distress. But you've bothered me all this week. And this morning there you were. I was watching some woman buy a book while I called my office." He grinned at the familiar book jacket, without telling her just how familiar it was. "And then I realized it was you. It was crazy, like something in a movie. For a week I'm haunted by a vision of you, as you sit crying on the stairs, and then suddenly there you are, looking just as beautiful."

This time she smiled in answer, he was sweet and he seemed very young; in a funny way he suddenly reminded her of her brother, who had been in love every other week when he was fifteen. "And then you disappeared again," he went on despairingly. "I hung up the phone and you had vanished into thin air." She didn't want to tell him that she had stepped into a private office and was taken by several secluded corridors to the plane. But he looked puzzled for a moment. "I didn't even see you board the plane." And then he lowered his voice conspiratorially. "Tell me the truth, are you magic?" He looked like an overgrown child and she couldn't surpress a grin.

Her eyes began to dance as she looked at him, no longer angry, no longer afraid. He was a little mad, a little young, and a lot romantic, and she could sense that he didn't wish her any harm. He was just sweet, and somewhat foolish. And now she nodded to him with a small smile. "Yes, I am."

"Aha! I thought so. A magic lady. That's terrific." He sat back in his seat with a broad smile and she smiled back. It was an amusing game. And no harm could come to her, after all she was on the plane. He was a stranger, and she would never see him again. The stewardesses would whisk her away almost instantly when the plane reached New York and she would be safe again, in familiar hands. But just this once it was amusing to play this game with a stranger. And she did remember him now from the night when she had been so desperately lonely and had fled the house and sat, crying, on the long stone steps that led down the hillside. She had looked up and seen him, and before he could approach her, she had fled through the garden roof. But as she thought of it she noticed that Alex was smiling at her again. "Is it difficult being a magic lady?"

"Sometimes." He thought he heard an accent as he listened but he wasn't sure. And then, lulled by the safety of the game, he decided to ask her.

"Are you an American magic lady?"

Still smiling at him in return, she shook her head. "No, I'm not." Although she had married John Henry, she had remained a citizen of both France and Spain. She didn't see what harm could come of talking to Alex, who seemed to be staring at the collection of rings on both her hands. She knew what he was wondering, and knew also that he would have a hard time finding out what he wanted to know.

Suddenly she didn't want to tell him, didn't want to be Mrs. John Henry Phillips, just for a while. For a little while she wanted to be just Raphaella, a very young girl.

"You haven't told me where you're from, Magic Lady." His gaze tore itself away from her hands. He had decided that whoever she was, she was successful, and he had been relieved not to find a solid band of gold on her left hand. He had decided for some reason that she probably had a wealthy father and maybe her old man had been giving her a hard time, maybe that was why she had been crying on the steps when he first saw her. Or maybe she was divorced. But the truth of it was that he didn't even care. All he cared about were her hands, her eyes, her smile, and the power he felt drawing him to her. He had felt it even at a distance, and it made him want to reach out to her again. And now he was much closer, but he knew he couldn't touch her. All he could do was play the game.

But she smiled at him openly now. For an instant they had become almost friends. "I'm from France."

"Are you? Do you still live there?"

She shook her head in answer, suddenly more sober. "No, I live in San Francisco."

"I thought so."

"Did you?" She looked up at him in surprise and amusement. "How did you know?" There was something very innocent about her as she said it. And yet at the same time her eyes were wise. Her way of speaking to him suggested that she had not been much exposed to the big bad world. "Do I look like a San Franciscan?"

"No, you don't. But I just had a feeling that you live here. Do you like it?"

She nodded slowly, but the bottomless sadness had come back to her eyes. Talking to her was like sailing a boat through difficult waters, he was never quite sure when he was about to run aground or when he was safe and could sail free. "I like it. I don't see very much of San Francisco anymore."

"Don't you?" He was afraid to ask a serious question, like why she didn't see much anymore. "What do you do instead?" His voice was so soft that it caressed her, and she turned to him with the largest eyes he'd ever seen.

"I read. A great deal." She smiled at him then and shrugged, as though embarrassed. Blushing faintly, she looked away and then back at him to ask a question. "And you?" She felt very brave, asking something so personal of this strange man.

"I'm an attorney."

She nodded quietly and smiled. She had liked his answer. She had always found the law intriguing, and somehow it seemed a suitable occupation for this man. She had guessed that he was around her own age. In truth he was six years older than she. "Do you like it?"

"Very much. And you? What do you do, Magic Lady, other than read?"

For a moment, with a touch of irony, she was going to tell him that she was a nurse. But that seemed an unwonted cruelty to John Henry, so she said nothing for a moment and only shook her head. "Nothing." She looked up at Alex frankly. "Nothing at all."

He wondered again what her story was, what her life was like, what she did all day long, and why she had been crying that night. Suddenly it bothered him more than ever. "Do you travel a great deal?"

"Now and then. Just for a few days." She looked down at her hands, her eyes fixing on the large gold and diamond knot on her left hand.

"Are you going back to France now?" He had assumed Paris, and was, of course, right. But she shook her head.

"New York. I only go back to Paris once a year, in the summer."

He nodded slowly and smiled. "It's a beautiful city. I spent six months there once and I loved it."

"Did you?" Raphaella looked pleased. "Do you speak French, then?"

"Not really." The broad boyish grin returned. "Certainly not as well as you speak English." She laughed softly then and fingered the book she had bought at the airport. Alex noticed it with a twinkle in his eye. "Do you read a lot of her?"

"Who?"

"Charlotte Brandon."

Raphaella nodded. "I love her. I've read every book she ever wrote." And then she glanced at him apologetically. "I know, it's not very serious reading, but it's a wonderful escape. I open her books and I am instantly absorbed into the world she describes. I think that kind of reading seems silly to a man, but it"—she couldn't tell him that the books had saved her sanity over the last seven years, he would think she was crazy—"it's just very enjoyable."

He smiled more deeply. "I know, I've read her too."

"Have you?" Raphaella looked at him in nothing less than amazement. Charlotte Brandon's books did not seem like the sort of thing a man would read. John Henry certainly never would have. Or her father. They read books of nonfiction, about economics, or world wars. "Do you like them?"

"Very much." And then he decided to play with her for a little longer. "I've read them all."

"Really?" Her huge eyes widened further. To her it seemed an odd thing for an attorney to do. And then she smiled at him again and held the book toward him.

"Have you read this one? It's the new one." Maybe she had found a friend after all.

He nodded as he glanced at the book. "I think it's her best. You'll like it. It's more serious than some of her others. More thoughtful. She deals very heavily with death, it isn't just a pretty story. She's saying a great deal." He knew that his mother had written it the previous year, before she'd had some fairly important surgery, and she had been afraid it would be her last book. She had tried to say something important with it, and she had. Alex's face was more serious as he looked at Raphaella. "This one means a lot to her."

Raphaella looked at him strangely. "How do you know? Have you met her?"

There was a moment's pause as the broad smile returned to his face, and he leaned over and whispered to Raphaella, "She's my mom." But this time Raphaella laughed at him; the sound was that of a silvery bell and it pleased his ears. "No, really, she is."

"You know, for a lawyer you're really very silly."

"Silly?" He tried to look outraged. "I'm serious. Charlotte Brandon is my mother."

"And the President of the United States is my father."

"Congratulations." He held out a hand to shake hers and she slid her cool hand gently into his and they shook firmly. "By the way, I'm Alex Hale."

"You see!" she said, laughing again. "Your name isn't Brandon!"

"That's her maiden name. She is Charlotte Brandon Hale."

"Absolutely." Raphaella couldn't stop laughing now as she stared at him and laughed more. "Do you always tell stories like this?"

"Only to total strangers. By the way, Magic Lady, what's your name?" He knew it was a little pushy, but he desperately wanted to know who she was. He wanted to lose their mutual anonymity. He wanted to know who she was, where she lived, where he could find her, so if she disappeared again into thin air, he'd be able to track her down.

But she hesitated in answer to his question, only for an instant, and then she smiled. "Raphaella."

He shook his head dubiously with a small smile. "Now that sounds like a story to me. Raphaella. That's not a French name."

"No, it's Spanish. I'm only half French."

"And half Spanish?" Her coloring told him that it was true, the raven-black hair and black eyes and porcelain-white skin were what he would have expected from Spain. Little did he know that she got her coloring from her French father.

"Yes, I'm half Spanish."

"Which half? Your mind or your heart?" It was a serious question and she frowned as she considered the answer.

"That's a difficult question. I'm not sure. I suppose that my heart is French, and my mind is Spanish. I think like a Spaniard, not because I want to so much but mostly out of habit. Somehow that whole way of life pervades everything that you are."

Alex looked over his shoulder suspiciously and then leaned toward her to whisper, "I don't see a duenna."

She rolled her eyes and laughed. "Ah, no, but you will!"

"Really?"

"Very much so. The only place I'm ever alone is on a plane."

"How strange, and rather intriguing." He wanted to ask her then how old she was. He guessed twenty-five or -six, and would have been surprised to learn she was thirty-two. "Do you mind being chaperoned all the time?"

"Sometimes. But without that it would probably seem very strange. I'm used to it. Sometimes I think it would be frightening not to be so protected."

"Why?" She intrigued him more than ever. She was different from every woman he had ever known.

"Then one would have no protection." She said it with great seriousness.

"From what?"

She paused for a long moment and then smiled at him and said gently, "People like you." He could only smile in answer, and for a long moment they sat together, with their own thoughts and questions each about the other's life. She turned to him after a little while, and her eyes were curious and happier than they had seemed before. "Why did you tell me that story about Charlotte Brandon?" She couldn't figure him out, but she liked him; he seemed honest and kind and funny and bright, as best she could judge.

But he was smiling at her now in answer. "Because it's true. She is my mother, Raphaella. Tell me, is that really your name?"

She nodded soberly in answer. "It is." But she had offered no other, no last name. Just Raphaella. And he liked that name a great deal.

"In any case she's really my mother." He pointed to the picture on the back of the book and then looked quietly at Raphaella, still holding the book in her hand. "You'd like her a lot. She's a remarkable woman."

"I'm sure she is." But it was obvious that she still didn't believe Alex's tale, and then with an expression of amusement he reached into his jacket and withdrew the narrow black wallet Kay had given him for his birthday the year before. It bore the same interlocking G's as Raphaella's black lizard bag. Gucci. He pulled out two dog-eared photographs and silently he handed them to her across the empty seat. She gazed at them for an instant, and then her eyes grew wide. One of the photographs was a miniature of the one on the back of the book, and the other was one of his mother laughing as he held an arm around her, and his sister stood at her other side with George.

"Family portrait. We took it last year. My sister, my brother-in-law, and my mother. Now what do you think?"

Raphaella was smiling and looking at Alex with sudden awe. "Oh, you must tell me about her! Is she wonderful?"

"Very much so. And as a matter of fact, Magic Lady"—he stood up to his full height, slipped the two files into the pocket of the seat in front of them, and sat down again in the empty seat next to hers—"I think you're pretty wonderful too. Now, before I tell you all about my mother, can I interest you in a drink before lunch?" It was the first time he had used his mother to woo a woman, but he didn't care. He wanted to know Raphaella as well as he could by the time the plane landed in New York.

They talked for the next four and a half hours, over two glasses of white wine and then over a fairly inedible lunch, which neither of them noticed, as they talked about Paris and Rome and Madrid, and life in San Francisco, and writing and people and children and law. She learned that he had a beautiful little Victorian house that he loved. He knew about her life in Spain at Santa Eugenia and listened with rapt fascination to her tales of a world that dated back centuries and was like nothing he had ever known. She told him of the children she loved so much, of the stories she told them, of her cousins, of ridiculous gossip about that kind of life in Spain. She told him about everything but John Henry and the life she led now. But it was no life, it was a dark, empty void, a nonlife. It wasn't that she wanted to conceal it from him, it was that she herself didn't want to think about it now.

When at last the stewardess asked them to fasten their seat belts, they both looked like two children who had been told that the party was over and it was time to go home.

"What will you do now?" He already knew that she was meeting her mother, her aunt, and two female cousins, in true Spanish fashion, and that she would be staying at the hotel with them in New York.

"Now? I will meet my mother at the hotel. They should already be there."

"Can I give you a ride in a cab?"

She shook her head slowly. "I'll be picked up. In fact"—she looked at him regretfully—"I will be doing my disappearing act as soon as I arrive."

"At least I can help you pick up your luggage." He sounded as if he were pleading.

But she shook her head again. "No. You see, I'll be escorted right off the plane."

He tried to smile at her then. "Are you sure you're not a jailbird, and you're traveling in custody or something?"

"I might as well be." Her voice was as sad as her

eyes. Suddenly the gaiety of the last five hours had faded for both of them. The real world was about to intrude on their little game. "I'm sorry."

"So am I." And then he looked at her seriously. "Raphaella . . . could I see you while we're in New York? I know you'll be busy, but maybe for a drink, a—" She was already shaking her head. "Why not?"

"It's impossible. My family would never understand."

"Why not, for God's sake, you're a grown woman."

"Precisely. And women from that world don't run around having drinks with strange men."

"I'm not strange." He looked boyish again and she laughed. "All right, so I am. Will you have lunch with me and my mother? Tomorrow?" He was improvising but he'd drag his mother to lunch if he had to haul her out of an editorial meeting by the hair. If Charlotte Brandon was required as a duenna in order to convince Raphaella to come to lunch with him, then that was who they would have. "Will you? The Four Seasons. One o'clock."

"Alex, I don't know. I'm sure I'll be—"

"Try. You don't even have to promise. We'll be there. If you can make it, fine. If you don't show, I'll understand. Just see." The plane had touched the runway and there was a sudden urgency in his voice.

"I don't see how—" She looked distressed as her eyes met his.

"Never mind. Just remember how much you want to meet my mother. The Four Seasons. One o'clock. You'll remember."

"Yes, but—"

"Shhh. . . ." He put a finger to her lips, and her eyes held his for a long time. Suddenly he leaned closer to her and was desperately aware of how much he wanted to kiss her. Maybe if he did, he would never see her again, and if he didn't, perhaps he would see her again. Instead he talked over the roar of the motors as they taxied toward the terminal. "Where are you staying?"

Her eyes were enormous as she looked at him, hesitating, unsure. In effect he was asking her to trust him, and she wanted to, but she wasn't sure if she should. But the words were out of her mouth almost as though she couldn't control them as the plane jolted to a sudden stop. "The Carlyle." And then, as though by a prearranged signal, two stewardesses stood in the aisle, one held her mink coat, the other pulled her tote bag from beneath her seat, and like an obedient child Raphaella asked Alex to hand her her hat from the overhead compartment, and without saying a word, she put it on, unfastened her seat belt, and stood up. She stood there, as he had first seen her in the airport, swathed in mink, her eyes veiled by the little black hat, her book and her handbag clutched in her hand. She looked at him, and then held out a black kid-gloved hand. "Thank you." The words were for the five hours he had given her, for the cherished moment, the flight from reality, for a taste of what her life might have been, could have been, and was not. Her eyes lingered on his for only a moment, and then she turned away.

The two stewardesses who had come for Raphaella had been joined by a steward, who stood firmly behind her now, and one of the spare exits was opened at the rear of the plane, near where she and Alex had sat, as the stewardesses announced on the PA system that passengers would be deplaning up front. The door at the rear opened briefly, and Raphaella and the three crew members stepped quickly out. The door was immediately shut again, and only a few of the passengers in the rear wondered what had happened and why the woman in the dark mink had been taken out. But they were busy with their own lives, their own plans, and only Alex stood there for a long moment, watching the door through which she had fled. Once more she had escaped him. Once more the woman of the dark, haunting beauty was gone. But now he knew that her name was Raphaella, and that she would be staying at the Carlyle.

Suddenly, with a sinking feeling, he realized that he didn't know her last name. Raphaella. Raphaella what? How could he ask for her at the hotel? Now his only hope was to see her the next day at lunch. If she showed up, if she could get away from her relatives . . . if . . . He felt like a small terrified schoolboy as he picked up his coat and his briefcase and began to make his way toward the front of the plane.

CHAPTER 6

The waiter at the Four Seasons escorted the tall, attractive woman across the floor to her usual table near the bar. The stark modern decor served as the perfect backdrop for the colorful people who populated the restaurant night and day. As she made her way to the table the woman smiled, nodded, acknowledged a friend who stopped a conversation just long enough to wave. Charlotte Brandon was a regular here. For her it was like having lunch at her club, and her tall, thin frame moved with ease in the familiar surroundings, her snow-colored hair peeking out from beneath a very becoming dark mink hat, which perfectly matched the beautiful mink coat she wore over a navy-blue dress. In her ears were sapphires and diamonds, and around her neck three strands of large beautiful pearls, and on her left hand a single sapphire, which she had bought herself for her fiftieth birthday, after she had sold her fifteenth book. The previous book had sold over three million copies in paperback, and she had decided to splurge and buy the ring.

It still amazed her to realize that her career had all started with the death of her husband when his plane crashed, and she had taken her first job, doing research for a very boring column she had never really enjoyed. But what she had enjoyed, she discovered quickly, was writing, and when she sat down to write her first novel, she felt as though she had come home at last. The first book had done nicely, and the second had done better, but the third book was a best-seller right off the bat, and from then on it was hard work but smooth sailing, and she loved her work more every year, with each book. For years now all that had really mattered to her were her books and her children and her grandchild, Amanda.

There had never really been anyone important in her life after her husband died, but eventually she had forced herself to go out with other men. There had been half a lifetime now of close friends, warm relationships, but never anyone she wanted to marry. For twenty years the children had been her excuse, and now it was always her work. "I'm too difficult to live with. My hours are impossible. I write all night and sleep all day. It would drive you crazy! You'd hate it!" Her excuses were numerous and not very valid. She was a well-organized, well-disciplined woman who was able to schedule her working hours like an army battalion going on a march. The truth was that she didn't want to get married again. She would never love anyone after Arthur Hale. He had been the bright light in her heavens, he had been the model for half a dozen heroes in her books. And Alexander looked so much like him, it always brought a lump to her throat just to see him, so dark, so tall, so long and lean and handsome. It filled her with pride to realize that this extraordinarily beautiful, intelligent, warm human being was also her son. It was a very different feeling from what she had when she saw her daughter. Kay always filled her with some secret guilt over what she had done wrong. Why had Kay turned out so bitter, so cold, and so angry? What could have made her that way? Was it her mother's long work hours? The death of her father? Sibling rivalry? For Charlotte there was always a sense of failure, of sorrow and misgiving, when she looked into those cold eyes so much like her own yet there was nothing happy reflected there.

She was so different from Alex, who stood to his full height now as he saw his mother, with genuine glee in his eyes and a warm happy smile.

"My God, Mother, you look gorgeous!" He stooped slightly to kiss her and she gave him a quick hug. It was the first time in several months that he'd come to New York from San Francisco, but she never really felt that they were very far apart. He called her often, to see how she was, to tell her some story, to inquire about her latest book, or to explain his most recent case. She had an ongoing sense of belonging in his life, yet with neither of them clinging too tight. It was a relationship that in every way she cherished. She sat down across the table from her son, and her joy to be seeing him showed in her eyes. "You look better than ever!" He smiled at her with obvious pride.

"Flattery, my darling, is wicked but delightful. Thank you." Her eyes danced into his and he grinned at her. At sixty-two she was still a glamorous woman, tall, graceful, elegant, with the smooth skin of a woman almost half her age. Cosmetic surgery had assisted her in maintaining the beautiful face and smooth complexion, but she had been a dazzling woman from the first. And as involved as she was in the promotion and publicity of her works, it wasn't surprising that she was anxious to stay young. Over the years Charlotte Brandon had become a large business. As the woman behind the pen, she knew her face was an important part of her image, as was her warmth and her vitality. She was a woman whom other women respected and who had won the devotion of her readers over three decades. "So what have you been up to? You look wonderful too, I might add."

"I've been busy. Nonstop in fact since I last saw you." But as he said it, his eyes strayed suddenly to the door. For an instant he had thought that he'd seen Raphaella. A dark head in a mink coat had come up the stairs, but he saw that it was a different woman, and his eyes returned rapidly to his mother's face.

"Expecting someone, Alex?" She was quick to see the look in his eyes and she smiled. "Or just tired of California women?"

"Who has time to meet any? I've been working night and day."

"You shouldn't do that." For a moment she looked at him sadly. She wanted more for him than just a half life. She wanted more than that for both her children, but so far neither had seemed to find what they wanted. Alex had had the abortive marriage to Rachel, and Kay was devoured by her passion for politics and the ambition that obscured everything else in her life. Sometimes Charlotte thought that she didn't understand them. She had managed to have both after all, a family and a career, but they told her that times were different, that careers could no longer be run as genteely as hers had been. Were they right or just kidding themselves about their own failures? She wondered now as she watched her son, questioning if he was happy with his solitary existence or if he wanted something different after all. She wondered if he had a serious relationship with a woman, someone he truly loved.

"Don't look so worried, Mother." He patted her hand with a smile and waved to the waiter. "Drink?" She nodded, and he ordered Bloody Marys for both of them, and then he sat back with a grin. He had to tell her. Now, in case Raphaella arrived on time. He told her one o'clock, and he had met his mother at twelve thirty. Then again there was the chance that Raphaella wouldn't come at all. His brow clouded for an instant, and then he looked into his mother's deep blue eyes. "I invited a friend to join us. I'm not sure she can make it." And then, looking boyish and embarrassed, he looked down for a moment and then back into the blue eyes. "I hope you don't mind." But Charlotte Brandon was already laughing, a youthful, happy sound that filled the air, and it always made him smile. "Stop laughing at me, Mother." But her laughter was always contagious, and he found himself grinning as amusement danced in her eyes.

"You look about fourteen years old, Alex. I'm sorry. Who in God's name did you invite to lunch?"

"Just a friend. Oh, dammit. A woman." He almost added, "I picked her up on a plane."

"Is she a friend of yours here in New York?" The questions weren't prying, they were friendly, as Charlotte continued to smile at her son.

"No. She lives in San Francisco. She's just here for a few days. We flew in on the same plane."

"That's nice. What does she do?" She took the first sip of her drink, wondering if she shouldn't ask, but she was always curious about his friends. Sometimes it was hard not to sound like a mother, but when she pushed too hard, he always told her gently to stop. She looked at him inquiringly now, but he didn't seem to mind. He looked happier than she'd seen him look in a long time, and there was something wonderfully warm and gentle about his eyes. He had never looked that way with Rachel, he had always looked so uncomfortable then and so worried. She suddenly found herself wondering if Alex had some kind of surprise in store.

But he was only grinning at her in amusement, in answer to her question. "You may find this difficult to believe, Famous Author Charlotte Brandon, but she doesn't seem to do a damn thing."

"My, my. How decadent." But Charlotte did not look disturbed, only curious at what she read in the eyes of her son. "Is she very young?" That would explain it. Very young people had a right to take some time to figure out what to do. But when they were a little older, Charlotte expected them to have found their way, at least to some kind of job.

"No. I mean, not that young. She's about thirty. But she's European."

"Ah." His mother said, understanding. "Now I see."

"It's strange though." He looked pensive for a moment. "I've never known anyone who's led that kind of life. Her father is French, and her mother is Spanish, and she has spent most of her life locked up, surrounded, escorted, besieged by relatives and duennas. It seems like an incredible life."

"How did you ever get her away from them all long enough to get to know her?" Charlotte was intrigued and took her attention away only long enough to wave vaguely at a friend halfway across the room.

"I haven't yet. But I plan to. That was one of the reasons why I invited her to lunch today. She adores your books."

"Oh, God, Alex, not one of those. For God's sake, how can I eat with people asking me questions about how long I've written and how many months it took to write each one of my books?" But her tone of reproach was playful, and she still wore a halfhearted smile. "Why can't you play with girls who prefer other authors? Some nice girl who likes to read Proust or Balzac or Camus, or adores reading the memoirs of Winston Churchill. Someone sensible."

He chuckled at the earnest look she wore and then suddenly over her shoulder he saw a vision enter the Four Seasons, and Charlotte Brandon thought she actually heard him catch his breath. Seeing the direction in which he was staring, she turned to see a remarkably beautiful, tall, dark-haired young woman standing at the top of the stairs, looking tremendously fragile and yet at the same time entirely self-possessed. She was a most beautiful woman and all eyes were turned toward her in frank admiration as they stared. Her posture was perfect, her head held high, her hair gleaming in a carefully woven knot of what looked like black silk. She wore a narrow dress of dark chocolate-brown cashmere, which was almost the same color as the rich fur. She had a creamy silk

Hermès scarf knotted loosely around her neck, there were pearls and diamonds in her ears. Her legs looked endless and graceful in chocolate-colored stockings and brown suede shoes. The bag she wore was in the same rich brown leather, and this time it was not Gucci but Hermès. She was the most beautiful creature that Charlotte had seen in years, and she suddenly understood the rapt expression of her son. What also struck her, as Alex excused himself from the table and approached her, was that there was something very familiar about the girl. It was a face that Charlotte had seen somewhere, or maybe it was only that she was so typical of the aristocracy of Spain. She had a grace and a presence as she moved toward the table that suggested the bearing of a young queen, yet at the same time from the look in her eyes one could sense a gentleness, a shyness, which were remarkable given her striking good looks. This time it was Charlotte who almost uttered an exclamation as she watched her. The girl was so beautiful that one could only observe her with awe. And it was easy to understand Alex's fascination. This was a very, very rare gem.

"Mother, I'd like to introduce you to Raphaella. Raphaella, my mother, Charlotte Brandon." For an instant Charlotte wondered at the absence of a surname, but the question was forgotten as she looked into the dark, haunted eyes of the girl. At close range one could see that she was almost frightened, and she was a little out of breath, as though she had run. She shook hands very properly with Charlotte, and let Alex take her coat as she sat down.

"I am so terribly sorry to be late, Mrs. Brandon." She looked Charlotte squarely in the eye, a faint blush on her creamy cheeks. "I was engaged. It was difficult to . . . get free." Her eyelashes veiled her eyes as she settled back in her seat, and Alex felt for an instant as though he would melt watching her. She was the most incredible woman he had ever seen. And as she looked at them side by side, Charlotte couldn't help thinking that they made a remarkable pair. Their dark heads close together, the big eyes, the splendid young limbs, the graceful hands. They looked like two young gods of mythology destined to make a pair. Charlotte had to force herself back into the conversation with a pleasant smile.

"Not at all, dear. Don't worry. Alex and I were just catching up. He tells me that you flew in from San Francisco last night also. To visit friends?"

"To meet my mother." Raphaella began to relax slowly, although she had declined a drink when she sat down.

"Does she live here?"

"No, in Madrid. She is passing through on her way to Buenos Aires. And she thought that . . . well, it gives me a chance to come to New York for a few days."

"She's lucky to see you. I always feel that way when Alex comes to town." All three of them smiled then, and Alex induced them to order lunch before they went on. It was after that that Raphaella confessed to Charlotte how much her books had meant to her over the years.

"I will admit that I used to read them in Spanish, and now and then in French, but when I first came to this country, my—" She blushed and lowered her eyes for a moment. She had been about to tell them that her husband had bought some of Charlotte's books for her in English, but suddenly she had stopped. It seemed dishonest, but she didn't want to talk about John Henry now. "I bought them in English, and now I read them all in English all the time." And then her eyes grew slowly sad again as she looked at Charlotte. "You don't know how much your work has meant to me. Sometimes I think it's what has"—her voice was so soft it was almost inaudible—"sometimes it's what has kept me alive." The agony in her voice was plainly apparent as Charlotte watched her, and Alex was reminded of the first time he had seen her crying on the stairs. Now in the splendor of the New York restaurant he found himself wondering what was the secret that weighed so heavily on her soul. But she only looked up at his mother, with a small smile of thanks, and without thinking, Charlotte reached out and touched her hand.

"They mean a lot to me when I write them. But the important thing is that they mean something to people like you. Thank you, Raphaella. It's a beautiful compliment, and in a sense it makes my life worthwhile." And then, as though she sensed something hidden, some distant wish, some dream, she looked hard at Raphaella. "Do you write too?"

But Raphaella only smiled and shook her head, looking very young and childlike and not as sophisticated as she had seemed at first. "Oh, no!" And then she laughed. "But I am a storyteller."

"That's the first step." In silence Alex watched them. He loved seeing them together, the richness of the contrast, two beautiful women, yet one so young and so fragile, the other so mature and so strong, one with white hair and one with black, one he knew so well and the other not at all. Yet he wanted to know her. He wanted to know her better than he had ever known anyone before. As he watched them he listened to his mother go on. "What kind of a storyteller are you, Raphaella?"

"I tell stories to children. In the summer. All my little cousins. We spend the summer together in our family house in Spain." But Charlotte's knowledge of such family "houses" told her that it was something more than that. "There are dozens of them, we are a very large family, and I always love to take the children in hand. And I tell them stories"—and she smiled happily—"and they listen, and giggle, and laugh. It's wonderful, it does something good to the soul."

Charlotte smiled at the younger woman's expression as she nodded, and then as she gazed at her, it was as though everything came into focus in her head. Raphaella . . . Raphaella . . . Spain . . . a family estate there . . . and Paris . . . a bank. . . . She had to fight an impulse to say something aloud. Instead she let Alex carry on the conversation as she looked again and again at the face of the girl. And as she looked she wondered if Alex knew the whole story. Something told her that he did not.

Only an hour after she had joined them, Raphaella looked regretfully but nervously at her watch. "I am so sorry . . . I'm afraid I must go back to my mother and my aunt and my cousins. They will probably think that I've run away." She didn't tell Alex's mother that she had feigned a headache to escape lunch with her own entourage.

She had desperately wanted to meet Charlotte Brandon, and to see Alex again, if only once. He offered now to escort her to a taxi, and leaving his mother with a fresh pot of *café filtre*, he promised to return immediately and left with his ravishing friend

on his arm. Before she left, Raphaella had said everything proper to Charlotte, and for a single moment
their eyes had met and held. It was as though Raphaella were telling her the whole story, and as
though Charlotte were telling her that she already
knew. It was one of those silent communications that
happen between women, and for as long as their eyes
held, Charlotte felt her heart go out to this lovely
young girl. She had remembered the whole story as
she sat there, only now it was no longer a tragic item
in the news, she had seen the living, breathing, lonely
young woman to whom the tragedy had occurred. For
an instant she had wanted to put her arms around her,
but instead she had only shaken the cool slender hand
and watched them go, her son so handsome and the
girl so startlingly lovely as they disappeared down the
stairs.

Alex was gazing at her with obvious pleasure as
they emerged onto the street and stood there for a moment, inhaling the cool autumn air and feeling happy
and young. His eyes danced and he couldn't help smiling as she looked up at him with something sad and
wise and yet also something happy lurking in her
eyes. "My mother adored you, you know."

"I don't know why she would. But I also adored her.
What a lovely woman she is, Alex. She has all the
qualities a woman should have."

"Yeah, she's a pretty nice old girl." He said it in
teasing fashion, but he wasn't thinking of his mother
as he looked into Raphaella's eyes. "When am I going
to see you again?"

But she looked away nervously before she answered, glancing into the street to see if there was a
passing cab. And then she looked back at Alex, her

eyes dark and troubled, her face suddenly inexplicably sad. "I can't Alex. I'm sorry. I must be with my mother . . . and—"

"You can't be with them day and night." He sounded stubborn, and she smiled. There was no way that he could understand it. He had never lived a life like hers.

"But I am. Every moment. And then I must go home."

"So must I. Then I'll see you there. Which reminds me, young lady, there was something you forgot to tell me when you told me you were staying at the Carlyle."

"What?" She looked suddenly troubled.

"Your last name."

"Did I do that?" It was difficult to tell if her innocence was real or feigned.

"You did. If you hadn't shown up today, I would have been forced to sit in the lobby of the Carlyle for the rest of the week, waiting until you walked by, and then I'd have thrown myself at your feet in front of your mother and embarrassed you royally, begging for your name!" They were both laughing as he said it, and he gently took her hand in his own. "Raphaella, I want to see you again." She looked up at him, her eyes melting into his, wanting everything he wanted, but knowing that she had no right. He bent slowly toward her, wanting to kiss her, but she turned away, burying her face in his shoulder and holding tightly to the lapel of his coat with one hand.

"No, Alex, don't." He understood that if her world were filled with duennas, then she wasn't likely to kiss a man in the street.

"All right. But I want to see you, Raphaella. What

about tonight?" There was a brief chuckle in his shoulder as she moved to look at him again.

"What about my mother, and my aunt and my cousins?" He was impossible, he was so stubborn, but he was also one of the nicest men she had ever met.

"Bring them along. I'll bring my mother." He was only teasing and she knew it, and this time she laughed out loud.

"You're impossible."

"I know. And I also won't take no for an answer."

"Alex, please!" She looked at her watch again and suddenly panicked. "Oh, my God, they'll kill me! By now they must be back from lunch."

"Then promise you'll see me tonight for a drink." He held tightly to her arm, and then suddenly remembered. "And what the hell is your last name?"

She flung a hand away from him and hailed a cab passing nearby. It shrieked to a stop next to them, and Alex held the one arm more tightly. "Alex, don't. I have to—"

"Not until—" It was half a game and half in earnest and she laughed nervously and looked into his eyes again.

"All right. All right. Phillips."

"Is that how you're registered at the Carlyle?"

"Yes, your honor." She looked meek for a moment and then nervous again. "But, Alex, I can't see you. Not here, and not in San Francisco, and not ever. This must be good-bye."

"For chrissake, don't be silly. This is just the beginning."

"No, it's not." She looked serious for a moment as she stood there, and the cabbie snorted impatiently while Alex glared. "This is not the beginning, Alex, it's the end. And I must go now."

"Not like that!" Alex looked suddenly desperate, and then regretted that he hadn't kissed her. "What? You just had lunch with me so you could meet my famous mother? Is that nice?" He was teasing but she looked at him in confusion and he knew that he had scored a hit.

"Oh, Alex, how could you—"

"Will you see me later?"

"Alex—"

"Never mind. Eleven o'clock tonight. The Café Carlyle. We can talk and listen to Bobby Short. And if you're not there, I'll come upstairs and pound on your mother's door." But he looked suddenly worried. "Can you get away from them by eleven?" Even he had to admit that it was funny. She was thirty-two years old and he was asking her if she could escape her mother. In fact it was utterly absurd.

"I'll try." She grinned at him, looking suddenly young again, but with a hint of something guilty about her eyes. "We shouldn't do this."

"Why not?"

She was about to tell him, but knew that she couldn't, standing on the sidewalk with an impatient cab driver beginning to snarl. "We'll talk about it tonight."

"Good." He grinned broadly. Then she'd be there. And with that, he pulled open the door to the cab and swept her a bow. "See you this evening, Miss Phillips." He bent slightly and kissed her on the forehead; a moment later the door was closed and the cab was speeding uptown as Raphaella sat in the backseat furious at her own weakness. She should never have misled him from the beginning. She should have told him the truth on the plane, and she should never have gone to lunch. But just once, just once, she told herself, she had a right to do something wild and romantic and amusing. Or did she have that right at all? What gave her that right when John Henry sat dying in his wheelchair? How dare she play such games? As the cab neared the Carlyle she vowed that that night she would tell Alex that she was married. And she was not going to see him again. After tonight . . . there was still one more meeting . . . and her heart fluttered just at the thought of seeing him one more time.

"Well?" Alex looked at his mother victoriously and sat down. She smiled at him, and as she did so she felt suddenly very old. How young he looked, how hopeful, how happy, how blind.

"Well what?" The blue eyes were gentle and sad.

"What do you mean, 'Well what?' Isn't she incredible?"

"Yes." Charlotte said it matter of factly. "She is probably the most beautiful young woman I've ever seen. And she is charming and gentle and lovely and I like her. But, Alex. . . ." She hesitated for a long moment and then decided to speak her mind. "What good is that going to do you?"

"What's that supposed to mean?" He looked suddenly annoyed as he took a sip of his cold coffee. "She's wonderful."

"How well do you know her?"

"Not very." He grinned at her then. "But I'm hoping to change that, in spite of her mother and her aunt and her cousins and her duennas."

"What about her husband?" Alex looked suddenly as though he had been shot. His eyes flew open as he stared at her, and then they narrowed again with rare distrust.

"What do you mean, 'her husband'?"

"Alex, do you know who she is?"

"She is half Spanish and half French, she lives in San Francisco, she is unemployed, thirty-two years old, I learned today, and her name is Raphaella Phillips. I just discovered her last name."

"That doesn't ring a bell?"

"No, and for chrissake, stop playing games with me." His eyes darted fire, and Charlotte Brandon sat back in her chair and sighed. She had been right then. The last name confirmed it. She wasn't sure why, but she had remembered that face, though she hadn't seen a photograph of her in the papers for years. The last time was perhaps seven or eight years ago, leaving the hospital, after John Henry Phillips had had his first stroke. "What the hell are you trying to tell me, Mother?"

"That she's married, darling, and to a very important man. Does the name John Henry Phillips mean anything?"

For a fraction of a second Alex closed his eyes. He was thinking that what his mother was telling him couldn't be true. "He's dead, isn't he?"

"No, not as far as I know. He had a series of strokes several years ago, and he must be almost eighty, but I'm sure he's still alive. We'd certainly all have heard about it if he weren't."

"But what makes you think she's his wife?" Alex looked as though an earthquake had struck him, right between the eyes.

"I remember reading the story, and seeing the photographs. She was just as beautiful then. It struck me as shocking at first that he was marrying such a young girl. I don't know, she was seventeen or eighteen, something like that. The daughter of some important French banker. But when I saw them together at a press conference I went to with a journalist friend and I saw some of the photographs, I felt differently. You know, in his day John Henry Phillips was an extraordinary man."

"And now?"

"Who knows. I know that he's bed-ridden and seriously impaired by his strokes, but I don't think the public knows much more than that. She has always been kept very much out of the public eye, which was why I couldn't place her at first. But that face . . . one doesn't forget it easily." Their eyes met and Alex nodded. He hadn't forgotten it easily either, and he knew that he never would. "I take it she hasn't told you any of this." He shook his head again. "I hope she does." His mother's voice was gentle. "She ought to tell you herself. Maybe I shouldn't have. . . ." Her voice trailed off and he shook his head again, and then stared miserably up at the woman who was his oldest friend.

"Why? Why should she be married to that ancient bastard? He's old enough to be her grandfather, and he's practically dead." The injustice of it tore at everything in his heart. Why? Why should he have Raphaella?

"But he isn't dead, Alex. I don't understand what she has in mind with you. Except that I'll tell you honestly I think that she herself is confused. She's not sure what she's doing with you. And you should keep in mind that she has led a totally sheltered life. John Henry Phillips has kept her totally concealed from the public for almost fifteen years. I don't think she's used to meeting brash young lawyers or having casual affairs. I may be wrong about her, but I don't think I am."

"I don't think you are either. Christ." He sat back in his chair with a long unhappy sigh. "Now what?"

"Are you seeing her again?"

He nodded. "Later tonight. She said she wanted to talk to me." He wondered if she would tell him then. And then what?

Alex realized as he sat staring into space across from his mother that John Henry Phillips might live for another twenty years—at which time Alex would be almost sixty, and Raphaella would be fifty-two. A lifetime of waiting for an old man to die.

"What are you thinking?" His mother's voice was very soft.

Slowly he dragged his eyes back to hers. "Nothing very pleasant. You know," he spoke slowly, "I saw her one night on the steps near her house. She was crying. I thought about her for days until I saw her again on the plane coming here. And we talked, and—" He looked up at his mother bleakly.

"Alex, you hardly know her."

"You're wrong. I do know her. I feel as though I know her better than anyone else. I know her soul and her mind and her heart. I know what she feels and how lonely she is. And now I know why. And I know something else." He looked long and hard at his mother.

"What's that, Alex?"

"That I love her. I know that sounds crazy, but I do."

"You don't know that. It's too soon. She's almost a complete stranger."

"No, she isn't." And then he said nothing further. He put his credit card down for the check, looked at his mother, and said, "We'll work it out." But Charlotte Brandon only nodded, thinking it unlikely that they would.

When Alex left her a few minutes later on Lexington Avenue, the look in his eyes told her that he was determined. And as he bowed his head in the stiff breeze and walked briskly north, he knew in his own mind that he didn't care what it would take to win Raphaella, but he would do it. He had never before wanted any woman as he wanted her. And his fight for her had just begun. It wasn't a fight that Alex Hale was willing to lose.

CHAPTER 7

At five minutes to eleven in the evening, after a brisk walk up Madison Avenue, Alex Hale turned right on 76th Street and walked into the Carlyle.

He had reserved a table for them in the Café Carlyle, with every intention of chatting with Raphaella for an hour and then enjoying Bobby Short's midnight show. He was one of the greater gifts of New York, and sharing him with Raphaella was a treat Alex had looked forward to all night. He checked his coat at the door and wove his way to the designated table, and then sat there for ten minutes, waiting for her to arrive. At eleven fifteen he began to worry, and at eleven thirty he wondered if he should call her room. But he realized that was impossible. Especially now that he knew about her husband. He realized that he had to wait for her quietly without creating a stir.

At twenty minutes before twelve he saw her staring through the glass door and looking as though she were poised to run. He tried to catch her eye but she didn't see him, and then, after a moment of scanning the room, she disappeared. Almost without thinking, Alex rose from the table and hurried to the door and out into the lobby in time to see her escaping down the hall. "Raphaella!" he called out softly, and she turned, her eyes huge and frightened, her face very pale. She was wearing a beautiful ivory satin evening dress that fell straight from her shoulders to its black-bordered hem at her feet. On her left shoulder she wore a huge elaborate pin with an enormous baroque pearl at its center, surrounded by onyx and diamonds, and she wore earrings to match. The effect was very striking, and Alex noticed once again how incredibly beautiful she was. She had stopped when he called her, and she stood very still now as he stood in front of her with a look of great seriousness in his eyes. "Don't run away yet. Let's have a drink and talk." His voice was very gentle, and he wanted to reach out to her, but he didn't even dare to touch her hand.

"I—I shouldn't. I can't. I came to tell you that . . . I'm sorry—it's so late . . . I—"

"Raphaella, it's not even midnight. Couldn't we talk for just half an hour?"

"There are so many people. . . ." She looked unhappy as they stood there, and suddenly he remembered the Bemelmans bar. He was sorry to miss out on Bobby Short with her, but it meant more to him to spend the time talking about what she had on her mind.

"There's another bar here where we'll be able to talk more quietly. Come on." And without waiting for an answer, he tucked her hand into his arm, and led her back down the hallway to a bar across from the Café Carlyle, and here they slipped onto a banquette behind a small table, and Alex looked at her with a slow, happy smile. "What would you like to drink? Some wine? Some sherry?" But she only shook her head in answer, and he saw that she was still very distressed. When the waiter had left them, he turned to her and spoke softly. "Raphaella, is something wrong?" She nodded slowly, first looking down at her hands, her perfect profile etched sharply in the darkened room as he watched her.

She looked up at him, her eyes seeking his, as though that alone caused her great pain. The look of sorrow on her face was the same that he had seen that first evening when he had found her crying on the steps. "Why don't we talk about it?"

She took a little breath and sat back against the banquette, still keeping her eyes locked in his. "I should have spoken to you about it earlier, Alex. I have been" —she hesitated on the words and then went on—"very deceitful with you. I don't know what happened. I think I was carried away. You were so nice on the plane. Your mother was so charming. But I have been most unfair to you, my friend. . . ." Her eyes were filled with sorrow and she gently touched his hand. "I have given you the impression that I am free, I have been very wrong to do so. And I must apologize to you now." She looked at him bleakly and withdrew her hand. "I am married, Alex. I should have told you that from the first. I don't know why I played this game with you. But it was very, very wrong. I can't see you again."

She was a woman of honor, and he was touched to the core by the earnestness with which she looked at him now, the tears dancing on the tips of her lashes, her eyes so very big, her face so very pale.

He spoke to her carefully and with great seriousness, as he did to Amanda when she was a very little girl. "Raphaella, I respect you very much for what you have just done. But must that affect our—our friendship? I can accept your situation. Couldn't we go on seeing each other in spite of that?" It was an honest question, and he wasn't about to let go.

She shook her head sadly. "I would like to see you . . . if—if I were free. But I am a married woman. It's not possible. It wouldn't be right."

"Why?"

"It would not be fair to my husband. And he is such"—she faltered on the words—"such a good man. He has been . . . so fair . . . so kind to me. . . ." She turned her face away and Alex saw a tear roll swiftly down one delicate, ivory cheek. He reached out a hand to smooth his fingertips across the satiny softness of her face, and suddenly he wanted to cry too. She couldn't mean it. She couldn't mean to be faithful to her husband for the rest of his life. The horror of that began to dawn on him as he watched her face.

"But, Raphaella . . . you can't be . . . the night I saw you on the steps . . . you're not happy. I know that. Why can't we see each other and just enjoy what we have?"

"Because I have no right to that. I'm not free."

"For God's sake—" He was about to tell her that he knew everything, but she stopped him with one hand held out as though to defend herself from an aggressor, and with one swift movement she stood up and looked down at him with the tears still running down her face.

"No, Alex, no! I can't. I'm married. And I'm very, very sorry for letting it go this far. I shouldn't have. I was dishonest to come to lunch with your mother. . . ."

"Stop confessing and sit down." He reached out gently for her arm and pulled her toward him back onto the seat, and for reasons that she herself did not understand, she let him, and then he wiped the tears from her cheeks with his hand. "Raphaella." He spoke very softly so that no one else could hear. "I love you. I know that sounds crazy. We hardly know each other, but I love you. I've been looking for you for years and years. You can't walk out on that now. Not for what you have with—with your husband."

"What do you mean?"

"I mean that from what I understand from my mother, your husband is very old, and very ill, and has been for years. I have to admit, I had no idea who you were when I met you, it was my mother who recognized you, she told me who you were and about—about your husband."

"Then she knew. She must think I'm awful." Raphaella looked deeply ashamed.

"No." He was definite and his voice sounded urgent as he leaned toward her. He could almost feel the warmth of her silky flesh next to his and he had never been as filled with desire as he was right then, but this was no time for passion. He had to talk to her, make sense to her, make her see. "How could anyone think you awful? You've been faithful to him, haven't you, all these years?" It was almost a rhetorical question and she nodded her head slowly and then sighed.

"I have. But there is no reason to stop now. I have no right to behave as though I'm free, Alex. I'm not. And I have no right to confuse your life or touch it with the sorrow of mine."

"The reason your life is so lonely is because that is how you are living it. Lonely and alone with a very sick, elderly man. You have a right to so much more than that."

"Yes. But it's not his fault things turned out as they did."

"Nor is it yours. Must you punish yourself?"

"No, but I cannot punish him." The way she said it told him that he was losing the battle again, and he felt a desperate sinking in his heart. And as he did she stood up again, but this time with great determination. "I must go now." His eyes begged her not to. "I must." And then, without saying anything further, she let her lips gently brush his brow as she kissed him softly and walked quickly from the bar. He made a single move to follow her, and she shook her head and held up a hand. He knew that once again she was crying, but he also knew that this time he had lost. To pursue her would only make her more unhappy and he knew that there was nothing that he could do. He had sensed that as she was speaking. She was bound to John Henry Phillips in marriage and in honor, and it was not a bond that Raphaella was prepared to break, nor would she even stretch it, and certainly not for a perfect stranger, a man she had met the day before on a plane.

Alex Hale paid for his drink at the bar at the Carlyle, forgot about the table he had reserved across the hall to see Bobby Short, and walked out onto Madison Avenue, his arm up for a cab to take him back to his hotel. And when he slid onto the seat, the cabbie glanced in his rearview mirror, chomped hard on his cigar, and looked surprised. "Must be cold out there, huh, buddy?" It was the only obvious explanation he could find for the tears spilling from Alex's eyes and rolling swiftly down his cheeks.

CHAPTER 8

Alex and his niece stood side by side for a long moment, watching the skaters circle gracefully below them in Rockefeller Center. They had just finished an early dinner at the Café Français and he had to get her home by eight o'clock if he was going to catch his plane.

"I wish I could spend my life like that, Uncle Alex." The small delicate blond girl with the China-blue eyes and soft halo of curls looked up at her uncle with a smile.

"What? Skating?" He smiled, as much at what she had said as at the tiny figure she was beside him. They had shared a pleasant evening, and as always the loneliness of the pretty teen-ager tore at his heart. She was like no one else in her family. Not her mother or father, not even her grandmother, or Alex himself. She was quiet and devoted, gentle and lonely and loyal. She reminded him in fact of Raphaella as they stood in the chill air. Perhaps they were both people who had suffered at the hands of life, and he wondered if they were almost equally lonely as he looked down at the young girl. He had also been wondering all evening what was on her mind. She had seemed quiet and troubled and now she watched the skaters with a look of longing, like a very hungry child. He wished suddenly that he weren't taking the night flight to San Francisco, and that he had more time to spend with her, maybe they could even have rented skates. But he already had his reservation and had given up his room at the hotel. "Next time I'm in town, we'll come do this."

She grinned up at him. "I'm real good now, you know."

"Oh, yeah?" His look was teasing. "How come?"

"I go skating all the time."

"Here?" He glanced down at the graceful girl with pleasure. And he was sorry again that he didn't have time to let her show him how "real good" she was.

But she was shaking her head in answer. "Not here. I can't afford this on my allowance." That in itself seemed to him absurd. Her father was one of the leading surgeons in Manhattan, and Kay certainly had a decent sum of her own money by now. "I skate in the park, Uncle Alex." It was only now and then that she still called him that.

"By yourself?" He looked horrified and she smiled at him with hauteur.

"Sometimes. I'm a big girl now, you know."

"Big enough not to get mugged?" He looked angry as they stood there and she shook her head and laughed.

"You sound just like Grandma."

"Does she know you go skating in Central Park

alone? Come to think of it, does your mother?" In the end Kay had gone back to Washington before he got there and he hadn't seen her this trip at all.

"They both know. And I'm careful. If I skate at night, I leave the park with other people, so I don't have to walk alone."

"And how do you know those 'other people' won't hurt you?"

"Why should they?"

"Oh, for chrissake, Mandy, you know what it's like here. You've lived in New York all your life. Do I have to explain to you what one doesn't do here?"

"It's not the same for a kid. Why would someone mug me? What would they get? Two rolls of Life Savers, three bucks, and my keys?"

"Maybe. Or"—he hated even to say it—"or maybe something much more precious. They could hurt you." He didn't want to say rape. Not to the innocent little face looking up at him with the funny smile. "Look, just do me a favor. Don't do it." And then, with a frown between his eyes, he reached into his pocket and pulled out his wallet, whence he took out a single brand-new hundred-dollar bill. He handed it to Amanda with a serious expression, and her eyes grew wide in surprise.

"What are you doing?"

"That is your skating fund. I want you to come here from now on. And when you run out, I want you to tell me and I'll send you some more. That's just between you and me, young lady, but I don't want you skating in Central Park anymore. Is that clear?"

"Yes, sir. But, Alex, you're crazy! A hundred dollars!" And then she grinned broadly and looked again about ten years old. "Wow!" And without further ado she stood on tiptoe, threw her arms around her uncle, kissed him soundly on the cheek, and stuffed the hundred-dollar bill into her little denim bag. The fact that she had taken it made him feel better, but what he didn't know and would have worried him severely was that as often as she skated, the money would only last for a few weeks. And she would have been embarrassed to ask him to send her more money. She just wasn't that kind of girl. She wasn't demanding. And she was always grateful for whatever she got without asking for more.

Reluctantly he looked at his watch and then down at Amanda. His regret was instantly mirrored in her face. "I'm afraid, young lady, that we're going to have to leave." She nodded and said nothing, wondering how soon she would see him again. His visits were always like a burst of sunshine for her. That and the time that she spent with her grandmother made her life a little more bearable and a lot more worthwhile. They walked slowly up the sloping promenade toward Fifth Avenue, and when they reached the street, he hailed a cab.

"Do you know how soon you'll be back, Alex?"

"I don't know. It won't be too long." He always had the same feeling of pain and remorse when he left her. As though he should have done more for her, and reproached himself that he had not. But how much could one do? How could one replace one blind parent and another who was unfeeling? How could one give a child what she had not had for almost seventeen years? And despite her diminutive size, she was no longer a child, even Alex could no longer ignore that. She was a singularly beautiful young girl. It was only amazing that she had not yet discovered that herself.

"Will you be back for Thanksgiving?"

"Maybe." He saw the imploring look in her eyes. "All right. I'll try. But I won't promise." They had by then reached her building, and Alex left her with a hug and a kiss on the cheek and a long hard squeeze. He could see that there were tears sparkling in her eyes as she left him, but her wave as he drove away in the taxi was a gallant one, and her smile was filled with all the promise of her sixteen and a half years. It always made him sad to leave her. Somehow she always reminded him of the opportunities he had missed, the children that he himself didn't have. He would have loved it if Amanda had been his daughter. And that thought in itself always made him angry. His sister didn't deserve a child as lovely as that.

He gave the driver the address of his hotel, where he picked up his luggage from the doorman, and then settled back in the seat with another glance at his watch and a long tired sigh. "Kennedy Airport, please. United." He realized then that it would be good to get home. He had only been in New York for two days but they had drained him. The exchange with Raphaella the night before had left him feeling bleak and lonely. His business had gone well, but it seemed eclipsed by the emotional turmoil he felt as they drove slowly uptown. He found himself thinking less and less of Amanda and more and more of Raphaella as he sat there. He was sorry for her, and yet at the same time angry. Why did she insist on being faithful to a husband who was old enough to be her grandfather and already half dead? It didn't make any sense. It was crazy. . . . He remembered the look on

her face as she had walked away from him the night
before. Yesterday. He had seen her only yesterday.
And then suddenly, with an inexplicable surge of
rage, he asked himself why he had to be understanding, why he had to accept what she said. "Go away"
was in effect what she had told him. But he had decided not to. All of a sudden. Just like that. "Driver."
Alex looked around him as though he had suddenly
woken up. They were on 99th Street on the East River
Drive. "Take me to the Carlyle."

"Now?"

Alex nodded emphatically. "Now."

"Not the airport?"

"No." To hell with it. He could always stay at his
mother's apartment if he missed the plane back to San
Francisco. She had gone to Boston for the weekend to
do some promotional appearances for her new book.
It was worth one more try, just to see her. If she was
there. If she would come downstairs to see him. If. . . .

In her room at the Carlyle, Raphaella was stretched
out on the large double bed in a pink satin bathrobe,
wearing cream-colored lace underwear underneath.
For the first time in what seemed like centuries, she
was alone. She had just said good-bye to her mother
and her aunt and her cousins, who were by now at the
airport, boarding the plane for Buenos Aires. She was
going back to San Francisco in the morning, but for
tonight she could relax at the Carlyle and do absolutely nothing. She didn't have to be charming, pleasant, patient. She didn't have to translate for her family
in a dozen elegant stores. She didn't have to order
meals for them or run around the city shopping. She
could just lie there with a book and relax, and in a

few moments room service would bring her dinner to her room. She would eat it in solitary splendor in the living room of the suite she always stayed in, and she looked around as she lay there, feeling a mixture of exhaustion and delight. It was so good not to hear them chattering, not to have to feign amusement or pretend to be happy every moment anymore. She hadn't had a minute to herself since she'd got there. Not that she ever did. That was the whole point. She wasn't supposed to be alone. Never. That was not the role of a woman. A woman had to be surrounded, protected, guarded. Except of course if it was just a matter of being alone overnight at the hotel as she was now, before going back to San Francisco in the morning. She would keep to her room, order room service, and in the morning leave for the airport in a limousine.

After all, one had to be careful, she reminded herself cynically in her room, if she wasn't, look what happened. As they had a thousand times in the last forty-eight hours, her thoughts flew to Alex, to the shape of his face, the look in his eyes, the broad shoulders, the softness of his hair—that was what happened. One got accosted by strangers on airplanes. One went to lunch with them. One went out for drinks. One forgot one's obligations. And one fell in love.

She reminded herself once more of her decision, consoled herself that it was the right thing to do, and forced her mind back to other things. There was no reason to think about Alex Hale anymore, she told herself. No reason at all. She would never see him again. She would never know him any better. And his declaration to her the night before was only the infatuation of a very foolish man. Foolish and foolhardy.

How could he expect her to see him again? What made him think that she was willing to have an affair? Her thoughts lingered over his face one more time as she lay there, and she found herself wondering if her mother had ever done anything like that. Had she ever met anyone like Alex? Had any of the women whom she knew in Spain? They seemed perfectly satisfied to lead sequestered lives, lives in which they constantly spent money, bought jewelry and furs and dresses, and went to parties, but lived surrounded by other women, behind carefully guarded walls. What was wrong with her? Why was she suddenly chafing at those traditions? The other women she knew in Paris and Madrid and Barcelona, they had the parties, and the amusements, and the gala events that made the years drift by.

And they had children . . . children . . . her heart always ached when she thought of babies. For years she had been unable to see a pregnant woman walk by her without wanting to burst into tears. She had never told John Henry how bereft she felt for the lack of children. But she always suspected that he knew. It was why he was always so lavish, why he spoiled her so much, and always seemed to love her so much more.

Raphaella forced her eyes shut and sat up in bed in her bathrobe, angry at herself for letting her thoughts take the turn they just had. She was free of that life for one more night, one day. She didn't have to think of John Henry, of his pain, of his strokes, of what would happen to her until he died. She didn't have to think of what she was missing, and what she had already missed. There was no point thinking of parties she would never go to, of people she wouldn't meet, and children she would never have. Her life was cut out for her. It was her destiny, her path, her obligation.

With the back of her hand, she wiped a tear from her cheek and forced herself to pick up the book that lay beside her on the bed. It was the Charlotte Brandon she had bought at the airport, and it was these thoughts that her books always kept her from. For as long as the books lasted, they kept everything but their intricate stories from her mind. They were her only haven, and they had been for years. With a comfortable sigh she opened the book again, grateful that Charlotte Brandon was still able to write two a year. Sometimes Raphaella read them over. She had read most of her books at least two or three times each. Sometimes she read them in different languages. But she had read only two or three pages when the phone rang and broke into the world into which she had fled.

"Hello?" It seemed odd that someone should call her. Her mother was supposed to be already on the plane. And they never called her from San Francisco, unless something had gone terribly wrong. And she had called John Henry that morning and the nurse had said that he was fine.

"Raphaella?" At first the voice was not familiar, and then suddenly her heart began to pound.

"Yes?" He could barely hear her.

"I—I'm sorry . . . I—I was wondering if I could see you. I know you explained it all to me last night, but I just thought that maybe we could talk about it more calmly, and . . . well, maybe we could just be friends." His heart was pounding as hard as hers. What if she said she didn't want to see him? He couldn't bear the thought suddenly that he might never see her again. "I . . . Raphaella. . . ." She hadn't answered, and he was instantly terrified that she might have hung up the phone. "Are you there?"

"Yes." It was as though she could barely speak now. Why did he have to do this? Why did he have to call her now? She was resigned to her obligations, to her duty, why did he have to taunt her in this terribly cruel way? "I am here."

"Could I . . . could we . . . could I see you? I— I'm leaving for the airport in a few minutes. I just thought I'd stop and see if I could see you." It was all he had wanted to do. Talk to her, once more, before catching the last plane.

"Where are you?" A frown crossed her face as she wondered.

"I'm downstairs." He said it with such an abashed tone of apology that she laughed.

"Here? In the hotel?" She was smiling. He was ridiculous, really. Like a very small boy.

"What do you say?"

"Alex, I'm not dressed." But it was a minor detail. And suddenly they both knew he had won. Even if only for a few minutes. But he had won.

"So what? I don't care if you wear a towel. . . . Raphaella . . . ?" There was a long silence between them. And then he heard the doorbell of the suite in the distance. "Is that your mother?"

"Not very likely. She just left for Buenos Aires. I think it's my dinner."

A second later the door to the suite opened slowly and the waiter rolled the cumbersome table into the room. She signaled that she would sign it, and did so as she returned her attention to the phone.

"So what are we going to do? Will you come downstairs, or do I have to come up and bang on the door of your room. Or I could masquerade as a waiter from room service. How about that?"

"Alex, stop it." And then she sounded serious again. "I said everything there is to say last night."

"No, you didn't. You didn't explain to me why you feel the way you do."

"Because I love my husband." She squeezed her eyes shut, denying what she was already beginning to feel for him. "And I have no choice."

"That's not true. You have a lot of choices. We all do. Sometimes we don't want them, but they're there. And I understand how you feel, and I respect it. But can't we at least talk to each other? Look, I'll stand in the doorway. I won't touch you. I promise. I just want to see you. Raphaella . . . please. . . ."

There were tears in her eyes and she took a deep breath to tell him that he had to go away, that he couldn't do this to her, that it wasn't fair, and then suddenly, not knowing why she did it, she nodded. "All right. Come up. But just for a few minutes." And when she hung up the phone, her hand was trembling and she felt so dizzy that she had to close her eyes.

She didn't even have time to slip into some clothes before he rang the doorbell. She just tightened her robe around her and smoothed down her hair. It was hanging long and heavy down her back, and she looked much younger than she did when she wore it in the elegant knot. She hesitated for an endless moment in front of the door before she opened it, reminding herself that she could still refuse to let him in. But instead she unlocked it and turned the doorknob, and then she stood there, staring up at the remarkably handsome man who stood waiting on the other side. He stood as silent as she did for a moment, and then she took a step backward and gestured inside. But there was no smile on her face now, only a very serious expression as her eyes followed him into the room.

"Hello." He sounded nervous and looked boyish and stood staring at her for a long moment from across the room. "Thank you for letting me come up here like this. I know it's a little crazy, but I had to see you." And as he looked at her, he wondered why he had come. What was he going to tell her? What could he possibly tell her except that everytime he saw her, he was more in love with her than he had been the time before. And when he didn't see her, she haunted him like a ghost he couldn't live without. Instead he just looked at her and nodded. "Thank you."

"It's all right." Her voice was very quiet. "Would you like something to eat?" She waved vaguely at the enormous wheeled table and he shook his head.

"Thank you. I already had dinner with my niece. I didn't mean to interrupt your dinner. Why don't you sit down and start." But she only shook her head and smiled at him.

"It can wait." After a moment's pause she sighed and walked slowly across the room. She looked out into the street with a distracted expression and then slowly back at him. "Alex, I'm sorry. I am deeply touched by what you feel, but there is nothing I can do." The voice that spoke to him was that of a lonely princess, aware always of her royal obligations and regretful that there was nothing more she could do. Everything about her was aristocratic, her posture, her expression, the way she stood there; even in the pink satin bathrobe Raphaella Phillips was regal to the very soles of her feet. The only thing that told him that she was human was the look of intense pain that could not be hidden in her eyes.

"What about what *you* feel, Raphaella. What about you?"

"What about me? I am who I am. I can't change that. I am the wife of John Henry Phillips. I have been for almost fifteen years. I have to live up to that, Alex. I always will."

"And for how many of those years has he been . . . the way he is now?"

"More than seven."

"Is that enough for you? Telling yourself that you are fulfilling an obligation? Does that console you for your lost youth? How old are you now? Thirty-two? You've lived like this since you were twenty-five, Raphaella. How can you? How can you go on?"

Slowly she shook her head in answer, her eyes brimming with tears. "I have to. That's all. It doesn't matter."

"Of course it matters. How can you say that?" He walked to her side and looked down at her gently. "Raphaella, we are talking about your life."

"But there are no choices, Alex. That is what you don't understand. Perhaps that is why the way my mother lives is better. Maybe that's why all of that makes sense. That way, there are no temptations. No one ever gets close enough to force you to make a choice. There are no choices then."

"I'm sorry that this is so painful. But why must it be a choice? Why must we talk about all that now? Why can't we just be friends, you and I? I won't ask anything of you. But we could meet as friends, maybe just for lunch." It was a dream and he knew it, and Raphaella did too as she shook her head.

"How long do you think that would last, Alex? I know how you feel. And I think that you know I feel the same way too." Something in his heart soared as she said it, and he wanted to take her in his arms, but he didn't dare.

"Can we forget that? Can we pretend it doesn't exist?" The look on his face said it was not possible.

"I think we have to." And then, with a small brave smile, "Perhaps in a few years we'll meet again."

"Where? At your family's home in Spain, after they lock you up again? Who are you kidding? Raphaella—" he walked to where she stood and put his hands gently on her shoulders as she looked up at him with those enormous, troubled black eyes that he already loved so much—"Raphaella, people spend a lifetime looking for love, wanting it, needing it, seeking it, and most of the time they don't find it. But once in a while, once in a great while, it comes to you, it throws itself in your lap, pounds on your door, and says 'Here I am, take me, I'm yours.' When it comes, how can you turn away from it? How can you say, 'Not now, maybe later'? How can you take that chance, knowing that the opportunity may never come again?"

"Sometimes taking that opportunity is a luxury, a luxury one can't afford. I can't afford it right now. It wouldn't be right and you know that."

"I don't know that. Would letting yourself love me really take something away from your husband? Would it really make any difference to him in the condition he's in?"

"It might." Her eyes didn't waver from Alex's and he hadn't taken his hands from her shoulders as they stood facing each other in the center of the room. "It might make a very big difference if I grew indifferent to his needs, if I was never around to see that he was properly cared for, if I became involved with you and forgot about him. Something like that could kill him. It might make the difference for him between life and death. I could never fail him like that."

"I would never ask you to. Never. Don't you understand that? I told you, I respect your relationship with him, I respect what you do and are and feel. I understand that. I'm just telling you that you have a right to something more, and so do I. And it doesn't have to change anything for you with your husband. I swear it, Raphaella. I just want to share something with you that neither of us has, maybe that we've never had. From what I can gather, you live in a vacuum. And so do I. In some ways I have for a long time."

Raphaella looked up at him with the painful look of decision still in her eyes. "How do you know we would even have anything, Alex? Perhaps what you feel is all an illusion, a dream. You don't know me. Everything you think of me is a fantasy."

But this time he only shook his head and lowered his mouth gently onto hers. For an instant he felt her stiffen, but his arms circled her so quickly and so firmly that she could not pull away, and moments later she didn't want to. She clung to him as though he were the last man left on earth, and her entire body began to pulse with a passion she had never known before. And then, breathlessly, she pulled herself from him and shook her head, turning away.

"No, Alex. No!" She turned to face him with a look of fire in her eyes. "No! Don't do this! Don't tempt me with what I cannot have. I can't have it, and you know that!" And then she turned away, her shoulders bent, her eyes filled with tears. "Please go."

"Raphaella. . . ." She turned slowly to face him then, her face distraught, her eyes huge in the sharply etched face. And then it was as though he saw her melt in front of his eyes. The fire went out of her eyes and she closed them for an instant and then walked toward him, her hands going around him, her mouth hungrily reaching for his.

"Oh, darling, I love you. . . . I love you. . . ." His words were gentle yet urgent, and she held him and kissed him with all the pent-up loving of more than seven years. And then, without thinking, he slipped the pink satin bathrobe from her shoulders and knelt to kiss her body as she stood before him, a goddess he had revered from the moment he had first seen her crying on the steps. This was the woman he had longed for, the woman he had needed and almost instantly loved. And as he held her and caressed her Raphaella knew that she was giving herself to him with all of her heart. It seemed hours before they stopped kissing and touching and holding and reaching out and running their hands over each other's skin. She felt her legs tremble below her and then suddenly he swept her into his arms, the pink satin robe left behind them on the carpet, and slowly he walked into the bedroom and deposited her on the bed. "Raphaella?" His mouth formed her name as a question and she nodded slowly, with a small hesitant smile, and he turned off the light and quickly slipped off his clothes and lay beside her.

He touched her hungrily again with his mouth and his hands. She felt now as though she were dreaming, as though this couldn't be happening, as though it couldn't possibly be real, and with an abandon she had never before known, she gave herself to him, her body arching and pulsing and throbbing with a desire she had never even dreamed. And with the same fervor Alex pressed himself to her, his body reaching deep inside her to her very soul, their arms intertwined, their legs part of one body, their mouths holding tight in one endless kiss, until suddenly the final moment of their pleasure burst from them, as together they seemed to soar.

Then they lay quietly together in the soft lamplight, and Alex looked at the woman he knew that he loved. For an instant he was suddenly frightened. What had he done, and what would she do now? Would she hate him? Would it be over? But as he saw the warmth dawning in her eyes, he knew that this was not the end, but the beginning, and as he watched her she leaned closer to him, kissed him softly on the lips, and ran a hand ever so slowly down his spine. His whole body began to tingle, and he kissed her again, and then lay on his side and watched her smile.

"I love you, Raphaella." The words were spoken so softly that only she could have heard him, and she nodded slowly, the smile spreading to her eyes. "I love you." He said it again, and her smile broadened.

"I know. And I love you too." She spoke as softly as he did, and suddenly he pulled her closer again, tightly into his arms, so she could never leave him. And as though she understood, she held him closer. "It's all right, Alex . . . shh . . . it's all right."

A few minutes later his hands began to caress her again.

CHAPTER 9

"Raphaella?" It was only a whisper, as he lay on one elbow looking at her. He wasn't sure if she was awake. But now her eyes fluttered open slowly in the first light of morning, and the first thing she saw was Alex, looking down at her with his eyes full of love. "Good morning, my darling." He kissed her then and smoothed the long silky black hair so much like his own. And suddenly she saw him grinning, and she smiled in return.

"What are you laughing about so early in the morning?"

"I was just thinking that if we ever had children and they ever had anything but jet-black hair, you'd be in big trouble."

"Oh, would I?" She looked at him in amusement as he nodded.

"Yes, you would." He looked at her pensively, a single finger tracing a line around her breasts and down the center of her body to where her legs joined, and then lazily he brought the finger back up again to circle her breasts. He stopped for a moment, a question in his eyes. "Don't you want children, Raphaella?"

"Now?"

"No. I mean ever. I was just wondering if—" He hesitated and then decided to ask her. "Can you?"

"I think so." She didn't want to betray John Henry's weakness, so she said no more as he watched her face.

"Did you not have any because you didn't want to, or because . . . for other reasons?" He had somehow sensed that she was being discreet.

"Other reasons."

He nodded quietly. "I wondered." She leaned toward him then and kissed him softly on the mouth. And then suddenly she sat up in bed with a look of terror, glanced at the clock, and stared at Alex with a hand over her mouth.

"What's the matter?"

"My God . . . I just missed my plane."

He grinned at her, looking unimpressed. "I missed mine last night. In fact"—the grin grew slowly—"I never even retrieved my luggage from the doorman."

But she wasn't listening to him. "What'll I do? I have to call the airline . . . I'm sure they have another— My God, when Tom goes to meet me at the airport—"

Alex's brow clouded as soon as she said the words. "Who is Tom?"

This time it was Raphaella who was smiling. "The chauffeur, silly."

"Good. Anyway, you can call home and tell them you missed the flight. Just tell them you'll catch—" He had been about to say "the next one," but suddenly he had a thought. "Raphaella . . . what if—" He was almost afraid to say it, and slowly he reached for her hand. "What if we don't go home until tomorrow, and we spend the weekend here together? We could."

"No, we couldn't. They expect me . . . I have to—"

"Why? You don't have anything to do at home. You said so yourself, and one day, or even two, can't make that much difference now. We won't be this free again for a long time. We're here, we're alone, we're together. . . . How about it? Until tomorrow?" He pulled her into his arms as he asked her, praying she'd say yes. But she pulled away again slowly, her face thoughtful, but unsure.

"I'd have to lie to them, Alex. And if—"

"If anything happens"—they both knew he meant to John Henry—"you can get the next plane back. It's no different than it was all week while you were here with your mother. The only difference is that now you'll be here with me. Please." He looked gentle and boyish, and she wanted nothing more than to be in New York with him, but what about her obligations . . . John Henry. . . . But suddenly she knew that she had to do something for herself this time. She looked up at Alex and nodded. She looked frightened, but excited, and he let out a whoop of joy. "Darling, I love you!"

"You're crazy!"

"We both are. I'll go take a shower, you order breakfast, and then we'll go out for a walk." But the awkwardness of ordering breakfast for two hadn't occurred to either of them, so she ordered an enormous breakfast from room service, but when they asked for how many, she promptly answered, "Service for one." She reported to him as he stood in the shower, and she found herself looking at his body with longing and admiration once again. He was so tall and strong and handsome, he looked like a statue of a young Greek god. "What are you looking at, madam?" He peeked out at her with water running down his face.

"You. You're beautiful, Alex."

"Now I know that you're crazy." And then he looked at her soberly for a moment. "Did you call home?" She shook her head like a recalcitrant schoolgirl and he stood very still in the shower, and the water running over his body made her want to follow it with her tongue. She couldn't think about home now. Home was not real. All she could think about was him. "Why don't you go do that now, babe." She nodded slowly and left the room. As she sat beside the telephone the beauty of his body seemed to fade. Suddenly she felt like Mrs. John Henry Phillips again. What lie would she tell them? The operator answered too quickly and she put the call through to San Francisco right away. It was only a moment later when she had the nurse on the line and was told that John Henry was still sleeping, it was only seven o'clock in the morning in San Francisco, and he had not yet woken up.

"Is he all right?" She was terrified. Perhaps she would be punished. Maybe he'd be worse now and it would be her fault. But the nurse's cheerful voice came across the line quickly.

"He's just fine. We had him in the chair for an hour yesterday. And I think he enjoyed it. I read the paper to him for a little while after dinner, and he went right to sleep." Then nothing was different, it all sounded the same as it had been when she left. She explained that she had been delayed in New York with her mother. And she would be flying back to

San Francisco the next day. She waited for an instant, almost expecting the nurse to call her a liar and a whore, but nothing happened, and she knew that her mother would never call from Argentina, so there was no reason to think that she would be found out. But she felt so terribly guilty, it seemed impossible that they wouldn't know. She asked the woman to tell Tom not to pick her up at the airport that day and told her that she would call the next morning to tell them what plane she'd be on. It occurred to her that she could take a cab from the airport with Alex, but if she did something like that, then they would wonder what she was up to. She had never taken a cab from an airport in her entire life. She thanked the nurse then, asked her to tell Mr. Phillips that she had called and to tell him that everything was fine, and then she hung up, her eyes quiet, her face grave.

"Something wrong?" Alex emerged from the bathroom, his hair combed and with a towel around his waist. She looked different than she had a few minutes before when he had told her to go and call home. "What happened?"

"Nothing. I—I just called them." She lowered her eyes.

"Is something wrong?" There was an obvious question in his voice and he looked worried, but she quickly shook her head.

"No, no. He's fine. I just—" She looked up at him miserably then. "I just feel so guilty. Alex, I should go back." It was an anguished whisper as he sat down beside her. He sat very still for a moment and then put an arm around her shoulders and held her tight.

"That's okay, if that's what you want to do. I told you. I understand. I always will." She looked at him with eyes full of confusion, and he pulled her close to him again. "It's okay, darling. Everything is fine."

"Why are you being so kind to me?" She buried her face in the bare flesh of his shoulder as she asked him.

"Because I love you. I told you that last night too." He smiled and kissed the top of her head.

"But you barely know me."

"Bullshit. I know you right down to the tips of your toes." She blushed then, but she also knew that he had meant it in another sense, a more important one. And oddly, though she had known him for such a short time, she believed him. He did know her. Better than anyone ever had. Even her husband.

"Will you be very angry if I go back today?" She sounded regretful and let out a long quiet sigh.

"No, I'll be very sorry. But not angry. If that's what you have to do, then it's okay."

"What will you do? Go back to see your mother or your sister?"

"No, my mother's in Boston, Kay is in Washington, and my niece has lots of plans for the weekend. I'll go home. Probably on the same flight with you, if we can get seats together. Would that be all right with you?" She nodded. "Good." He stood up slowly. "Then call the airline. I'll go shave." He sauntered back into the bathroom and closed the door as she sat there, feeling as though she had just given up the only thing she wanted in the world. Time with Alex. Together. Just the two of them. Alone. She sat there for a long moment and then walked to the closed door and knocked softly. "Yes?"

"May I come in?" He opened the door and looked down at her with a smile that told her again that he loved her.

"Of course you can, silly. You don't have to ask. Did you call the airline?"

She shook her head sheepishly. "I don't want to."

"Why not?" He felt his heart pound as he waited.

"Because I don't want to go back yet." She looked like a little girl as she stood there, her long hair falling over her shoulders, still tousled from the night before. "I want to stay here with you."

"You do, do you?" He couldn't keep the smile off his face, and he put down his razor and grabbed her with one hand, using the other to grab a towel and wipe the soap from his face. "Well, I'd like nothing better." He kissed her long and hard then and took her back to bed. It was half an hour before they had ended their lovemaking and the waiter from room service arrived.

They sat down to breakfast together after the waiter had left them, she in the pink satin robe and he in a towel, the two of them happy and smiling and making plans for the day. It was as though they had always been together, as they divided up the scrambled eggs.

"And then I want to go to the top of the Empire State Building, and I want to eat hot chestnuts, and I want to go skating. . . ."

He laughed at her. "You sound just like my niece. She loves to skate too."

"Then we can go together. But first I want to go to the Empire State Building."

"Raphaella!" he groaned as he finished his coffee. "Do you mean it?"

"I certainly do. I never get to do things like that!"

"Oh, baby." He leaned across the table to kiss her. "You are the most beautiful woman I have ever seen."

"Then you are blind and crazy and I love you." But she was wondering if she was the crazy one. This was absolute madness. And the maddest thing of all was that she felt as though she had known him all of her life.

Together they devised a scenario whereby Raphaella could retrieve Alex's luggage from the doorman, and when the bellboy brought it upstairs, Alex got dressed as Raphaella took a bath. They stood side by side in the huge closet arranging their things and chatting, and it was very much like a honeymoon, as she remarked to him on their way downtown. He dutifully took her to the top of the Empire State Building, to lunch at the Plaza, and then for a hansom carriage ride in the park. They spent two hours wandering through the wonders of the Metropolitan Museum, and they wandered into Parke-Bernet to watch an auction of French antiques in full swing. And then, happy and relaxed and more than a little tired, they crossed the street to the Carlyle and rode the elevator back up to her room. She was yawning as she took off her coat and hung it up in the closet, and Alex was already lying on the bed with his jacket and shoes off, holding out his arms to her.

"I don't know about you, lady, but I'm exhausted. I don't think I've done that much in one day since I was a kid."

"Me too." She found herself suddenly wishing then that she could take him to Paris, and to Barcelona and Madrid, where she could show him all her favorite things there. And then she wanted to take him to Santa Eugenia, to see the place where she had spent all her summers, and where they could visit with all of the children whom she loved so much. It was strange to think of them sometimes. The children she had told stories to when she had first married were getting married and having babies of their own now. Sometimes it made her feel very old, as though an important part of life had passed her by.

"What were you thinking just then?" For an instant he had seen the old sorrow lingering in her eyes.

"I was thinking about Santa Eugenia."

"What about it?" He probed further.

"I was thinking about the children there. . . . Oh, Alex . . . you don't know how I love them."

In a firm, quiet voice he spoke to her and reached for her hand. "One day we'll have children of our own." She said nothing, it was a subject she didn't like to discuss. She had put it away from her fourteen years before.

"It doesn't matter."

"Yes, it does. Very much. To both of us. I wanted children very much with my wife."

"Could she not have them?" Raphaella looked hopeful and curious as she asked him, as though they would have that in common, as though they had both been robbed by the same turn of fate.

"No." He shook his head and looked pensive. "She could have had them. But she didn't like children. Funny, how you look at things differently as time moves on. If I met a woman who felt that way now, I don't think I could love her. I thought I could talk Rachel into it. But I couldn't. She was too involved in her work. Looking back, I guess it's just as well we didn't have kids."

"What did she do?"

"She was an attorney." Raphaella looked impressed and he kissed her softly on the lips. "But she wasn't much of a woman, Raphaella, don't look like that."

"Did you leave her?"

He shook his head again. "No. She left me."

"For a man?"

"No." He smiled now, and there was no bitterness as he did so. "For a job. That's all that mattered to her. Ever. It's just as well things worked out as they did." They lay side by side like old friends and seasoned lovers, and Alex smiled.

"Is she very successful?"

"Probably."

She nodded slowly. "Sometimes I wish I were. The one thing I think I would have been good at was denied me, and everything else . . . well . . . there's nothing much I can do."

"You tell stories to children."

She smiled and looked embarrassed. "That's hardly a life's work."

He was studying her quietly, remembering something his mother had said. "Why don't you write down the stories? You could write children's books, Raphaella." Her eyes shone for a moment as she considered the suggestion, but then he went to her and took her in his arms. "I hope that you know that if you never do a damn thing except love me, that will be enough."

"Will it? Won't you be bored?" She actually looked worried.

"Never. It's funny. All my life I've been surrounded by ambitious women, professional women, women with all kinds of careers. I never thought I could understand a woman who was any different. And suddenly I realize that what I've wanted all along was someone like you. I don't want to wrestle and compete, and fight over who makes the bigger living. I just want to be myself with someone I care about, someone warm and kind and intelligent and nice to be with. . . ." He nuzzled her neck. "You know, that sounds kind of like you."

She looked at him for a long moment and then tilted her head to one side. "You know what's strange? Right now, I feel as though this is my life. Here. With you. As though nothing else ever existed, as though my life in San Francisco isn't even real. Isn't that odd?" She looked puzzled and he touched her face gently before kissing her on the mouth. And then he pulled away from her slowly with a small smile.

"No. As a matter of fact I don't find it odd at all." His arms were around her again then, and he kissed her hungrily as her hands gently touched his thighs.

CHAPTER 10

The stewardess's voice droned on endlessly announcing their arrival in San Francisco, and Alex was aware of a feeling of depression stealing over him as the plane descended slowly toward the ground. Their two days together had been so perfect, so idyllic. They had gone to dinner the night before, and then gone to listen to Bobby Short as he had originally planned. And she had loved it. After that they had sat up and talked until almost four o'clock. Alternately discovering each other's bodies, and then lying side by side telling each other about their respective lives. When the sun came up on Sunday morning, she knew all about Rachel, his mother, and his sister. She told him about her father, Julien, the brother who had died at sixteen playing polo, and her marriage to John Henry, in the beginning, and now. It was as though they had always been together, as though they had always been meant to be. And now they were coming back to San Francisco and he was going to have to let her go, at least for a while. And he would have to content himself with what little time she could spare him when she stole away from her other life in her husband's house. At least that was what they had discussed the night before.

"What are you thinking? You look awfully serious." He looked at her gently as they prepared to land. He sensed easily that she was feeling the same sadness he was. Their few days together had seemed like a lifetime, and now once again everything was going to change. "Are you all right?"

She looked at him sadly and nodded. "I was just thinking. . . ."

"What about?"

"Us. About how things will be now."

"It'll be all right." He spoke near to her ear, in a quiet, intimate way that thrilled her, but now she shook her head.

"No, it won't."

He took her hand in his own and held it, searching her eyes and suddenly not liking what he saw. He suspected that she was feeling besieged by guilt again, but that was to be expected, after all they were nearing home turf. It would be harder to put aside her obligations here. But she didn't really have to. There would be room for both men in her life.

"Alex. . . ." Her voice faltered on the words. "I can't do it." As her eyes met his they filled with tears.

"What do you mean?" He tried to fight his own panic and maintain at least an outward appearance of calm in the face of what he thought she had just said.

"I can't."

"You don't have to do anything right now, except relax." It was his best professional voice, but it didn't seem to soothe her, as the tears spilled onto her cheeks and rolled slowly until they fell onto their clasped hands. "We can work all of this out later, as we go along."

But again she shook her head, and her next word was only a whisper. "No . . . I was wrong. . . . I can't do it, Alex . . . not here. Not in the same town with him. It's just not right."

"Raphaella, don't . . . just give yourself a little time to adjust."

"To what?" For an instant she looked angry. "Betraying my husband?"

"Is that what it is?"

She shook her head again, her eyes begging him to understand. "What can I do?"

"Wait. Try to live with the joy we have. Be fair to him and to yourself. That's all I want for all of us. . . ." She nodded slowly and he squeezed her hand tightly in his own. "Will you give it a chance?"

It seemed an eternity before she answered. "I'll try."

The plane landed a moment later and when it stopped at the gate, two stewardesses appeared, one carrying her fur coat, and Raphaella stood up quietly and put it on, giving no sign that the man she'd been seated next to had been anyone important to her at all. She picked up her tote bag, buttoned her coat, and then nodded. Only her eyes said "I love you" as she walked away and disappeared out of the rear exit in the plane as she had done before. The exit was closed again after she'd gone through it, and Alex felt a loneliness engulf him, the likes of which he'd never known. He suddenly felt as though everything he cared about had been stolen from him, and a wave of terror swept through him. What if he never saw her again? He had to fight panic as he waited to deplane with the others, and then walked zombielike to the baggage claim to pick up his bag. He spotted the long black limousine waiting at the curb outside the building and the chauffeur who stood with the others, still waiting for her bags. Alex left the terminal quickly with his bags and stood for a moment looking at the long black car. The reflection of the bright lights on the window hid her from his vision but he couldn't bring himself to move away, and as though Raphaella had sensed this, one of the rear windows rolled down slowly as she pressed the little button with one finger. She looked anxiously out at him, wanting in some way to touch him again. Their eyes held for an endless moment and then, as though the sun had just risen for them again, he smiled gently at her and turned and walked toward the garage. In his heart he was whispering "Tomorrow" and wishing it were tonight.

CHAPTER 11

It was almost eight fifteen as he sat there, his foot tapping gently, in the den. The wine was standing open next to the cheese and fruit he had set out on the table, the fire was crackling brightly, the music was playing, and he was a nervous wreck. She had said any time after seven thirty, but he had not heard from her all day, and now he wondered if for some reason she had been unable to get out. She had sounded as lonely as he had when she had called him the previous evening, and his whole body had ached with the longing of wanting to take her in his arms. And now as he stood frowning down at the fire, wondering if anything had happened, he jumped at the sound of the phone.

"Alex?" His heart pounded and then skipped a beat in disappointment. It wasn't Raphaella, it was Kay.

"Oh. Hi."

"Something wrong? You sound uptight."

"No, I'm just busy." And he wasn't in the mood to talk to her.

"Working?"

"Sort of. . . . No . . . nothing . . . never mind. What's up?"

"Jesus. Talk about the bum's rush. I wanted to talk to you about Amanda."

"Something wrong?"

"Not yet, thank God. Fortunately I know more about teen-agers than you do. That hundred dollars you gave her, Alex. No go."

"What do you mean?" His face tightened as he listened to his sister.

"I mean that she's sixteen years old, and the only thing kids that age do with money is buy drugs."

"Did she tell you why I gave it to her? And by the way, how did you find out, I thought that was just between the two of us."

"Never mind how I found it. I was going through some of her things and it turned up."

"Christ, what do you do to the kid, Kay, frisk her?"

"Hardly. But you forget how delicate my position is, Alex. I don't want her keeping dope in my house."

"You make her sound like a goddamn junkie."

"Horseshit. But if I'd let her, she'd keep a box of joints around like you and I would keep Scotch."

"Have you ever just simply asked her not to?"

"Sure. You really think kids do what you say?" Her total disrespect for her daughter drove him crazy and he felt the urge to explode as he listened to the innuendos in his sister's voice.

"I think your attitude toward her is disgusting. I think she is one kid you can trust. And the reason I gave her the money is so that she could go skating at

Rockefeller Center. She tells me that she goes skating a lot, and she skates at Wollman Rink in the park. I don't know if you're aware of it, but that kid could get murdered going in and out of Central Park. As her uncle, I'd like to treat her to the skating sessions. I had no idea you'd take the money away from her though or I'd have arranged it some other way."

"Why don't you just let me handle my own daughter, Alex?"

"Why don't you admit that as a mother you stink?" His voice bellowed across the room as he stood there wishing that there were something he could do for the child. "I want you to let Amanda keep that money."

"I don't give a damn what you want. I sent you a check in that amount today."

"I'll take this up myself with Amanda."

"Don't bother, Alex." Kay's voice was like ice. "I check her mail." His own sense of frustration only mirrored what he knew Amanda must have felt in dealing with Kay.

"You are a vicious bitch, do you know that? And you have no right to harass that child."

"And where do you come off judging how I treat my daughter? You have no children, damn you. What the hell do you know?"

"Maybe nothing, Sis. Maybe nothing at all. And I may not have children, dear Congresswoman Willard. But you dear lady, have no heart."

She hung up on him then and at the same moment he heard the doorbell ring, and he felt a rush of emotions swirl around him like a riptide. It was Raphaella, he knew it. She had come after all. And suddenly his heart was soaring, but he had not yet forgotten the exchange with his sister about Amanda, and he also

knew that he wanted to speak to the girl himself. He
ran down the flight of stairs from his den to the front
door and pulled it open and stood looking at Raphaella for a moment, happy, confused, and slightly
harassed.

"I was worried that something had happened." She
shook her head and said not a word, but the smile
that she wore spoke for her, and then carefully she
stepped inside. As he closed the door behind her Alex
swept her into his arms and held her very tight. "Oh,
baby, how I missed you. . . . Are you all right?"

"Yes." It was a tiny word buried beneath the fur
coat she wore and his own body as he hugged her.
She was wearing the lynx coat that she had worn that
night on the steps. And then she hugged him again,
under her own steam this time, and when she did, he
saw that there was something tired and sad in her
eyes. She had left a note in her bedroom saying only
that she was going for a walk to visit friends, just in
case they came to find her. That way none of the servants would panic and call the police when she didn't
come back immediately from her walk. They were always uneasy about her evening strolls anyway, and
John Henry would have had a fit if he knew. "I
thought today would go on forever. I waited and I
waited and I waited, and every hour felt like two
days."

"That's how I felt today at the office. Come on." He
took her by the hand and walked her to the stairway.
"I want to show you around upstairs." As they made
their way through the house she was aware of the
emptiness of the living room, yet in contrast she was
overwhelmed by the warmth of his bedroom and the
den. The two rooms were filled with creamy wools

and soft leathers, huge plants, and endless shelves of books. There was a fire burning brightly in his bedroom and Raphaella felt instantly at home.

"Oh, Alex, it's so pretty! And so comfortable and so warm." She rapidly shed the heavy fur coat and curled up on the floor beside him in front of the fire, the thick white rug beneath them, and before them on a low glass table were the wine and the cheese and the pâté he had stopped to buy for her on the way home.

"Do you like it?" He looked happily around him. He had put together the decor himself when he bought the house.

"I love it." She smiled, but she was oddly quiet, and he sensed again that something was wrong.

"What is it, Raphaella?" His voice was so gentle that it brought tears to her eyes. For all the pleasant patter about his house, he had sensed from the first moment that she was deeply upset. "What's wrong?"

She closed her eyes for a moment, and then opened them again as she reached out instinctively for Alex's hand. "I can't do this, Alex. . . . I just can't. I meant to . . . I was going to . . . I had it all planned, how every day I could spend with John Henry, and every night I could slip out for a 'walk' and then come here to be with you. And when I thought of it"—she smiled sadly again—"my heart flew. I felt young and excited and happy, like"—she faltered, her voice barely audible, her eyes damp—"like a bride. . . ." Her eyes roved slowly toward the fire, but she left her hand in his. "But I'm not any of those things, Alex. I'm not young anymore, at least not that young. And I have no right to that kind of happiness, not with you. And I'm not a bride. I'm a married woman. And I have a responsibility to a very sick man." Her voice grew stronger and she pulled her hand away from his. "I can't come here anymore, Alex. Not after tonight." Now when she faced him, her voice was resolute.

"What made you change your mind?"

"Coming home. Seeing him. Remembering who I am."

"Did you forget me in all that?" It sounded pathetic to his own ears and he was angry at himself for saying it, but it was what he felt. Life had just dealt him a cruel blow. A woman he wanted desperately, and was not destined to have.

But she brought his hand gently to her lips and kissed it as she shook her head. "I didn't forget you, Alex." And then, "I never will." Almost as she said it she rose to go. He sat there watching her for a long moment, wanting to stop her, to fight her, yet knowing that there was nothing he could do. He had wanted to make love to her again, to talk to her, to spend the night with her . . . to spend his life with her. Slowly he got to his feet.

"I want you to know something, Raphaella." He reached out and pulled her into his arms. "I love you. We barely know each other and yet I know that I love you. I want you to go home and think about what you're doing, and if you change your mind, even for a moment, I want you to come back. Next week, next month, next year. I'll be here." He held her tight for a long, long time, wondering how long it would be before he would see her again. He couldn't bear the thought that perhaps he never would. "I love you. Don't forget that."

"I won't." There were tears streaming from her eyes now. "I love you too."

They walked downstairs then, as though they both knew that there was no point staying in the house anymore, it would be too painful for them both. And with an arm around her shoulders, and her eyes filled with tears, he walked her home. She turned only once on her doorstep, waved once, and then disappeared.

CHAPTER 12

For the next two months Raphaella moved as though underwater. Her every step seemed to be weighted, heavy, slow. She couldn't move, she couldn't think, she couldn't walk, she could barely even talk to her husband, who puzzled at length over what might have happened in New York. Some ghastly episode of hostility with her mother, some kind of family argument or feud. It was weeks before he decided to broach the subject, but when he did, Raphaella seemed almost not to hear.

"Did something happen with your mother, little one? Was she insisting that you start to spend more time in Spain?" In vain he sought an answer, unable to imagine what could have brought such pain to Raphaella's eyes.

"No, no . . . it was nothing." There had been something then. But what?

"Is anyone ill?"

"No." She smiled bravely. "Not at all. I'm only very

tired, John Henry. But you mustn't trouble yourself. I
should take more air." But even the endless walks
didn't help her. In vain she walked from one end of
the Presidio to the other, down to the little pond at the
Palace of Fine Arts, and even to the edge of the bay,
then struggled back up the hill. But no matter how
tired or how breathless or how exhausted or how
much she pressed herself, she couldn't forget him. She
found herself wondering day and night what he was
doing, if he was well, or happy, if he was working, or
in the pretty little house on Vallejo. It seemed as
though every hour of the day she wanted to know
where he was. And yet she knew that in all likelihood
she would never see him again, never touch him,
never hold him. The realization of that made her ache
to her very core, until at last she had felt so much pain
that she was numb and her eyes were almost glazed.

Thanksgiving Day she sat with John Henry, moving
like a robot, her eyes distant and dull. "More turkey,
Raphaella?"

"Mm?" She stared at him in answer, seeming not to
understand what he had just said. One of the maids
had been standing by with the platter, attempting in
vain to catch her attention, until John Henry finally
spoke up. They were sharing Thanksgiving dinner in
his bedroom, served on trays, so that he could remain
in bed. His health had failed again slightly in the past
two months.

"Raphaella?"

"Yes? Oh . . . no . . . I'm sorry. . . ." She looked
away and shook her head, and then she sat there,
trying to make conversation with him, but tonight he
was too tired. A half hour after dinner his chin nodded down gently onto his chest, his eyelids closed, and

he let out a soft snore. The nurse, who had been standing by, gently lifted the tray away from him and lowered him further into the bed, signaling to Raphaella that she might as well go. And then slowly, slowly, Raphaella walked down the endless hall to her own rooms, her mind filled with thoughts of Alex, and then, as though mesmerized, she walked to the phone. It was wrong, and she knew it. But she could call to wish him a happy Thanksgiving after all. What was wrong with that? Everything, if what she had to do was avoid him, and she knew that she did. She knew that even the sound of his voice, the look in his eyes, his touch, all of it could weave her into the same delicious web again, and she had tried so hard to flee. Out of honor, out of a sense of duty, she had desperately tried, and now, as she dialed his number, she knew that she had failed. She didn't want to stay away from him for a moment longer. She couldn't. She just couldn't. Her heart pounded as she dialed the phone. It seemed an eternity before he answered, but now that she had dialed, she would not hang up.

"Hello?" She closed her eyes when she heard it, relief and pain and excitement sweeping over her all at once.

"Hello." He didn't recognize her for a moment, and then suddenly his eyes widened, and at his end he looked as though he might go into shock.

"Oh, my God."

"No." She smiled softly. "It's only me. I called to wish you a happy Thanksgiving."

There was a pause. "Thank you." He sounded strained. "How are you?"

"I—I'm fine. . . ." And then suddenly she decided to tell him. No matter if he had changed his mind, if he no longer loved her, if he had met someone else. She had to tell him. Even if only just this once. "I'm not fine . . . it's been awful . . . I can't—" She almost gasped with the remembered pain and emptiness of the last two months. "I can't live like this any longer. I can't bear it . . . oh, Alex. . . ." Without meaning to, she had begun to cry, from sorrow as much as from relief. At least she was speaking to him again. She didn't give a damn if the world ended then and there. She was happier than she had been in months.

"Where are you?" His voice sounded tense.

"I'm at home."

"I'll meet you on the corner in five minutes."

She was going to say no, she was going to tell him that she couldn't do that, but she didn't have the strength to fight it anymore. She didn't want to. Silently she nodded her head, and then, "I'll be there."

She ran into the bathroom, splashed cold water on her face, and then dried it hurriedly in one of the huge Porthault towels, ran a comb through her dark hair, pulled open her closet, grabbed her lynx coat, and then literally ran from her room, down the stairs, and out the door. This time she had left no message, no explanation, and she didn't know how long she would be gone. Maybe five minutes, maybe an hour. But John Henry didn't need her just now. He was sleeping, he had his nurses, his servants, his doctors, and just this once, she wanted something more, much, much more. She found it as she ran hastily toward the corner, her dark hair flying behind her, the coat open, her lips suddenly caught in a half-smile, as a sparkle came to her eyes that hadn't been there in months. As she rounded the corner, suddenly she saw him there, in dark slacks and thick sweater, his hair tousled, his eyes bright, and slightly out of breath. He ran toward her so quickly and pulled her into his arms with such force that they almost collided and could easily have knocked each other out. Instead he crushed his mouth down on hers, and they seemed to stand there that way forever. It was an outrageous chance to take, there on the corner, but fortunately no one saw them, and for once in her life Raphaella didn't really care.

As though by silent agreement they began to walk slowly toward his house a few minutes later, and as he closed the door quietly behind them, Raphaella looked around her and let out a long sigh.

"Welcome home." He didn't tell her then how much he had missed her. He saved that until they lay side by side in his bed. It was as though for two months they had both lived in limbo, barely alive, barely existing, between numbness and constant pain. The two months they had just endured were among the worst moments Raphaella could remember. For Alex they had been much the same, yet now it was as though none of it had ever happened, as though they had never been apart and never would be again. He wanted to ask her what would happen, but he didn't quite dare. He decided simply to cherish the moment and pray that she was ready now for something more than they had had in the past two months.

"Happy Thanksgiving, my darling. . . ." He pulled her once more into his arms and they made love yet again. It was after ten o'clock when he finally remembered the turkey he had left cooking in the oven. It was an hour overcooked, but when they went down to the kitchen to find it, neither of them cared. Raphaella wore his bathrobe, and Alex wore blue jeans

and a shirt, and together they ate and they talked and
they laughed. It was indeed a homecoming, and unlike her first Thanksgiving dinner earlier that evening,
this time Raphaella ate as though she hadn't seen food
in years.

"And your work? It's going well?" She looked so
happy as they sat there, she was smiling like a relaxed,
happy child.

"I wouldn't say that." He looked sheepish. "If I
worked for someone else, I'd probably have lost my
job in the last two months."

"I don't believe that, Alex."

"It's true. I haven't been able to keep my mind on
anything."

She looked momentarily sobered. "Neither have
I. . . ." And then she looked at him again and her
eyes gentled. "Except you. It was like a kind of madness which took me and just wouldn't let me go."

"Did you want it to?"

"Yes. If only to stop the pain. It was"—she looked
away, embarrassed—"it was a very difficult time for
me, Alex. I have been wrestling with my conscience
since the last time I saw you."

"And what happened tonight? What made you
call?"

"I couldn't bear it any longer. I felt as though I
might die if I didn't speak to you right then." He nodded, knowing the feeling only too well. And then he
leaned across the table to kiss her.

"Thank God you called. I don't think I could have
stood it much longer. I wanted to call you so badly. A
hundred times I had the phone in my hand. Twice I
even called, but you didn't answer, so I just hung up.
God, I thought I'd go nuts." She nodded in silent un-

derstanding, and as he watched her he decided to take the next step. "And now?" They were terrifying words, but he had to ask her. He had to know sooner of later, and he wanted to know now. "Do you know what you want to do now, Raphaella?" He was leaving it to her, but he had already decided that he wouldn't let her go as easily this time. Not after what they had both been through. But this time he didn't have to fight her. She smiled softly at him and touched his hand with her own.

"We'll do what we have to . . . to be together as much as we can."

He sat watching her for a moment, as though he were afraid to believe what she had just told him. "Do you mean that?"

"Yes. Do you still want me? I mean the way you did before?"

But what he did next answered her question. He pulled her from her seat and took her in his arms with such force and passion that she could barely breathe.

"Alex!"

"Does that answer your question?" There was fire and joy and excitement suddenly in his eyes. "My God, woman, how I love you. Yes, I want you. I love you, I need you. And I'll accept any way we have to work things out, so we can be together as much as we can, without hurting you, or—or—" She nodded. He didn't want to say John Henry's name. "In fact—" He stood up suddenly again and strode across the kitchen where he pulled open a drawer and fished out a single key. He walked back to where she sat, reached for her hand, and carefully put the key in it. "That's the key to this house, my darling, and I want you to be here whenever you can, as much as you want to, whether I'm here or not." Her eyes filled with tears then, and he pulled her gently into his arms, and a few moments later they wandered slowly upstairs again. She had the key to the house in the dressing gown pocket, and there was a smile in her eyes that had never been there before. She had never been happier in her life.

They spent the next three hours making love to each other again and again, and at last, as they lay side by side, still not totally sated, yet infinitely content, Raphaella jumped in surprise as she heard the phone. Alex frowned as he listened, shrugged, and then picked it up, sitting up slowly in the bed. And then, as he listened, the frown deepened, and without thinking, he stood up, still holding the phone, with an expression of horror on his face. "What . . . when . . . ? Oh, my God. How is she?" He knit his brows and his hand trembled as he grabbed a pen. The conversation went on in garbled monosyllables for a few more minutes and then he hung up and dropped his head into his hands with a soft moan. Raphaella stared at him in horror. All she could think of was his mother.

"Alex. . . ." Her voice was fearful and gentle. "Darling . . . what is it? What happened . . . ? . . . Tell me . . . please . . ." Her hands were gentle on his shoulders, and then softly she stroked his head and his neck as he began to cry. It seemed like hours before he looked up at her.

"It's Amanda, my niece." The words were a hoarse croak as she sat there. And then, with enormous effort, he told her the rest. "She's been raped. They just found her." He took a deep breath and closed his eyes for a moment before opening them again and going on. "After Thanksgiving dinner this afternoon she went skating . . . alone . . . in the park, and—" His voice faltered. "She was beaten, Raphaella. Her arms are broken, and my mother said—" He cried openly again as he spoke. "They beat up her face, and—and"—his voice dropped to a whisper—"they raped her . . . little Mandy. . . ." He couldn't go on then and Raphaella took him in her arms with tears flooding her eyes.

It was an hour later before they caught their breath and she went to get him a cup of coffee. He sat in bed sipping it slowly, smoking a cigarette. Raphaella looked over at him worriedly with a small frown between her eyes. "Can you still catch a plane tonight?" Her eyes were large and dark and damp, and her face was lit as though with some magical light from within. It was as though suddenly her face took away his anger, as though all the fury drained from his being, just from being with her. Without answering her question, he moved toward her and pulled her into his arms, where he held her tightly, as though he might never let go. They lay like that for a long moment as Raphaella stroked his back with one graceful hand. They said nothing and then, pulling carefully away from her, he looked down into her face again. "Will you come to New York with me, Raphaella?"

"Now?" She looked stunned. In the middle of the night? What would she say to her household, to John Henry? How could she go with him? She had had no time to prepare anyone. Her mind raced. But no one had prepared Amanda either, the poor child. There was a look of despair in her eyes as she looked up to answer his question. "Alex . . . I want to . . . I'd like to. But I can't." She had taken such a big step tonight. She wasn't yet ready for more. And she couldn't just leave John Henry.

He nodded slowly. "I understand." He turned to look again at this woman that he borrowed, who was someone else's, not his, and yet whom he loved so much. "I may be gone for a while." She nodded slowly. She wanted desperately to go with him, but they both knew she could not. Instead she held him tightly in her arms, wordlessly, and offered whatever comfort she could.

"I'm sorry, Alex."

"So am I." He was more composed now. "My sister should be horsewhipped for the way she takes care of that child."

"It can't be her fault." Raphaella looked shocked. "Why was the child alone? Where *was* her mother, dammit? Her father . . . ?" He began to cry again and Raphaella held him tightly.

They called the hospital three more times that evening, and Amanda was still listed as critical when at last Raphaella went home. It was by then a little after four thirty and they were both exhausted, but they had done the little they could do, and Raphaella had helped pack his bags. They had sat and talked for hours, staring into the fire, as Alex told her what Amanda had been like as a little girl. What had become clear to Raphaella was how he loved her, and how much it pained him that her parents had never taken time with her as a child.

"Alex . . . ?" She looked at him pensively in the firelight. It was the only light that had remained in the dark room. "Why don't you bring her back here when she's better?"

"To San Francisco?" He looked startled. "How could I do that? I'm not prepared . . . I don't have—" He sighed softly. "I'm at my office all day. I'm busy."

"So is her mother, and the difference is that you love her." Raphaella smiled softly in the glow from the embers, and he thought that he had never seen her look as beautiful as she did now. "When my brother died and my mother went back to Santa Eugenia with her sisters, all my father and I had were each other." She looked very far away for a long moment. "And I think we helped each other a lot."

Alex looked pensive as he watched her. "I doubt very much that her parents would let me bring her out."

Raphaella looked at him quietly. "After what happened do they really have a choice? Isn't it a little bit their fault that they weren't taking better care of their daughter, that they let her go there, that maybe they didn't even know where she was?"

Silently he nodded. It was what he had been thinking all evening. He blamed it all on his sister. And her insane ambition that had long since blocked everyone else from her view. "I'll think it over." And then he looked at her pensively. "We could fix up the third floor for her, couldn't we?"

She grinned at him then. "Yes, 'we' could. I could easily get it all ready in a few days. But, Alex. . . ."

There was an unspoken question in her eyes now, and this time it was Alex who smiled. "She'd love you. You're everything her mother has refused to give her."

"But her mother may not like it, Alex. After all I'm— we're not—" She faltered and he shook his head.

"So? Does it really make a difference? Does it to us?" She shook her head.

"But to other people, people who matter to Kay, it would seem wrong."

"I don't care." His voice was harsh now. It was then that he had looked wistfully once more at Raphaella, thinking of his family and the trip to New York. "I wish you were coming with me." He had said it yet again as he had watched her dress to go home that morning, and now he whispered it one last time as she prepared to leave him and walk the last block to her house alone.

Her eyes were damp now in the gray before the morning, and she wasn't sure but she thought that his were too. In their own way they had been keeping a vigil for Amanda, staying awake, keeping her alive in their thoughts and their conversation, reaching out to the child who lay so bruised and battered so far away in New York. But it wasn't of Amanda that Raphaella was thinking as she kissed Alex again and touched his face for a last time. "I wish that I were coming too." She felt once again the cruelty of her situation, the push and pull of obligations she had to fulfill for John Henry, yet she was so grateful to have Alex back in her life again, to be sharing even a night or a moment with him. All that she really regretted was not being able to help him make the difficult journey to New York. "Will you be all right there?" He nodded, but he wasn't smiling. He would be all right. But would Amanda? They had talked of bringing her home to San Francisco, but what if she didn't survive? The thought crossed both their minds now as Raphaella's lips gently touched his eyes. "May I call you?" He nodded, this time with a smile.

They both knew that a great deal had changed between them in one evening. It was a leap that they had made together, hand in hand.

"I'm going to be staying at my mother's."

"Give her my love." Their eyes met and held for a long moment and she kissed him for a last time. "And don't forget how much I love you."

He kissed her long and hard then, and finally with a last move she was gone. The heavy oak door closed a block away a few minutes later, and Alex walked quickly back to his house to shower and dress before catching the seven-o'clock flight to New York.

CHAPTER 13

Charlotte Brandon waited nervously downstairs in the hospital lobby, staring at the reception desk and the vending machines that sold candy and coffee, as Alex went upstairs to see Amanda for the first time. The last report he had had when he called from the Carlyle was that she was doing better and she was a little less sedated, but now she was in considerable pain. Visits were not encouraged, but since Alex had come so far to see her, they would let him into the intensive-care unit, on the hour, for five or ten minutes, but no more.

And now Alex had vanished into the elevator as his mother sat numbly, watching the passersby. But the faces were all blank and unfamiliar as they hurried in and out of the lobby, carrying flowers, presents, shopping bags with slippers and bedjackets. Twice she had watched hugely pregnant women amble in slowly with tense faces, holding tightly to their husbands, who clutched little overnight bags in their other hands. Charlotte remembered with tenderness moments like that in her own life, but tonight she felt very old and tired and all she could think of was her grandchild, lying in a bed on another floor. And Kay had not yet been to see her. She was due in from Washington in a few hours. George had come in, of course, but he only checked the charts and spoke to the resident and the nurses and offered little comfort to the child.

George was really not the right man to be a father to his daughter in this circumstance. He was too uncomfortable with her feelings.

"Mother?" She jumped at the sound of Alex's voice speaking her name and turned to see the look of grief in his eyes. It struck fresh terror in her heart.

"How is she?"

"The same. And where the hell is Kay?"

"I told you, she's in Washington, Alex. George called her immediately after the police called him, but she couldn't get away until tonight." It had been more than twenty-four hours since the nighmare had occurred. And Alex's eyes blazed.

"She should be goddamn shot. And George, where the hell is he? The nurse up there says he keeps coming and going, just to check the charts."

"Well, there isn't much else he can do. Is there?"

"What do you think?" They both fell silent. He didn't tell her that Amanda had been sobbing so hysterically when he'd gotten there that they'd had to give her another shot. But as least she had recognized him, and she had clung so desperately to his hand. Just looking at him now, Charlotte Brandon's eyes filled with tears once again, and she sat down in one of the orange vinyl lobby chairs and blew her nose.

"Oh, Alex, how do things like this happen?"

"Because there are crazy people out there, Mother. And because Amanda has two parents who don't give a damn."

Charlotte spoke softly as Alex sat down in the chair next to hers. "Do you really believe that, Alex?"

"I don't know what I believe. But I do know one thing. Whatever Kay feels for her child, in her heart, she still has no right to be the one to bring her up. Even if she thinks she loves her—and I'm not even convinced that she does—she still has absolutely no idea of what's involved, no idea of what she owes that child as her mother. And George is just as bad." Charlotte nodded her head slowly. She had thought so before, but she had never anticipated anything like this. She looked into Alex's eyes, and she saw something there she had never seen before.

"Are you going to do something about this, Alex?" She had suddenly sensed it. It was as though she knew.

"I am." He spoke with quiet determination.

"What do you have in mind?" Whatever it was, she knew it would be radical, and for Amanda's best interest. She had a great deal of faith in her only son.

"I'm taking her back with me."

"To San Francisco?" Charlotte Brandon looked momentarily stunned. "Can you do that?"

"I'm going to. Just let them try to stop me. I'll make the biggest stink you've ever seen, and see how my darling political sister enjoys that." He had Kay over a barrel and they both knew it. His mother nodded her head.

"Do you think you can take care of her out there,

Alex? It isn't as though she's had a skating accident. There are going to be emotional repercussions from all this as well."

"I'll do my best. I'll get her a good shrink and give her all the loving I can. It can't hurt. And it's more than she has here."

"I could keep her with me, you know."

"No, you couldn't." He looked at her honestly. "You're no match for Kay. She'd threaten you into letting her come back to them in a week."

"I'm not sure of that." Charlotte looked only slightly miffed.

"Why risk it? Why not make a nice clean break? San Francisco is a long way off."

"But you'll be alone out there with her, Alex. . . ." And then, as she said the words, she suddenly understood, and her eyes bore into her son's asking a silent question, as slowly he began to smile. He knew his mother well.

"Yes?" He had nothing to hide from his mother. He never had before. They were friends, and he trusted her, even with the secret of Raphaella.

This time Charlotte smiled too. "I'm not quite sure how to phrase what I'm thinking. Your . . . er . . . young friend . . . the . . . uh—"

"Good God, Mother!" He chuckled softly. "If you mean Raphaella, yes, I'm still seeing her." He didn't want to admit that she had just returned to him after two months of agonizing separation. He didn't want his mother, or anyone, to know that Raphaella had ever had doubts. It hurt his pride as much as his soul, but the fact that he was involved with a married woman, and one as well-known as Raphaella, was not a secret he would keep from her. His face sobered as he looked at his mother. "We talked about all this last night, before I left. I think she could give a great deal to Amanda."

"I don't doubt it," Charlotte sighed softly. "But Alex, she has . . . other responsibilities. . . . Her husband is a very sick man."

"I know that. But they have nurses. She won't be able to be with Amanda day and night, but she'll be with us some of the time." At least he prayed that she would. "And regardless of Raphaella, Mother, this is something I have to do for Amanda, and for myself. I won't be able to live with myself if I leave that child here with Kay gone all the time and George lost in the clouds. She's withering from the lack of attention. She needs more than they have to give her."

"And you think you can?"

"I'm sure as hell going to try."

"Well"—she took a deep breath and looked at her son—"I wish you well, darling. I think what you're doing is probably right."

"Thank you." There was a mist in his eyes as he kissed her cheek and stood up. "Come on, I'll take you home, and then I'll come back to see her again."

"You must be exhausted after the trip." She looked at him worriedly, there were dark circles under his eyes.

"I'm fine." And he was even more so a few minutes later as his mother opened the door of the apartment and the phone was ringing determinedly. Without asking permission to answer it, Alex pounced on it and then instantly beamed. It was Raphaella.

"How is she?"

The smile faded slowly as his thoughts reverted again to his niece. "About the same."

"Have you seen your sister?"

"Not yet." His voice hardened on the words. "She's not coming in from Washington until tonight." At her end Raphaella looked shocked, but Alex couldn't see.

"But you're all right?"

"I'm well. And I love you."

Raphaella smiled. "So do I." She had missed him unbearably all day and had gone on several long walks. She had already been to his house twice. And it did not feel like intruding into the house of a stranger, it felt like coming home. She had carefully cleaned up all the debris from the Thanksgiving dinner and watered all his plants. It was amazing how naturally she felt herself fitting into his life. "How's your mother?"

"Fine."

"Give her my love." They talked on for a few moments and then Alex told her that he had decided to bring Amanda home.

"What do you think?"

"What do I think?" She sounded a little surprised to be asked. "I think it's wonderful. You're her uncle and you love her." And then, shyly, "Alex . . . could I— could I fix up her room?" He nodded slowly, thinking. He wanted to tell her to wait, until they knew if Amanda would make it, but he couldn't bring himself to say the words. Instead he only nodded again, as though wanting to force the fates.

"Go ahead." And with that he looked at his watch and realized that he had to get back to the hospital. "Call me later, if you can. I have to go back." It was wonderful, her presence in his life now. No more silence, no more waiting, no more agony, or ghastly sense of loss. She was there as though she had always been and always would be. "I love you."

"I love you too, darling. Take good care."

He gently put the phone back on its cradle, and with a soft smile his mother quietly disappeared into the kitchen to make tea. When she returned a few minutes later with two steaming cups, she saw that Alex was already wearing his coat.

"You're going back now?" He nodded soberly, and without saying more, she picked up her own coat again. But Alex instantly stopped her. She had been at the hospital all night the previous night.

"I want you to get some rest."

"I can't, Alex." And when he saw the look in her eyes, he said nothing more. They each took a sip of their tea and went outside to hail a cab.

CHAPTER 14

He was looking down at Amanda from the doorway, and all he could see was the narrow bundle huddled in the white sheets and blue blankets on the bed. From the angle at which the girl was lying, Charlotte could still not see her face. But as she walked around the bed to stand next to Alex, she had to fight her own reactions so that they wouldn't show in her face. She had felt the same way again and again the night before.

What she saw before her was a tiny young girl who looked more like nine than seventeen, but only by her shape and the size of her hands and arms could one distinguish vaguely what was her sex and age. Her arms were mostly encased in plaster, her hands lay exposed and immobile, like two small sleeping birds, and the face that they looked at on the pillow was only a blur of swelling and bruises in purples and blues. Her hair framed her face like a soft curly halo, and the eyes that opened were of a clean, bright blue.

They looked a little like Charlotte's, and a little bit like Alex's, but it was hard to tell now, they looked so anguished and rapidly filled with tears.

"Mandy?" His voice was a whisper, and he didn't dare touch even her hand now for fear that it would hurt. She nodded slowly in answer, not saying a word. "I'm back, and I brought Grandma with me." Amanda's eyes went to her grandmother as two steady rivers of tears flowed into the pillow beneath her head. There was no sound for a long moment as the heart-rending blue eyes looked at the familiar faces, and then once again there were sobs as Alex gently stroked her hair. There was a communication between them that went beyond words, and Alex only stood there, his eyes gentle, his hand soft and smooth on the girl's hair. And in a moment Amanda closed her eyes again and fell asleep. A nurse signaled to them a moment later, and Charlotte and Alex left the room. They both looked exhausted and desperately worried, but in Alex's eyes there was a growing seed of fury for his sister, Kay. It didn't explode from him until they reached Charlotte's apartment, and when they did, he was almost too angry for words.

"I know what you're thinking, Alex." His mother's voice was gentle. "But right now it won't help."

"Why not?"

"Why don't you take it easy until you can talk to Kay. You can get it all out of your system then."

"And when will that be? When do you suppose Her Majesty will finally turn up?"

"I wish I knew, Alex."

As it turned out, it was the next day.

Alex was sipping coffee from a plastic cup, and

Charlotte had gone home for a few hours to have a nap. They moved Amanda that morning out of intensive care into a little brightly painted pink room. And now she lay looking just as battered and broken, but there was something a little bit more lively in her eyes. Alex had been talking to her about San Francisco, and once or twice she had almost looked as though she cared.

It was at the end of the day that she finally spoke of her fears to her uncle.

"What am I going to tell people? How can I explain what happened? I know my face is all messed up. One of the nurses' aides said so." They hadn't allowed her a mirror. "And look at my arms." She looked at the two cumbersome plaster casts molded around her elbows, and Alex glanced at them but failed to look impressed.

"You're going to tell them that you had a car accident on Thanksgiving. That's all. It's perfectly plausible." And then with a look of intense meaning he looked straight at Amanda and put a hand on her shoulder. "Darling, no one ever has to know. Not unless you tell them, and that's up to you. But other than that, no one knows. Only your parents, your grandmother, and I."

"And whoever reads the papers." Then with another look of despair at Alex, "Was I on the news?"

He shook his head in answer. "No, you were not. I told you. No one has to know. You haven't been shamed. You're no different than you were before you came in here. You're the same, Amanda. You had a terrible accident, and horrible experience, but that's all it was. It didn't change *you*. It wasn't *your* fault.

People won't respond to you differently, Amanda. You haven't changed." It was what the therapist had stressed to him that morning, that they had to insist to Amanda that she was not different now and that it was not in any way her fault. Apparently it was common among rape victims to think that they were in some way responsible for what had happened, and afterward to think that they had been altered in some major way. Admittedly in Mandy's case she was perhaps more altered than others. She had lost her virginity to a rapist. There was no doubt that the experience would affect her severely, but with treatment and a great deal of understanding, the psychiatrists felt that she had a good chance of coming out of it whole. His only regret, he had mentioned to them that morning, was that he had not been able to meet with Amanda's mother, and unfortunately Dr. Willard didn't have time for a consultation either, but his secretary had called to tell the psychiatrist to go ahead and meet with the girl.

"But it's not just the victim in these cases who needs help," he had stressed to Alex. "It's the family who needs help as well. Their outlook, their view of what happened, will color the victim's attitude about herself forever." And then he had looked at him with a small smile. "But I'm awfully glad that you could talk to me this morning. And I'm seeing Amanda's grandmother this afternoon." And then he had added sheepishly the rejoinder that Alex had heard for most of his life. "You know, my wife reads all her books."

But right now his mother's books were not foremost on his mind. He had also asked Amanda's doctor how soon she could go home, and he had said that he felt certain that she could be released by the end of the week. That meant Friday, if not before, which suited him perfectly. The sooner he got Amanda back to San Francisco, the happier he would be. And it was that that he was thinking of as Kay walked into the room, looking lanky and chic in a brown suede pantsuit trimmed with red fox.

Their eyes met and held for a long moment, and Kay said not a word. They had suddenly become opponents in the ring, and each one was aware of just how lethal the other could be.

"Hello, Kay." Alex spoke first. He wanted to ask her how she could explain how long it had taken her to show up at the hospital, but he didn't want to make a scene in front of his niece. He didn't really have to. Everything he felt, all his fury, was easy to read in his eyes.

"Hello, Alex. Nice of you to come East."

"Nice of you to come up from Washington." Round one. "You must be very busy." Amanda was watching them, and Alex saw her face go pale. He hesitated for only a moment and then he left the room. When Kay emerged again a few moments later, he was waiting for her in an alcove down the hall. "I want to talk to you for a minute."

She looked at him with mock amusement. "I figured you would. Such a nervous little uncle, coming all the way to New York."

"Are you aware, Kay, that your child almost died?"

"Perfectly. George checked her charts three times a day. If things had gotten worse, I'd have come home. As it was, if it's any of your goddamn business, I couldn't."

"Why not?"

"I had two meetings with the President. Satisfied?"

"Not really. On Thanksgiving?"

"That's right. At Camp David."

"Do you expect me to be impressed?"

"That's your business. But my daughter is mine."

"Not when you totally abdicate your responsibilities, Kay. She needs a hell of a lot more than just George looking at her charts. She needs love, for chrissake, and tenderness, and interest, and understanding. My God, Kay. She's just a child. And she's been beaten and raped. Can't you even conceive of what that means?"

"Perfectly. But nothing I do now will change that. And two days didn't make any difference. She's going to have to live with this for a lifetime."

"And how much of that time are you going to devote to her?"

"That's none of your fucking business."

"I've decided otherwise." His eyes were like steel.

"And just what exactly does that mean?"

"I'm taking her back with me. They said she could travel by Friday."

"The hell you are." Kay Willard's eyes blazed. "You take that child anywhere and I'll have you in jail for kidnapping."

"You filthy bitch." His eyes narrowed as he looked down at her. "As a matter of fact, my dear, unless you are fully prepared to answer to charges of child abuse, I wouldn't do a damn thing if I were you. Kidnapping, my ass."

"What do you mean, child abuse?"

"Just that, and criminal negligence."

"You really think you'd have a chance of making that stick? My husband is one of the most prominent surgeons in New York, a great humanitarian, dear Alex."

"Fine. Prove it in court. You'd love that, wouldn't you? It would look sensational in the papers."

"You son of a bitch." She had finally begun to realize that he meant it. "Just what exactly do you have in mind?"

"Nothing elaborate. Amanda is coming to California with me. Permanently. And if you need something to tell your constituents, you can explain that she had a severe accident and needs extensive rest in a warm climate. That ought to do the trick."

"And what do I tell George?"

"That's your problem."

She looked at him with a kind of morbid fascination. "You really mean it, don't you?"

"I do."

"Why?"

"Because I love her."

"And you think I don't?" She didn't even look hurt, just annoyed.

Alex sighed softly. "I don't think you have time to love anyone, Kay. Except maybe the voters. You care whether or not they'll cast their lot with you. I don't know what makes you tick anymore, and I don't really care. All I do know is that it's destroying that child, and I won't let it . . . I won't let you."

"And you're going to save her? How touching. Don't you think it would be a little healthier for you to use your spare emotional energy on a grown woman and not a seventeen-year-old girl? You realize that all of this is a little sick, don't you?" But she didn't look genuinely worried and he knew she wasn't. She was just mad as hell, and she had no way out.

"Why don't you keep your seamy little insinuations to yourself, along with your ambitions in regard to my ex-wife."

"That has nothing to do with it." But it was obvious that she was lying. "I think you're an ass, Alex. And you're playing games just like Amanda."

"You think getting raped was a game?"

"Maybe. I'm not too clear on the details yet. Maybe this is what she wanted. To be rescued by her big handsome uncle. Maybe this is all her little plot."

"I think you're sick."

"Do you? Well, Alex, it doesn't worry me what you think. And I'll let you play your little game for a while. It might do her good. But I'm coming out to get her in a month or two, and that'll be the end of it. So if you think you're going to hang on to her, you're crazy."

"Am I? Are you willing to face those charges I mentioned?"

"You wouldn't."

"Don't try me." They stood there for a moment, equal in their antagonism, Alex having won for the moment. "Unless something back here changes radically, she's staying with me."

"Have you told her that you're planning to save her from me?"

"Not yet. She was hysterical until this morning." Kay said nothing, and then with a last venomous look she started to walk away. She stopped for a moment and leveled a vicious glare into her brother's eyes.

"Don't think you can play your hero role forever, Alex. You can have her out there for now, but when I want her home, she's coming. Is that clear?"

"I don't think you understand my position."

"I don't think you understand mine. It's a dangerous one. What you're doing could affect me politically, and that's something I won't tolerate, not from my own brother."

"Then you'd better keep your ass in line, lady, and stay out of my hair. And that's a warning." She wanted to laugh at him then, but she couldn't. For the first time in her life she was afraid of her younger brother.

"I don't understand why you're doing this."

"You wouldn't. But I do. And so will Amanda."

"Remember what I said, Alex. When I need her to come home, she comes back here."

"Why? To impress the voters with what a great mother you are? That's a crock of shit." But as he said it she took a step toward him as though to slap him. He grabbed her wrist first and the look in his eyes was terrifying. "Don't do it, Kay."

"Then get the hell out of my life."

"With pleasure." His eyes glinted with victory, and she turned on her heel and walked away as quickly as she could, disappearing a moment later around a bend and into the elevator, and only moments after that into the limousine that waited for her at the curb.

When Alex walked back into Amanda's room, she was sleeping and he gently stroked her hair on the pillow, picked up his coat, and left. But as he walked quietly through the lobby he decided that he couldn't wait till he got to his mother's apartment to call. It was taking a chance to call her, but he had to. He had to share it with someone, and he only wanted to share it with her. With a businesslike voice he asked to speak to Mrs. Phillips. And she came on the line a moment later.

"Raphaella?"

"Yes." And then a sharp intake of breath as she realized who it was. "Oh. Is—" She sounded frightened, as though she thought it meant that Amanda had died.

"No, no, everything's fine. But I had to let you know that my niece and I will be coming to San Francisco at the end of the week, and your father wanted me to say hello when I reached the States." If anyone was listening, it sounded like a perfectly respectable call. And Raphaella had fully caught his meaning. She was beaming from ear to ear.

"Will your niece be with you for long?"

"I . . . uh . . . believe so. Yes." He grinned. "I do."

"Oh. . . ." She had almost said his name in her excitement "I'm so pleased!" And then she thought of the room she had promised to put together for him. "I'll take care of the accommodations as quickly as I can."

"Wonderful. I'd be very grateful. And of course I'll reimburse you as soon as I get to San Francisco."

"Oh, shut up." She was grinning into the phone, and a few minutes later they both hung up. Friday, he had finally told her, or maybe Saturday. It didn't give her much time.

CHAPTER 15

The next two days were a kind of frenzy for Raphaella. She spent the morning reading quietly to John Henry and holding his hand as he drifted off to sleep, and then she would hurry downtown to go shopping, telling the chauffeur not to wait, she would prefer to go home in a cab. And if Tom found her behavior a trifle eccentric, he was too well trained to mention it as she raced into the nearest store. Each afternoon she emerged carrying enormous bundles, and the bigger items she had sent directly to the house. She was buying floor samples and pieces in funny little thrift shops, like a wonderful old washstand from a decorator, and a whole set of Victorian wicker from a garage sale she'd passed on the street as she raced home in a cab. By the end of the second day she had created total chaos, and she almost cried with relief when Alex apologetically told her on the phone that he wouldn't be back until Sunday night, but he had very good news. He had seen George that morning and everything had gone smoothly. George had agreed that it would do Amanda good to get away. They hadn't discussed the length of her visit, but once she was in California, it would be easy to extend it, she would already be away. For the moment he had casually mentioned "a few months" and George hadn't demurred. Alex had called the best of the private high schools in San Francisco and, having explained the severity of her "accident," read them a transcript of her grades, and explained who her mother and grandmother were, it had not been very difficult to get her into the school. She was to start after the first of the year. In the meantime she would rest at home, go for walks, get her health back, and do whatever she had to, to get over the shock of the rape. She had a month to recuperate slowly before going back to school. And when Raphaella asked how Kay had taken it, Alex sounded strained. "It was less pleasant with her than with George."

"What does that mean, Alex?"

"It means I didn't give her any choice."

"Is she very angry?"

"More or less." He changed the subject quickly then, and as Raphaella hung up the phone her thoughts were filled with the young girl, wondering what she was like, if she would like her.

It was as though Raphaella had suddenly acquired not just a new man, but a new family as well. And there was Kay to consider. Alex had mentioned that his sister would be coming out to San Francisco at some point to check on Amanda. And Raphaella hoped that eventually they could all become friends. They were, after all, civilized people. Kay was undoubtedly an intelligent woman, and Raphaella was sorry that she and Alex were at odds. Perhaps, eventually, she could do something to still the troubled waters. In the meantime, after the phone call, she bustled about setting everything right on the third floor of Alex's house. She had told him that he could reach her there while she worked on the room for Amanda, and when she was through with her labor of love, she sat down on the bed with a broad, happy grin. In a few days she had wrought a minor miracle, and she was very pleased.

She had turned the bedroom into an airy haven, a room filled with pink flowered fabrics and Victorian wicker, a huge flowered rug she had bought right off the floor at Macy's, and the antique washstand with the white marble top. She had put a large pink azalea in the old sink, and there were delicate flowered prints in gold frames on the walls. The bed was a four-poster with a white canopy and pink bows, which they had delivered only that morning. There was a huge pink satin quilt on the bed, and a little fur throw rug over a nearby chair. There was more of the flowered fabric and the wicker in the little study beyond. She had even found a small pretty desk that sat in front of the windows, and the bathroom had also been filled with pretty feminine things. The fact that she had been able to do it at all in so few days was nothing less than extraordinary, and that she had been able to bribe and cajole everyone into making deliveries still amazed her.

She had bought all of her purchases with the huge roll of cash she had gotten at the bank on Wednesday morning, she didn't want her checks to record any of those purchases. All of her accounts were balanced at John Henry's old office and it would have been impossible to explain what the checks had been for. This way she only had a single sum that had been withdrawn, and she would find some way to explain it, like a shopping spree, or perhaps in time the secretary wouldn't remember if it had been before or after her trip to New York.

The only one she had to account to now was Alex, and she was a little bit nervous about what he would say. In truth she had not spent a great deal of money, and he had asked her if she could see if she could order a bed. She had of course done a great deal more than that in the upstairs bedroom, but much of it was in fact simple. It was just done with a great deal of caring and style and good taste. The lavish profusion of flowers, the little white curtains she had sewn and trimmed with pink ribbons, the cushions she had thrown here and there, and the wicker she herself had spray-painted late one night made the difference. The extra touches that now looked so expensive in fact were not. But she hoped that Alex would not be angry at the extent of the decorating, she had just found as she went along that she couldn't stop until she had turned it into the perfect room for the battered young girl. After the horror of what had happened to the child, Raphaella wanted to help provide her with something special, a home she could sink into with a long, happy sigh, a place where she would be loved and could relax. She closed the door softly now and went back downstairs to Alex's bedroom, looked around, straightened the bedspread, picked up her coat, and walked down the stairs and out the front door.

With a sigh Raphaella opened the door to John Henry's mansion and walked slowly upstairs with a thoughtful look and a slow step. She looked around her at the velvet hangings, the medieval tapestries, the chandeliers, the grand piano in the foyer, and she realized once again that this was her home. Not the cozy little house on Vallejo, not the place where she had just spent almost a week like a crazy woman decorating a room for a young girl who also was not her own.

"Mrs. Phillips?"

"Mmm?" Raphaella looked up, startled, as she turned to go down the hall to her room. It was almost time for dinner and she still had to dress. "Yes?" The nurse from the second shift was smiling at her.

"Mr. Phillips has been asking for you for the last hour. Perhaps you'd like to spend a moment with him before you change."

Raphaella nodded quietly and murmured, "Yes." She walked slowly to the door of his room, knocked once, turned the knob, and walked in without waiting for him to bid her to enter. The knock was only a formality, like so many others in their lives. He was lying tucked into bed, with a blanket over him, his eyes were closed and the light in the room was very dim. "John Henry?" Her voice was only a whisper as she stared at the broken old man who lay in his bed. This was the room that had once been their bedroom, the room he had also long ago shared with his first wife. At first it had bothered Raphaella, but John Henry was a man of tradition, and he had wanted to bring her here. And somehow the ghosts had all faded as they had lain there. It was only now that she thought of them all again. Now that he almost seemed to be one of them. "John Henry. . . ." She whispered his name again and he opened his eyes. When he saw her, he opened them fully, smiled his crooked smile, and patted a place next to him on the bed.

"Hello, little one. I asked for you earlier but they said you were out. Where were you?" It was not an interrogation, only a friendly question, but something inside her flinched nonetheless.

"I was out . . . shopping. . . ." She smiled at him. "For Christmas." He didn't know that her packages for Paris and Spain had all been shipped a month before.

"Did you buy anything pretty?" She nodded. Oh, yes, she had. She had bought lovely things . . . for Amanda, her lover's niece. The realization of what she was doing struck her once again like a physical blow. "Anything pretty for you?" She shook her head slowly, her eyes very wide.

"I didn't have time."

"Then I want you to go shopping tomorrow and get something for yourself." She looked at the long, angular frame of the man who was her husband and she was once more devoured by her own guilt.

"I'd rather spend the day here with you. I—I haven't seen you very much lately. . . ." She looked apologetic and he shook his head and waved a tired hand.

"I don't expect you to sit here with me, Raphaella." He shook his head again, closed his eyes for a moment, and then opened them again. There was something infinitely wise in the eyes that gazed out at the young woman. "I never expect you to sit here with me waiting, little one . . . never. . . . I am only sorry that it is so long in coming." For a moment she wondered if his mind were wandering, and she looked at him with sudden concern in her eyes. But he only smiled. "Death, my darling . . . death. . . . It has been a long wait for the final moment. And you have been a very brave girl. I will never forgive myself for what I've done."

"How can you say that?" She looked at him in horror. "I love you. I wouldn't be anywhere else." But was it true now? Wouldn't she rather be with Alex? She asked herself as she reached for John Henry's hand and took it very gently in her own. "I have never regretted anything, my darling, except"—she felt a lump rise in her throat as she watched him—"that this has happened to you."

"I should have died when I had the first stroke. I would have, if life were a little more fair, and if you and that young fool doctor you hired had let me go."

"You're being crazy."

"No, I'm not, and you know it. This is no life for anyone, not for me and not for you. I keep you here year after year as my prisoner, you're still almost a child, and I am wasting your best years. My own are long gone. I was—" He closed his eyes briefly as though he were in pain and the frown on Raphaella's face deepened as she watched him. He very quickly reopened his eyes and looked at her again. "I was wrong to marry you, Raphaella. I was too old."

"John Henry, stop it." It frightened her when he spoke like that, and he didn't do it often, but she suspected that many of his thoughts centered on this theme. She kissed him gently and looked at him closely as he leaned forward. He looked deathly pale as he lay in the huge double bed. "Have they had you out in the garden for any air this week, darling? Or on the terrace?"

He shook his head with a crooked little smile.

"No, Miss Nightingale, they haven't. And I don't want to go. I'm happier here in my bed."

"Don't be silly. The air does you good, and you like going out in the garden." She sounded quietly desperate, thinking that if she hadn't been spending so much time away from him, she would have been aware of what the nurse was doing for him. They should have been taking him out. It was important that they keep him moving, that they keep him as alive and interested as they could. Without that she knew that he would stop trying and sooner or later he would just simply give up. The doctor had told her as much many years earlier, and she could see now that he had come to a very bad spot. "I'll take you out tomorrow."

"I don't want you to." He looked querulous for a moment. "I told you, I want to stay in bed."

"Well, you can't. So how's that?"

"Pesty child." He glared at her, but he smiled then and raised her hands to brush them with his lips. "I still love you. So much more than I can tell you . . . so much more than you know." His eyes looked faintly misty. "Do you remember those first days in Paris" —he smiled to himself and she smiled with him— "when I proposed to you, Raphaella." He looked at her clearly. "My God, you were only a child." They looked at each other tenderly for a moment, and she leaned forward to kiss his cheek once again.

"Well, I'm an old woman now, my darling, and I'm lucky you still love me." And then she stood up, still smiling. "But I'd best change for dinner or you may throw me out and find yourself another young girl!" He chuckled at this and when she left the room with a kiss and a wave, he felt better, and she berated herself all the way back to her room for having neglected him so terribly for the past week and a half. What had she been doing, running around buying furniture and fabric and curtains and carpets for almost a whole week? But as she closed the door to her bedroom she knew what she had been doing. She had been thinking of Alex, of his niece and of setting up her bedroom, of the other life that she wanted so badly. As she stared into the mirror for a long moment, tormenting herself for having neglected her husband for almost ten days, she wondered if she had a right to what she had with Alex. This was her destiny with John Henry. She really had no right to ask for anything more. But could she give it up now? After two months she was no longer sure that she could.

With a deep sigh she opened her closet, and pulled out a gray silk dress she had bought with her mother in Madrid. Black pumps, the exquisite necklace of gray pearls that had belonged to John Henry's mother, matching earrings, and a delicate gray slip. She threw it all on the bed and walked into her bathroom, lost in thought over what she'd been doing, thinking of the man she had almost forgotten, and the one that she never could, yet knowing that both men needed her. John Henry more than Alex of course, but they both needed her, and more than that, she knew that she needed them both.

Half an hour later she stood in front of her mirror, a vision of elegance and grace in the pale gray silk dress, her hair smoothly combed into the knot she wore at the nape of her neck, the pearls on her ears lighting up her face. And as she looked into the mirror she had no answers. There was no way to see the end of the story. All she could hope for was that no one would get hurt. But as she closed the door to her bedroom she felt a tremor of fear run through her, knowing that that was almost too much to ask.

CHAPTER 16

On Sunday evening the nurse put John Henry to bed
at eight thirty, and Raphaella walked slowly and
thoughtfully to her room. She had been thinking
about Alex and Amanda all evening, making a mental
note of when they would be leaving the city, boarding
the plane. Now they were only two hours from San
Francisco, but she felt for the first time in ages that
they might have been in another world. She had spent
the day with John Henry, gotten him out to the garden in the morning, carefully wrapped in blankets and
wearing a warm scarf and a hat as well as a black
cashmere coat over his silk robe. In the afternoon she
had pushed the wheelchair out on the terrace, and by
the end of the day she had to admit to herself that he
looked better, and he was relaxed and tired that evening when they put him to bed. This was what she
was supposed to be doing, this was her duty, he was
her husband. "For better or worse." But again and
again her mind wandered back to Alex and to

Amanda. And more and more as she sat in the brick palace she felt as though she lay buried in a tomb. But she was shocked at her own feelings, and suddenly the evil of what she was doing had risen to haunt her. She was no longer sure it was right.

At ten o'clock she sat staring sadly, knowing that their plane had just landed, that they would be collecting their luggage and looking for a cab. At ten fifteen she knew they were on their way to the city, and with every ounce of her being she found herself wishing that she could be there. But suddenly the fact that she had fallen in love with Alex seemed wrong to her, and she was afraid that in the long run John Henry would pay the price, in lack of attention, lack of her company, lack of a certain feeling, and without that she knew that John Henry would not stay alive. But can't you do both? she found herself silently asking. She wasn't sure that she could. When she was with Alex, it was as if no one else in the world existed and all that she wanted was to be with him and forget everyone else. But she couldn't afford to forget John Henry. If she forgot him, she might as well put a gun to his head.

She sat there staring silently out the window, and eventually she got up and turned off the light. She still sat there in her dress from dinner, which she had eaten on a tray in his room while they talked and he dozed between bites. He had been exhausted from all the fresh air. But now she sat very still, as though she were watching, looking for someone, for something, as though Alex would suddenly appear outside. It was eleven o'clock when she heard the phone ring, and she started and picked it up, knowing that all the servants would be in bed except for John Henry's nurse. She couldn't imagine who would call. But when she picked it up, it was Alex, and she trembled at the sound of his voice.

"Raphaella?" It frightened her to be talking to him here, but she wanted desperately to reach out to him. After their two-month separation after New York, and then his trip to see about Amanda, now suddenly she ached to be with him again.

"The room for Amanda is incredible." He spoke softly and for a moment she was frightened that someone might hear, but there was such joy in his voice that she couldn't resist.

"Does she like it?"

"She's in seventh heaven. It's the first time in years I've seen her look like that."

"Good." Raphaella felt pleased as she tried to imagine the young girl discovering the pink and white room. "Is she all right?"

He sighed in answer. "I don't know, Raphaella. I suppose so. But how all right could she be after what happened? Her mother made an outrageous scene before we left. She tried to make her feel guilty for leaving. And then, of course, she admitted that she's afraid of what it will look like to the voters if her daughter is living with an uncle instead of with her."

"If she handles it right, it could just seem that she's very busy."

"I said pretty much the same thing. Anyway, it got ugly, and Mandy was so exhausted that she slept all the way out here on the plane. Seeing that beautiful room you put together for her was the happiest thing that happened to her all day."

"I'm glad." But as she said the words Raphaella felt unbearably lonely. She would have liked to see Amanda's face as she walked into the room. She would have liked to have been there at the airport, to have come home with them in the car, and to have walked into the house with them, to have shared each moment, seen their smiles, helped make Amanda feel welcome in the house that Raphaella had been in and out of a dozen times in the past week. Suddenly she felt left out and as she listened to Alex's voice on the telephone, she felt desperately alone. It was an almost crushing burden, and she was reminded of the night when she had cried in similiar loneliness on the steps near the house . . . the night she had first seen Alex. . . . It seemed a century ago as she thought of it now.

"You got very quiet. Is something wrong?" His voice was deep and alluring as Raphaella closed her eyes and shook her head.

"I was just thinking of something . . . I'm sorry. . . ."

"What was it?"

She hesitated for a moment. "That night on the stairs . . . the first time I saw you."

He smiled too. "You didn't see me in the beginning though. I saw you first." But as they reminisced about their first meeting Raphaella began to get nervous again about the phone. If any of the servants were awake, they could pick it up at any moment, and she was worried about what they might hear or think.

"Perhaps we should talk about this tomorrow."

He understood her. "Will we see you then?"

"I'd like that." The prospect warmed her, and for an instant the loneliness dimmed.

"What would be a good time for you?"

She laughed softly, she had nothing to do now that the room for Amanda was done. It had been her only project in years. "Just tell me when. I'll come over. Or would it be better if—" She suddenly worried about Amanda. Perhaps it was too soon to meet the girl. Perhaps she would resent meeting Alex's lover, maybe she wanted her beloved uncle all to herself.

"Don't be silly, Raphaella. If I could talk you into it, I'd love it if you'd come over now." But they both knew that Amanda was tired and it was too late. "Why don't you join us for breakfast? Can you come over that early?"

Raphaella smiled. "How about six? Five fifteen? Four thirty?"

"That sounds great." He laughed as he closed his eyes. He could envision every detail of her face. He was aching to see her again, to touch her, to hold her, to let their bodies entwine as though they had always been one. "As a matter of fact, with the time difference, I probably will be up at six. Why don't you just plan on coming over when you get up. You don't even have to call. I'm not going in to the office tomorrow morning. I want to make sure that the woman who's coming to help Amanda is okay." With two broken arms, the girl was virtually helpless, and he had had his secretary make arrangements for a combination light housekeeper-practical nurse. And then after a moment, "I'll be waiting for you." The longing in his voice was as clear as the hunger in Raphaella's own.

"I'll come early." And then, forgetting her anxiety about who might be listening in on the phone, "I've missed you, Alex."

"Oh, baby." The sound of his voice said it all. "If you only knew how I've missed you."

They hung up a few moments later, and Raphaella sat for a long time staring at the phone with a radiant

smile. She glanced at her watch as she stood up to
undress. It was after midnight, and in six or seven or
eight hours she would be with him again. The very
thought of it made her eyes dance and her heart race.

CHAPTER 17

Raphaella had set her alarm for six thirty, and an hour later she slipped quietly out the front door. She had already spoken to one of John Henry's nurses and had explained to her that she was going to an early Mass and then for a long walk. It seemed like a wholesome explanation for what would undoubtedly be an absence of several hours. At least she hoped it would be as she hurried along the street in the December fog and the early-morning chill, with her coat pulled tightly around her and a pearly gray light bathing everything she could see. She reached the cozy little house on Vallejo in a matter of moments, and was pleased to see that most of the lights were already on. That meant that Alex was awake then, and she hesitated for a moment, facing the big brass knocker, wondering if she should knock, ring the doorbell, or use her key. In the end she opted for a quick ring, and then stood there, breathless, excited, waiting, a smile dawning on

her face, before his hand even touched the door, and
then suddenly there he was, so tall and handsome,
with a smile on his own lips, his eyes bright. Without
saying a word, he pulled her quickly inside, closed the
door, and folded her tightly into his arms. They said
nothing for a long moment, but his lips found hers and
they clung together that way for what seemed like a
very long time. Afterward he just held her, sharing the
warmth of his body and letting one hand stroke her
shining black hair. He looked down at her almost with
amazement, as though he still found it remarkable that
he knew her at all.

"Hello, Alex." She looked up at him happily with a
twinkle in her eyes.

"Hello." And then as he stood back just a little, "My
God, you look lovely."

"Not at this hour." But she did. She looked absolutely radiant. Her eyes were big and bright like onyx
flecked with diamonds, and her face was pink from
the brisk walk. She had worn a pale peach-colored
silk shirt and beige slacks with the lynx coat. And beneath the slacks he could just see cinnamon suede
Gucci shoes. "How is Amanda?" Raphaella glanced toward the upstairs and Alex smiled again.

"Still asleep." But he wasn't thinking of Amanda.
The only thing he could think of this morning was the
incredibly beautiful woman who stood before him in
the front hall, and as he looked at her he wasn't sure
whether to take her downstairs to the kitchen and offer her coffee or rush her upstairs with far less social
pursuits in mind.

But as she watched him struggle with the decision,
Raphaella grinned. "You look positively wicked this
morning, Alex." With a spark of mischief of her own

she took off the heavy lynx coat and dropped it on the newel post at the foot of the stairs.

"Do I?" He feigned innocence. "I wonder why."

"I can't imagine. Can I make you coffee?"

"I was just thinking about doing that." But he obviously looked disappointed and she laughed.

"But?"

"Never mind . . . never mind." He began to usher her downstairs, but they didn't get past the first step when he turned to kiss her, and they dawdled there for a long time as he held her tightly in his arms. It was thus that Amanda found them as she wandered sleepily down the stairs in a blue flowered nightgown, her blond hair a halo around the pretty young face, and the bruises fading slightly around her eyes.

"Oh." It was a single sound of surprise, but Raphaella heard it instantly and almost jumped out of Alex's arms. She turned, blushing slightly, to see Amanda looking at her with a host of questions in her eyes. She glanced at Alex then, as though there she would find an explanation. As she watched them Raphaella thought that she looked very much like a little girl.

Raphaella turned and walked toward her with a soft smile and held out her hand, only to touch gently the fingers exposed at the end of Amanda's casts. "I'm sorry to intrude on you so early in the morning. I—I wanted to see how you were." She was mortified to have been caught necking on the stairs, and suddenly all her fears about meeting Amanda surged up in her again, but the girl looked so fragile and guileless that it was impossible to imagine her as any kind of threat. It was Raphaella who felt threatening, afraid that she might have upset the girl.

But Amanda smiled then, a soft blush creeping into her cheeks. "It's okay. I'm sorry, I didn't mean to walk in on you and Uncle Alex." It had pleased her to see them kissing. She never saw any warmth in her own home. "I didn't know anyone was here."

"I don't usually go visiting this early, but—"

Alex cut in quickly, he wanted Amanda to know who Raphaella was and just how important she was to him. She was old enough to understand that. "This is the fairy godmother who decorated your room, Mandy." His voice was tender, and so were his eyes, as he looked at them both, the three of them hovering near the stairs.

"You are? You did?"

Raphaella laughed at the amazement in the girl's eyes. "More or less. I'm not much of a decorator, but it was fun to put together your room."

"How did you do it so quickly? Alex said there was nothing in it at all when he left."

"I stole everything." They laughed and she grinned. "Do you like it?"

"Are you kidding? It's terrif!" This time it was Raphaella who laughed at both the excitement and the slang.

"I'm so glad." She wanted to hug her then, but she didn't quite dare.

"Can I offer both of you ladies breakfast?" Alex was beaming down at them both.

"I'll help you." Raphaella volunteered as she followed him down the stairs.

"Me too." Amanda seemed happily engaged for the first time since the tragedy. And she looked even happier an hour later as the three of them sat around the kitchen table, chuckling over the remains of fried eggs and bacon and toast. Mandy had even managed to butter the toast with her casts on, Raphaella had made the coffee, and Alex had seen to the rest.

"Excellent teamwork!" He commended the two women as they teased him again about being a very imperious chef. But what was evident above all as Raphaella cleared the table was that the three of them were comfortable together, and she felt as though she had just been given a priceless gift.

"Can I help you get dressed, Mandy?"

"Sure." The girl's eyes lit up, and half an hour later, with Raphaella's help, she was dressed. It was only when the new housekeeper came at nine that Alex and Raphaella were once again alone.

"What a wonderful girl she is, Alex."

He beamed at her. "Isn't she? And . . . God, Raphaella, it's amazing how she's recovering from the— From what happened to her. It's only been a week." His face had sobered as he remembered.

Raphaella nodded slowly, thinking back over the past week. "I think she'll be fine. Thanks to you."

"Maybe thanks to both of us." He hadn't been oblivious of the gentle, loving way she had of handling the girl. He had been touched by her obvious warmth and the way she had reached out to Amanda, and he hoped that it meant good times for the three of them in days to come. Amanda was part of his life now, but so was Raphaella, and it meant a great deal to him for the three of them to be close.

CHAPTER 18

"What do you mean you don't like the angel?" Alex looked at her with a crooked grin as he perched on the top of a ladder in the empty living room. Raphaella and Mandy were standing beneath him, and Mandy had just told him that the angel looked dumb.

"Look at him, he's grinning. He looks silly."

"If you ask me, you guys look pretty silly too." They were both lying on the floor playing with the trains Alex had brought up from the basement. They had been his father's and then his.

Alex clambered down the ladder and observed the fruit of his labors. He had already strung the lights and Mandy and Raphaella had done most of the decorating while he had gotten things started, assembling the trains. It was the day before Christmas, and his mother had promised to come out for a visit in two days. In the meantime it was just he and Amanda and Raphaella. She had been spending as much time as she could with him, but she had her own things to do.

She had been attempting to make things a little bit festive for John Henry, and Alex had even gone with her to pick out a small tree. She had spent a week planning a party for the servants, wrapping gifts, and putting up funny red stockings with their names. They were always amused by her thoughtful gestures, and the gifts she had bought them were always useful as well as expensive, gifts they were happy to get and would enjoy for many long years. Everything was done with a kind of generous fervor, a zeal all her own. The presents were beautifully wrapped, carefully selected; the house looked lovely, filled with poinsettias and pinecones, little pine plants; and there was a huge handsome wreath on the front door. Just that morning she had taken John Henry around the house in his wheelchair, and afterward she had disappeared and returned with a bottle of champagne. But this year she noticed that he viewed it all with less interest. He seemed far removed from any Christmas joy.

"I'm too old for all this, Raphaella. I've seen it too often. It doesn't matter anymore." He seemed even to struggle with the words.

"Don't be silly. You're just tired. Besides, you don't know what I bought you." She had picked out a silk robe with his monogram. But she knew even that wouldn't bring him around. He was increasingly lethargic, increasingly morbid, and had been this way for months now, as though he no longer cared.

But with Alex she found the Christmas spirit, and in Amanda she saw the childlike joy she loved so much in her little cousins in Spain. For Amanda there were long strands of red berries, arrangements of holly, long strings of popcorn they made for the tree, there were decorations they baked and cut out and painted.

There were gifts that they made as well as the ones they bought. For weeks it had been an exhausting proposition and now it was culminated with the decoration of the tree. Just before midnight they were finished, and the presents were stacked in little piles all over the floor. In the empty parlor the tree looked gigantic, the lights splendid, and the little train tooted freely around the floor.

"Happy?" Alex smiled lazily at her as they stretched out in front of the fireplace in his room, a pile of logs burning.

"Very. Do you think Mandy will like her present?"

"She'd better or I'm sending her back to Kay." He had bought her a little lamb jacket like Raphaella's and had promised her driving lessons as soon as the casts were off her arms. They were due off in another two weeks. Raphaella was giving her ski boots, which she had begged Alex for, a bright blue cashmere sweater, and a whole stack of books.

"You know." Raphaella smiled happily up at him. "It's not like buying for my cousins. It feels like"—she hesitated to say it, feeling foolish—"like having a daughter, for the first time in my life."

He grinned down at her with a sheepish smile. "I feel the same way. It's nice, isn't it? Now I realize how empty the house was. It's so different now." And as though to prove it, the impish little face poked through the door. The bruises were gone now and the look of devastation was fading slowly from her eyes. In the month that she'd been in San Francisco, she had rested, gone for long walks, and talked almost daily to a psychiatrist, who was helping her to live with the fact that she had been raped.

"Hi, you guys. What are you up to?"

"Nothing special." Her uncle looked at her happily. "How come you're not in bed?"

"I'm too excited." And with that, she walked into the room and took two large cumbersome packages from behind her back. "I wanted to give you both these." Raphaella and Alex looked at her with surprise and pleasure and sat up on the floor as she held out the gifts. She looked as though she were going to explode with the excitement, and she sat down on the edge of the bed, swinging her long blond hair away from her face.

"Should we open them now?" Alex was teasing. "Or should we wait. What do you think, Raphaella?" But she was already opening hers, with a smile, until she pulled away the paper, and then she caught her breath and let out a little gasp.

"Oh, Mandy. . . ." She looked at the young girl with amazement. "I didn't know you could paint." And with casts on. It was amazing. But she shielded the gift from Alexander, suspecting that his gift was the mate to hers, and a moment later she saw that she was right. "Oh, they're so lovely. Mandy . . . thank you!" Her pleasure was written all over her face as she embraced the girl she had come to love, and for a long startled moment Alex just sat and stared at his gift. Mandy had sketched them without their realizing it and done their portraits in watercolors. The paintings were stunning, both in composition and attitude. Then she had them framed and had given the one of Alex to Raphaella and the one of her to Alex. It was at a perfect reflection of Raphaella that he now stared. And it wasn't only accurate in detail and feature but in the spirit she had caught, the warmth and the sorrow and the loving of the rich black eyes, the softness of the face, the creaminess of her complexion. One had a sense of precisely how the woman thought and breathed and moved. And she had done just as good a job with Alex, catching him when he wasn't aware. Raphaella had been harder because she was around Mandy less often, and Amanda hadn't wanted to press herself on them when they had so little time alone. But it was clear from the awed faces of the recipients that her gifts were an enormous success.

Alex stood up to kiss and hug her tightly, and after that the three of them sat on the floor by the fire and talked for hours. They talked about people, about life, about dreams and disappointments. Amanda talked openly now about the pain inflicted by her parents. Alex nodded and tried to explain what Kay had been like as a young girl. They talked about Charlotte and what it had been like to have her for a mother, and Raphaella talked about the rigidity of her father, and how little suited she had felt for the life imposed on her with her mother in Spain. In the end they even talked about her and Alex, speaking openly to Amanda about how grateful they were for whatever they could have of each other, in whatever little bits of time. It surprised them both that she understood it, that she wasn't shocked by Raphaella's marriage, and Raphaella herself was startled to realize that Amanda thought her something of a hero for sticking by John Henry until the end.

"But that's what I'm supposed to be doing. He's my husband, even if—even if everything is changed."

"Maybe, but I don't think many women would do that. They'd go off with Alex just because he's young and handsome and they loved him. It must be hard to stay with your husband like that, day after day." It was the first time they'd discussed it openly and for a moment Raphaella had to force herself not to change the subject, but to face it with these two people she loved.

"It is hard." She sounded very soft and very sad as she thought of her husband's worn face. "Very hard sometimes. He's so tired. It's as though I'm the only thing that makes him want to go on. Sometimes I'm not sure I can carry the burden of that another step. What if something were to happen to me, what if I had to go away, what if . . . ?" She looked mutely at Alex and he understood. She shook her head slowly. "I think then he would die."

Amanda was looking at her face, as though searching for an answer to a question, as though seeking to understand this woman she had come to admire and love so much. "But what if he did die, Raphaella? Maybe he doesn't want to live anymore. Is it right to force him?" It was a question as old as the ages, and not one which could be answered in one night.

"I don't know, darling. I just know I have to do whatever I can."

Amanda looked at her in open admiration as Alex watched them both with pride. "But you do so much for us too."

"Don't be silly." Raphaella's embarrassment was obvious. "I don't do anything. I just turn up here every evening like a bad fairy, peering over your shoulders, asking if you did the laundry"—then she grinned at Alex—"telling you to clean up your room."

"Yup, that's all she does, folks." Alex was teasing as he stepped in. "In fact she doesn't do a damn thing except eat our food, hang around in our bedrooms, decorate the house, occasionally feed us, polish the copper, read the briefs I sweat over, teach Amanda to knit, weed the garden, bring us flowers, buy us presents." He looked at her, prepared to go on.

"It really isn't very much." Raphaella was blushing, and he tugged at a lock of the jet black hair.

"Well, if it isn't, pretty lady, I'd hate to see you at full speed." They kissed softly for a moment, and Amanda tiptoed to the door.

Amanda smiled at them from the doorway. "Good night, you two."

"Hey, wait a minute." Alex stretched out a hand to pull her back. "Don't you want your presents now too?" She giggled in answer and he stood up and pulled Raphaella to her feet. "Come on, you guys, it's Christmas." He knew that Raphaella wouldn't be with them the next day until late.

The three of them trooped downstairs, laughing and talking, and pounced on the presents with their names on them with obvious glee. Alex had a beautiful Irish sweater from his mother, a set of pens from Amanda, in addition to the painting she'd given him upstairs, a bottle of wine from his brother-in-law, nothing at all from his sister, and a Gucci briefcase from Raphaella, along with a tie and a beautifully bound old leather book, which was the book of poems he had told her about a month before.

"My God, woman, you're crazy!" But his reproaches were interrupted by Amanda's squeals as she opened her gifts. But then it was Raphaella's turn. She had a little bottle of perfume from Amanda, and a pretty scarf from Charlotte Brandon, which touched her a great deal, and then there was a small flat box that Alex handed her with a mysterious smile and a kiss. "Go on, open it."

"I'm afraid to." Her voice was a whisper and he saw her hands tremble as she pulled off the paper and stared at the dark green velvet box. Inside, there was a creamy satin lining and on it nestled an exquisitely simple circle of black onyx and ivory banded in gold. She saw instantly that it was a bracelet, and then noticed in amazement that there were earrings and a beautiful onyx and ivory ring to match. She slipped the whole set on and looked in the mirror at herself in stupefaction. It all fit perfectly, even the black and white ring. "Alex, you're the one who's crazy! How could you?" But they were so lovely, she could hardly reproach him for the expensive gift. "Darling, I love them." She kissed him long and hard on the mouth as Amanda smiled and started the little train.

"Did you look inside the ring?" She shook her head slowly and he took it off her right hand. "It says something." Quickly she held the ring up and looked at the engraving on the gold band that lined the ring, and she looked up at him with tears standing in her eyes. It said SOMEDAY. Only that. Just one word. His eyes pierced into hers now, filled with meaning. It meant that someday they would be together, for always. Someday she would be his, and he would be hers.

She stayed until three o'clock that morning, an hour after Amanda finally went to bed. It had been a beautiful evening, a wonderful Christmas, and as Alex and Raphaella lay side by side on the bed, staring into the fire, he looked at her and whispered it again. "Someday, Raphaella, someday." The echo of his words still rang in her head as she walked the last block home and disappeared through the garden door.

CHAPTER 19

"Well, children, if old age doesn't kill me, undoubtedly my own gluttony will. I must have eaten enough for ten people." Charlotte Brandon stared around the table with a look of happy exhaustion, and the other three looked much the same. They had devoured a mountain of cracked crab for dinner, and Raphaella was serving espresso in little gold and white cups. They were among the few nice things that Rachel had forgotten when she'd left for New York.

Raphaella put the cup of coffee in front of Alex's mother and the two women exchanged a smile. There was a quiet understanding between them, based on a compatible sharing of someone they both loved a great deal. And now they had two such bonds to bring them closer. There was Amanda as well.

"I hate to ask, Mother, but how's Kay doing?" Alex looked only slightly tense as he inquired. But Charlotte looked at him frankly, and then at her only grandchild.

"I think she's still very upset that Amanda's out here. And I don't think she's given up hope that Amanda will come back." Charlotte's audience immediately wore tense faces, but she was quick to reassure them on that head. "I don't think she's going to do anything about it, but I think she realizes now what she's lost." Amanda hadn't yet heard from her mother in the four weeks since she'd left New York. "But I don't really think she has time to pursue it. The campaign is beginning to get under way." She fell silent and Alex nodded, glancing at Raphaella, who wore a worried smile.

"Don't look so uptight, pretty lady." He spoke to her softly. "The wicked witch of the East isn't going to hurt you."

"Oh, Alex." The four of them laughed, but Raphaella was always uneasy about her. She had an odd sense that if she had to Kay would do anything to get what she wanted out of life. And if what she wanted was to separate Alex from Raphaella, perhaps she would find a way to do just that. Which is why they made sure she knew nothing about them and they led a totally hidden life. They never went out in public. They only met in the house. And there was no one who knew about them, except Charlotte, and now Amanda.

"Do you think she'll win the election, Mother?" Alex looked searchingly at his mother as he lit one of his rare cigars. He only smoked Havanas when he could get them, long, narrow, pungent, aromatic wonders, which he got from a friend who flew in and out of Switzerland, where he bought the Cuban cigars from another old friend.

"No, Alex, I don't. I think this time Kay has bitten

off more than she can chew. The incumbent is a great deal stronger than she is. But she's certainly trying to make up for it with a lot of hard work and a great many tough speeches. She's also fighting for an endorsement from every powerful politician she can find."

Alex looked at his mother oddly. "Including my ex-father-in-law?"

"Of course."

"God bless her. She's incredible. She's got more goddamn nerve than anyone I know." And then he turned to Raphaella. "He's a powerful man in politics, and he's one of the reasons Kay was so pissed off when I got divorced from Rachel. She was afraid that the old man would be mad. And he was." He grinned at Raphaella in amusement. "He sure as hell was." Then he looked at his mother again. "Is she seeing Rachel?"

"Probably." Charlotte sighed. Her daughter would stop at nothing to get what she wanted. She never had.

Alex turned to Raphaella again and took her hand in his. "See what an interesting family I come from. And you think your father is peculiar. You should only know some of my cousins and uncles. Christ, at least half of them are nuts."

Even Charlotte laughed in amusement, and Amanda slipped into the kitchen and began to clean up. Alex noticed it after a moment and raised an eyebrow in Raphaella's direction. "Something wrong?"

She whispered softly. "I think it upsets her to talk about her mother. It brings back some difficult memories."

For an instant Charlotte Brandon looked worried,

and then she gave them both the news. "I hate to tell you this, now, children, but Kay said she was going to try to be here by the end of the week. She wanted to see Amanda around Christmas."

"Oh, shit." Alex sat back in his chair with a slump and a groan. "Why now? What the hell does she want?"

His mother looked at him bluntly. "Amanda. What do you think? She thinks it's hurting her politically to have Mandy out here. She is afraid that people think there's a secret, maybe the girl's pregnant or she's coming off drugs."

"Oh, for chrissake." As he said it Raphaella disappeared into the kitchen to chat with Mandy as they cleared. She could see that the child was distressed by the conversation, and at last she put an arm around her shoulders and decided to tell her, so that she, too, would be prepared.

"Amanda, your mother is coming out here."

"What?" The girl's eyes flew wide. "Why? She can't take me back with her. I won't go . . . I'll . . . she can't. . . ." Her eyes filled instantly with tears and she clung to Raphaella, who held her tight.

"You don't have to go anywhere, but you should see her."

"I don't want to."

"She's your mother."

"No, she's not." Amanda's eyes went cold and Raphaella looked shocked.

"Amanda!"

"I mean it. Giving birth to a baby doesn't make a woman a mother, Raphaella. Loving that child and caring for it and about it, sitting with it when it's sick, and making it happy and being its friend, that's what makes a mother. Not getting votes and winning elections. Christ, you're more my mother than she ever was." Raphaella was touched but she didn't want to come between them. She was always careful about that. In her own way she couldn't be more than an invisible partner in their lives, not for her or for Alex. She had no right to take Kay's place.

"Maybe you're not being fair to her, Amanda."

"No? Do you have any idea how often I see her? Do you know when I see her, Raphaella? When some newspaper wants to take pictures of her at home, when she's going to some goddamn youth group and needs me as a prop, when I make her look good somewhere, that's when I see her. That's the only time I see her." And then the final damnation. "Has she called me here?"

But Raphaella knew better. "Would you have wanted her to?"

Amanda was honest. "No, I would not."

"Maybe she sensed that."

"Only if it suited her purposes." And then, with a shake of her head, she turned away, suddenly no longer a perceptive, angry young woman, but once more a child. "You don't understand."

"Yes, I do." More than she wanted to admit to Amanda. "I'm sure she's not an easy woman, darling, but—"

"It's not that." Amanda turned to face her with tears in her eyes. "It's not that she's difficult. It's that she doesn't give a damn about me. She never did."

"You don't know that." Raphaella's voice was gentle. "You will never know what's happening inside her head. She may feel a great deal more than you think."

"I don't think so." The young girl's eyes were bleak,

and Raphaella shared her pain. She walked over to her and held her for a long moment.

"I love you, darling. And so does Alex, and so does your grandma. You have all of us."

Amanda nodded, fighting back tears. "I wish she weren't coming."

"Why? She can't hurt you. You're perfectly safe here."

"It doesn't matter. She scares me. She'll try to take me away."

"Not if you don't want to go. You're too old to be forced to go anywhere. And besides, Alex won't let that happen."

Amanda nodded sadly, but when she was alone in her bedroom, she sobbed for two hours. The prospect of seeing her mother again filled her with dread. And after Alex left for the office the next morning, she sat staring mournfully out at the fog hanging over the bay. It looked like an omen of dreadful things coming, and suddenly, as she watched it, she knew that she had to do something, before her mother came.

It took her half an hour to find her, and when she did, her mother sounded curt on the phone. "To what do I owe this honor, Amanda? I haven't heard from you in a month."

She didn't remind her mother that she hadn't called or written either. "Grandma says you're coming out."

"That's right."

"Why?" Amanda's voice trembled. "I mean—"

"Just what do you mean, Amanda?" Kay's voice was like ice. "Is there some reason why you don't want me to come out there?"

"You don't need to. Everything is just fine."

"Good. I'll be happy to see that."

"Why? Dammit, why?" Without meaning to, Amanda started to cry, "I don't want you to come out here."

"How touching, Amanda. It's alway nice to know that you're just thrilled."

"It's not that, it's just—"

"What?"

"I don't know." Amanda's voice was barely more than a whisper. "It'll just remind me of New York." Of her loneliness there, of how little time her parents gave her, of how empty the apartment always was, of the Thanksgiving she had spent alone . . . and then been raped.

"Don't be childish. I'm not asking you to come here. I'm coming to see you out there. Why should that remind you of New York?"

"I don't know. But it will."

"That's nonsense. And I want to see for myself how you are. Your uncle has hardly gone out of his way to let me know."

"He's busy."

"Oh, really? Since when?" Her voice rang with contempt and Amanda bristled instantly at the words.

"He's always been busy."

"Not since he lost Rachel, darling, not Alex. What's he have to be busy with?"

"Don't be a bitch, Mother."

"Stop it, Amanda! You may not speak to me like that. As it so happens, you're so goddamn blind about your Uncle Alex that you wouldn't notice his shortcomings. It's no wonder he wants you around. After all, what else does he have to do! Rachel tells me he's so stuck on himself, he has no friends. Except now of course he's got you."

"What a stinking thing to say." As always when she

was confronted by her mother, she began to seethe with rage. "He has a damn good law practice, he works very hard, and he has lots of things in his life."

"And how would *you* know, Amanda?" There was a vicious implication in the words, which made Amanda catch her breath.

"Mother!" She sounded very young and very shocked.

"Well?" Kay pressed in for the kill. "It's true, isn't it? Once you're back with me, he'll be alone again. No wonder he hangs on so tight."

"You make me sick. He happens to be involved with a perfectly wonderful woman, who is worth ten of you, and is a better mother to me than you've ever been or ever will be."

"Really?" Kay began to sound intrigued and suddenly Mandy's heart raced. She knew she shouldn't have told her, but she couldn't stand the implications her mother was making. It had just been too much. "And who is she?"

"That's none of your business."

"Is that right? I'm afraid I don't agree with you, my dear. Is she living with the two of you?"

"No." Amanda sounded nervous. "No, she's not." Oh, God, what had she done? She instinctively sensed that telling her mother had been a terrible thing to do, and she was suddenly frightened, for Raphaella and Alex, as much as for herself. "It doesn't matter. I shouldn't have said anything."

"Why not? Is it a secret?"

"No, of course not. For God's sake, Mother, ask Alex. Don't pump me."

"I will. Of course I'll see for myself when I'm out there." And so she did.

The following evening, at nine thirty, with no prior warning the doorbell rang and Alex bounded down the stairs. He couldn't imagine who it could be that late in the evening, and Raphaella was in the kitchen chatting over tea and cookies with Amanda and his mother. They were in no way prepared for the vision that appeared only a moment later at the foot of the stairs. Amanda's mother stood in the kitchen doorway, watching them with considerable interest, her red hair freshly coifed in a dark gray mohair coat with a matching skirt. It was a perfect outfit for a politician. It looked serious and somehow managed to make her look both competent and feminine all at the same time. But it was her eyes that intrigued Raphaella as she stood for the introduction and held out a graceful hand.

"Good evening, Mrs. Willard. How do you do?" Kay greeted her mother curtly with a peck on the cheek before taking the proffered hand, which she shook hard, and then moved away from the perfectly etched cameo face. It was a face that she somehow thought she remembered, it was familiar, yet not a face she had met before, at least she didn't think so. Had she seen her somewhere? Seen her picture somewhere? It troubled her as she walked slowly to where her daughter stood. Amanda had not come toward her, and as far as anyone knew, they had had no contact since Amanda left New York. She hadn't had the heart to admit to anyone that she had called her mother the day before, and spilled the beans about Raphaella.

"Amanda?" Kay looked at her questioningly, as though she were asking if Amanda would say hello.

"Hello, Mother." Reluctantly she forced herself to

approach her and then stood looking uncomfortable and unhappy only a foot away.

"You look very well." She gave her a perfunctory kiss on the forehead and looked over her shoulder. It was obvious that her interest in Raphaella was greater than her interest in anyone else in the room. There was an air of distinction and of elegance about Raphaella that intrigued Alex's older sister more than anyone knew.

"Would you like coffee?" Alex poured her a cup, and Raphaella forced herself not to move. She had grown so used to playing lady of the house in the past month that she had to remind herself now not to do anything that might give her away. She sat quietly at the table, like any other guest.

The conversation went on inanely for another half hour, and then, after a private word with Alex, Raphaella excused herself and left, explaining that it was getting late. It was shortly after ten o'clock. And as soon as the door closed behind her Kay's narrowed eyes fell on her brother, and she wore a tight little smile.

"Very interesting, Alex. Who is she?"

"A friend. I introduced you." He looked intentionally vague, and he didn't see that Amanda blushed.

"Not really. All you told me was her first name. What's her last name? Is she anyone important?"

"Why? Are you soliciting campaign funds out here? She doesn't vote in this country, Kay. Save your energy for someone else." His mother looked amused and coughed over her cup of tea.

"Something tells me that something about her isn't kosher." Just the way she said it annoyed Alex, and he looked up with an irritated glance. He was also un-

comfortable about not having escorted Raphaella
back to her house, but he agreed with Raphaella that
it was best not to make a big show of their relationship to his sister. The less she knew, the better off
they'd all be.

"That's a stupid thing to say, Kay."

"Is it?" Christ, she'd been in his house for less than
an hour and she was already driving him nuts. He
tried not to let it show, but it did. "Then what's the
big secret about her? What's her name?"

"Phillips. Her ex-husband was American."

"She's divorced?"

"Yes." He lied. "Anything else you want to know?
Her criminal record, job references, scholastic
achievements?"

"Does she have any?"

"Does it matter?" As their eyes met they each knew
that they were still at war. What Kay wondered
was why. The purpose of her trip, and her alleged interest in her daughter, was forgotten as she ferreted
for information about her brother's intriguing friend.
"And more importantly, Kay, is it any of your business?"

"I think so. If she's hanging around my daughter,
I'd like to know who and what she is." The perfect
excuse. The virtues of motherhood. It covered her like
an umbrella and Alex sneered.

"You never change, do you, Kay?"

"Neither do you." In neither case was it a compliment. "She looks empty to me." He fought himself not
to react. "Does she work?"

"No." But he hated himself instantly for answering.
What business was it of hers, dammit? It wasn't, and
she had no right to ask.

"I suppose you think that's terribly feminine, not working, I mean."

"I don't think about it one way or the other. It's her business. Not mine. Or yours." And with that, he rose with his cup of coffee and looked pointedly at the three women in the room. "I assume, Kay, that you came to visit your daughter, so I'll leave you two together, much as I hate to leave the child alone with you. Mother, do you want to come upstairs with your cup of tea?" Charlotte Brandon nodded quietly, looked searchingly at her daughter and then her grandchild, and followed her son out of the room. It wasn't until they got upstairs that she saw him relax again. "Christ, Mother, what the hell does she think she's doing with that inquisition of hers?"

"Don't let it bother you. She's just checking you out."

"Christ, she's unbearable." Charlotte Brandon said nothing in answer, but she was clearly upset.

"I hope she isn't too hard on Mandy. I thought she looked terribly upset when Kay came into the room."

"Didn't we all." He stared into the fire with a distant look in his eyes. He was thinking of Raphaella, and wished she hadn't left when she did. But after her having been faced with Kay's interrogation he was just as glad she was gone.

It was fully an hour later when Amanda knocked on the door of her uncle's den. Her eyes were damp and she looked exhausted as she sat down heavily in a chair.

"How'd it go, sweetheart?" He patted her hand and her eyes filled with tears.

"The way it always goes with her. Shitty." And then

with another desperate sigh, "She just left. She said she'd call us tomorrow."

"I can hardly wait." Alex looked rueful and reached out to rumple his niece's hair. "Don't let her get to you, love. You know how she is, and there isn't a damn thing she can do to you here."

"Oh, no?" Amanda looked suddenly irate. "She told me that if I didn't come home by the beginning of March she was going to have me put away in some kind of institution and claim that I was out of my mind and had run away."

"What's happening in March?" Alex looked troubled, but not as much as his niece thought he should.

"She's going to start campaigning around the colleges after that. She wants me to come along. She thinks that if they think she can relate to a sixteen-year-old then she can relate to them. They should only know! Christ, I'd rather be locked up in an institution." But when she turned to him, her eyes looked ten years old. "Do you really think she'd do that, Alex?"

"Of course not." He smiled at his niece. "How do you think that would look in the papers? Hell, it looks a lot better to have you out here."

"I didn't think about that."

"That's what she counted on. She's just trying to scare you."

"Well, she did." She thought then about telling Alex that she had told her mother on the phone about Raphaella, but for some reason she just couldn't bring herself to broach the subject, and maybe the fact that she'd thrown Raphaella in her mother's teeth wouldn't matter that much after all.

As it happened, it didn't. Until five o'clock that

morning when Kay woke up slowly in her bed at the
Fairmont Hotel. It was eight o'clock in the morning,
by eastern time, and she awoke as she always did, out
of habit, only to realize that in San Francisco it was
only five A.M. She lay there quietly, thinking about
Amanda and her brother, and then thinking about
Raphaella . . . the dark eyes . . . the black hair . . .
that face. And suddenly, as though someone had put
the photograph before her, she remembered the face
she had seen the night before. "My God," she said it
aloud and sat up brusquely, staring at the far wall, and
then lying down again, her eyes narrow. Could it . . .
it couldn't . . . but it could. . . . Her husband had
come to address some special congressional commit-
tee. It had been years before, and he had already
been a very old man, but one of the most respected
financiers in the country, and she remembered dis-
tinctly now that he had made San Francisco his home.
She had spoken to him only briefly and had been introduced, for only a moment, to his remarkably beautiful young wife. She had been scarcely more than a
child bride then, and Kay had been fairly young herself. She hadn't been particularly impressed with the
dark-eyed young beauty, but she had been overwhelmed by the power and intensity of the man. John
Henry Phillips . . . Phillips . . . Raphaella Phillips,
Alex had told her . . . her ex-husband, he had said.
And if that was the case, the girl was probably worth
a bundle. If she had divorced John Henry Phillips, she
could be worth millions. Or could she? Had she divorced him? Kay found herself suddenly wondering.
She hadn't heard about a divorce. She waited an hour
then and called her secretary in Washington.

It would be easy to get the information, she figured. And she was right. Her secretary called her back half an hour later. As far as anyone knew—and she had spoken to several people who should have had the information—John Henry Phillips was still alive and had never been divorced. He had been a widower for several years and was married to a Frenchwoman now, by the name of Raphaella, the daughter of an important French banker named Antoine de Mornay-Malle. She was thought to be in her early thirties. The couple lived in seclusion on the West Coast. Mr. Phillips had been very ill for several years. So he had, echoed Kay as she hung up the phone in her darkened hotel room in San Francisco.

CHAPTER 20

"Are you totally out of your goddamn mind, you incredible ass?" Kay had raged into his office only moments after he'd arrived himself.

"My, my, aren't we charming this morning." He was in no mood for his sister, and particularly not for the performance she was delivering on the other side of his desk. "May I ask what you're referring to?"

"The married woman you're involved with, Alex. That's what I'm referring to."

"I would say you've made two fairly presumptuous assumptions. Wouldn't you?" He looked cool but angry as he sat there and watched her storm around the room until she finally stopped and stood facing him across his desk.

"Is that right? Can you tell me that that was not Mrs. John Henry Phillips I met last night? And that you are not involved with her?"

"I don't have to tell you a damn thing." But he was stunned by the accuracy of his sister's information.

"Don't you? And you don't have to tell her husband either?"

"Her husband, and she, and I, are none of your goddamn business, Kay. The only thing out here that is your business is your daughter and that's it!" He stood up to face her now. But he knew that she had a score to even. She had lost her daughter to him, probably for good and he had threatened to expose her shortcomings publicly. That was not going to win him her friendship now. But he didn't give a damn. He didn't want her friendship. But he did want to know what she knew about Raphaella and how she had found out. "Just what exactly are you referring to in all this?"

"I'm referring to the fact that my daughter tells me there's a woman in your life. who is 'worth ten of me,' as she puts it. and I find out she's another man's wife. I have a right to know who is around my daughter, Alex. I'm her mother, no matter what you think of me. And George isn't going to put up with your keeping her forever either. especially with your little affair going on. She's his daughter too."

"I'd be surprised to hear that he remembered that."

"Oh, shut up for chrissake. You and your smartass pious comment. It's easy for you to come in and pick up the pieces. You haven't had to take care of her for seventeen years."

"Neither have you."

"Bull. The point is, Alex, just exactly who do you have around her now? That was something I wanted to know when I got here."

"And you found Mrs. Phillips unsuitable?" He almost laughed in his sister's face.

"That's not the point either. The point, my dear, is that you seem to be shacking up with the wife of one of the most influential men in this country, and if anyone finds that out, I am going to be politically dead. Not because of anything I've done, but by association, because of you and your lousy scandal, and I have no intention of letting you ruin me politically for a lousy piece of ass."

But what she had just said was too much for Alex. Without thinking, he leaned across the desk and grabbed her arm. "Now listen here, you lousy political slut. That woman is worth not ten of you, but ten thousand. She is a lady from the top of her head to the soles of her feet, and my involvement with her is none of your goddamn business. In what affects your child, she is nothing but wonderful to her, and as for me, I'll do what I goddamn well want to do. It is none of your goddamn business. I don't give a shit about your political career and I never have. You would like it one hell of a lot better if I had stayed married to Rachel and done you some good. Well, tough shit, big sister, tough shit. I didn't stay married to her, and I am never going back to her, and she is almost as big a bitch as you are, my dear. But the woman I am currently involved with is an extraordinary human being, and she happens to be married to a bed-ridden old man who is damn close to eighty. Any day now he is going to die and I'm going to marry that woman you met last night, and if you don't like it, old girl, you can bloody well shove it."

"How adorable, Alex, and how fluent." She tried to wrench her arm free, but he didn't let her go. He only tightened his grip as his eyes hardened still more.

"The fact is, my dear, that the old boy is not dead yet, and if anyone finds out what you're up to, it'll be the biggest scandal in the country."

"I doubt that. And I don't really give a shit, Kay, except for Raphaella."

"Then you better start thinking." Her eyes glinted evilly at him. "Because I may take care of the matter for you myself."

"And commit political suicide?" He laughed bitterly at her and let go of her arm to walk around the desk to where she stood. "I'm not worried about that."

"Maybe you should be, Alex. Maybe all I'd have to do to take care of it for you is to tell the old man myself."

"You couldn't get near him."

"Don't be so sure. If I want to, I'll get to him. Or to her." She stood there, measuring her brother, and he had to fight himself not to slap her face.

"Get out of my office."

"With pleasure." She started toward the door. "But if I were you, I'd think twice about what I was doing. You're playing a big game, for high stakes, and you won't win this one, Alex, not if it could cost me my ass. I've got too much riding on this next election to let you play with dynamite over some little French whore."

"Get out of my office!" This time he roared at her, and she flinched as he grabbed her arm again, almost dragged her to the door, and threw it open. "And stay out. Stay away from all of us, damn you! You're nothing better than filth!"

"Good-bye, Alex." She looked him squarely in the eye as she stood in the doorway. "Remember what I said. I'll get to him if I have to. Remember that."

"Get out." This time he lowered his voice, and she turned on her heel and left. And he found that he was shaking violently when he sat down at his desk. For the first time in his life he had actually wanted to kill someone. He had wanted to throttle her for every lousy word she had said. It made him sick to remember that she was his sister. And as he sat there he began to worry about Amanda, thinking that perhaps Kay might try to force her to go back to New York with her. After half an hour of intense deliberation he told his secretary that he was leaving for the day. And just as he left his office, in her house Raphaella was picking up the phone. It was Alex's sister, and Raphaella frowned as she took the call.

"No, nothing's wrong. I thought maybe we could meet for coffee. Could I perhaps come over on my way to see Mandy later—" Raphaella blanched.

"I'm afraid not, my—" She had been about to tell her that her husband was ill. "My mother isn't well. She's staying with me just now." And how had she gotten the number? From Alex? From Mandy? From Charlotte? The frown on Raphaella's face deepened still more.

"I see. Then could we meet somewhere?"

Raphaella suggested the bar at the Fairmont and met Kay there shortly before lunchtime, where they both ordered drinks. But Kay didn't wait until the drinks arrived before explaining her purpose in seeing Raphaella. She made no bones at all about why she had come.

"I want you to stop seeing my brother, Mrs. Phillips."

Raphaella looked stunned as she sat there, awed by the sheer nerve of the woman. "May I ask why?"

"Do you really have to? You're married, for God's sake, and to a very important man. If your involvement with Alex became known, it would be a scandal for all of us, wouldn't it?" It was Raphaella's first taste of the true evil in the woman's eyes. She was hateful to her very core.

"I imagine it would be quite a scandal for you. That's it, isn't it?" She spoke politely and with a delicate smile.

But when Kay answered, she smiled too. "I would think the greatest scandal would be for you. I can't imagine that your husband, or your family in Europe, would be terribly pleased with the news."

Raphaella paused for a moment, trying to catch her breath, as their drinks arrived and the waiter disappeared once again. "No, I wouldn't enjoy that, Mrs. Willard." Her eyes sought Kay's now, as one woman reaching out to another. "I didn't enter into this lightly. I didn't want to get involved with Alex, as much for his sake, as for my own. There is very little I can give him. My life belongs entirely to my husband, and he is a very sick man." Her voice was weighted down with sorrow as she spoke, and her eyes were full. "But I'm in love with your brother. I love him very much. I love my husband, too, but—" She sighed and looked immensely European and lovelier than ever, strong and at the same time very frail. Kay hated everything about her. Because she was everything that Kay would never be. "I can't explain what happened with Alex, or why. It just did. And we're trying to work it out as best we can. I can assure you, Mrs. Willard, we are above all discreet. No one will ever know."

"That's nonsense. My mother knows. Mandy knows.

Other people do and will find out. You can't control that. And you're not playing with fire. You're playing with the atom bomb. At least as far as I'm concerned."

"So you expect us to end it?" Raphaella looked tired and annoyed. What a dreadful, selfish woman she was. Amanda was right. She thought only of herself.

"Yes, I do. And if he isn't strong enough to, then you do it. But it has to end. Not just for my sake, but for yours too. You can't afford to get found out, and if I have to, I'll tell your husband." Raphaella looked at her, shocked.

"Are you mad? He's paralyzed, bed-ridden, attended by nurses, you would tell him something like this? You'd kill him!" She was outraged that Kay would dare make such a threat, and she looked like the kind of woman to do it.

"Then you'd better think of that. If it would kill him, he would in effect die by your hand. It's in your power to stop this now, before anyone finds out. Besides which think of what you're doing to my brother. He wants children, he needs a wife, he's lonely. What can you give him? A few hours now and then? A roll in the sack? Shit, lady, your husband could live for another ten or fifteen years. Is that what you're offering Alex? An illicit affair for the next ten years? And you claim that you love him? If you loved him, you'd let him go. You have no right to hang on to him and ruin his life." What she was saying cut Raphaella to the quick. It didn't occur to her at that precise moment that Kay Willard's interest was not in Alex's life, but her own.

"I don't know what to say to you, Mrs. Willard. It has never been my intention to hurt your brother."

"Then don't." Raphaella nodded dumbly, and Kay

reached for the check, signed her name and the number of her room, and stood up. "I think we've finished our business with each other. Don't you?" Raphaella nodded again, and without saying another word, she walked away and hurried past the doorman with tears streaming from her eyes.

Kay went to see Mandy that morning. Alex was already back from the office, and he and Mandy were sitting quietly in the den when she arrived. There was no way she could take Mandy back with her now. Her interest in her daughter had already waned. She had decided that she had to get back to Washington. She reminded her only to think about March, said goodbye stiffly to Alex, and told her mother she would see her in New York. Charlotte was leaving the following afternoon.

And it was obvious that there was a sense of relief in the house as Kay's rented limousine pulled away. It was only as Alex realized that Raphaella hadn't called him all afternoon that the relief began to ebb. And then suddenly he understood what had happened, and he called her house instead.

"I—I'm sorry . . . I was busy . . . I couldn't call . . . I . . ." He knew it for sure then, from the sound of her voice.

"I need to see you right away."

"I'm afraid I—" Tears streamed down her cheeks as she fought to keep her voice normal.

"I'm sorry, Raphaella. I must see you . . . it's Mandy. . . ."

"Oh, my God . . . what happened?"

"I can't explain it till I see you."

She was at the house twenty minutes later, and he

apologized profusely for the deception, but he had known that it was imperative that he get to her right away, before she pulled away again, before she cut herself off from what they both needed so much. He told her honestly what happened with his sister, and he forced from her a description of Raphaella's hour with Kay at the Fairmont bar.

"And you believe her? Do you really think you're depriving me? Hell, darling, I haven't been this happy in years, or in fact ever in my life."

"But do you think she would?" She was still worried about the threat to John Henry.

"No, I don't. She's a bitch. But she's not completely crazy. There's no way she could get to him."

"She could, you know. I have no control over his mail, for instance. His secretaries bring it to the house and give it directly to him."

"She's not going to put something like that in a letter, for God's sake. She's too concerned with her own neck."

"I suppose that's true." Raphaella sighed lengthily and let herself melt into his arms. "My God, what an incredible woman she is."

"No," he said softly, "what an incredible woman you are." He looked down at her carefully then. "Shall we forget that any part of the last two days ever happened?"

"I'd like that, Alex. But should we? How do we know that all of her threats are idle?"

"Because there's only one thing my sister cares about, Raphaella, and that is her career. In the end that's the only thing that matters to her, and to get at us, she would have to jeopardize that, and she won't.

Believe me, darling. I know she won't." But Raphaella was never quite as sure. She and Alex and Amanda went on with their lives but the threats of Kay Willard seemed to ring in Raphaella's ears like an echo for months. She only hoped that Alex was right in believing that Kay's threats were empty.

CHAPTER 21

"Amanda?" Raphaella's voice rang out in the house as
she closed the door behind her. It was four o'clock but
she knew that Amanda was due from school. In the
months since Amanda had settled into living with
Alex, Raphaella had taken to dropping by in the after-
noons, sometimes before Mandy got home from her
classes, to tidy up the house, fix her a snack, and sit
peacefully in the sunshine in the garden, waiting for
the young girl to come home. They would have long
talks sometimes about whatever they thought was important, now and then Mandy told a funny story
about Alex, and lately Raphaella had been showing
her drafts of the children's book she had started after
Christmas. She had worked on it for five months now,
and she hoped to have it in final draft form when she
left for Spain in July.

But today it wasn't her manuscript she had brought
with her, but a copy of *Time* magazine. On the cover

was a photograph of Kay Willard, and beneath it the caption: THE WHITE HOUSE IN 1992 . . . '96 . . . 2000? Raphaella had read the article thoughtfully and then brought it with her when she came to see if Mandy was home from school. Her daytime visits to the house on Vallejo had begun to happen slowly, and now Mandy expected her to be there every day. She usually came when John Henry slept in the afternoon. And lately he had been sleeping longer and longer, until finally they had to wake him for his dinner at six.

"Amanda?" Raphaella stood silent for a long moment, her dark hair tucked into a neat little straw fedora, and she was wearing an exquisitely cut cream-colored linen suit. "Mandy?" For a moment she had thought that she heard a noise as she walked slowly upstairs.

It was on the third floor that Raphaella found her, sitting in one of the wicker chairs in her bedroom, her feet tucked under her and her chin on her knees, as she stared sullenly at the view.

"Amanda? . . . Darling?" Raphaella sat down on the bed, the magazine and her beige lizard handbag still tucked under her arm. "Did something happen at school?" She sat down on the bed and reached out to take the girl's hand. And then slowly Amanda turned to face her, her glance instantly taking in the magazine under Raphaella's arm.

"I see that you read it too."

"What? The article about your mother?" The pretty sixteen-year-old nodded. "Is that why you're upset?" It was unusual in the extreme for Mandy not to come running downstairs at the sound of her voice, laughing and smiling and filled with tales of what had happened in school. But the girl only nodded again. "I didn't think it was a bad piece."

"Except for the fact that none of it's true. Hell, did you read the part about my having a terrible car accident last winter, and recuperating slowly on the sunny West Coast with my uncle, while my mother comes out to see me in every spare moment she has?" She glared unhappily at Raphaella. "Shit, I'm just glad she's never come back here since Christmas." As it turned out, she wouldn't have had much choice. After her one explosive visit Alex had been fully prepared to tell her to stay away but Kay had never turned up again anyway. In fact after the first few months she hardly ever called. "Christ, Raphaella. She's such a bitch and I hate her."

"No, you don't. Maybe in time you'll come to understand each other better." Raphaella didn't know what else to say. She sat peacefully with her for a few minutes and then touched her hand gently. "Do you want to go for a walk?"

"Not really."

"Why not?"

She shrugged her shoulders, obviously depressed, and Raphaella understood. She had her own fears about Kay Willard. Nothing more had happened between them, but Raphaella was always aware that it still could. Kay's last conversation with Alex had been filled with more ugliness, but she'd agreed to leave Amanda where she was for the time being.

Half an hour later Raphaella managed to force Amanda out into the brilliant May sunshine, and arm in arm they walked back down to Union Street, and wandered in and out of all the shops, stopping at last for an iced cappuccino at the Coffee Cantata, the seat next to them laden with packages filled with silly things.

"Think Alex will like the poster?" Amanda looked over her iced coffee at Raphaella, and they both grinned.

"He'll love it. We'll have to put it up in his study before he comes home." It was a large poster of a woman on a surfboard in Hawaii, which only a teen-ager could have loved. But the important thing was that their shopping had completely taken Amanda's mind off her mother, and Raphaella was relieved. They didn't get back to the house until five thirty, and Raphaella hastily left Amanda, promising to return as always, later that night. Then she began the short walk to her own home, thinking of how totally her life had meshed with Mandy and Alex in the past six months. It was a balmy beautiful evening and the sun was shooting golden lights onto all the windows as the late afternoon sky began to give off a soft glow. She was halfway home when she heard a horn behind her, and turned around, startled to see a black Porsche, and then she quickly noticed Alex at the wheel.

She stopped walking for a long moment and just stood there, their eyes meeting and holding as though seeing each other for the first time. He pulled the car up slowly behind her and leaned back against the red leather seat with a smile. "Want a ride, lady?"

"I never talk to strangers."

Neither of them spoke for a moment as they smiled. And then his brow creased a little bit. "How's Mandy?" It was like having a teen-age daughter of their own now. She ate into their thoughts as well as their time alone. "Did she see the piece in *Time*?" Raphaella nodded slowly, her face sobering as she came closer to the car.

"She came home from school this morning, Alex. I don't know what to tell her. She gets more violent about her mother all the time." And then, after she frowned and he nodded, she looked at him worriedly. "What are we going to tell her about July?"

"Nothing yet. We can tell her later."

"How much later?"

"We'll tell her in June." But he looked worried too.

"What if she won't go?"

"She has to. At least this once." And then he sighed. "Just one more year until she turns eighteen, we might as well humor Kay a little. A court battle would hurt everyone now. If Mandy can put up with just this one visit, it should help keep the peace. You know, considering the fact that this is an election year for her, and that she thinks Amanda is essential to her winning the election, it's a goddamn miracle she didn't have her kidnapped and brought home. I suppose we should be grateful for small things."

Raphaella looked at him honestly. "Mandy wouldn't have stayed with her mother if she'd forced her to go back."

"That's probably why she didn't try. But there isn't a damn thing we can do about this summer. She'll just have to go." Raphaella only nodded in answer. It was something they had agreed to a month before. Amanda would go home to her mother just before the Fourth of July weekend, spend a month with her at their summer home on Long Island, and then go to Europe with her grandmother for a month in August, before returning to San Francisco for another year of school.

Alex had thought it a major victory to get Kay to agree to her coming back to San Francisco, but he knew that his niece would go through the roof at the prospect of going home. But he had called her psychiatrist, who felt that she could handle the confrontation with her mother, and he felt that most of the psychological damage from the rape had also been put to rest. They all knew that she was going to have a fit at the idea of leaving Alex and going home to George and Kay. Raphaella planned to fly East with her and leave her in New York, where she herself would spend a night at the Carlyle before flying on to Paris for a week and then Spain for another two. It was her annual pilgrimage to see her parents and spend a little time at Santa Eugenia. And this year it meant even more to her than it had before. She was going to try out the final draft of her children's book on all her little cousins, and she could hardly wait to see how it would go. She would simply translate the stories in Spanish as she read them. She had done it before when she brought books with her from the States. But this year was more important because the stories were her own, and if the children liked them, she was going to send the collection to Charlotte's agent and see if anyone would buy them in the fall.

When Raphaella looked at him, he was grinning at her. "What's so funny, Alexander?"

"We are." He smiled more gently at her now, a warm light kindling in his eyes. "Listen to us, discussing our teen-age daughter." He hesitated for a minute and then gestured to the empty seat next to his. "Want to get in for a minute?" She hesitated only briefly, glancing at her watch, and then absentmindedly looked around to see if anyone she knew was nearby.

"I really should get home. . . ." She wanted to be with John Henry when they brought him his tray at six o'clock.

"I won't push you." But his eyes were so gentle, his face so handsome, and they hadn't had a moment alone in such a long time. It seemed as though Amanda were always with them. And when she went upstairs at midnight, they had so little time left before Raphaella had to go home.

Now she smiled and nodded. "I'd love to."

"Do we have time for a quick ride?"

She nodded, feeling wayward and mischievous, and he rapidly put the car in gear and sped off, heading down the hills toward the speeding traffic on Lombard Street and then into the wooded seclusion of the Presidio, sweeping down to the water until they sat next to the small fortress beneath the Golden Gate Bridge at Fort Point. Above them traffic was hurrying across the bridge into Marin County, and there were sailboats on the water, a ferry, several small speedboats, and a brisk breeze that whipped Raphaella's hair as she took off her straw hat.

"Want to get out?" He kissed her and she nodded, and they stepped out side by side. Two dark-haired, tall, handsome people holding hands, looking out at the bay. For a time Raphaella felt very young as she stood there, thinking of the months they had already shared. They had grown so close and spent so many nights together, whispering, talking, sitting by the fire, making love, running down to the kitchen at two in the morning to make omelets or sandwiches or milk shakes. They had so much and yet so little . . . so many dreams . . . so little time . . . and such endless hope. As they stood side by side looking at the last of the sunlight shimmering on the boats, Raphaella turned to look at Alexander, wondering if they would ever have more. A few minutes, an hour, the hours before sunrise, stolen moments, and never much more than that. Even the child that they shared was only borrowed and in another year she would be gone. She was already thinking of what colleges to apply to, and Raphaella and Alex were already having pangs, feeling the loss before it hit them, wishing her there with them for many more years.

"What were you thinking just then, Raphaella?" He looked down at her gently and brushed the hair from her eyes with one careful hand.

"About Amanda." She hesitated and then kissed the hand as it brushed near her lips. "I wish that she were ours."

He nodded silently. "So do I." He wanted to tell her then that there would be others, someday, in a few years, children of their own. But he didn't say it, knowing how it hurt her not to have children. But it was a recurrent theme between them, her guilt at keeping him from marrying someone else and having children of his own.

"I hope she'll be okay this summer." They began to walk slowly along the edge of the road as the spray splashed up toward them, stopping just short of where they stood.

He turned to her then. "I hope you'll be okay too." They hadn't said much about it but in six weeks she was leaving for Spain.

"I will." They stopped walking, and she held his hand tightly. "I'll miss you terribly, Alex."

He pulled her close. "I'll miss you too. God . . ." He thought for a moment. "I don't know what I'll do without you." He had gotten so used to seeing her every night and now he couldn't imagine a life without her.

"I won't be gone for more than three weeks."

"That will feel like an eternity, especially with Mandy gone too."

"Maybe you'll get some work done for a change."

He grinned softly at her and with the boats passing slowly by them they kissed, and then they walked on arm in arm. They wandered along for another half hour and then regretfully got back into the car. It had been a pleasant ending to a golden afternoon, and when he dropped her off two blocks from her own home, she touched his lips softly with her fingertips and blew him a kiss before stepping out of the car.

She watched him drive away toward Vallejo and smiled to herself as she walked the last two blocks toward home. It was extraordinary how much her life had altered in the past seven months since she'd met Alex. It had changed subtly, but it had changed a great deal. She was the mistress of a wonderful, handsome, charming young lawyer; the "daughter-in-love," as Charlotte called her, of a novelist she had always admired; she was the stand-in mother for a lovely seventeen-year-old girl; and she felt as though she had a home in the house on Vallejo with the funny little overgrown garden and the brick kitchen filled with copper pots. And yet, at the same time, she was still who she always had been, Mrs. John Henry Phillips, the French-born wife of a celebrated financier, the daughter of the French banker, Antoine de Mornay-Malle. She was going, as she always did, to Santa Eugenia to see her mother, she was doing everything as she always had before. Yet there was so much more to her life now, it was so much richer, so much fuller, so different, so happy. She smiled to herself as she turned the last corner before she reached the house. What she had didn't hurt John Henry, she reassured herself firmly as she put her key in the front door. She still spent several hours in the morning with him, saw to it that the nurses were attentive and careful, that his meals were as he liked them, and she read to him for at least an hour every day. But the difference was that there was so much more now.

After her mornings with John Henry, she spent two or three hours in her room, working on the children's book she was going to try out on the children in Spain. And around four o'clock every afternoon, she walked slowly down to Vallejo, while John Henry took his nap. She almost always managed to be at the house before Amanda, so that the girl came home to someone who loved her and she didn't have to be alone in the house. And often Alex got home just before Raphaella left to go back to her own house. They would kiss and greet each other like married people, the only difference was that then Raphaella had to rush off, to spend another hour or two with John Henry, chat if he felt like talking, tell him some amusing story, or turn his wheelchair so that he could see the boats on the bay. They always had dinner together, only now they no longer used the dining room. John Henry ate in bed, on a tray. And once she was sure that he was comfortably settled, that the nurse was in charge, and that the house was quiet, she waited in her room for half an hour and then she went out.

She was almost sure that the servants had their suspicions about where she went and how long she stayed, but no one ever dared to mention her nightly disappearances, and the sound of a door closing at four or five in the morning was something no one questioned anymore. Raphaella had finally found a life she could live with, after eight years of intolerable loneliness and pain, and it was a life in which no one suffered, no one was hurt, in which she inflicted no pain. John Henry would never know about Alex, and she and Alex had something that meant a great deal to them both. The only thing that occasionally bothered her was that Kay had said so long ago that she was keeping Alex away from someone who could give him more. But he said that it was what he wanted, and by now Raphaella knew that she loved him too much to give him up.

As she ran up the stairs to her bedroom, she mentally prepared what she would wear. She had just bought a turquoise silk dress at I. Magnin's, and with her creamy skin and dark hair it made a sparkling impression as she put it on and clasped diamond and turquoise earrings to her ears.

She was only ten minutes late when she knocked on the door and opened it to see John Henry with the tray set before him as he sat propped against pillows in his bed. As he sat there with his eyes burned deep into their sockets, his face lined, with one side of his face limply hanging down, one eye drooping, and his tall frame and lean arms so bent and so frail, it suddenly stopped her where she stood in the doorway. It was as though she hadn't seen him in a very long time. He looked as if he had slowly begun to lose the tenuous grip on life to which he had clung for almost eight years.

"Raphaella?" He looked at her strangely as he said

the word in the garbled fashion he had said it for the past eight years, and Raphaella looked at him almost in astonishment, remembering once again to whom she was married, what were her duties, and how far she was from ever being Alex's wife.

She turned to shut the door softly behind her, brushing the tears from her eyes with one hand.

CHAPTER 22

Raphaella said her good-byes to Alex at five o'clock in the morning, when she left him to go home to her own house. She had already packed her bags the night before, and now all she had to do was go home, leave a few memos for the servants, dress, have breakfast, and say good-bye to John Henry before she left. Her leave-taking would be simple and solemn, a kiss on the cheek, a last look, a touch on his hand, and always the vague guilt that she shouldn't be leaving, that she should be with him and not going to Spain. But it was a ritual that they were both used to, and it was something that she had done every year for fifteen years. It was leaving Alex that was so much more painful, it was wrenching just to know that she wouldn't see him for a day. But the next weeks seemed almost unbearable as they clung to each other before the first light of dawn. It was almost as though they were afraid that something would come between them forever, as though they would never find each other again. Raphaella clove to him like a second skin as they stood there and she made no move to leave him at the foot of the stairs. She looked at him sorrowfully then, her eyes filled with tears, shaking her head with a small girlish smile.

"I can't make myself leave you."

He smiled and pulled her still closer to him. "You never leave me, Raphaella. I'm with you always, wherever you go."

"I wish you were coming with me to Spain."

"Maybe someday." Always someday . . . someday . . . but when? It was a line of thought she never liked pursuing because it always made her think that when their "someday" came, John Henry would be dead. It was almost like killing him just to think it, so she didn't, and lived in the present instead.

"Maybe. I'll write to you."

"May I write to you?" She nodded in answer.

"Don't forget to remind Mandy about the extra suitcase and her tennis racket."

He smiled at her then. "Yes, little mother. I'll tell her. What time do I have to get her up?"

"At six thirty. The plane leaves at nine." He was going to take Mandy to the airport but it was unlikely that he would even see Raphaella there once they arrived. She would as usual be deposited by the chauffeur and spirited onto the plane. But they had ordered Mandy's ticket for the same flight, and at the other end Raphaella was giving Mandy a lift to the Carlyle in her rented limousine. It was there that Charlotte would come to get her and accompany her to Kay's apartment. Amanda had flatly stated that she wasn't going to face her mother alone. She hadn't seen her since the explosive exchange after Christmas, and

she was feeling very skittish about going home at all.
Typically her father was at a medical convention in
Atlanta and he wouldn't be there to cushion the blow.
"Alex." Raphaella looked at him longingly for a last
time. "I love you."

"So do I, babe." He held her close. "Everything's
going to be all right." She nodded silently, not sure
why she felt so uneasy about the trip, but she hated
leaving him. She had lain awake beside him all night.
"Ready to go?" She nodded, and this time he walked
her almost all the way home.

She did not see him at the airport, but it was like
finding a piece of home as she saw Mandy get on the
plane, wearing a wide-brimmed straw hat, a white
cotton dress, and white sandals they'd bought together and carrying the tennis racket Raphaella had
been afraid she'd forget.

"Hi, Ma." Mandy grinned at her and Raphaella
laughed at the pretty young girl. Had she been taller
and looked a little less elfin she might have looked
more like a woman. But as it was, she still looked like
a girl.

"It sure is good to see you. I was already getting
lonely."

"So is Alex. He burned the eggs, spilled the coffee,
forgot the toast, and almost ran out of gas on the way
to the airport. I don't think his mind was on what he
was doing, to say the least." The two exchanged a
smile, it was comforting to Raphaella just to hear
about Alex, as though it brought him a little closer, as
they made their way across the country to New York.
Five hours later they finally got there in the heat and
the confusion and the fetid furor of a New York summer. It was as though San Francisco didn't exist,

and they would never find their way back. Raphaella and Mandy looked at each other with exhaustion and longed to go home.

"I always forget what it's like here."

Mandy looked around the airport in amazement. "Christ, so have I. Jesus, it's awful." But with that, the chauffeur found them, and in minutes they were ensconced in the back of the air-conditioned limousine. "Maybe it's not so bad after all." She grinned happily at Raphaella, who smiled and took her hand. She would have given anything to be riding in the Porsche with Alex and not sitting in the back of a limousine in New York. For months now the trappings of her life with John Henry had irked her, the servants, the protection, the enormous house. She wanted something so much simpler like the little house on Vallejo and her life with Amanda and him.

When they got to the Carlyle, there was a message from Charlotte that she had been delayed at a meeting with a publisher and she was going to be late. Amanda and Raphaella went up to the suite, took off their shoes and their hats, sat down on the couch, and ordered lemonade.

"Do you believe how hot it is out there?" Mandy looked at her miserably and Raphaella smiled. Amanda was already finding every reason to hate New York.

"It won't be so bad on Long Island. You'll be able to go swimming every day." It was like reconciling a child to the prospect of camp, but Amanda did not look reconciled for a moment as the bell rang at the door of the suite. "It must be our lemonades."

She walked quickly to the door with her handbag in her hand, the bright red silk suit she had worn on the

plane only slightly wrinkled, and she looked very
beautiful in the rich red with her white skin and dark
hair. It always startled Amanda how beautiful Raphaella was. It was something one never quite got
used to, that breathtaking face and those enormous
dark eyes. Alex certainly didn't take her for granted,
she had noticed, he looked nothing less than dazzled
every time she walked in the door. And she was always so beautifully put together, impeccably chic.
Now, as Amanda watched her, she pulled open the
door with a small impersonal smile and an air of authority, prepared to see a waiter with a tray bearing
two long, cool lemonades. What she saw instead was
Amanda's mother standing in the door of the suite,
looking hot and rumpled in an ugly green linen suit
and a strange self-satisfied little grin. As though she
had won. Amanda felt a ripple of fear rush through
her and Raphaella looked polite but strained. The last
time they had seen each other was at the Fairmont
bar six months before, when she had threatened to re-
veal the affair with Alex to John Henry.

"My mother couldn't make it, so I thought I'd pick
Mandy up instead." She stared for a moment at Raphaella and stepped into the suite.

Raphaella closed the door after Kay entered, and
watched as she crossed the room to her only child,
who stood staring nervously at her mother, making no
move toward her and saying nothing, her eyes opened
wide.

"Hello, Mandy." Kay spoke to her first as she approached her, and still Amanda said nothing. Raphaella noticed that Amanda looked more than ever
like a frightened child. She looked desperately unhappy as she stood there and the tall redhead ap-

proached. "You look fine. Is that a new hat?" Amanda noticed and Raphaella invited Kay to sit down just as the bell rang again and the lemonades arrived. She offered one to Kay who declined it and handed the other one to the girl, who accepted it mutely, with eyes that pleaded with Raphaella, and then she lowered them into her lap as she sipped her drink. It was a strange, awkward moment, and Raphaella was quick to fill the gap with small talk about the trip. It was nonetheless an awkward half hour as they sat there, and Raphaella was relieved when Kay rose to go.

"Will you be going straight to Long Island?" Raphaella asked, wishing she could comfort Mandy.

"No. As a matter of fact Mandy and I are going to be taking a little trip." At this she instantly caught her daughter's attention, and the girl watched her with hostile eyes.

"Oh, really? Where?"

"To Minnesota."

"Something to do with your campaign, Mother?" The words were her first to her mother and an accusation filled with scorn.

"More or less, it's a county fair, but there are some things I should go to. I thought you'd enjoy it." Her face said she was angry, but she didn't dare let it show in her words. Raphaella glanced at Amanda, who she noticed looked tired and miserable. All the child wanted was to be back in San Francisco with Alex, and Raphaella had to admit that it would have been a lot more pleasant for her as well. Only her manners and breeding had induced her to be more than civil to Kay.

Amanda picked up her single suitcase and her tennis racket and faced Raphaella. They stood for just an instant like that, and then Raphaella folded her rapidly into her arms. She wanted to tell her to be patient, to be gentle, yet to be strong and not let her mother hurt her; she wanted to tell her a thousand things but it was no longer the place or the time. "Have a good time, darling." And then more softly, "I'll miss you."

But Amanda said it openly, with tears in her eyes. "I'll miss you too." She was crying silently as she fled into the hallway of the Carlyle, and Kay paused for a moment in the doorway, seeming to take stock of every inch of Raphaella's face.

"Thank you for bringing her in from the airport."

There was no mention of the rest of what Raphaella had done for her, the six months of loving and motherly care, as she helped Alex with the niece they had both come to love so much. But Raphaella wanted no thanks from this woman. All she wanted was her assurance that she wouldn't hurt the girl. But there was no way to get that, no way to admonish Kay to be kind to her own child.

"I hope it's a good month for you both."

"It will be." Kay said it with a curious little smile as she watched Raphaella. And then, almost grinning over her shoulder, she tossed back at the dark-haired beauty, "Have a good time in Spain." With that, she stepped into the elevator with Amanda, and Raphaella, feeling suddenly empty and bereft, found herself wondering how Kay knew that she was going to Spain.

CHAPTER 23

The next morning as Raphaella boarded the plane to Paris she wasn't even looking forward to seeing the children. All she wanted was to go home. This leg of her journey only carried her further away from where her heart was, and she felt tired and lonely. She closed her eyes and tried to pretend that she was on her way to California and not to France.

It was a flight that she was certainly used to, and from sheer boredom she slept halfway across the Atlantic. She did a little reading, ate lunch and dinner, and thought smilingly of when she had met Alex on the trip to New York the previous fall, but it seemed inconceivable now to her to speak to a stranger, as inconceivable as it had seemed to her before. She couldn't help smiling to herself as they prepared to land in Paris. He certainly wasn't a stranger anymore. "And how did you two meet?" She could imagine her father asking. "On a plane, Papa. He picked me up." "He what?" She almost laughed openly as she fastened her seat belt and prepared to land. She was still amused at the idea as she was taken off the plane before the others and whisked through customs, but she was no longer amused by anything as she reached the gate and saw her father's face. He looked stern and almost angry and he stood like a statue, watching her come toward him in an outfit that would have brought an appreciative smile to any man's eyes. She wore a black suit with a white silk shirt and a little black straw hat with a veil. As she saw him her heart suddenly fluttered. It was obvious that something had happened. He had bad news for her . . . perhaps her mother . . . or John Henry . . . or a cousin . . . or . . .

"*Bonjour, Papa.*" He barely bent as she reached up to kiss him, and his substantial frame seemed more rigid than rock. His face was old and lined, and the eyes looked at her coldly as she peered into his ice-blue eyes with a look of fear on her face. "Has something happened?"

"We will discuss that at home." Oh, God . . . it was John Henry. And he didn't want to tell her here. Suddenly all thought of Alex left her mind. All she could think of was the elderly man she had left in San Francisco, and as always she reproached herself for leaving him at all.

"Papa . . . please. . . ." They stood in the airport looking at each other. "Is it—is it"—her voice sank to a whisper—"John Henry?" He only shook his head. After not seeing her for an entire year, he had nothing to say to her. He remained a wall of granite as they climbed into his black Citroën. He nodded to the driver, and they started home.

Raphaella sat frozen in terror for the entire drive

into Paris, her hand trembling when at last they
stopped outside his house. The chauffeur held open
the door for them, his black uniform suiting her father's expression and Raphaella's mood. There was an
odd kind of feeling as she walked into the enormous
foyer filled with gilt mirrors and marble-topped Louis
XV tables. There was a magnificent Aubusson tapestry hanging on one wall, and a view of the garden
through the French windows beyond, but the overall
feeling was one of arctic splendor and it somehow
made things worse as her father glared at her in dis-
pleasure and waved in the direction of his study up a
tall flight of marble stairs. It was suddenly like being
a child again, and as though somehow, in some way,
unbeknownst to her, she had erred.

She merely followed him up the steps, carrying her
handbag and her hat in one hand, waiting until her
private audience to discover what was so upsetting to
him. Perhaps it was something to do with John Henry
after all. As she walked hurriedly up the stairs she
couldn't imagine what it could be, unless it was something that had occurred while she was in New York.
Perhaps another stroke? But it didn't seem like bad
news he was going to share with her. But rather some
terrible censure over something she had done. She remembered that particular expression on his face from
her youth.

He marched solemnly into his study and Raphaella
followed suit. It was a room with enormously high
ceilings, wood paneling, walls covered with book-
cases, and a desk large enough for a president or a
king. It was a handsome example of Louis XV furniture, dripping with gilt, and highly impressive, and he
took his chair behind the desk.

"*Alors. . . .*" He glared at her and waved to a chair across from the desk. There had been not a moment of kindness between them. Not a kind word, and barely an embrace. And although her father was not a warm man or given to excessive demonstration, he was certainly being, even for him, excessively stern.

"Papa, what is it?" Her face had grown very white during the long drive from the airport, and now she seemed even more pale as she waited for him to begin.

"What is it?" His eyebrows drew together, and his face looked fierce as he stared first at his desk and then at her. "Must we play games?"

"But, Papa, I have no idea."

"In that case"—he almost bellowed the words at his daughter—"you are totally without conscience. Or perhaps very naive, if you think you can do anything you wish, in any corner of the world, and not have it known." He let the words sink in for a moment and Raphaella's heart began to race. "Do you understand me?" He lowered his voice and looked at her pointedly as she shook her head. "No? Then perhaps I should be more honest with you than you are with me, or your poor husband, lying sick at home in his bed." His voice was filled with reproach and contempt for his only daughter, and suddenly, like a child caught in a terrible misdemeanor, she felt awash with shame. The pale cheeks were suddenly suffused with a flush and Antoine de Mornay-Malle nodded his head. "Perhaps now you understand me."

But her voice was clear when she answered. "No, I do not."

"Then you are a liar, as well as a cheat." The words rang out like bells in the large austere room. "I received," he said deliberately, as though he were addressing Parliament instead of his only surviving child, "several weeks ago a letter. From an American congresswoman, Madame Kay Willard." He searched Raphaella's face and she felt her heart stop.

Raphaella waited, barely able to breathe. "It was, I must tell you, a very painful letter for me to read. Painful for a number of reasons. But most of all because I learned things about you, my daughter, that I had never hoped to hear. Shall I go on?" Raphaella wanted to tell him not to, but she didn't dare. He went on anyway, as she knew he would. "She not only explained to me that you are cheating on your husband. A man, may I remind you, Raphaella, who has been nothing but good to you since you were barely more than a child. A man who trusts you, who loves you, who needs your every waking moment, your every thought, every breath, to keep him alive. If you give him anything less than that, you will kill him, as I'm quite sure you are aware. So, not only are you destroying this man who has loved you, and who is my oldest and dearest friend, but you are apparently destroying as well the lives of several other people, a man who apparently had a wife who loved him and whom you have estranged, keeping him from a decent woman, as well as having children, which apparently is something dear to his heart. I also understand from Madame Willard that after a serious accident her daughter has gone to California to recover and to live with this man you have stolen from his wife. Apparently you are corrupting this child as well with your shocking behavior. In addition Madame Willard is in the Congress and from what she tells me, she will lose all chance to continue her life's work if this scandal comes out. In fact she tells me that she is going to retire immediately if you and her brother don't stop, because she cannot face the disgrace such a scandal would bring to her, and to her husband, her aging mother, and her child. I might add as well that if such a matter were to become public you would disgrace me and the Banque Malle as well, which does not even bring into consideration how your behavior would be viewed in Spain. Not to mention what they would make of you in the press."

Raphaella felt as though she had just been crucified, and the enormity of what had happened, of the accusations, of what Kay had done, and what her father had just said to her were almost more than she could cope with as she sat there. How could she tell him? Where would she begin? The truth was that Kay was a vicious, hungry politician who would stop at nothing to get what she wanted and that she was not retiring but running for election again, this time as senator. That Amanda had not been "corrupted" by her and Alex but deeply loved, that he hadn't been married to Rachel when she had met him, that he didn't want Rachel back, and that she herself was still giving everything she could to John Henry, but that she loved Alex too. But her father only sat there, staring at her with disapproval and anger in his eyes. As she looked at him, feeling powerless before him, the tears spilled from her eyes and ran down her cheeks.

"I must also tell you," he continued after a moment, "that it is not in my character to believe the word of a total stranger. At considerable inconvenience and great expense I hired a detective who, for the past ten days, has chronicled your activities and seems to verify what this woman says. You came home"—he glared at her in fury—"no earlier than five o'clock in the morning, every single night. And even if you don't care what you are doing to those around you, Raphaella, I should think that your own reputation would matter to you more than that! Your servants must think you a slut . . . a whore! A piece of garbage!" He was roaring at her and left his seat to pace the room. She had still said not a word. "How can you do such a thing? How can you be so dishonored, so disgusting, so cheap?" He turned to face her and she shook her head mutely and dropped her head into her hands. A moment later she blew her nose in the lace handkerchief she extracted from her handbag, took a deep breath, and faced her father from across the room.

"Papa, this woman hates me . . . what she has said—"

"Is all true. The reports from the man I hired say so."

"No." She shook her head vehemently and stood up as well. "No, the only accurate thing is that I love her brother. But he is not married, he was divorced when I met him—" He instantly cut her off.

"And you are a Catholic, or had you forgotten? And a married woman, or had you forgotten that too? I don't care if he was a priest or a Zulu, the fact is that you are married to John Henry and you are not free to whore around as you choose. I will never be able to look at him again after what you have done here. I cannot face my oldest friend, because the daughter I gave him is a whore!"

"I am not a whore!" She shouted the words at him, with sobs clutching at her throat. "And you didn't give me to him. I married him . . . because I wanted to . . . I loved him. . . ." She didn't go on.

"I don't want to hear your nonsense, Raphaella. I want to hear only one thing. That you will not see this man again." He glared at her angrily and walked slowly toward her. "And until you do that, and give me your solemn promise, you are not welcome to be in my house. In fact"—he looked at his watch—"your flight to Madrid is in two hours. I want you to go there, to think about this, and I will come to see you in a few days. I want to know then that you have written to this man and told him that it's over. And to assure that you keep your promise, I intend to keep the surveillance on you for an indefinite time."

"But why, for God's sake, why?"

"Because if you have no honor, Raphaella, I do. You are breaking every promise you ever made when you married John Henry. You are disgracing me as well as yourself. And I will not have a whore for a daughter. And if you refuse to comply with what I'm asking, I will tell you simply that you leave me no choice but to tell John Henry what you've done."

"For God's sake, Papa . . . please. . . ." She was sobbing almost hysterically now. "This is my life . . . you'll kill him . . . Papa . . . please. . . ."

"You're a disgrace to my name, Raphaella." He stared at her without coming closer and then went to his chair behind the desk again and sat down.

She looked at him, understanding the horror of what had happened, and for the first time in her life hating someone as she never had before. If Kay had stood in the same room with her at that moment, she would have killed her, gladly, and with her bare hands. Instead she turned to her father with a look of despair.

"But, Papa . . . why—why must you do this? I'm a grown woman . . . you have no right—"

"I have every right. You have obviously been too long in America, my dear. And perhaps, also, you have been too long on a loose leash, while your husband has been sick. Madame Willard tells me that she tried to reason with you but that you and this man persist. She tells me that if it were not for you, he would go back to his wife, that if it were not for you, he could settle down and have children." He looked at her reproachfully. "How can you do that to someone you pretend to love?" His words and the look on his face were like a knife cutting through her, and his gaze never wavered from her eyes. "But my concern is not with this man, it is with your husband. It is to him that you should feel the strongest allegiance. And I'm quite serious, Raphaella, I will tell him."

"It will kill him." She spoke very quietly, her eyes still pouring tears down her face.

"Yes," her father said curtly. "It will kill him. And his blood will be on your hands. I want you to think about that in Santa Eugenia. And I want you to know why I made arrangements for you to leave tonight." He stood up and there was suddenly an air of dismissal on the granitelike face of her father. "I will not have a whore under my roof, Raphaella, not even for one night." He walked to the door of his study then, pulled it open, bowed slightly, and waved her outside. He stared at her long and hard for an endless moment as she shivered, looking ravaged by what had passed between them, and he only shook his head and spoke two words to her. "Good afternoon." And then he shut the door firmly behind her, and she had to walk to the nearest chair and sit down.

She felt so sick and shaky that she felt sure she would faint in a moment. But she just sat there, dazed, horrified, hurt, embarrassed, angry. How could he do this to her? And had Kay known what she was doing? Could she possibly have known the cataclysmic effect her letter would have? Raphaella sat stunned for more than half an hour, and then, glancing at her watch, she realized that since her father had changed her flight she would have to leave the house then and there.

She walked slowly to the staircase, with a backward glance toward her father's study. She had no desire to say good-bye to him now. He had said everything he had to say, and she knew that he would turn up at Santa Eugenia. But she didn't give a damn what he did, or threatened or said, he had no right to interfere with her life with Alex. And she didn't give a damn what he threatened to do to her. She wouldn't give Alex up. She marched down the stairs to the front hallway, put on the little black straw hat with the veil, and picked up her bag. She realized now that her valises had never been taken out of the Citroën and that the chauffeur was still standing just outside the door. In effect she had been banished from her father's house, but she was so angry that she didn't care. He had treated her all her life like an object, a piece of furniture, some kind of chattel, and she would not let him do that.

CHAPTER 24

In San Francisco, at the same time as Raphaella was being driven back to the airport outside Paris, Alex had just received a most unusual call. He sat staring at his folded hands at his desk and wondered why he had received the call. It most certainly had to do with Raphaella, but more than that he did not know. And he felt an odd and terrible weight as he waited for the appointed hour. At five minutes after nine that morning, he had received a call from one of John Henry's secretaries and had been asked to come to the house that morning, if he could. He had told him only that Mr. Phillips wanted to see him on a personal matter of considerable importance. Further explanation was not offered and he didn't dare ask. Immediately after he had hung up, he had dialed his sister, but Congresswoman Willard was not available that morning, and he knew that there was nowhere else to seek an answer. He would have to wait until he saw John Henry in another two hours. He feared above all that someone had told him and now the old man was going to tell him not to see Raphaella again. Perhaps he had already spoken to her himself and she hadn't told Alex. Perhaps he had already arranged with her family to keep her in Spain. But he sensed something terrible about to happen, and due to John Henry's advanced age and the obvious gravity of the situation, he couldn't refuse to go and see him, but he would have liked to, he thought as he parked his car across the street from the house.

Slowly he crossed to the enormous oak door he had seen so often. He rang the bell and waited, and a moment later a serious-faced butler appeared. Alex felt, for a moment, as though each member of the household knew his crime and was about to pass judgment on him. He was a small boy about to be scolded for stealing apples—but no, this was much, much worse. If he had allowed himself, he would have been truly terrified. But he felt that this was an instance in which he had absolutely no choice. He owed it to John Henry Phillips to appear before him, no matter what the old man chose to do or say.

The butler led him to the main hall, where a maid escorted him upstairs; and outside John Henry's suite of rooms an elderly man walked toward Alex, smiled benignly, and thanked him for coming to see Mr. Phillips on such short notice. He identified himself as Mr. Phillips's secretary, and Alex recognized the voice he had heard on the phone.

"Very kind of you to come so quickly. This is most unusual for Mr. Henry. He hasn't asked anyone to come here to see him in several years. But I gather that this is a somewhat urgent personal matter, and he thought that you might be able to help him." Once again Alex felt apprehensive.

"Certainly." He found himself muttering inanities to the ancient secretary and wondered if he was going to faint as they waited for a nurse to usher them inside. "Is he very ill?" It was a stupid question he knew as the man nodded, since he knew from Raphaella just how sick John Henry was, but he found himself totally unnerved just from being here outside John Henry's bedroom doorway, in "her" home. These were the halls she walked every day. This was the house in which she had breakfast each morning, to which she came after she left him, after they had made love.

"Mr. Hale . . ." The nurse had opened the door and the secretary beckoned. For a moment Alex seemed to falter, and then he walked toward the doorway, feeling like a man going to his own execution, but at least he was going in style. He would not disgrace her, neither by proving himself a coward in refusing to come here or by looking less than appropriate when he did. He had stopped at home to change his clothes for a dark pin-striped suit he had bought in London, white shirt, and Dior tie but even that didn't help as he crossed the threshold and looked at the shrunken figure in the massive antique bed.

"Mr. Phillips?" Alex's voice was barely more than a whisper, as behind him both the secretary and the nurse instantly disappeared. They were alone now, the two men who loved Raphaella, one so beaten and so old and so broken, the other so young and tall as he stood looking at the man Raphaella had married fifteen years before.

"Please come in." His speech was garbled and difficult to understand, but it was as though Alex sensed his words with ease, so attuned was he to what was coming. He had felt more of a man because he had come so willingly to accept whatever anger or insults John Henry chose to hurl at him, but he felt less of a man now when he realized how small and pained his opponent was. John Henry waved vaguely toward a chair near the bed, indicating to Alex to take it, but there was nothing vague about the sharp blue eyes that watched him, taking his measure, inch by inch, hair by hair. Alex sat down cautiously in the chair, wishing that he would wake up in his bed to find that this had only been an anxious dream. It was one of those moments in a lifetime that one would like to wish away.

"I want to . . . " He labored with his speech but his eyes never left Alex as he did so, and even now there was about him the aura of command. There was nothing overbearing about him, just a kind of quiet strength, even in his broken condition; one sensed that this had once been a great man. It was easier now to understand what he might once have been to Raphaella, and why she still loved him now. There was more than loyalty here, there was someone very special, and for an instant Alex felt shame at what they had done. "I want . . . " John Henry struggled on, fighting with the side of his mouth that no longer chose to move, "to thank you . . . for coming." It was then that Alex realized that the eyes were not only piercing but also kind. Alex nodded at him, not quite sure what to say. "Yes, sir" would have seemed appropriate. He felt in awe of this man.

"Yes. Your secretary said that it was important."

They both knew that this was the understatement of the year. Despite the crippled mouth John Henry attempted to smile.

"Indeed, Mr. Hale . . . indeed." And then after a brief pause, "I hope . . . I did not . . . frighten you . . . in asking you . . ." He seemed barely able to finish but determined to do so. It was rough going for them both. ". . . to come here. It is very important," he said more clearly, "to all three . . . of us . . . I do not need to explain."

"I—" Should he deny it? Alex wondered. But there had been no accusation. There had only been the truth. "I understand."

"Good." John Henry nodded, looking pleased. "I love my wife very much, Mr. Hale. . . ." The eyes were strangely bright. "So much so that it has pained me . . . terribly . . . to keep her trapped here, while I . . . I am a prisoner of this useless, finished body . . . and she goes on . . . chained to me . . ." He looked grief stricken as his eyes reached out toward Alex ". . . like this. It is not a life for a . . . young . . . woman . . . yet . . . she is very good to me."

Alex couldn't stop himself then. And his voice was hoarse as he spoke. "She loves you a great deal." He felt ever more the intruder. They were the lovers. He was the interloper. It was the first time he had truly understood. She was this man's wife, not his. And by virtue of what they felt for each other, she belonged here. And yet, could he truly believe that? John Henry was a very old man, approaching death by infinitely small, measured steps. As he himself seemed to know, it was a cruel existence for her. He looked at Alex helplessly now.

"This has been a terrible thing to do . . . to her."

"You didn't wish it."

There was the ghost of a smile. "No . . . I did not
. . . but . . . it happened . . . and still . . . I live
on . . . and I torment her."

"That's not true." They sat here like two old friends,
each acknowledging the other's existence and importance, it was a very strange moment in both men's
lives. "She doesn't resent one moment of her time with
you." Again he had had to fight the urge to add "Sir."

"But she should . . . resent it." He closed his eyes
for a moment. "I do." He opened his eyes again and
they were as sharp as before. "I resent it . . . for her
. . . and for me. . . . But I did not ask you here to
tell you my regrets . . . and my sorrows . . . I called
you here to ask you . . . about you."

Alex's heart pounded and he decided to take the
bull by the horns. "May I ask you how you know of
me?" Had he known all along? Did he have her followed by servants as a routine?

"I received . . . a letter."

Alex felt a strange flame within him begin to glow.
"May I ask from whom?"

"I do not . . . know."

"It was anonymous?"

John Henry nodded. "It told me only . . . that . . .
you and . . . " He didn't seem to want to say her
name in Alex's presence, it was enough that they sat
here together, speaking the truth. "That you and she
had been involved for . . . almost a year." He began
to cough softly, and Alex worried, but John Henry
waved his hand to indicate that all was well, and a
moment later he went on. "It gave me your address
and telephone number, explained that you . . . are
. . . an attorney . . . and it said quite clearly . . .

that I would be wise . . . to put a stop to this." He looked at Alex with curiosity. "Why is that so? Was the letter . . . from your wife?" He seemed disturbed, but Alex shook his head.

"I don't have a wife. I've been divorced for several years."

"Is she . . . still . . . jealous?" He fought to go on.

"No. I believe the letter you received was from my sister. She's a politician. A congresswoman, in fact. And she is a dreadful, selfish, evil woman. She thinks that if any word of this—my—er—our involvement ever leaked out it would damage her politically, because of the scandal."

"She is probably . . . right." John Henry nodded his head. "But does anyone know?" He found that hard to believe. Raphaella would always—above all— be discreet.

"No." Alex was adamant. "No one. Only my niece, and she adores Raphaella and is very able to keep our secret."

"Is she a small child?" John Henry seemed to smile.

"She is seventeen and she is the daughter of that same sister. In recent months Amanda, my niece, has been staying with me. She was injured on Thanksgiving Day and while her mother has been most unkind to her, your—er—Raphaella"—he decided to go ahead and say it—"has been wonderful to her." His eyes lit with warmth as he said the words, and John Henry smiled again.

"She would be wonderful . . . in a case like that. She is a most . . . unusual . . . person." On that they both agreed, and then his face grew sad. "She should have had . . . children." And then, "Perhaps . . . one day . . . she will." Alex said nothing. At last

John Henry went on. "So, you think it is . . . your sister."

"I do. Did she threaten you in any way in the letter?"

"No." He looked shocked. "She only relied . . . on . . . my . . . ability to put a stop . . . to it." He looked suddenly amused and waved at his useless limbs beneath the sheets. "What confidence to have . . . in a very old man." But he didn't seem so old in spirit as his eyes met Alex's. "Tell me, how . . . may I ask . . . how did it begin?"

"We met on a plane, last year. No, that's not true." Alex frowned and closed his eyes for a moment, remembering the first time he had seen her on the stairs. "I saw her one night . . . sitting on the steps, looking out at the bay." He realized that he didn't want to tell John Henry she'd been crying. "I thought she was incredibly beautiful, but that was all. I never expected to see her again."

"But you did?" John Henry looked intrigued.

"Yes, on the plane I mentioned. I glimpsed her in the airport and she disappeared."

John Henry smiled at him benignly. "You must . . . be a romantic."

Alex blushed slightly, with a sheepish smile. "I am."

"So is she." He spoke as her father, and he didn't offer the information that he had been a romantic too. "And then?"

"We spoke. I mentioned my mother. She was reading one of her books."

"Your mother . . . writes?" His interest seemed to grow.

"Charlotte Brandon."

"Most . . . impressive. . . . I read some of her early . . . books . . . I would have liked to meet her." Alex would have liked to tell him that he would, but they both knew that that would not happen. "And your sister is . . . a congresswoman. . . . Quite a group." He smiled benevolently at Alex and waited for the rest.

"I invited her to lunch with my mother in New York and—" He faltered for only the fraction of a second. "I didn't know who she was then. My mother told me after lunch."

"She knew?"

"She recognized her."

"I'm . . . surprised. . . . Few people know her. . . . I have kept her well hidden from . . . the press." Alex nodded. "She had not . . . told you . . . herself?"

"No. The next time I saw her, she told me only that she was married and could not get involved." John Henry nodded, seemingly pleased. "She was very definite, and I'm afraid that I—I pressed her."

"Why?" John Henry's voice was suddenly harsh in the still room.

"I'm sorry. I couldn't help it. I . . . as you said, I'm a romantic. I was in love with her."

"So soon?" He looked skeptical, but Alex held firm.

"Yes." He took a deep breath. It was difficult to be telling it all to John Henry. And why? Why did the old man want to know it all? "I saw her again, and I believed she was drawn to me too." It was none of his business that they had gone to bed in New York. They had a right to their privacy too. She was not only his, but Alex's as well. "We flew back to San Francisco on the same plane, but I only saw her once more here. She came to tell me that she couldn't see me again. She didn't want to be unfaithful to you."

John Henry looked stunned. "She is an . . . amazing . . . woman." Alex clearly agreed. "And then? You pressed her again?" It was not an accusation, only a question.

"No. I left her alone. She called me two months later. And I think we had both been equally unhappy."

"It began then?" Alex nodded. "I see. And how long has that been?"

"Almost eight months."

John Henry nodded slowly. "I used . . . to wish . . . that she would find someone. She's been so lonely . . . and I can do nothing . . . about it. After a time I stopped thinking . . . about it. . . . She seemed so set in living her life . . . like this." He looked at Alex once again without accusation.

"Is there any reason . . . why . . . I should stop it? Is she . . . unhappy?" Alex slowly shook his head. "Are you?"

"No." Alex sighed softly. "I love her very deeply. I'm only sorry that this had to come to your attention. We never meant to hurt you. She above all couldn't have borne that."

"I know." John Henry looked at him gently. "I know . . . and you . . . have not . . . hurt me. You have taken nothing from me. She is as much my wife as she has ever been . . . as much as she can be . . . now. She is as kind to me as ever . . . as gentle . . . as loving. And if you give her something more, some sunshine . . . some joy . . . some kindness . . . some love . . . how could I begrudge her that? It is not right . . . for a man of my age . . . to keep a

beautiful young woman locked in a trap. . . . No!"
His voice echoed powerfully in the room. "No . . . I
will not stop her!" And then his voice softened again.
"She has a right to happiness with you . . . just as
she once had a right to happiness with me. Life is a
series of moving seasons . . . moving stages . . .
moving dreams . . . we must move with them. To
stay locked in the past will condemn her to the same
fate as mine. It would be immoral to allow her to do
that . . . that would be the scandal"—he smiled gently at Alex—"not what she shares with you." And then
almost in a whisper, "I am grateful to you . . . if
you . . . have made . . . her happy, and I believe
that you have." And then he waited for a long moment. "And now? What do you plan with her, or do
you?" He looked worried again, as though trying to
settle the future for a beloved child.

Alex wasn't sure what to tell him. "We seldom talk
about it."

"But do you think . . . about it?"

"I do." Alex was honest with him. He had been too
kind not to be.

"Will you"—his eyes filled with tears on the words—
"take care of her . . . for me?"

"If she will let me."

John Henry shook his head. "If they will . . . let
you. . . . If anything happens to me, her family will
come and get her . . . and take her away." He sighed
softly. "She needs you . . . if you will be good to her,
she needs you very much . . . just as once . . . she
needed me."

Alex's own eyes were damp now. "I promise you. I
will take care of her. And I will never, never pull her
away from you. Not now, not later, not in fifty years

or ten years or two. I want you to know that." He reached out and took John Henry's frail hand in his own. "She is your wife, and I respect that. I always have. I always will."

"And one day you will make her . . . yours?" Their eyes met and held.

"If she lets me."

"See that . . . she does." He squeezed Alex's hand hard, and then his eyes closed, as though he were exhausted. He opened them a moment later with a small smile. "You're a good man, Alexander."

"Thank you, sir." He had finally said it. And he felt better. It was as though they were father and son.

"You were brave to come here."

"I had to."

"And your sister?" His eyes questioned Alex and Alex only shrugged.

"She can't really make trouble between us." He looked at John Henry. "What more can she do? She told you. She can't make it public, the voters would find out then." He smiled. "She has no power at all."

But John Henry looked worried. "She could hurt . . . Raphaella." He said it so gently, it was almost a whisper. But he had said her name at last.

"I won't let her." And Alex sounded so strong as he said it that John Henry looked completely at peace.

"Good." And then after a moment, "She will be safe with you."

"Always."

He looked at Alex for a long time and then stretched out his hand again. Alex took it in his and John Henry pressed it and whispered softly, "You have my blessing, Alexander . . . tell her that . . . when the time comes." There were tears in Alex's eyes as he kissed the frail hand he held, and a few minutes later he left the old man to rest.

He left the stately mansion with a feeling of peace he had never before known. Without meaning to, his sister had bestowed on him an infinitely precious gift. Rather than ending the affair with Raphaella, she had given them the key to their future. In a strange, old-fashioned way, in the ritual of bestowing a blessing, John Henry Phillips had passed on Raphaella to Alexander Hale, not as a possession or a burden, but as a precious treasure that each, in his own time, had vowed to love and protect.

CHAPTER 25

"Raphaella, darling." Her mother threw her arms around her as Raphaella came off the plane in Madrid. "But what is this madness? Why didn't you stay in Paris for the night? When your father told me you were going to come straight through like this, I told him it was quite mad." Alejandra de Mornay-Malle looked at the dark circles forming under her daughter's eyes and scolded her gently, but the way she did it told Raphaella that she had no idea why her plans had changed. Obviously her father had said nothing about the letter from "Madame Willard," or the affair with Alex, or that she was in disgrace.

Raphaella smiled tiredly at her mother, wanting to feel happy to see her, wanting a feeling of homecoming, of a haven from her father's anger. Instead all she felt was exhaustion, and all she could hear was the echo of her father's words. "I will not have a whore under my roof, Raphaella, not even for one night."

"Darling, you look exhausted, are you sure you're

not ill?" The striking flaxen beauty that had made
Alejandra de Santos y Quadral famous as a girl had
dimmed only slightly with the onset of middle age.
She was still a remarkably beautiful woman, her
beauty impaired only by the fact that she was insipid
and the brilliant green eyes held no very interesting
light. But as a statue she would have been lovely, and
as a portrait she had been very beautiful, quite a
number of times. But she had none of Raphaella's
smoky beauty or the stark contrast of her jet-black
hair and ivory skin. There was none of Raphaella's
depth in her mother, none of her intelligence or her
wit or her excitement. Alejandra was just a very elegant woman with a very lovely face, a kind heart, excellent breeding, good manners, and an easy, gracious
way.

"I'm fine, Mother. I'm just very tired. But I didn't
want to waste time in Paris, since I can't stay for very
long."

"Can't you?" Her mother looked dismayed at the
prospect of a short visit. "But why not? Is John Henry
ill again, darling?"

Raphaella shook her head as they wended their way
from the airport toward Madrid. "No. I just don't like
to leave him for very long." But there was a look of
strain and anguish about her daughter, which Alejandra noticed about her again as they left for Santa Eugenia the next day.

The night before, she had excused herself early,
saying that all she needed was a night of rest and she
would be fine. But her mother had sensed a reserve,
almost a recalcitrance, that made her worry, and on
the trip to Santa Eugenia the next day Raphaella said
not a word. It was then that Alejandra became almost

frightened and called her husband in Paris that night.

"But, Antoine, what is it? The girl is positively mourning over something. I don't understand it, but everything is very wrong. Are you sure it's not John Henry?" After eight years of his illness it seemed odd that Raphaella should be feeling it so much now. It was then with a sigh of regret that Antoine told her and that she listened with dismay. "Poor child."

"No, Alejandra, no. There is nothing here to pity. She is behaving abominably, and it will become known very shortly. How will you feel when you read about it in the gossip columns or when you see a photograph of her in the papers somewhere, dancing at a party with a strange man?" He sounded very old and very stuffy, and at her end of the phone Alejandra only smiled.

"That doesn't sound like Raphaella. Do you suppose she really loves him?"

"I doubt it. It doesn't really matter. I put things to her very clearly. She has absolutely no choice." Alejandra nodded again, wondering, and then shrugged. Antoine was probably right. He almost always was, as were her brothers, at least most of the time.

But later that night she broached the subject to Raphaella, who had been taking a long quiet walk on the elaborately sculptured grounds. There were palm trees and tall dark cypress, flower gardens and fountains, and hedges in the shapes of birds, but Raphaella saw none of it as she walked along thinking of Alex. All she could think of was the letter Kay had sent her father and that she would not give in to his threats, no matter how adamant he was. She was, after all, a grown woman. She lived in San Francisco, was married, and led her own life. But the truth of how much

her family still controlled her came back to her again
and again as she pondered her father's words.

"Raphaella?" She jumped when she heard her name
and then saw her mother, wearing a long white evening dress and an endless rope of perfectly matched
pearls. "Did I frighten you? I'm sorry." She smiled and
gently took her daughter's arm. She was good at con-
soling and advising other women, she had had a lifetime of that in Spain. "What were you thinking when
you were walking?"

"Oh . . ." Raphaella exhaled slowly. "About nothing special . . . some things in San Francisco. . . ."
She smiled at her mother, but her eyes stayed tired
and sad.

"Your friend?" Suddenly Raphaella stopped walking, and her mother slipped an arm around her daughter's shoulders. "Don't get angry. I talked to your father tonight. I was very worried . . . you look so
upset." But there was no reproach in her voice, only
sorrow, and gently she led Raphaella along down the
winding path. "I'm sorry that something like that has
happened."

Raphaella didn't say anything for a long time, and
then she nodded. "So am I." She wasn't sorry for herself, but in a way she was sorry for Alex. She always
had been, right from the start. "He's a wonderful man.
He deserves much more than I can give him."

"You should think about that, Raphaella. Weigh it
in your conscience. Your father is afraid of the disgrace, but I don't think that's what is really so important. I think you ought to think if you're ruining someone's life. Are you destroying this man? You know"—
she smiled gently and squeezed Raphaella's shoulders
again—"everyone once or twice in a lifetime commits

an indiscretion. But it's important that there not be someone who can be hurt by it. Someone you know well usually makes more sense, sometimes even a cousin, maybe someone else who is also a married man. But to play with people who are free, who want more from you, who have hopes for something you can't give is a cruelty, Raphaella. More than that it's irresponsible. If that is what you are doing, then it is wrong for you to love this man."

Her mother had just added yet another burden to the enormous weight she had felt pressing down on her since she'd arrived. After she had recovered from her anger at the words of her father, she had been overwhelmed with depression at the truth of at least some of his accusations. The fact that she might be taking something from John Henry, in the way of time or spirit or devotion or even just a fraction of a feeling, had worried her all along, and the fact that she was keeping Alex from something more productive had been her other regret about the relationship from the first.

Now her mother was telling her to have an affair with a cousin or someone as married as she was but not with Alex. She was telling her that loving Alex was being cruel. And suddenly, as the emotions poured over her, Raphaella couldn't bear it for a moment longer. She shook her head, squeezed her mother's arm, and ran back along the pathway all the way to the house. Her mother followed more slowly, with tears in her eyes for the anguish she had seen on Raphaella's face.

CHAPTER 26

The days Raphaella spent at Santa Eugenia that summer were among the unhappiest she had ever spent there, and each day weighed on her like a yoke of cast iron that she wore around her neck. This year even the children didn't enchant her. They were loud and unruly, constantly playing practical jokes on the grown-ups and annoying Raphaella in every possible way. The only bright spot was that they had loved her stories, but even that didn't seem to matter to her very much now. She put the manuscripts back in her suitcase after her first few days there and refused to tell them any more stories during the rest of her stay. She wrote two or three letters to Alex, but suddenly they all seemed stilted and awkward. It was impossible not to tell him what had happened, and she didn't want to do that until she had resolved it all in her own mind. Each time she tried to write to him, she felt more guilty, each day she felt more oppressed by her father and mother's words.

It was almost a relief when after the first week her father came for the weekend, and after a formal luncheon at which everyone at Santa Eugenia was present, thrity-four people that day, he told Raphaella he wanted to see her in the small solarium that adjoined his room. When she joined him there, he looked as ferocious as he had in Paris, and she unconsciously sat down in a striped green and white chair as she would have as a child.

"Well, have you come to your senses?" He came directly to the point, and she fought with herself not to tremble at his words. It was ridiculous that at her age he should impress her, but she had spent too many years taking orders from him not to be impressed by the power he wielded, because he was her father and because he was a man. "Have you?"

"I'm not sure I know what you mean, Father. I still don't agree with your position. What I've been doing has not hurt John Henry, however much you may disapprove."

"Really? Then how is his health, Raphaella? It was my understanding that he was not doing very well."

"He's not doing badly." Her voice faltered and then she got out of the chair and walked around the room, finally coming to a stop to face her father with what was the truth. "He is seventy-seven years old, Papa. He has been bed-ridden, more or less, for almost eight years. He has had a number of strokes, and he has very little desire to go on living the way he is. Can you really blame that on me?"

"If he has so little desire to go on living, can you dare to take a chance with the little desire he has left?

Can you dare to take the chance that someone will tell him, and that for him it will be the last straw? You must be a very brave woman, Raphaella. In your shoes I would not take that chance. If only because I would not be entirely certain that I could live with myself if I killed him . . . which, I will add, your circumstances might. Or hadn't that thought occurred to you?"

"It has. Often." She sighed softly. "But, Papa . . . I love . . . this man."

"Not enough to do what's best for him though. That saddens me. I thought there was more to you than that."

She eyed him sadly. "Must I be so perfect, Papa? Must I be so very strong? I have been strong for eight years . . . for eight—" But she couldn't go on, she was crying again, and then she looked up at him tremulously, "Now this is all I have."

"No." He spoke firmly. "You have John Henry. You have no right to more than that. One day, after he is gone, then you can consider other possibilities. But those doors are not open to you now." He looked at her sternly. "And I hope, for John Henry's sake, that they are not open to you for a long time." She bowed her head for a moment and then looked up and walked to the door of the little room.

"Thank you, Papa." She said the words very softly and left the room.

Her father left for Paris the next day, but it was obvious to him, as well as to her mother, that some of what they had said to Raphaella appeared to have taken hold. Much of the fight had gone out of her, and finally after four more days at Santa Eugenia, and five more sleepless nights, she got out of bed at five o'clock one morning, went to the desk in her room, and pulled out a piece of paper and a pen. It was not that she would no longer fight her parents, it was that she could no longer fight the inner voice that they had spawned. How could she know that what she was doing was not hurting John Henry? And what they said of Alex was true as well. He had a right to more than she could give him, and perhaps she would not be free to give him more for many years.

She sat at her desk, staring down at the blank paper, knowing what she had to say. Not because of her father or her mother or Kay Willard, she told herself, but because of John Henry and Alex and what she owed them. It took her two hours to compose the letter, which she could hardly see when she finally signed it with a last stroke of her pen. The tears were pouring down her face so copiously that it was only a blur before her, but the meaning of her words to him was anything but a blur. She had told him that she did not wish to continue, that she had given it all a great deal of thought during her vacation in Spain, that there was no point in their dragging on a love affair that had no future. She had realized now that he was not suited to her, nor to the life she would lead one day when she was free. She told him that she was happier in Spain with her family, that this was where she belonged, and that since he was divorced and she was a Catholic she could never marry him anyway. She drew on every lie and excuse and insult she could find, but she did not want to leave him with a single doubt about continuing. She wanted to free him completely so that he could find another woman and not wait for her. She wanted to know that she had given him the final gift of freedom, and if she had to do that by sounding unkind in the letter, then she was willing to do that, for Alex. It was her last gift to him.

But the second letter she wrote was almost harder. It was a letter to Mandy, which she sent to Charlotte Brandon's address in New York. It explained that things had changed between her and Alex, that they wouldn't be continuing to see each other when she got back to San Francisco, but that she would always love Mandy and treasure the months that they had shared.

By the time she finished both letters, it was eight o'clock in the morning, and Raphaella felt as though she had been beaten from midnight until dawn. She put on a thick terry-cloth robe and ran silently to the main hall, where she left the two letters on a silver platter. Then she walked slowly outside and across the grounds to a remote spot on the beach that she had discovered as a child. She stripped away the robe and the nightgown beneath it, kicked off the sandals she had worn, and threw her body into the water with a vengeance, swimming as hard and as far as she could. She had just renounced the one thing she lived for, and now she didn't give a damn if she lived or died. She had saved John Henry for another day or a year or a decade or even two, had freed Alex to marry and have babies, and she had nothing, except the emptiness that had consumed her for the last lonely eight years.

She swam as far out as she could manage, and then swam back, until every inch of her body screamed. Slowly she walked out of the water and back to the bathrobe, and she lay down on it on the sand, her long lean, naked limbs gleaming in the morning sunlight as her shoulders shook and she sobbed. She lay there like that for almost an hour, and when she went back to the house, she saw that the servants had removed her two letters from the giant silver salver and taken them into town to mail. It was done.

CHAPTER 27

When she left Spain and returned to San Francisco, the days seemed endless to Raphaella. She sat by John Henry's side for hours every day, reading, thinking, sometimes talking. She read him parts of the newspaper, tried to unearth books that once pleased him, sat in the garden with him, and read books of her own while he napped more and more. But each hour, each day, each moment, dragged past her with lead weights attached to them. It seemed to her each morning that she would never get through one more day. And by nightfall she was exhausted by the effort it had taken, just to sit there, barely moving, her own voice droning in her ears, and then his soft snore as he slept while she read.

It was the life of slow torture to which she felt condemned now. It was different than it had been before she'd met Alex the previous year. Then she hadn't known anything different, she hadn't had the joy of fixing up a room for Mandy, hadn't baked bread or puttered in the garden or waited impatiently for him to come home, she hadn't raced laughing up the stairs beside Mandy or stood looking at the view with Alex just before the dawn. Now there was nothing, only endlessly bleak days during the warm summer, sitting in the garden watching great puffs of white clouds roll by overhead, or sitting in her room late at night listening to the foghorns bleating on the bay.

Sometimes she was reminded of her earlier summers in Santa Eugenia, or even summers she had spent away with John Henry some ten years before. But now there was no swimming, no laughing, no running on a beach with the wind in her hair. There was nothing, no one, only John Henry, and he was different, too, than he had been a year before. He was so much more tired, worn out really, and introverted, so much less interested in the world beyond his bed. He didn't care anymore about politics, about large oil deals with the Arabs, or about potential disasters that in his earlier life would have been so intriguing to him. He didn't give a damn about his old firm or any of his partners. He really didn't care about anything, and he was querulous suddenly if the least little thing went wrong. It was as though he resented everything and everybody, hating them finally for the agonies of the past eight years. He was tired of dying slowly, he told Raphaella one morning. "If I'm going to die sooner or later anyway, then I might as well do it right now."

He talked constantly now of wishing it were over, of hating the nurses, of not wanting to be pushed around in his chair. He didn't want to be bothered by anyone, he insisted, and it was only with Raphaella that he made the supreme effort, as though he didn't want to punish her for the way he felt. But it was obvious to everyone who saw him that he was desperately unhappy, and it never failed to remind Raphaella of her father's words. Maybe he'd been right after all that John Henry needed her full attention. Certainly he did now, even if he hadn't before. Or maybe it was because she had nothing else to do now that he only seemed to need her so much more. But he seemed to swallow up every moment, and she felt obliged to sit with him, to be near him, to sit and watch him while he slept. It was as though she had made one last commitment, to give up her whole life for this man. And at the same time it was as though John Henry had finally given up his will to live. Raphaella felt that weigh on her more now too. If he was tired of living, what could she do to make him want to stay alive? To infuse him with her youth, with her own vitality, with her will to live? But her life was no happier than John Henry's. Since she had given up Alex, there was no longer any reason that Raphaella could see that justified her existence, except as a kind of life-giving serum for John Henry. There were days when she thought that she couldn't bear it anymore.

She almost never went out anymore, and when she did, she had the chauffeur drive her somewhere so that she could take a long walk. She hadn't been downtown since returning from Spain earlier that summer, and she was afraid to wander in the neighborhood, even in the evening, for fear that somehow, somewhere, Alex would be there. He had gotten her letter the day before she had left Santa Eugenia, and she had sat terribly still for a long moment when the butler told her there was a call from America, wanting it to be Alex, and yet fearing that at the same time. She didn't dare refuse the call for fear that it was something about John Henry.

So she went to the phone with her heart pounding and her hands trembling, and when she had heard his voice at the other end, she had closed her eyes tightly and tried to fight back the tears. She told him very quietly and calmly that she had come to her senses here at Santa Eugenia and that there was nothing more to say that she hadn't already said in the letter he had just received. He had accused her of being crazy, said that someone must have pressured her into it, asked her if it had anything to do with something Kay might have said in New York. She assured him that it was none of those things, that it was her own decision, and when she had hung up the phone, she had cried for several hours. Giving up Alex was the most painful decision of her lifetime, but she could no longer take a chance that her divided allegiance would kill John Henry, nor would she continue to deprive Alex of all that he deserved to have with someone else. In the end her father and Kay had won. And now all that remained was for Raphaella to live up to it for the rest of her days. By the end of the summer she saw the years stretching ahead of her like a series of bleak, empty rooms.

In September, as John Henry began to sleep for several hours in the morning, just to keep herself busy she picked up the manuscripts of the children's books again. She chose the one she liked the best, and, feeling silly for even putting it together, she finally typed it and sent the final version to a publisher of children's books in New York. It had been an idea Charlotte Brandon had given her, and it seemed vaguely foolish to even do it, but she had nothing to lose, and even less to do.

With the book completed, Raphaella was once again haunted by her memories of last summer. Above all, there were times when she resented her father terribly, and she doubted she would ever forgive him for the things he had said. He had only relented slightly when she told him on the phone from Santa Eugenia that she had taken care of everything in San Francisco. He had told her that it was nothing she should be praised for, that it was only her duty, and that it had pained him to have to use such force to alter a course that she should have altered herself long before. He pointed out that she had disappointed him severely, and even her mother's gentler words left her, in the end, with a sense of failure.

It was this feeling that she carried with her into the autumn in San Francisco and that made her turn down her mother's offer to meet her in New York for a few days when she was there on her way to Brazil with the usual horde. Raphaella no longer felt that she should do things like go to New York to meet her mother. Her place was with John Henry, and she would not leave him again until the day he died. Who knew if her months of ricocheting between her own home and Alex's had not in some way sped John Henry toward his death. It would have been useless, of course, to tell her that any speed in that direction would have been welcomed by no one as much as by John Henry himself. Now she almost never left him except for her occasional walks.

Her mother had been vaguely disturbed at Raphaella's refusal to join her at the Carlyle and wondered briefly if she was still angry at her father for what had passed between them in July. But Raphaella's letter of refusal didn't sound as if she were pouting. It sounded more as though she were oddly withdrawn. Her mother promised herself that she would call her from New York and make sure that nothing was the matter, but with her sisters and her cousins and her nieces and their constant errands and shopping and the time difference, she left for Buenos Aires without ever having had a chance to call.

It wouldn't have mattered to Raphaella anyway. She had no desire to talk to her mother or her father and had decided that summer that she would not return to Europe again either until after John Henry had passed on. He seemed to be living in a state of suspended animation, sleeping most of the time, depressed when he wasn't, refusing to eat, and seeming to lose whatever abilities had remained. The doctor told her that all of it was normal in a man of his age with the shocks he had suffered from the strokes. It was only surprising that the determination of his spirit had not been more acutely affected before. It seemed only ironic to Raphaella that now as she devoted herself to him fully he seemed to be at his worst. But the doctor told her that he might also get a little better, that perhaps after a few months of lethargy he might inexplicably perk up. It was certainly obvious that Raphaella was doing everything to entertain him, and now she even began to cook small gourmet dishes in order to tempt his palate and induce him to eat. It was a life about which most people would have had nightmares, but which Raphaella seemed not even to notice. Having given up the only thing that she had cared about and relinquished the only two people she had

loved in a long time, Alexander and Amanda, she felt
it no longer mattered to her what she did with her time.

November disappeared like the months before it,
and it was December when she got the letter from the
publishing house in New York. They were enchanted
with the book she had sent them, surprised that she
didn't have an agent, and wanted to pay her two thousand dollars as an advance for the book, which they
would have illustrated and hoped to release the following summer. For a moment she stared at the letter
in amazement, and then for the first time in a long
time she broke out in a broad smile. Almost like a
schoolgirl she raced up the staircase with the letter to
show John Henry. When she got there, she found him
sleeping in his wheelchair, his mouth open, his chin
on his chest, making a soft purr. She stood there for a
time, watching him, and then suddenly felt desperately lonely. She had wanted so much to tell him, and
there was no one else to tell. Once again she felt a
familiar pang for Alex, but she pushed the thought
instantly away, telling herself that by now he had
found someone else to replace her, that Mandy was
happy, and that Alex might even be married or engaged. In another year he might even have children.
She felt that perhaps indeed, she had done the right
thing for everybody concerned.

She folded the letter and went back downstairs. She
realized, too, that John Henry had known nothing
about the stories she'd been concocting for the children, and he would find it very strange if she brought
him the news of a book now. It was better to say
nothing. And of course her mother wouldn't be interested, and she had no desire to write to tell her father.
In the end there was no one to tell, so she sat down

and answered the letter, thanked them for the advance, which she accepted, and then later wondered why she had. It was an ego trip that suddenly seemed very foolish, and after she gave the letter of acceptance to the chauffeur to mail, she was sorry she had done it. She was so used to denying herself everything she wanted that even that little treat now seemed out of place.

Feeling annoyed with herself for doing something so silly, she later asked the chauffeur to drive her out to the beach, while John Henry slept away the afternoon. She just wanted to walk in the fresh air and see the dogs and the children, feel the wind on her face, and get away from the stale air of the house. She had to remind herself that it was almost Christmas. But it didn't really matter this year. John Henry was too tired to care if they celebrated it or not. Briefly she found herself dwelling on the Christmas she had shared with Alex and Mandy and then once again forced the memories out of her head. She seldom even allowed herself even those now.

It was almost four o'clock when the chauffeur pulled the car up alongside the vans and the pickups and the old jalopies, and smiling at the incongruous vision she knew she presented, she slid into a pair of loafers she often wore at Santa Eugenia and slipped out of the car into the stiff breeze. She was wearing a little curly lamb jacket with a red turtleneck sweater and a pair of gray slacks. She didn't dress as elaborately as she used to anymore. To sit beside John Henry while he slept or dine from a tray in his room as he gazed sightlessly at the news on the television, there didn't seem to be much point in getting dressed.

Tom, the chauffeur, watched Raphaella disappear down the stairs onto the long sandy beach, and then he glimpsed her again as she wandered near where the surf broke. Eventually he could no longer distinguish her from the others, and he climbed back into the car, turned on the radio, and lit a cigarette. By then Raphaella was far down the beach, watching three Labradors chase each other in and out of the water, and a group of young people wearing blankets and blue jeans were drinking wine and playing their guitars.

The sound of their singing followed her further down the beach as she wandered, and at last she sat down on a log and took a deep breath of the salt air. It felt so good to be there, to be out in the world for a few moments, to at least see others living even if she could not do much living herself. She just sat there and watched people passing, arm in arm, kissing, side by side, talking and laughing or jogging past each other. They all seemed to be bent on going somewhere and she wondered where they all went when the sun went down.

It was then that she found herself watching a man who was running. He came from far down the beach in a straight line, running almost like a machine, without stopping, until finally, still moving with the smoothness of a dancer, he slowed to a walk and kept coming down the beach. The fluidity of his movement in the distance had intrigued her, and as he came closer she kept her eyes on him for a long time. She was distracted by a group of children, and when she looked for him again, she saw that he was wearing a red jacket and was very tall, but his features were indistinct until he came closer. Suddenly she gasped. She just sat there staring, startled, unable to move or turn so that he wouldn't see her face. She just sat there watching as Alex came closer and then stopped when his eyes fell on her. He didn't move for a long time, and then slowly, deliberately, he walked toward where she sat. She wanted to run away, to vanish, but after seeing him run down the beach, she knew she didn't have a chance and she had ventured quite far from where she had left the car. Now relentlessly, with his face set, he came toward her, until he stood before her, looking down at her sitting on the log.

Neither of them spoke for a long moment and then, as though in spite of himself, he smiled. "Hello. How are you?" It was difficult to believe that they hadn't seen each other in five months. As Raphaella looked up at the face she had seen in her mind so clearly and so often, it seemed as though they had been together only the day before.

"I'm fine. How are you?"

He sighed and didn't answer. "Are you fine, Raphaella? I mean really. . . ." She nodded this time, wondering why he hadn't answered when she asked him how he was. Wasn't he happier? Hadn't he found someone to replace her? Wasn't that why she had released him? Surely her sacrifice had instantly borne fruit. "I still don't understand why you did it." He looked at her bluntly, showing no inclination to leave. He had waited five months to confront her. He wouldn't have left now if they'd dragged him away.

"I told you. We're too different."

"Are we? Two different worlds, is that it?" He sounded bitter. "Who told you that? Your father? Or someone else? One of your cousins in Spain?"

No, she wanted to tell him, *your sister fixed it for us. Your sister, and my father with his goddamn surveillance and threats to tell John Henry, whether it killed him or not . . . that, and my conscience. I want you to have the babies that I'll never have. . . .*

"No. No one told me to do it. I just knew it was the right thing to do."

"Oh, really? Don't you think we might have discussed it. You know, like grown-ups. Where I come from, people discuss things before they make major decisions that affect other people's lives."

She forced herself to look at him coldly. "It was beginning to affect my husband, Alex."

"Was it? Strange that you only noticed that when you were six thousand miles away from him in Spain."

She looked at him pleadingly then, the agony of the past five months beginning to show in her eyes. He had already noticed how much thinner her face was, how dark were the circles beneath the eyes, how frail were her hands. "Why are you doing this now, Alex?"

"Because you never gave me the chance to in July." He had called her four or five times in San Francisco, and she had refused to take the calls. "Didn't you know what that letter would do to me? Did you think of that at all?" And suddenly, as she saw his face, she understood better. First Rachel had left him, giving him no chance to win against an invisible opponent, a hundred-thousand-dollar-a-year job in New York. And then Raphaella had done almost the same thing, flaunting John Henry and their "differences" as an excuse to walk out. Suddenly she saw it all differently and she ached at what she saw in his eyes. Beneath his piercing gaze she dropped her eyes now and touched the sand with one long thin hand.

"I'm sorry . . . oh, God . . . I'm so sorry. . . ."
She looked up at him then and there were tears in her
eyes. And the pain he saw there brought him to his
knees beside her on the sand.

"Do you have any idea how much I love you?"

She turned her head away then and put up a hand
as though to stop him from speaking, whispering
softly, "Alex, don't. . . ." But he took the hand in his
own and then with his other hand brought her face
back until she looked at him again.

"Did you hear me? I love you. I did then, and I do
now, and I always will. And maybe I don't understand
you, maybe there are differences between us, but I
can learn to understand those differences better, Raphaella. I can if you give me the chance."

"But why? Why only a half life with me when you
can have a whole one with someone else?"

"Is that why you did it?" At times he had thought
so, but he had never been able to understand why she
had severed the tie so quickly, so bluntly. It had to be
more than just that.

"Partly." She answered him honestly now, her eyes
looked in his. "I wanted you to have more."

"All I wanted was you." And then he spoke more
softly. "That's all I want now." But she shook her head
slowly in answer.

"You can't have that." And then after a long pause,
"It's not right."

"Why not, dammit?" There was fire in his eyes
when he asked the question. "Why? Because of your
husband? How can you give up all that you are for a
man who is almost dead, for a man who, from what
you yourself have told me, has always wanted your

happiness, and would probably love you enough to set you free if he could?"

Alex knew John Henry had in a sense set Raphaella free already. But he couldn't tell Raphaella of that meeting. Her face bore witness to the terrible strain under which she was suffering. To add to that, to tell her that John Henry knew of their relationship, was unthinkable.

But Raphaella wouldn't listen. "That wasn't the deal I made. For better or worse . . . in sickness and in health . . . until death do us part. Not boredom, not strokes, not Alex. . . . I can't let any of that hinder my obligations."

"Fuck your obligations." He exploded and Raphaella looked shocked and shook her head.

"No, if I don't honor what I owe him, he'll die. I know that now. My father told me that this summer and he was right. He's barely hanging on now, for God's sake."

"But that has nothing to do with you, dammit, don't you see that? Are you going to let your father run your life too? Are you going to be pushed around by your 'duties' and 'obligations' and your sense of noblesse oblige? What about *you*, Raphaella? What about what *you* want? Do you ever allow yourself to think of that?" The truth was that she tried not to think of it. Not anymore.

"You don't understand, Alex." She spoke so softly that he could barely hear her in the wind. He sat next to her on the log, their bodies so close that it made Raphaella shiver. "Do you want my jacket?" She shook her head. And then he went on. "I do understand. I think you did something insane this summer, you made one giant sacrifice in order to atone for what you thought was one giant sin."

But again she shook her head. "I just can't do it to John Henry." Alex could not, try as he might, tell her that the one constant in her life—her relationship with her husband—had already been altered.

"Do what, for God's sake? Spend a few hours away from the house? Do you have to chain yourself to his bedpost?"

She nodded slowly. "For the moment, yes." And then, as though she owed it to him to tell him, she went on. "My father was having me folllowed, Alex. He threatened to tell John Henry. And that would have killed him. I had no choice."

"Oh, my God." He stared at her in amazement. What she hadn't even told him was that the surveillance was due to a letter from his sister, Kay. "Why would he do a thing like that?"

"Tell John Henry? I'm not sure he would. But I couldn't take the chance. He said he would, so I had to do what I did."

"But why would he have you followed?" She shrugged and looked him in the eye.

"It doesn't really matter. He just did."

"And now you sit there and wait."

She closed her eyes. "Don't say it like that. I'm not waiting. You make it sound as though I'm waiting for him to die, and I'm not. I'm simply doing what I set out to do fifteen years ago—be his wife."

"Don't you think circumstances warrant a little bending of the rules on this one, Raphaella?" His eyes pleaded with her, but once again she shook her head. "All right, I won't push you." He realized again how much pressure she must have been under in

Spain. It was hard to imagine her father having her followed and threatening to tell her husband that she was having an affair.

Alex pondered with well-hidden fury what he would have liked to do to Raphaella's father, and then he looked her in the eye. "I'm going to just leave it open. I love you. I want you. On any terms you want, whenever you can. If that's tomorrow, or in ten years. Come knock on my door and I'll be there. Do you understand that, Raphaella? Do you know that I mean what I'm saying?"

"I do, but I think it's crazy for you to do that. You have to lead a life."

"And you don't?"

"That's different, Alex. You're not married, I am." They sat silent for a while on the log, looking out at the sea. It felt good just being there together again, after so long. Raphaella wanted to prolong the moment, but the light was already growing dim and the fog was beginning to roll in.

"Is he still having you followed?"

"I don't think so. There's no reason to now." She smiled gently at Alex and wished that she could just touch his cheek. But she knew that she couldn't let herself do that. Never again. And what he was saying was madness. He couldn't sit around waiting for her for the rest of his life.

"Come on." He stood up and held out a hand to her. "I'll walk you back to your car." And then he smiled at her. "Or is that not such a great idea?"

"It's not." She smiled in answer. "But you can walk me back part of the way." It was getting dark quickly enough that she was not enchanted at the prospect of walking back to the car alone. She looked up at him with a gentle look of inquiry, her brows knit, her eyes seeming even larger now that her face was thinner than it had been. "How is Amanda?"

Alex looked down at Raphaella with a gentle smile. "She misses you . . . almost as much as I do. . . ."

Raphaella didn't answer. "How did the summer go?"

"She lasted exactly five days with Kay. My darling sister had planned the entire month so that she would be showing Mandy off to the voters every moment. Mandy tried it on for size and told her to shove it."

"Did she come home?"

"No, my mother took her to Europe early." He shrugged. "I think they had a nice time."

"Didn't she tell you?"

He looked long and hard at Raphaella. "I don't think I heard anything anyone told me until about November." She nodded, and they walked on. And then at last she stopped.

"I should walk on alone from here."

"Raphaella—" He hesitated, but then decided he had to ask her. "Can I see you sometime? Just for lunch . . . or a drink. . . ."

But she shook her head. "I couldn't do that."

"Why not?"

"Because we'd both want more than that and you know it. It has to be the way it is now, Alex."

"Why? With me so lonely for you, I can't see straight, and you wasting away? Is that how it has to be? Was that why your father threatened to tell John Henry, so he could be assured that we'd both live like this? Don't you want more, Raphaella?" And then, unable to stop himself, he reached out and took her gently in his arms. "Don't you remember how it was?"

Her eyes filled with tears and she buried her face in his shoulder, nodding, but not wanting to see his face. "Yes . . . yes . . . I remember . . . but that's over. . . ."

"No, it's not. I still love you. I will always love you."

"You must not do that." She looked up at him finally, with agony in her eyes. "You must forget all that, Alex. You have to."

Alex said nothing and only shook his head. "What are you doing on Christmas?" It was an odd question and Raphaella looked at him, puzzled, not understanding what he had in mind.

"Nothing. Why?"

"My mother is taking Amanda to Hawaii. They leave at five in the afternoon on Christmas Day. Why don't you come over in the evening for a cup of coffee? I promise I won't push you or bug you, ask you for any promises. I just want to see you. It would mean a lot to me. Please, Raphaella. . . ." His voice trailed off and she stood there, and then finally, painfully, agonizingly, she forced herself to shake her head.

"No." It was barely more than a whisper. "No."

"I won't let you do this. I'll be there. Alone. At my place on Christmas night. Think about it. I'll be waiting."

"No, Alex . . . please."

"It doesn't matter. If you don't come, it's all right."

"But I don't want you to sit there. And I won't come."

He said nothing but there was a hopeful light in his eyes. "I'll be there." He smiled. "Good-bye now." He kissed the top of her head then and patted her shoulders with his big hands. "Take care, babe." He stood there and she said nothing, then slowly she turned away.

She turned back once to see him standing there in his red parka with the wind in his dark hair. "I won't come, Alex."

"It doesn't matter. I want to be there. In case you do." And as she walked away toward the stairway that would lead her back to the car, he shouted after her, "See you on Christmas."

As he watched her climb the stairs he thought of her devotion to John Henry, to him, to all her obligations. He would let her make her own decision.

But he could not stop loving her.

CHAPTER 28

The small tree they had put on the card table across the room twinkled merrily as Raphaella and John Henry ate their turkey on the all-too-familiar trays. He seemed quieter than usual, and Raphaella wondered if the holiday depressed him, if it reminded him of ski vacations in his youth, or the trips he had taken with Raphaella, or the years when his son had been a boy and there had been a giant tree in the foyer downstairs.

"John Henry . . . darling . . . are you all right?" She leaned over and spoke to him gently, and he nodded, but he didn't answer. He was thinking of Alex and their talk. Something was wrong, but he'd been so depressed over the last months that Raphaella's condition had remained unnoticed. She usually fooled him with her extraordinary determination to keep his spirits up, camouflaging her own pain. He lay back against the pillows with a sigh.

"I'm so tired of all this, Raphaella."

"What, Christmas?" She looked surprised. The only sign of it was the tiny tree in his bedroom, but maybe the light hurt his eyes.

"No, all of it. Living . . . eating dinner . . . watching the news when nothing is ever new. Breathing . . . talking . . . sleeping. . . ." He looked at her bleakly, and there was no sign of anything even remotely happy in his eyes.

"You're not tired of me, are you?" She smiled gently at him and made a move to kiss his cheek, but he turned away.

"Don't . . . do that." His voice was soft and sad, muffled by his pillows.

"John Henry . . . what's wrong?" She looked surprised and hurt as she watched him, and slowly he turned to face her again.

"How can you ask that? How can you . . . live like this . . . anymore? How can you bear it? Sometimes I think . . . about the old men . . . who died in India . . . where they burned . . . their young wives on the funeral pyre. I'm no better than that, Raphaella."

"Don't say that. Don't be silly. . . . I love you. . . ."

"Then you're crazy." He didn't sound amused, but angry. "And if you are, then I'm not. Why don't you go somewhere? Take a vacation . . . do something for God's sake . . . but don't just sit here wasting your life. Mine is over, Raphaella. . . ." His voice dropped to a whisper. "Mine is gone. It has been for years."

"That's not true." Tears sprang to her eyes as she tried to convince him. The look on his face broke her heart.

"It is true . . . and you have . . . to face it. I've been dead . . . for years. But the worst part of it is

. . . I'm killing you too. Why don't you go home to Paris for a while?" He had again wondered what was happening between her and Alex but he didn't want to ask. He didn't want her to know that he knew.

"Why?" She looked astonished. "Why Paris?" To her father? After what had happened during the summer? The very idea made her ill. But John Henry looked adamantly at her from his bed.

"I want you . . . to go away . . . for a while."

She shook her head firmly. "I won't go."

"Yes, you will." They were like children arguing, but neither of them was amused, and neither of them smiled.

"No, I will not."

"Dammit, I want you to go somewhere."

"Fine, then I'll go for a walk. But this is my home too and you can't send me away." She took the tray from him and set it down on the floor. "I think you're just bored with me, John Henry." She tried to tease him, but his eye would not catch the sparkle of mischief beginning to glow in hers. "Maybe what you need is a new sexy nurse." But he wasn't amused. He just lay there glowering, it was part of his querulousness that she noticed more and more.

"Stop talking rubbish."

"I'm not talking rubbish." She spoke to him gently, leaning forward earnestly in her chair. "I love you and I don't want to go away."

"Well, I want you to go away."

She sat back in silence for a while as he watched her, and then suddenly he spoke softly in the quiet room. "I want to die, Raphaella." He closed his eyes as he continued to speak. "That's all I want to do. And why don't I . . . God, why don't I?" He opened his eyes and looked at her again. "Tell me that. Where the hell is justice?" He looked at her accusingly. "Why am I still alive?"

"Because I need you." She said it softly and he shook his head and turned his face away again. He said nothing for a very long time then, and when she approached the bed carefully, she saw that he had fallen asleep. It made her sad to realize how unhappy he was. It was as though she weren't doing enough.

The nurse came in on tiptoe and Raphaella motioned to her that John Henry had fallen asleep. They stepped out for a whispered conference. The consensus was that he was probably asleep for the night. He had had a long, difficult day, and Christmas had made no difference. Nothing really did anymore. He was sick of it all.

"I'll be in my room if you need me." She whispered it to the nurse and then walked pensively down the hall. Poor John Henry, what a rotten existence. And in Raphaella's mind the injustice was not that he was still living, but that he had had the strokes at all. Without them, at his age, he could still have been vital. Slower perhaps than he had been at fifty or sixty, a little more tired, but happy and busy and alive. But the way things were, he had nothing, and he was right in a way. He was barely alive.

She walked slowly into her little study, thinking of him and then letting her mind drift to other things. Her family celebrating Christmas at Santa Eugenia, her father, and then inevitably the Christmas she had shared with Alexander and Amanda the year before. And then for the hundredth time since that morning she remembered what he had said to her three weeks before on the beach. "I'll be waiting . . . I'll be there. . . ." She could still hear him say it. And as she sat there, alone in her study, she wondered again if he really was. It was only seven thirty, a respectable hour, and she could easily have gone for a walk, but where would it lead her? What would happen if she went there? Was it smart, was it wise? Did it make sense at all? She knew that it didn't, that her place was there in John Henry's huge empty house. As the hours ticked slowly onward, she suddenly felt she had to go there, just for a moment, for half an hour, just to see him. It was madness and she knew it, but at nine thirty she flew out of her chair, unable to stay in the house a moment longer. She had to go.

She quickly slipped a red wool coat over the simple black dress she had been wearing, put on long narrow black leather boots, slipped a black leather handbag on her shoulder, and ran a comb through her hair. She felt her heart flutter at the prospect of seeing him, reproaching herself for going but suddenly smiling as she thought ahead to the moment when he would open the door. She left a note in her room that she had gone for a walk and to drop in on a friend, in case someone came to find her, and her feet fairly flew as she hurried the few blocks to the little house she hadn't seen in five and a half months.

When she saw the house, she simply stood there looking at it, and she sighed softly. She felt as though she had been lost for almost half a year and she had finally found her way home. Unable to suppress the smile on her face, she crossed the street and rang the doorbell, and then suddenly there was the rapid thumping of his footstep on the stairs. There was a pause, and then the door opened and he stood there, unable to believe what he saw, until suddenly the smile in her eyes was matched by his.

"Merry Christmas." They said it in unison and then laughed together as he stood aside with a bow and then rose to face her with a warm smile. "Welcome home, Raphaella." Saying not a word, she walked inside.

There was furniture in the living room now. He and Mandy had put it together, gone to auctions and garage sales and department stores and art galleries and thrift shops, and what they had put together was a comfortable combination of French provincial and Early American. The room was decorated with a handsome fur throw, soft French Impressionist paintings, lots of silver and some pewter, and some handsome old books. There were huge jugs filled with flowers on the tables, and there were plants in every corner and crawling all over the little marble mantelpiece in the double parlor. The couch was off-white, the little throw cushions were made of fur and tapestry, and there were several needlepoints that Amanda had made for Alex while they were doing the house. With Raphaella gone she was even closer to her uncle and felt an obligation to take care of him now that there was no one else who would. She nagged him about eating the right foods, taking his vitamins, getting his sleep, driving too fast, working too hard, and not weeding the garden. He teased her about her boyfriends, her cooking, her makeup, her wardrobe, and yet somehow managed to make her feel that she was the prettiest girl alive. Together they ran a nice little household, and as she stepped across the threshold,

Raphaella could feel the love that they shared, it exuded from every corner of the room.

"Alex, this is lovely."

"Isn't it? Mandy did most of it after school." He looked proud of his absent niece as he led Raphaella into the living room, and it was something of a relief to sit in a room that had not been one they had shared. She had been somewhat nervous that he would take her up to the bedroom to sit in front of the fireplace and she couldn't have borne the memories there, or in the study, or even in the kitchen downstairs. This was perfect, because it was warm and pretty, and it was new.

He offered her coffee and brandy. She accepted the former, declined the latter, and sat down on the pretty little couch, admiring the details of the room again. He was back in a minute with the coffee, and she saw that his hands were trembling as badly as hers when he set down the cup.

"I didn't really know if you'd be here," she began nervously, "but I decided to take a chance."

He eyed her seriously from a chair next to the couch. "I told you I would be. And I meant it, Raphaella. You should know that by now." She nodded and sipped the hot espresso.

"How was Christmas?"

"All right." He smiled and shrugged. "It was a big event for Mandy, and my mother flew in last night to take her to Hawaii. She's been promising her that trip for years, and this seemed a good time. She just finished a book and she could use the rest too. As the saying goes, she's not getting any younger."

"Your mother?" Raphaella looked both shocked and amused. "She'll never be old." And then she remembered something she had forgotten to tell him when they met on the beach. "I'm having a book published too." And then she blushed and laughed softly. "Though nothing as important as a novel."

"Your children's book?" His eyes lit up with pleasure and she nodded.

"They just told me a few weeks ago."

"Did you use an agent?" She shook her head.

"No. Just beginner's luck, I guess." They smiled at each other for a long moment and then Alex sat back in his chair.

"I'm glad you're here, Raphaella. I've wanted to show you this room for a long time."

"And I've been wanting to tell you about the book." She smiled gently. It was as though they had both retrieved a friend. But what would they do now? They couldn't resume what they once had. Raphaella knew that. It would rock the boat too badly, with Kay, with her father, her mother, John Henry. She wished that she could tell him what the previous summer had been like, what kind of a nightmare it had been for her.

"What were you thinking about just then?" She had looked devastated as she stared into the fire.

She looked up at him honestly. "Last summer." She sighed softly. "It was such an awful time."

He nodded, looking pensive too, and then he sighed with a small smile. "I'm just happy you've come back at all, and that we can talk. That was the hardest part for me, not being able to talk to you anymore . . . or see you . . . knowing you wouldn't be here when I got home. Mandy said that was the hardest part for her too." What he said turned the knife in Raphaella's heart and she looked away from him so he wouldn't see the pain in her eyes. "What do you do now, Raphaella?" His voice was gentle, and she stared pensively into the fire.

"I'm with John Henry most of the time. He hasn't been well at all in the past few months."

"It must be hard for both of you."

"Mostly for him."

"And you?" He eyed her pointedly and she didn't answer. But then, without saying more, he leaned toward her and gently kissed her lips. She didn't stop him, she didn't think about what they were doing. She just kissed him, gently at first, and then with the passion and the sorrow and the loneliness and the aching for him that had drowned her since the summer before. It was as though it all washed over her with that first kiss, and she could feel him battling his own passions too.

"Alex . . . I can't. . . ." Not again. She couldn't start this again. He nodded.

"I know. It's all right." They sat there for a while, talking, looking into the fire, talking about themselves, about each other, about what had happened to them, and what they had felt, and then suddenly they were talking about other things, about people, about things that had amused them, about funny moments, as though for six months they had stored it all. It was three in the morning when Raphaella left him at the corner around the bend from her house. He had insisted on walking her home. And then, like a schoolboy, he hesitated briefly and decided to plunge in. "Can I see you again, Raphaella? Just like this . . . ?" He didn't want to frighten her away again, and he had just glimpsed the pressures she lived with, both real and in her own mind. She seemed to think about it, but only briefly, and she nodded.

"Maybe we could go for a walk on the beach?"

"Tomorrow?"

She laughed at the question and nodded. "Very well."

"I'll meet you here and we can go in my car." It would be Saturday, and he was free. "Twelve o'clock?"

"All right." Feeling very young and girlish, she smiled at him and waved, and then she was gone, grinning to herself all the way home. She didn't think of John Henry, or her father, or Kay Willard, or anyone else. She thought only of Alexander . . . Alex . . . and of seeing him at noon the next day and going to the beach.

CHAPTER 29

By the end of a week Alex and Raphaella were meeting every afternoon, either for a walk on the beach or to sit lazily in front of the fire, drinking espresso and talking about life. She showed him her contract for the book when it arrived from New York, and he told her about his latest cases, and they went back to Fort Point. They shared afternoon hours when he wasn't working, and a few hours in the evening after John Henry went to bed. They were always hours when she couldn't be with John Henry because he was sleeping, so she didn't feel that she was stealing a single precious life-giving moment from him. She gave to Alex the time that was her own, a half hour here, an hour there, a spare moment, to walk and breathe and think and be. They were some of the happiest hours they had spent together, hours in which they discovered each other once again. Only this time they discovered more than they had a year earlier, or perhaps it was that they had both grown so much in the time they were alone. In both cases the sense of loss had been staggering, yet it had prodded each of them in different ways. But the relationship between them was still very tenuous, it was all very new and they were both afraid. Raphaella was terrified to create the same cataclysmic disaster she had once before, arousing his sister's ire and her father's, and the problem of keeping Alex from a fuller relationship with someone else still remained. But Alex was only frightened of scaring her off again. He had, after all, John Henry's blessing, so he had no guilt at all. They advanced carefully, inching slowly toward each other, until the day after New Year when she came over at two in the afternoon, after John Henry had declared that he wanted to sleep all day, and he seemed bent on doing just that.

Raphaella wandered over to see Alex, rang the doorbell, not even sure that he was home, and he opened it to her in jeans and a comfortable old turtleneck sweater, with a look of immense pleasure to see her standing at the door.

"What a nice surprise. What are you doing here?"

"I just thought I'd come to visit. Am I disturbing you?" With a blush she suddenly realized that she had taken a great deal for granted, he could have had a woman upstairs in his room. But he instantly read the look on her face and chuckled.

"No, madam. You are not 'disturbing' me at all. Want a cup of coffee?" She nodded and followed him downstairs to the kitchen.

"Who's been doing those?" She waved a hand at the shining copper pots as she slid into a kitchen chair.

"I have."

"Have you really?"

"Of course." And then he smiled at her. "I have many talents you don't know about yet."

"Really? Like what?" He handed her a cup of warm coffee and she took a sip as he watched her happily from his chair.

"I'm not sure I should give up all my secrets at once."

They sat quietly together for a while, sipping their coffee and enjoying each other's company, and then they began, as always, to discuss a dozen different things. Their time together always seemed to pass so quickly. Then suddenly he remembered the manuscript to his mother's book.

"Oh, Alex, can I read it?" Raphaella's eyes shone.

"Sure. I have it upstairs. It's all over my desk."

Her eyes danced with pleasure at the prospect, and abandoning their coffee, they hastily went upstairs. She glanced at a few pages, loved what she was reading, and smiled up at Alex. She suddenly realized that this was her first time back in his room. Cautiously then she glanced across the hall at his bedroom, and then silently their eyes met and held. He kissed her then, slowly, artfully, hungrily, and her back arched with pleasure as he held her in his arms. He was waiting for her to stop him, but she didn't and he let his hands begin to rove, and then, as though by mutual agreement, they wandered slowly across the hall.

For the first time in his adult life he was frightened, of what he was doing, of the consequences of what they had just found again. He was so desperately afraid of losing her, but it was Raphaella who whispered softly to him. "It's all right, Alex." And then as he peeled off her sweater, "I love you so much." It seemed like a ballet as he slowly unclothed her, and she took off his clothes as well. They tasted and felt and held and caressed and lingered and it seemed to take them all afternoon to make love, but when at last they lay with each other and their bodies were sated and their minds and hearts were full, they both looked happier than they ever had with each other. Propped on one elbow Alex looked down at her with a smile that she had never seen before.

"Do you know how happy it makes me to see you here?"

She smiled softly. "I missed you so much, Alex . . . in every possible way." He nodded and lay down beside her, his fingers roving, his mouth hungry, his loins beginning to tingle, and suddenly he knew that he wanted her again. It was as though he couldn't get enough now, as though she might leave him again and there would never be more. They made love again and again and again into the evening, and then they took a warm bath together, and Raphaella sat in it dreamily with her eyes closed.

"Darling, you are exquisite."

"And very sleepy." She opened one eye and smiled. "I have to wake up and go home." But it seemed odd to be going anywhere, odder still to call the other house home. This was home again, where Alex was, where they shared their lives and their souls and their bodies and their loving. And she didn't give a damn what her father threatened this time. She would never let Alex go. Let Kay write him another damn letter. Let them all go to hell. She needed this man. And she had a right to him after all.

He kissed her again as they sat there soaking and she teased him that if he touched her again she would call the police. But he was as tired as she was, and as he drove her home, he yawned happily, kissed her once more, and then as always, let her walk the last block alone.

When she let herself into the house, there was a strange stillness, as though all the clocks had stopped somewhere, as though some sound that had existed subliminally in the huge mansion had somehow stopped. She decided that it was only her imagination and pure exhaustion, and with a grin and a yawn she began to climb the stairs. But as she reached the first landing she suddenly saw two of the maids and two of the nurses clustered in a small group outside John Henry's door. For an instant her heart skipped a beat and she wondered, and then she stopped at the head of the stairs as they saw her.

"Is something wrong?"

"It's—" The nurse looked red-eyed as she faced Raphaella. "It's your husband, Mrs. Phillips."

"Oh, my God." She said it softly. She knew as she saw them there was no mistaking the looks on their faces.

"Is he—" She couldn't finish the sentence and the nurse nodded.

"He's gone." But then, overcome by her own emotions, she burst into tears again and was instantly taken into the other nurse's arms.

"How did it happen?" Raphaella approached them slowly, her back very straight and her voice very soft. Her eyes looked enormous. John Henry had died while she lay in bed with Alex, playing and cavorting and making love. The indecency of it struck her like a slap across the face and in a single instant she remem-

bered the impact of her father's words the previous
summer. He had called her a whore. "Did he have another stroke?"

For an instant the foursome stood frozen, and then
the nurse who had been crying cried louder, and the
two maids seemed to instantly disappear. It was then
that the second nurse looked at Raphaella, and she
knew that something had gone very wrong while she
was gone.

"The doctor wants to speak to you, Mrs. Phillips.
He's been waiting for two hours. We didn't know
where you were, but we found the note in your room
and assumed that you'd be home soon." Raphaella felt
sick as she stood there.

"Is the doctor still here?"

"He's in Mr. Phillips's room, with the body. But
they'll be coming to take him away soon. He wants an
autopsy just to be certain." Raphaella stared at her
dumbly and then hurried into John Henry's room. She
stood very still as she came to the bed and saw him
lying there. He looked as though he were sleeping,
and once she thought that she saw him move his hand.
She didn't even see the doctor as she stood there. All
she could see was John Henry, so tired, so shriveled,
so old, and looking only as though he were asleep.

"Mrs. Phillips . . . ? Raphaella?"

Raphaella spun quickly when she heard the voice
beside her, and then sighed when she saw who it was.
"Hello, Ralph." But then, as though drawn by a mag-
net, her eyes went back to the face of the man she had
been married to for fifteen years. She wasn't even sure
what she felt yet. Sorrow, emptiness, regret, grief,
something, but she was not yet sure what. She didn't
really understand that he was gone. Only a few hours

before, he had said that he was tired, and now he looked like he had gone to sleep.

"Raphaella, let's go in the other room."

She followed the doctor into the dressing room, which the nurses had so often used, and they stood there together like two conspirators, but he looked unhappy as he stared at Raphaella and it was clear that he had something to say.

"What is it? What is it that no one is telling me? It wasn't a stroke, was it?" Suddenly she instinctively knew. And the doctor shook his head and confirmed her worst fears.

"No, it wasn't. It was a horrible accident. A terrible mistake, an almost unforgivable thing, except that it wasn't done maliciously, and no one could have known how he felt."

"What are you trying to tell me?" Her voice was rising, and she felt as though something in her head were going to explode.

"That your husband . . . John Henry . . . the nurse gave him a sleeping pill, and she left the bottle on the night table. . . ." There was a long pause as she stared at him in horror. "He took the pills, Raphaella. The whole bottle. He committed suicide. I don't know how else to tell you. But that's what happened." His voice faltered, and Raphaella felt herself wanting to scream. He had killed himself . . . John Henry had killed himself while she was out screwing Alex. . . . She had killed him . . . killed him as though she had done it with her bare hands. Was it that he knew about Alex? Was it that he sensed something? Could she have stopped it if she'd been there? Could it . . . would it . . . what if . . . her mind raced as her eyes grew wide with what she was thinking, but she could not make a sound. She could say nothing. Her father had been right. She had killed him. John Henry had committed suicide. At last she brought herself to look at the doctor.

"Did he leave me a note?" He shook his head in answer.

"Nothing."

"Oh, my God." She said it almost to herself and then sank to the floor at his feet, in a dead faint.

CHAPTER 30

Antoine de Mornay-Malle arrived from Paris at six o'clock the following evening and he found Raphaella sitting staring out at the bay. As she heard his voice behind her she rose from her chair and turned to greet him, and when she did so, he saw that her eyes were almost glazed. She had not gone to bed the previous evening, and despite the doctor's offers of a sedative she had refused. Now she stood looking very tired and very thin in a black wool dress that seemed to shrink her further, her hair pulled severely back, her eyes huge and almost gouged into the ghostly pale face. When he glanced at her legs he saw that she wore the black stockings of mourning, and she was bereft of jewelry except for the heavy gold knot she had worn for fifteen years on her left hand.

"Papa. . . ." She came toward him slowly as he approached her and his eyes searched her face. He had known from her voice when she called him that something was desperately wrong, more than just the death of her husband. There was something about it that she had not yet revealed.

"Raphaella, I'm very sorry." He unbent a little and settled himself in a chair next to hers. "Was it—was it quick?"

She said absolutely nothing, staring out at the bay and holding tightly to his hand. "I don't know . . . I think so. . . ."

"You weren't with him?" He stared at her face and began to frown. "Where were you?" His voice was suddenly filled with suspicion and she couldn't bear to look him in the eye.

"I was out for a little while."

Her father nodded. "It was another stroke . . . or did his heart just give out?" Like many people his age he wanted to know exactly how the end had come, possibly so that when it came to him, he would know what he should be expecting. But still he found something odd about the look on his daughter's face. As she sat there she was seriously thinking of not telling him, but she also knew that it was pointless to lie to him. Knowing her father, she was certain he would engage in conversation with everyone, the servants, the nurses, the doctor. Accidentally or on purpose he would discover the truth. Everyone in the household already knew it. The doctor had agreed with her to say absolutely nothing about the circumstances of John Henry's passing, but the nurses told the maid who mentioned it to the butler who gave the news to the chauffeur with a look of astonishment and dismay. And it wouldn't be long before one of them told a friend in one of the other houses, and eventually word would be out all over town. John Henry Phillips had committed suicide. And somehow Raphaella knew that her father would find it out too.

"Papa. . . ." Slowly she turned to face him, and at last she met his eyes. "It wasn't a stroke. . . ." She closed her eyes tightly for a moment, gripped her chair, opened her eyes again, and went on. "It was . . . he took pills, Papa. . . ." Her voice was barely audible as he looked at her, not understanding what she was trying to say. "I . . . he . . . he's been so depressed lately . . . he hated being sick . . . he's been—" She faltered as tears filled her eyes and a sob clutched her throat.

"What are you trying to tell me?" He stared at her, not moving at all in his chair.

"I'm telling you that—" She took a big gulp of air. "The nurse left the sleeping pills next to him on the table . . . and he took them . . . all of them." She said it clearly now.

"He killed himself?" Her father looked horrified, but slowly she nodded. "My God, where were you? Why didn't you see that the nurse put the medication away? Why weren't you here?"

"I don't know, Papa . . . but no one knew that he wanted to die. I mean, I knew it . . . he was so tired, and lately he was so sad from having been sick for so long. But no one thought . . . I didn't think . . . I never thought he would—"

"My God, are you crazy? How could you not be more careful? How could you not watch everything the nurses did? It was your responsibility . . . your duty. . . ." He prepared to go on but Raphaella leaped from her chair, looking as though she were about to scream.

"Stop it, Papa! Stop it! I couldn't help it. . . . Nobody could! It was no one's fault . . . it was—"

"You'll bring charges against the nurse, won't you?" He looked businesslike as he watched her from his chair. But Raphaella shook her head, once again looking broken and bereft.

"Of course not. She couldn't know . . . it was an accident, Papa."

"An accident that killed your husband." Their eyes met and held for a long time. As if he sensed something more that she hadn't told him, he narrowed his eyes as he watched her. "Is there more, Raphaella? Something you haven't told me?" And then, as though it had come to him more clearly, not as a guess, but as a certainty of her guilt, he sat very straight in his chair and stared at his daughter. "Where were you when he did this, Raphaella?" She looked woefully at her father, feeling not like a woman but more like a child. "Where were you?" He put horrible emphasis on the words when he asked the questions, and there was nothing she could say.

"I was out."

"With whom?"

"No one." But it was useless. He had already sensed it and she knew that he knew. She looked at him now, her face an agony of self-recrimination that told its own tale.

"You were with *him*, weren't you, Raphaella? Weren't you?" His voice rose ominously, and unable to see her way clear of the obstacle before her, she simply nodded her head. "My God, then, you killed him. Do you understand that? Do you know why he took those pills?" Her father looked at her in open revulsion, but again Raphaella shook her head.

"He didn't know about it, Papa. I'm sure of that."

"How can you be? The servants must have known it, they must have told him."

"They wouldn't have done that to him, and I don't think they knew." She walked listlessly toward the window. The worst was over now. He knew the truth. He couldn't say anything more. It was all out on the table, her perfidy, her betrayal, her failure of John Henry that had ended up in his death by pills, instead of by the hand of God.

"Then you lied to me when you said you wouldn't see him anymore?"

"No, I told you the truth." She turned to face him again. "I didn't see him again, until about two weeks ago. We met accidentally."

"So of course you climbed right back into his bed."

"Papa . . . please. . . ."

"Didn't you? Isn't that what killed your husband? Think about it. Can you really live with that? Can you?"

Her eyes filled with tears again and she shook her head. "No, I can't."

"You're a murderess, Raphaella." He slid the words out of his mouth like snakes, their venom poisoning all within reach. "A murderess as well as a whore." And then, drawing himself to his full height, he faced her. "You have disgraced me, and in my heart I disown you, but for my own sake, and the sake of your mother, I will not let you disgrace me again. I have no idea what you plan to do about your lover. I'm sure you would like nothing better than to run off with him the minute they put John Henry in the ground. But that, my dear girl, is not going to happen. Not for a moment. What you do later is none of my business, and as you keep pointing out, you're a grown woman. A repulsive one, an immoral one, but grown you certainly are. So in a year, after a decent period of mourning, you are welcome to go about your whoring again. But in the meantime, for one year, you will be decent, to me, to your mother, and to the memory of a man I loved a great deal, even if you did not. After the funeral you will fly to Spain with your mother. And you will stay there for one year. I will attend to all the business matters that come up in relation to the estate, it will take almost that long to settle it anyway, and after a year you can come back here and do whatever you want. But one year, one year you owe the man whom you murdered. If you went to prison, it would be for the rest of your life. And the fact is, young woman, that what you have done you will have to live with for the rest of your days." He walked solemnly to the door and turned around. "Be prepared to leave on the day of the funeral. I won't discuss it with you further. A year of decent mourning for a man you drove to suicide is a small price to pay." As she stood there and watched him leave the room, the tears slid slowly down her face.

It wasn't until the next morning that she heard from Alex. They had kept it out of the papers for a day, but on the following morning it was there, on the first page. John Henry Phillips was dead. It explained that he had been bed-ridden since his first illness, that he had had several strokes and had been incapacitated for eight years. The article barely mentioned Raphaella, except to mention that he was survived by no children, but by his second wife, the former Raphaella de Mornay-Malle y de Santos y Quadral; after that it mentioned the corporations he had founded, the fortune he had inherited, the important international deals he had consummated over the years. But that was not what had interested Alex. He had stared at the paper in amazement when he picked it up outside on his way to work.

He had stood there, motionless, reading, for several minutes, and then had run back inside to call Raphaella. He had wondered why she hadn't come to see him the night before, and he had been terrified that she might have had second thoughts about resuming their relationship and that their lovemaking the night before had filled her with guilt and driven her away again. Now he wondered what it would mean to her that John Henry had died while she was with him. He could figure out that much from what he had read. It mentioned the night that he had died, and Alex knew that he had either died while Raphaella was out or shortly after she got home. He tried to imagine the scene that had met her when she returned from their hours together, and he shuddered to himself as he dialed the phone. It had taken her several minutes to come to the phone herself after the butler answered, and when she did, her voice sounded lifeless and flat. But at her end, when she picked up the receiver and heard his voice, she felt a tremor run through her. It was like a brutal reminder of what she had been doing when her husband had taken the lethal pills.

"Raphaella?" His voice was gentle and it was obvious that he was upset. "I just read the paper. I am so sorry. . . ." And then after a moment's pause, "Are you all right?" She had said nothing so far except hello.

"Yes." She spoke very slowly. "I am." And then, "I'm sorry . . . I was busy just now when you called." She had been selecting the suit they would put on John Henry, and her father had been standing by wearing an expression that mingled accusation and grief for his lost friend. "The funeral is tomorrow." What she told him sounded bleak and disjointed and he sat on the stairs with the phone in his hand and closed his eyes. It was obvious what had happened. She was consumed with guilt over the death of her husband. He had to see her. To talk to her. To find out how she really was.

"Can I see you after the funeral, Raphaella? Just for a minute? I just want to know that you're all right."

"Thank you, Alex. I'm fine." She sounded like a zombie and he was suddenly frightened. It sounded as though she were heavily sedated, or worse yet, as though she were in some kind of shock.

"Can I see you?"

"I'm leaving tomorrow for Spain."

"Tomorrow? Why?"

"I'm going back with my parents. My father felt I should spend the period of mourning there."

Oh, Jesus. Alex shook his head. What had happened? What had they done to her? What had they told her? "How long is the period of mourning?"

She answered him expressionlessly. "One year."

He stared at the floor in stupefaction. She was going away for a year? He had lost her again and he knew it, and he also knew that this time it was for good. If she associated John Henry's death with their reunion, then their affair would remain always an ugly moment she would want to forget. And all that he knew was that he had to see her. For a minute, ten seconds, anything, to bring her back to reality, to remind her that he really loved her, that they had done nothing wrong, and that they had not caused John Henry's death. "Raphaella, I have to see you."

"I don't think I can." She glanced over her shoulder and could see her father in the next room.

"Yes, you can." Then Alex thought of something. "On the steps, where I first saw you, outside your garden. Just go down there and I'll meet you. Five minutes, Raphaella . . . that's all . . . please?"

There was such a tone of pleading in his voice that she pitied him, but she felt nothing for anyone anymore. Not for herself, not for Alex, maybe not even for John Henry. She was a murderess now. An evil woman. She was numb. But it wasn't Alex who had killed John Henry. She had. There was no reason to punish him.

"Why do you want to see me?"

"To talk to you."

"What if someone sees us?" But what did it matter? She had already committed the ultimate sin. And her father knew about Alex, knew she had been with him when John Henry took the pills. What difference would it make now if it made things easier for Alex? She was leaving the next day for Spain.

"They won't see us. And I won't stay more than a few minutes. Will you meet me?"

She nodded slowly. "Yes."

"Ten minutes. I'll be there."

They hung up, and ten minutes later he was waiting nervously at the bottom steps where he had first seen her, her face silhouetted in the lamplight, the lynx coat swathing her in softness, but that in no way prepared him for the vision that came to him now as she walked down the flight of stairs. Everything about her was rigid and dark and depressing. She wore a severe black dress, no makeup, black stockings, black shoes, and a look in her eyes that frightened him to his very core. He didn't even dare to approach her. He simply stood there and waited as she came to him and then stood before him, with that haunting look of agony in her black eyes.

"Hello, Alex." It was almost as though she were dead too. Or as if someone had killed her, which in effect her father had.

"Raphaella . . . oh, baby. . . ." He wanted to reach out to her but he didn't dare, instead he just watched her with a look of anguish in his own eyes. And then, "Let's sit down." He let himself down on the steps and motioned to her to join him. Like a little robot she did, hugging her knees close to her chest in the chill air on the cold steps. "I want you to tell me what you're feeling. You look so bottled up that it scares me, and I think you're blaming yourself for something you had nothing to do with. John Henry was old, Raphaella, and sick, and very tired. You told me that yourself. He was sick of living, he wanted to die. The timing was only coincidental."

Raphaella smiled bleakly at him and shook her head, as though she pitied him for being such a fool. "No, not coincidental, Alex. I killed him. He didn't die in his sleep as it said in the papers. Or he did, but it was not a natural sleep. He took a bottle of sleeping pills." She waited for it to sink in as she watched him with her own lifeless eyes. "He committed suicide."

"Oh, my God." He looked startled, as though someone had slapped him, but now he understood what he had heard in her voice and what he now saw in her face. "But do you know that for certain, Raphaella? Did he leave a note?"

"No, he didn't have to. He just did it. But my father is sure that he knew about us, so in effect I killed him. That's what my father says, and he's right." For an instant Alex wanted to kill her father, but he said nothing to her.

"How does he know that?"

"Why else would John Henry do it?"

"Because he was so damn tired of living like a dead man, Raphaella. How often had he told you that himself?" But she only shook her head now. She wouldn't listen. Alex was proclaiming their innocence, while she knew only too well the extent of their guilt. And if not his, then assuredly her own. "You don't believe me, do you?"

She shook her head slowly. "No, I don't. I think my father is right. I think someone must have seen us and told him, maybe one of the servants, maybe a neighbor when we came home one night."

"No, Raphaella, you're wrong. The servants didn't tell him." He looked at her gently. "My sister did, when you were in Europe last summer."

"Oh, my God." Raphaella looked as though she might faint, but he reached out and took her hand.

"It wasn't like that. Kay meant it to be, but it wasn't. One of his secretaries called and asked me to come to the house."

"And you did?" She looked shocked.

"I did. He was a wonderful man, Raphaella." There were tears in his eyes now, as well as hers.

"What happened?"

"We talked for a long time. About you. About me, I guess. About us. He gave me his blessing, Raphaella." The tears spilled from Alex's eyes. "He told me to take care of you, afterward. . . ." He reached out to her then but she pulled back. The blessing didn't count now. Even Alex knew it. It was too late for that. "Raphaella, darling, don't let them hurt you. Don't let them take something away that we both want, that even John Henry respected, something that is so right."

"We're not right. We were very, very wrong."

"Were we?" He faced her squarely as they sat there. "Do you really believe that?"

"What choice do I have, Alex? How can I believe differently? What I did killed my husband, drove him to suicide. Can you really tell me that I've done nothing wrong?"

"Yes, and so would anyone else who knew the story. You're innocent, Raphaella. No matter what your father says. If John Henry were alive, I'm sure he would tell you the same thing. Are you sure he didn't leave you a letter?" He searched her eyes as he asked her. It seemed odd that John Henry had left nothing, he seemed like the kind of man who would. But she only shook her head again.

"Nothing. The doctor checked when he got there, and so did the nurses. There was nothing."

"You're sure?" She nodded again. "So now what? You go to Spain with your mother to atone for your sin?" She nodded once more. "And then what? You come back here?" He mentally resigned himself to a long, lonely year.

"I don't know. I'll have to come back to settle things. I'll put the house on the market after the estate has been cleared. And then"—she faltered and stared at her feet as she spoke in a monotone—"I suppose I'll go back to Paris, or maybe Spain."

"Raphaella, that's crazy." He couldn't keep his

hands from hers anymore. He clasped her long thin fingers in his own. "I love you. I want to marry you. There's no reason for us not to. We haven't done anything wrong."

"Yes, Alex." She pulled away from him very slowly, retrieving her hand from his. "We have. *I* have done something very wrong."

"And for the rest of time you'll bear that burden, is that it?" But more to the point he knew as he sat there that for the rest of time he would remind her of what she considered her great sin. He had lost her. To a quirk of fate, of timing, to the insanity of a tired old man, to the evil interpretations of her father. He had lost her. And then, as though she knew what he was thinking, she nodded and stood up. She stood looking at him for a long moment, and then softly she whispered, "Good-bye." She didn't touch him, or kiss him, and she didn't wait for an answer. She simply turned and walked slowly down the stairs as Alex watched her, aghast at what he was losing, at what she was doing. In her unrelenting black garb she looked like a nun. This was the third time he had lost her. But this time he knew it was for good. When she reached the well-concealed garden door, she pushed it open and closed it behind her. She did not look back at Alex, and there was no sound after the door had closed. Alex just stood there for what felt like hours, and then slowly, aching and feeling as though he were dying, he walked painfully up the stairs, got into his car, and drove home.

CHAPTER 31

The funeral was as private as they could keep it, but there were still well over a hundred people in the pews of the little church. Raphaella sat in the front pew with her mother and father. There were tears on her father's cheeks, and her mother sobbed openly for a man she had barely known. In the pew immediately behind them were the half-dozen relatives who had accompanied her mother from Spain. Alejandra's brother and two of her sisters, a cousin and her daughter and son. The group had allegedly come to lend support to Raphaella as well as Alejandra, but Raphaella felt more as though they were the prison guards, come to escort her back to Spain.

It was she who sat dry eyed through the funeral, staring blindly at the coffin covered in a blanket of white roses. Her mother had taken care of the flowers, her father the rest of the arrangements. Raphaella had had to do nothing, except sit in her room and think of

what she had done. Now and then she thought of
Alex, of his face when she had last seen him, of what
he had told her. But she knew that he was wrong in
what he was thinking. It was all so obviously her
fault, as her father had told her, and Alex was only
trying to assuage her guilt. It was strange to realize
that she had lost both of them at the same time. She
had lost Alex as much as she had John Henry, and she
knew as she sat there stiffly, listening to the music,
that she would never see either of them again. It was
then that the tears began to flow slowly, rolling mer-
cilessly down her cheeks beneath the thick black veil
until they fell silently onto her delicate hands folded
in her lap. She never moved once during the entire
ceremony. She only sat there, a criminal at a tri-
bunal, with nothing to say in her own defense. For a
single mad moment she wanted to jump up and tell
them that she hadn't killed him on purpose, that she
was innocent, that it was all a mistake. But she wasn't
innocent, she reminded herself silently. She was
guilty. And now she would have to pay.

When it was over, they drove to the cemetery in silence. He was to be buried beside his first wife and
their son, and Raphaella knew as she looked at the
grassy knoll where they were buried that she would
never rest there with him. It was unlikely that she
would ever again live in California. She would return
for a few weeks, in a year, to pick up her things and
sell the house, and then one day, she would die and
be buried in Europe. It seemed more fitting somehow. She had no right to lie here with him. She was
the woman who had killed him, his murderess. It
would have been blasphemy to bury her in his plot.
And at the end of the prayer said by the priest at the

gravesite, her father glanced at her as though saying the same thing.

They drove back to the house once again in silence, and Raphaella returned to her room. Her packing was almost done. She had nothing to do and she didn't want to speak to or see anyone. No one seemed particularly anxious to speak to her. The whole family knew what had happened. Her aunts and uncles and cousins did not know about her affair, but they knew that John Henry had committed suicide, and their eyes seemed almost accusing to Raphaella, as though they were saying again and again that it was her fault. It was easier for her not to see them, not to see their faces or their eyes, and now she sat in her room, again like a prisoner, waiting and envying John Henry for his courage. If she had had the same bottle of pills, she would have taken them too. She had nothing left to live for and she would have been grateful to die. But she also knew that she had to be punished, and dying was too easy. She would have to live on, knowing what she had done in San Francisco and enduring the looks and whispers of her family in Spain. She knew that forty or fifty years later they would still tell the story and suspect that there was more that they didn't know. By then perhaps word of Alex's existence would have accompanied the rest of the story. People would talk about Tia Raphaella who had cheated on her husband . . . you remember, he committed suicide . . . I don't know how old she was . . . maybe thirty . . . you know, she was really the one who killed him.

As she heard the words in her head, she dropped her face in her hands and began to cry. She cried for the children who would never know her or know the truth about what had happened to her here, she cried for Alex and what had almost been, for Mandy whom she would never see again, and at last for John Henry . . . for what he had done . . . for what he had once been . . . for the man who had loved her so long ago and proposed to her as they walked along the Seine. She sat alone in her room and cried for hours, and then silently she walked to his bedroom and looked around for a last time.

At nine o'clock her mother came upstairs to tell her that it was time to leave the house to catch their plane. They were taking the ten-thirty night flight to New York, which would get them in around six in the morning, New York time, and at seven o'clock they would catch the flight to Spain. The plane would arrive at eight o'clock that evening local time in Madrid. She had a long journey ahead of her, and a very long year. As the man who did their heavy cleaning picked up her two bags and took them downstairs, she walked slowly down the main staircase, knowing that she would never live here again. Her days in San Francisco were over. Her life with John Henry was gone now. Her moments with Alex had ended in disaster. Her life was, in a sense, over.

"Ready?" Her mother looked at her gently, and Raphaella looked at her with the empty eyes Alex had seen that morning, nodded, and walked out the door.

CHAPTER 32

In the spring she received, via San Francisco, a copy
of her children's book, which was due out sometime
late in July. She eyed it quietly, with a sense of distance. It seemed a thousand years since she had
started that project, and it seemed so unimportant
now. She felt nothing for it at all. As little in fact as
she now felt for the children, for her parents, her
cousins, or even for herself. She felt nothing for anyone. For five months she had moved like a zombie,
gotten up in the morning, dressed in her black clothes
of mourning, gone to breakfast, returned to her bedroom, answered the scores of letters they were still
forwarding to her from San Francisco, all of them letters of condolence to which she responded on the
heavily black-bordered stationery suited to the task.
At lunchtime she would emerge again from her bedroom, and immediately afterward she would once
again disappear. Now and then she would take a solitary walk before dinner, but she was careful to dis-

courage companionship and to beg off if someone insisted on coming along.

It was clear that Raphaella wanted to see no one, and that she was taking her year of mourning very much to heart. She had even decided immediately after her arrival that she had no desire to stay on in Madrid. She went to sequester herself at Santa Eugenia, to be alone, and at first her parents agreed. In Spain her mother and the rest of the family were accustomed to the business of mourning, they did it for a year, and the widows and children of the dead always wore solid black. And even in Paris it wasn't an entirely unusual thing. But the zeal with which Raphaella threw herself into her mourning struck everyone strangely. It was as though she were punishing herself and atoning for countless unspoken sins. After the first three months her mother suggested she go to Paris, but the suggestion met with an instant refusal. She wanted to stay at Santa Eugenia, she had no desire to go anywhere else. She shunned everyone's company, even her mother's. She did nothing anyone knew of except stay in her room, write her endless letters in response to the cards and letters of condolence, and go for her solitary walks.

Among the letters that came after her arrival was a long and heartfelt one from Charlotte Brandon, reaching out to the young woman. She told her bluntly but kindly that Alex had explained the circumstances of John Henry's passing and that she hoped that Raphaella would be wise enough not to blame herself. There was a long philosophical part of the letter, in which she wrote that she had known of him as a young man and she had gathered over the years that his infirmities must have come as a spirit-crushing blow, that in light of what he had been and then had become, in

light of his affection for Raphaella, his life must have
been a prison that he had longed to flee, and that what
he had done, while certainly difficult for those who
survived him to understand, may well have been the
final blessing for him. "Although a selfish act," Charlotte wrote to Raphaella, "it is one that I hope you will
come to accept and understand, without the ego-
centricity of self-accusation and self-flagellation." She
urged Raphaella to simply accept it, be kind to his
memory, and to herself, and move on. It was a plea to
Raphaella to be good to herself, whatever that might
mean.

It was the only letter to which Raphaella did not
respond immediately as she sat by herself for endless
hours in her ivory tower. The letter from Charlotte
languished for weeks on the desk, unanswered. Raphaella simply did not know what to say. In the end
she answered simply, expressing her gratitude for the
kind words and the woman's thoughts and hoping that
if she found herself in Europe she would stop at Santa
Eugenia and say hello. However painful for Raphaella
the mental association of Charlotte and Alex, she had
been fond enough of Charlotte in her own right, and
in time she would like to see her again. But when she
made the suggestion, she did not anticipate a note
from Charlotte in late June. She and Mandy had just
flown to London, as usual, to promote Charlotte's latest book. There was also going to be a movie tie-in so
she was very busy. She was scheduled to fly on to
Paris and then Berlin, but as long as she was in Europe, she was thinking of flying to Madrid to see some
friends. She and Mandy were longing to see Raphaella
and wondered if they could either lure her to Madrid
or drive to Santa Eugenia to see her for an afternoon.

They were willing to undertake the trip to see her, and Raphaella was deeply touched. Enough so that she didn't dare refuse to see them, but attempted to discourage them with kind words. She explained that it was awkward for her to leave Santa Eugenia, that her assistance was needed to keep an eye on the children and see that things ran smoothly for her mother's innumerable guests, none of which was true of course. Since the rest of the family had begun to arrive for the summer, Raphaella had been more elusive than ever, and often took her meals on a tray in her room. To the emotional Spaniards around her it didn't seem an unusual posture during mourning, but nonetheless her mother was growing increasingly concerned.

The letter that Raphaella addressed to Charlotte in Paris was put on the same silver salver where the family left all of its outgoing mail. But on the particular day Raphaella left it, one of the children scooped it all up in his knapsack to mail it in town when he went shopping for candies with his sisters and brothers, and the letter to Charlotte slipped out of his hand before he reached the box. Or at least that was the only explanation Raphaella could discover when Charlotte called her three weeks later, in July, having heard not a word.

"May we come to see you?" Raphaella faltered for a long moment, feeling at the same time rude and trapped.

"I . . . it's so hot here, you'd hate it . . . and you know, it's so awkward to get here, I hate to put you to so much trouble."

"Then come to Madrid." Charlotte's voice had been filled with good cheer.

"I really can't leave here, but I'd love to." It was a blatant lie.

"Well, then it looks as though we have no choice, do we? How about tomorrow? We can rent a car and come down after breakfast. How does that sound?"

"A three-hour drive, just to see me? Oh, Charlotte . . . I feel awful. . . ."

"Don't. We'd love to. Is that all right for you?" For a moment she wasn't sure if Raphaella really wanted them, and she suddenly wondered if she was pressing herself on her and Raphaella would rather not see them at all. Perhaps the link with Alex was still too painful for her to bear. But she sounded well to Charlotte, and when she answered again, she sounded as though she'd be pleased to see them.

"It'll be wonderful to see you both!"

"I can hardly wait to see you, Raphaella. And you'll barely recognize Mandy. Did you know she's going to Stanford in the fall?"

At her end of the conversation Raphaella smiled gently. Mandy . . . her Amanda . . . it pleased her to know that she would still be living with Alex. He needed her as much as she needed him. "I'm glad." And then she couldn't help asking. "And Kay?"

"She lost the election, you know. But you must have known that before you left. That was last year." As it so happened, she had known it, because she had seen it in the papers, but Alex had refused to discuss his sister with her during the brief revival of their relationship. For him there had been an irreparable break between them over Amanda, and Raphaella had often wondered what he would have done if he had known about Kay's letter to her father. He would probably have killed her. But Raphaella had never told him. And now she was just as glad. What did it matter? Their life together was over, and Kay was his sister after all. "Darling, we'll catch up on all this tomorrow. Can we bring you anything from Madrid?"

"Just yourselves." Raphaella smiled and hung up, but for the rest of the day she paced her room nervously. Why had she let them talk her into it? And what would she do when they came? She didn't want to see Charlotte or Amanda, didn't want any reminders of her past life. She was leading a new life now at Santa Eugenia. This was all she would allow herself to have. What was the point of staying in touch with the past?

When she came down to dinner that evening, her mother noticed the nervous tremor of her hands, and she made a mental note to herself to speak to Antoine. She thought that Raphaella should see a doctor. She had been looking ghastly for months. Despite the brilliant summer sunshine she stayed in her room and remained ghostly pale, she had lost fifteen or twenty pounds since she'd arrived from San Francisco, and she looked frankly unhealthy compared to the rest of her family, with her huge dark, unhappy eyes in the painfully gaunt, waiflike face.

She mentioned in passing to her mother however that she was having two guests from Madrid the next day. "Well, actually they're from the States."

"Oh?" Her mother looked at her warmly. It was a relief that she was seeing someone. She hadn't even wanted to see her old acquaintances in Spain. It was the most earnest period of mourning Alejandra had ever seen. "Who are they, darling?"

"Charlotte Brandon and her granddaughter."

"The writer?" Her mother looked surprised. She had read some of her books translated into Spanish and she knew that Raphaella had read them all. "Would you like them to spend the night?" Raphaella shook her head absently and went back upstairs to her room.

She was still there late the next morning when one of the servants came upstairs and knocked softly on her door. "Doña Raphaella . . . you have guests." She hardly even dared to disturb Raphaella. The door opened and the fifteen-year-old girl in the maid's uniform visibly quailed.

"Thank you." Raphaella smiled and walked to the stairs. She was so nervous that her legs felt like wooden posts beneath her. It was odd, but she hadn't seen any friends in so long that she didn't know what to say. Looking serious and a little frightened, in one of the elegant black summer dresses her mother had bought her in Madrid and still wearing the black stockings, she walked down the stairs, looking frighteningly pale.

At the foot of the stairs Charlotte waited, and she gave an unconscious start when she saw Raphaella approach. She had never seen anyone looking so anguished and unhappy, and she looked like a portrait of sorrow in her black dress with her huge grief-stricken eyes. There was instantly a smile there for Charlotte, but it was more like a sad reaching-out across an unbridgeable chasm. It was as though she had slipped into another world since she had last seen her, and as she watched her, Charlotte felt an almost irresistible urge to cry. She managed somehow to quell it and took the girl in her arms with a warm, tender hug. She realized as she watched the gaunt beauty hug Amanda that in some ways she was even more beautiful than before but it was the kind of beauty one only looked at, one never touched, and one never really came to know. Throughout their visit she was hospitable and gracious, charming to them both, as she showed them the house and the gardens, the historical chapel built by her great-grandfather, and introduced them to all the children who were playing with their nannies in a special garden built just for them. It was an extraordinary place to spend a summer, Charlotte found herself thinking, and it was a relic of another life, another world, but it was no place for a young woman like Raphaella to be buried, and it frightened her when Raphaella told her that she planned to stay there.

"Won't you go back to San Francisco?" Charlotte looked upset.

But Raphaella shook her head quickly. "No. Eventually I have to go back to close the house of course, but I may even be able to do that from here."

"Then won't you want to move to Paris or Madrid?"

"No." She said it firmly and then smiled at Amanda, but Amanda had said almost nothing. She had only stared at Raphaella for the most part since they had arrived. It was like seeing the ghost of someone they had once known. This wasn't Raphaella. It was a kind of broken dream. And like Charlotte, Mandy spent the afternoon trying not to cry. All she could think of were the times with Alex, when he and Raphaella had been so happy, when she had been there when Mandy got home from school every day. But now, as she looked at this woman, she was a stranger, someone different and foreign. She reminded Mandy of Raphaella, but nothing more than that. It was a relief when at last Raphaella suggested she go swimming, and as Raphaella had so long ago, she tried to work out her feelings with a long exhausting swim, which gave Charlotte an opportunity to be alone with Raphaella, something she had longed for all day. Now, as they sat side by side in comfortable chairs in a secluded corner of the garden, Charlotte looked at her with a tender smile.

"Raphaella . . . may I speak to you as an old friend?"

"Always." But the look of the frightened doe came to her quickly. She didn't want to answer any questions, didn't want to have to explain her decisions. This was her life now. And she didn't want it exposed to anyone but herself.

"I think you are tormenting yourself beyond anything that anyone can imagine. I see it in your face, in the haunted look in your eyes, in the way you speak. . . . Raphaella . . . what can I tell you? What can anyone say to set you free?" She had gone right to the heart of the matter in a single minute, and Raphaella turned her face away so that the older woman would not see the shimmer of tears in her eyes. She appeared to be looking at the garden, but slowly, sadly, she shook her head.

"I will never be free again, Charlotte."

"But you are imprisoning yourself in this life. You are wrapped in guilt over something I will never believe was your doing. Never. I will always believe that your husband was tired of living, and if you let yourself, I think you'd know that too."

"I don't know that. I never will. It doesn't matter anyway. I had a full life. I was married for fifteen years. I want nothing more. I am here now. I have come home."

"Except that it's not home to you anymore, Raphaella. And you're talking like an old woman."

Raphaella smiled. "That's how I feel."

"That's crazy." And then, on the spur of the moment, she looked Raphaella in the eye. "Why don't you come to Paris with us?"

"Now?" Raphaella looked shocked.

"We're going back to Madrid tonight and we fly back to Paris tomorrow. How does that sound?"

"Slightly mad." Raphaella smiled gently. It appealed to her not at all. She hadn't been to Paris in a year now, and she had absolutely no desire to go.

"Will you think about it?" Raphaella shook her head sadly.

"No, Charlotte. I want to stay here."

"But why? Why must you do this? It's not right for you."

"Yes," she said, nodding slowly, "it is." And then finally she dared to ask the question that had been on her mind all day long. "How is Alex? Is he all right now?" He had written to her twice and she had not answered, but she had seen in his letters that he was distraught over what had happened, and it was compounded by her removal, her silence, and her original insistence that they would not meet again.

Charlotte nodded slowly. "He's coping." But this had been much harder than his separation from Rachel, and she was no longer entirely certain that he would ever be quite the same. She wasn't sure whether or not she should say that to Raphaella. She wasn't sure that Raphaella could bear any more guilt than she was already carrying around. "You never wrote to him, did you?"

"No." She looked Charlotte squarely in the eye. "I thought it would be better for him if I cut the cord all at once."

"That was what you thought once before, wasn't it? And you were wrong that time too."

"That was different." Raphaella looked vague, remembering the scene in Paris with her father only a year before. How intense it had all been, how important, and now everything had changed and none of it mattered anymore. Kay had lost her precious election, she had lost Alex, John Henry was dead. . . . Raphaella glanced up at Charlotte now. "Kay wrote a letter to my father, telling him about the affair with Alex, begging him to stop us, which he did." Seeing how shocked she was by this revelation, she decided not to add the information about the letter to John Henry, which had been an even crueler act. She smiled at Alex's mother. "He threatened to tell my husband and he had me followed. He also insisted that I was being selfish and destroying Alex's life by keeping him from marrying and having children." She sighed softly. "That time I really felt I had no choice."

"And this time?"

"My father wanted me to come here for a year. He thought it was the least I could do"—her voice dropped to barely more than a whisper—"after killing John Henry."

"But you didn't kill him." A moment passed between them, and then, "What happens after the year? Will your family be unhappy if you leave here?"

"I don't know. It doesn't make any difference, Charlotte. I won't. This is where I belong. This is where I will stay."

"Why do you belong here?"

"I don't want to discuss it."

"Stop punishing yourself, dammit!" She reached out and took Raphaella's hands in her own. "You're a beautiful young woman with a fine mind and a good heart, you deserve a full, happy life, a husband, children . . . with Alex, or with someone else, that's up to you, but you can't bury yourself here, Raphaella."

Raphaella pulled her hands slowly out of Charlotte's. "Yes, I can. I can't live anywhere else with what I've done. Whoever I touched, whoever I loved, whoever I married, I would think of John Henry and of Alex. One man I killed and the other I nearly destroyed. What right do I have to touch the life of anyone else?"

"Because you have neither killed nor destroyed anyone. God, I wish I could get that across to you." But she knew that it was almost hopeless. Raphaella was locked in her private dungeon and could barely hear what was being said. "Then you won't come to Paris?"

"No." She smiled gently. "But I thank you for the invitation. And Mandy looks wonderful." It was the signal that Raphaella no longer wished to talk about herself. She was no longer willing to discuss her decisions. She suggested instead that they visit the rose gardens at the far end of the estate. After that they rejoined Amanda, and a little while later it was time for them to go. She watched them leave with a look of regret and then walked back into the big house and across the pink marble hallway and made her way slowly up the stairs.

As Charlotte drove their rented car through the main gates of Santa Eugenia, Amanda burst into tears. "But why wouldn't she come to Paris?"

There were tears in Charlotte's eyes as well. "Because she didn't want to, Mandy. She wants to bury herself alive here."

"Couldn't you talk to her?" Mandy blew her nose and dabbed at her eyes. "God, she looked awful. She looks like she died, not him."

"In a way I think she did." Charlotte let the tears roll down her cheeks as she turned onto the highway to Madrid.

CHAPTER 33

It was in September that Alejandra began to push Raphaella. The rest of the family had gone back to Barcelona and Madrid, and Raphaella was determined to sit out the winter at Santa Eugenia. She insisted that she wanted to work on another children's book, but it was a lame excuse. She had no interest in writing anymore and she knew it. But her mother insisted that Raphaella return with her to Madrid.

"I don't want to, Mother."

"Nonsense. It'll be good for you."

"Why? I can't go to the theater or the opera or any dinner parties."

Her mother looked pensive as she gazed at the wan, tired face before her. "It's been nine months, Raphaella. You could go out with me once in a while."

"Thank you. . . ." She looked bleakly at her mother. "But I want to stay here." The discussion had gone nowhere for over an hour, and as usual, afterward Raphaella had disappeared to her room. She would sit there for hours, looking out at the gardens, thinking, dreaming. There were fewer letters to answer now. And she never read books anymore. She just sat there, thinking, sometimes about John Henry, sometimes about Alex, and about moments they had shared. Then she would think about the trip to Paris, when her father had thrown her out of his house and called her a whore. After that she would think of the scene she had found when she came home that night, after John Henry . . . and then her father's arrival . . . his calling her a murderess. She would simply sit there, living in her memories and staring outside, seeing nothing, going nowhere, doing nothing, as she dwindled away. Her mother was even afraid to leave Santa Eugenia, there was something frightening about the way Raphaella behaved. She was so removed, so distracted, so distant, so indifferent. She never seemed to eat anymore, never spoke to anyone unless she had to, never entered into jokes or discussions or moments of laughter. It was ghastly to see her that way. But at the end of September her mother finally insisted.

"I don't care what you say, Raphaella. I'm taking you back to Madrid. You can lock yourself up there." Besides, she was tired of the dreary autumn in the country. She herself was hungry for amusement, she couldn't understand how a young woman of thirty-four could bear the life she led. So Raphaella packed her bags and went with her, saying nothing on the drive and then going upstairs to the large suite of rooms she always occupied in her mother's house. No one even seemed to notice her anymore as she drifted among them. The aunts or the cousins or the brothers or the uncles. They had simply come to accept her the way she now was.

Her mother began the season with a round of parties, there was music and dancing and laughter in the house. She endorsed several benefits and took large groups to the opera, gave large and small dinners, and seemed to constantly entertain an army of friends. By the first of December Raphaella could no longer stand it. It seemed as though every time she went downstairs there were forty people waiting there in evening dresses and black ties. And her mother had flatly refused to allow her to continue to eat in her rooms. She insisted that it was unhealthy, and even though she was in mourning, she could at least eat with her mother's guests. Besides, it did her good to see people, her mother insisted, but Raphaella didn't agree. At the end of the first week of December she decided to get away and picked up the phone. She made a reservation on a plane to Paris, figuring that a few days in the solemnity of her father's quarters would be something of a relief. She always wondered how the two of them had stood each other, her mother so gregarious, so flighty, so social, her father so serious and so austere. But the answer of course was that her mother lived in Madrid, while her father stayed in Paris. Nowadays he very seldom came to Spain. He felt he was too old for Alejandra's frivolous entertainments, and Raphaella had to admit that she had come to feel that way herself.

She called her father to let him know that she was coming, but assumed that it would present no particular problem for him. She had a room in his house too. He was not home when she called his number, but the phone was answered by a new maid. She decided then to surprise him and reminded herself that she hadn't been in the house since the year before when he had confronted her about the affair with Alex. But now for nine months she had atoned for at least some of her sins, with her agonizing monastic life in Spain. She knew that her father approved of what she was doing, and after the ferocity of his accusations it was a relief to know that he might approve of her a little more now.

The plane to Paris was half empty. She took a taxi in from Orly Airport and stood for a moment looking up at the splendor of her father's house when she arrived. In a way it always felt odd to be back there. This was the house she had lived in as a child, and she could never quite return without feeling somehow as though she weren't a woman but was once more that small child. The house also reminded her of John Henry, his early trips to Paris, their long walks in the Luxembourg Gardens, and their meandering along the Seine.

She rang the doorbell and the door was opened, again by an unfamiliar face. It was a maid in a starched uniform with a sour face and thick black eyebrows who looked at her inquiringly as the taxi driver brought her bags inside.

"Yes?"

"I am Madame Phillips, Monsieur de Mornay-Malle's daughter." The little maid nodded at her, looking neither impressed nor interested in her arrival, and Raphaella smiled. "Is my father at home?"

The young woman nodded with an odd look in her eyes. "He's . . . upstairs." It was eight o'clock in the evening and Raphaella hadn't been entirely sure that she would find her father at home. But she knew that he would either be in, dining alone, or out for the evening. She ran no risk of encountering a party like those at her mother's, with dancing, laughing couples drifting through the halls. Her father was a good deal less social and he preferred to meet people in restaurants instead of at home.

Raphaella nodded pleasantly again at the woman. "I'll go up to see him. Would you be so kind as to have one of the men bring the bags up to my room in a while?" And then, realizing that the woman might not know which one it was, "The big blue bedroom on the second floor."

"Oh," said the maid, and then suddenly she clamped her mouth shut as though she couldn't bring herself to say more. "Yes, madame." She nodded her head at Raphaella and hurried back to the pantry as Raphaella walked slowly up the stairs. There was no particular joy for her in coming back here, but it was peaceful at least, and it was a relief after the constant movement in the house in Spain. She realized as she reached the second landing that after she sold the house in San Francisco she would have to set up an establishment of her own. She was thinking of buying a little piece of land near Santa Eugenia and putting up a small house adjoining the main grounds. While it was under construction, she could live peacefully at Santa Eugenia. It would give her the perfect excuse not to be in town. All of that was part of what she wanted to discuss with her father. He had been handling the estate for her since she had left San Francisco, and now she wanted to know where things stood. In a few more months she wanted to go back to California and close up the house for good.

She hesitated for a moment in front of her father's

study, looking at the elaborately carved double doors, and then she walked on quietly to her own room, to take off her coat, wash her hands, and comb her hair. There was no rush to see her father. She assumed that he would probably be reading in his library or going over some papers, smoking a cigar.

Without stopping to think of what she was doing, she turned the large brass knob and stepped into the anteroom of her old room. There were two sets of double doors that sealed off the entrance, and she passed through one set and then casually opened the next one and walked into the room. But there was the suddenly startling feeling of having walked into the wrong apartment. There was a tall heavyset blond woman seated at her dressing table, wearing a blue lace peignoir ringed with a soft fluff of feathers around the neck, and when she stood up to face Raphaella with a look of audacious inquiry, Raphaella saw that her blue satin slippers matched her robe. For an endless moment Raphaella only stood there, not able to understand who the woman was.

"Yes?" With an air of authority she gazed at Raphaella, and for a moment Raphaella thought that she was going to be told to leave her own room. And then suddenly she realized that it was quite obvious that her father had house guests, and here she had arrived totally unannounced. But it was no problem really. She could sleep in the large yellow and gold guest room on the third floor. It did not occur to her as she stood there that it was odd that her father's houseguests did not have that room instead of hers.

"I'm terribly sorry. . . . I thought—" She didn't know whether to advance and introduce herself or back out saying nothing at all.

"Who let you in here?"

"I'm not sure. There seems to be a new maid." She smiled pleasantly and the woman advanced on her angrily, and for a moment Raphaella got the feeling that this was the heavy-set woman's house. "Who are you?"

"Raphaella Phillips." She blushed faintly and the woman stopped in her tracks. And as Raphaella watched her she got the feeling that she had met this woman somewhere before. There was something vaguely familiar about the heavily lacquered blond helmet, the set of her eyes, something about her, but Raphaella couldn't place it, and with that, her father came in through the boudoir door. He was wearing a dark red silk bathrobe, and he looked pomaded and clean and perfectly groomed, but all he wore was the bathrobe, hanging slightly open, his legs and feet bare, and the gray tufts on his chest peeking through the open robe. "Oh. . . ." Raphaella backed toward the door as though she had walked into a room she should never have entered. As she did so she realized that it was exactly what she had done. She had walked right into an assignation, and as the realization of that hit her the woman's identity struck her with full force. "Oh, my God." And then Raphaella just stood there, staring at her father and the blond woman, who was the wife of the most inportant Cabinet minister in France.

"Please leave, us Georgette." His tone was austere but his face looked nervous, and the woman flushed and turned away. "Georgette. . . ." He spoke to her softly, nodding toward the boudoir, and she disappeared and he faced his daughter, pulling the robe tightly closed. "May I ask what you're doing here like this, unannounced, and in this room?"

She looked at him for a long time before answering, and suddenly the rage that she should have felt a year earlier washed over her with a force she could neither stop nor resist. Step by step she advanced toward him with a light in her eyes he had never seen there before. Instinctively his hand went out to the back of the chair near him, and something inside him trembled as he faced his child.

"What am *I* doing here, Papa? I came to visit you. I thought I'd come to see my father in Paris. Is that surprising? Perhaps I should have called, and spared Madame the embarrassment of being recognized, but I thought it might be more amusing to come as a surprise. And the reason I am standing in this room, Father, is because it used to be mine. But I think what is far more to the point is what *you* are doing in this room, Father. You with the saintly morals and the endless speeches. You who threw me out of this house over a year ago and called me a whore. You who called me a murderess because I 'killed' my seventy-seven-year-old husband who had been almost dead for nine years. And what if Monsieur le Ministre has a stroke tomorrow, Papa, then will you be a murderer too? What if he has a heart attack? What if he finds out he has cancer and kills himself because he can't bear it, then will you bear the guilt and punish yourself as you've punished me? What if your affair with his wife ends his political career? And what about her, Papa? What about her? What are you keeping her from? What right do you have to this while my mother sits in Madrid? What right do you have that I did not have a year ago with a man I loved? What right . . . ? How dare you! How dare you!" She stood before him, trembling and shouting in his face.

"How dare you have done to me what you did last year. You threw me out of this house and sent me to Spain that night because you said you would not have a whore under your roof. Well, you have a whore under your roof, Papa." She pointed hysterically at the boudoir, and before he could stop her, she strode to the door, where she found the minister's wife sitting on the edge of a Louis XVI chair, crying softly into a handkerchief as Raphaella looked down at her. "Good day, madame."

Then she turned to her father. "And good-bye. I will not spend a night under the same roof as a whore either, and you, Papa, are the whore, not Madame here, and not I. You are . . . you are. . . ." She began to sob hysterically. "What you said to me last year almost killed me . . . for almost a year I've tortured myself over what John Henry did, while everyone else told me that I was innocent, that he did it because he was so old and so sick and so miserable. Only *you* accused me of killing him and called me a whore. *You* said that I disgraced you, that I had risked a scandal that would destroy *your* good name. And what about *you*, damn you? What about *her?*" She waved vaguely at the woman in the blue peignoir. "Don't you think this would be a scandal to top all scandals? What about *your* servants? What about Monsieur le Ministre? What about the voters? What about your clients at the bank? Don't you care about them? Or is it that *I* am the only one who can be disgraceful? My God, what I did was so much less than this. And you have a right to this, if it's what you want. Who am I to tell you what you can and can't do, what's wrong and what isn't? But how dare you call me names. How dare you do what you did to me." She hung her head for a moment, sobbing, and then glared at him again. "I will never forgive you, Papa . . . never. . . ."

He looked like a broken man as he stared at her, his aging body hanging loosely in the bathrobe, his face registering the pain of what she had just said. "Raphaella . . . I was wrong . . . I was wrong. . . . This happened afterward. I swear it. It started this summer. . . ."

"I don't give a damn when it started." She fired the words at him as he stood looking at her and at his mistress, crying in her chair. "When I did it, you called me a killer. Now that it's you, it's all right. I would have spent the rest of my life at Santa Eugenia, eating out my soul. And do you know why? Because of what you said. Because I believed you. Because I felt so desperately guilty that I accepted all the misery you heaped on my head." She shook her head then and walked out of the boudoir to the door of the main room. He followed her, looking lamely after her, and she stopped for only an instant at the door to look back at him with an expression of scorn.

"Raphaella . . . I'm sorry. . . ."

"What are you sorry about, Father? That I found you out? Would you have come to tell me? Would you have told me that you had changed your mind, that I hadn't killed my husband? Would you have let me know that you'd thought things over and perhaps you were wrong? Just when would you have told me? If I hadn't walked in on you, just when would you have come to me and said that? When?"

"I don't know. . . ." His voice was a hoarse whisper. "In time . . . I would have. . . ."

"Would you?" She shook her head firmly. "I don't believe you. You'd never have done it. And all the

while you'd have been carrying on here with your
mistress and I would have buried myself in Spain.
Can you live with yourself knowing that? Can you?
The only one who has destroyed anyone's life, Father,
is you. You almost destroyed mine."

And with that, she slammed the door. She was
down the stairs in a moment and saw her bags still
standing in the hall. With a trembling hand she picked
up a bag in each hand, slipped her handbag over her
shoulder, opened the door, and marched out of the
house to find the nearest taxi stand. She knew there
was one around the corner, and she didn't give a
damn if she had to walk to the airport, she was going
back to Spain. She was still trembling and shaken
when she finally found a taxi, and when she told the
driver to take her to Orly, she put her head back on
the seat and closed her eyes as she stealthily wiped
the tears from her cheeks.

She was suddenly filled with hatred and anger for
her father. What a bastard he was, what a hypocrite.
What about her mother? What about all the accusations he'd made? All the things he'd said . . . ? But as
she raged silently to herself all the way to the airport,
she found herself thinking that in truth he was only human, as human as her mother probably was, as human
as she herself had been, maybe as human as John
Henry himself had been once upon a time. Maybe she
really hadn't killed John Henry. Maybe in fact he simply hadn't wanted to go on.

As she flew home to Madrid she stared into the
night sky and mulled it all over, and for the first time
in close to a year she felt free of the agonizing weight
of her own burdens of guilt and pain. She found herself feeling sorry for her father and suddenly laughing

softly to herself at the vision of him in his red robe, and the heavyset middle-aged mistress in the peignoir with the feathers around her fat neck. As the plane landed in Madrid she was laughing softly, and she was still grinning when she got off the plane.

CHAPTER 34

The next morning Raphaella came down to breakfast, and although her face was as pale and gaunt as it had been for a year, there was a different light in her eyes, and as she drank her coffee she answered her mother lightheartedly that she had discussed all her business with her father and had decided to come home.

"But in that case why didn't you just call him?"

"Because I thought it would take longer than it did."

"But that's silly. Why didn't you stay and visit with your father?"

Raphaella put down her coffee cup quietly. "Because I wanted to get back here as soon as I could, Mother."

"Oh?" Alejandra sensed something brewing and carefully watched her daughter's eyes. "Why?"

"I'm going home."

"To Santa Eugenia?" Alejandra looked annoyed.

"Oh, not that again, for heaven's sake. At least stay in Madrid until Christmas, and then we'll all be there together. But I don't want you there now. It's much too dreary at this time of year."

"I know it is, and that's not where I'm going. I meant San Francisco."

"What?" Her mother looked stunned. "Is that what you discussed with your father? What did he say?"

"Nothing." Raphaella almost smiled at the memory of the red bathrobe. "It's my decision." What she had learned about her father had finally freed her. "I want to go home."

"Don't be ridiculous. This is your home, Raphaella." She waved around her at the elaborate house that had been in the family for a hundred fifty years.

"Yes, partly. But I have a home there too. I want to go back there."

"And do what?" Her mother looked unhappy. First she had hidden at Santa Eugenia like a wounded animal, and now she wanted to flee. But she had to admit that there was something alive there. It was only a glimpse . . . a glimmer . . . but it was a reminder of the woman Raphaella had once been. She was still strangely quiet, oddly private, even now she would not say what she was going to do. Alejandra found herself wondering if she had heard from that man again, if that was why she was going, and if that was the case, she was not very pleased. It wasn't quite a year since the death of her husband after all. "Why don't you wait until the spring?"

Raphaella shook her head. "No. I'm going now."

"When?"

"Tomorrow." She decided as she said it and put down her coffee cup and looked her mother in the eye. "And I don't know how long I'll stay, or when I'll be back. I may sell the house there, I may not. I just don't know. The only thing I do know is that when I walked out on everything I had there I was in shock. I have to go back." Her mother knew that it was true. But she was afraid to lose her. She didn't want Raphaella to stay in the States. She belonged in Spain.

"Why don't you just let your father take care of everything for you?" It was what Alejandra would have done herself.

"No." Raphaella looked at her firmly. "I'm not a child anymore."

"Do you want to take one of your cousins?"

Raphaella smiled gently. "No, Mother. I'll be fine."

She attempted to discuss it several more times with Raphaella, but to no avail, and it was too late when Antoine received her message. The next day, with trembling hands, he picked up the phone and called Spain. He thought that perhaps Raphaella had told her, that his own marriage was going to explode now in a burst of flame. But what he learned was only that Raphaella had flown back to California that morning. It was too late to stop her, but Alejandra wanted him to call her and tell her to come home.

"I don't think she'll listen, Alejandra."

"She'll listen to you, Antoine." He heard the words with a sudden vision of the scene Raphaella had walked in on two days before and he found himself suddenly very grateful that she hadn't told her mother. Now he only shook his head.

"No, she won't listen to me, Alejandra. Not anymore."

CHAPTER 35

The plane landed at San Francisco Internationl Airport at three o'clock in the afternoon on a brilliantly clear December day. The sun was shining brightly, the air was warm, the wind brisk, and Raphaella took a deep breath, wondering how she had survived without that crisp air. It felt good in her soul just to be there, and when she checked her bags out of customs herself, she felt strong and free and independent as she walked outside with the porter and hailed a cab. There was no limousine waiting for her this time, there had been no special exit from the plane. She hadn't asked to be escorted through customs. She had come through just like everyone else, and it felt good. She was tired of being hidden and protected. She knew that it was time she took care of herself. She had called ahead to tell John Henry's staff that she was coming, there were only a few people at the house now anyway. The others had all been let go by her father, some with pensions, some with small sums left to them by John Henry, but all with regret at the era they saw close. They all believed that Raphaella would never come back again, and it was with amazement that the remaining few had heard that she was on her way.

When the cab pulled up in front of the mansion and she rang the doorbell, she was greeted with warmth and friendly smiles. They were all happy to see her, happy to have someone in the house again besides each other, although they all suspected that her return was an omen of further change. That evening they fixed her a handsome dinner, with turkey and stuffing, and sweet potatoes and asparagus, and a wonderful apple pie. In the pantry they all commented on how painfully thin she had gotten and how unhappy she looked, how tired, and how they had never seen such sad eyes. But she looked better than she had looked at Santa Eugenia for the past year, not that any of them could have known that.

To please them she had eaten in the dining room, and afterward she wandered slowly around the house. It looked sad somehow, empty, unloved, a relic of another era, and as she looked around her she knew that it was time to bring it to a close. If she stayed in San Francisco, which she was not at all sure of, she would have no need of a house like this. She knew as she wandered slowly upstairs that it would always depress her. She would always remember John Henry here, diminished as he had been in his last years.

In a way she was tempted to stay in San Francisco, but if she did, she would need a much smaller house . . . like Alex's house on Vallejo. . . . Despite all her efforts not to let it do that, her mind drifted once again back to him. It was impossible to walk into her bedroom and not think of all the nights when she'd waited impatiently to go to him. She thought of it now as she stood looking around her, wondering how he was, what had happened, what he'd done with his life in the last year. She had never heard again from Amanda or Charlotte, and she somehow suspected that she would not again. Nor did she plan to contact them . . . or Alex. . . . She had no intention of calling him to tell him she was back. She had come to face the memories of John Henry, to close the house, to pack up his belongings, to face herself. She no longer thought of herself entirely as a killer, but if she was going to live with what had happened, she knew that she had to deal with it, where it had happened, and face it all squarely before she went on, to stay in San Francisco or to go back to Spain. Where she stayed was no longer important. But how she felt about what had happened would determine the whole course of her life. She knew that all too well, and she roved restlessly from room to room now, trying not to think of Alex, not to let her mind wander, not even to allow herself to feel guilty again for the way that John Henry had died.

It was almost midnight when she finally had the courage to walk into his bedroom. She stood there for a long moment, looking around, remembering the hours she had spent with him, reading to him, talking, listening, eating dinners on trays. And then for some reason she remembered the poems he had been so fond of, and as though she had always meant to do that, she walked slowly to the bookcase and began to look over the books. She found the slim volume on the bottom shelf where someone had put it. Much of the time he had kept it on the night table next to his bed.

She remembered now that she had seen it there the next morning . . . the night after. . . . She found herself wondering now if he had been reading it when he died. It was an odd, romantic notion that was not very likely to have had much to do with the truth, but she felt close to him again as she sat down near the bed, holding the slim volume and remembering the first time they had read it together, on their honeymoon in the South of France. This was the same volume he had bought when he was a very young man. Now, smiling softly, she began to leaf through it and stopped suddenly at a familiar passage where the book had been marked with a single blue page. As the book opened to where the paper had been inserted, her heart suddenly leaped strangely as she realized that the single sheet was covered in the shaky scrawl John Henry had developed in his final years. It was as though he had left her something, some message, some last words. . . . And then, as she began to read, she realized that that was precisely what he had done, and glancing at the foot of the letter, her eyes filled with tears.

She read the words again as the blur of tears began slowly to spill down her cheeks.

My darling Raphaella,

It is an endless evening, at the conclusion of an endless lifetime. A rich lifetime. A richer one because of you. What a priceless gift you have been, my darling. One perfect, flawless diamond. You have never ceased to fill me with awe, to bring me pleasure, to give me joy. Now I can only beg you to forgive me. I have thought of this for so long. I have wanted for such a long time to be

free. I go now, without your permission, but I
hope with your blessing. Forgive me, my darling.
I leave you with all the love I have ever had to
give. And think of me not as gone, but as free.
With all my heart,

John Henry.

She read the words again and again. "Think of me
not as gone, but as free." He had left her a letter after
all. The relief was so overwhelming that she could
barely move. He had asked her to forgive *him*. How
absurd it all was. And how wrong she had been. Not
gone . . . but free. She thought of him that way now,
and she blessed him, as he had begged her to a year
before. And the blessing was returned. Because suddenly, for the first time in a year, Raphaella felt free
as well. She walked slowly through the house, knowing they were both free. She and John Henry. He had
moved on, as he had wanted to so badly. He had cho-
sen the path that was right for him. And now she was
free to do the same. She was free to leave . . . to
move on. . . . She was whole again. And suddenly
she wanted to call Alex to tell him about the letter,
but she knew that she could not. It would have been a
cruelty beyond words to step back into his life after
all that time. But she wanted so much to tell him.
They hadn't killed John Henry after all. He had simply
moved on.

As she walked slowly back to her bedroom at three
o'clock that morning, she thought of both men, tenderly, lovingly, and she loved them both more than
she had in a long time. They were all free now . . .
all three of them. At last.

* * *

She called the real-estate agent the next morning, listed the house, called several museums, the libraries at both the University of California and Stanford, and a moving company, asking for several men and some boxes and tape. It was time to go now. She had made up her mind. She wasn't sure where she was going, or what she would do, but it was time to get out of the house that had been John Henry's and never hers. Maybe it was even time to go back to Europe, but of that she was not yet sure. With John Henry's letter she was absolved of her "sin." She folded it neatly and put it in her handbag. She wanted to put it in the bank with some of her important papers. It was the most important piece of paper she had ever owned.

By the end of the week she had made her endowments to the museums, and the two universities she had called had divided up the books. She kept only a handful of the ones she had shared with John Henry, and of course the book of poems in which he had left the last letter to her the night he died. She had already gotten a phone call from her father and she told him about the letter. There had been a long silence at his end of the phone then, and when he spoke to her again, his voice was husky as he apologized for all that he had said. She assured him that she bore him no malice, but as they hung up they each wondered how one got back a year, how one took back words that could never be unsaid, how one put balm on wounds that might never heal. But it was John Henry who had bandaged up Raphaella's anguish, he who had given her the finest gift of all with the letter—the truth.

It all seemed like a dream as Raphaella and the servants packed the last of the boxes. It had taken them a little less than two weeks, and by the following week, on Christmas, Raphaella planned to be back in Spain. There was really no reason for her to be here. The house was all but sold to a woman who was madly in love with it, but whose husband needed just a little more time to make up his mind about their final bid. The furniture was all going to auction, except for a few small pieces she was sending to her mother in Spain. There was really nothing left for her to do there, and in a few days Raphaella would move to a hotel for her last nights before leaving San Francisco for good. Only the memories remained now, drifting through the house like old ghosts. Memories of dinners in the dining room with John Henry, Raphaella wearing silk dresses and pearls . . . of evenings in front of the fire . . . of the first time she had seen the house. She would have to pack up the memories and take them with her, she told herself as they finished packing, exactly one week before Christmas, at six o'clock. It was already dark out and the cook had made her a dinner of eggs and bacon, which was precisely what she wanted, and with a stretch and a sigh she looked around John Henry's mansion as she sat on the floor in a pair of old khaki slacks. Everything was ready for the movers to take to the auctioneers and to the shipping company, which would be sending on to Spain the few things that she wanted. But as she sat finishing the last of her eggs and bacon, her mind drifted again to Alex and the day they had met again on the beach, exactly a year before. She wondered if she would see him again if she went back there, but she smiled to herself at the improbability of it. That dream was over now too.

When she finished the eggs, she took her plates back to the kitchen. The last of the help would be leaving in a few days, and it was strangely pleasant, she had discovered, to take care of her own needs in the oddly dismantled house. But now there were no books to read, no letters to write, no television to watch. She thought, for the first time, of going to a movie but decided instead to go for a brief walk and then go to bed. She still had some things to do the next morning and she had to go down to the airline to get her return ticket to Spain.

Glancing at the view now and then, she wandered slowly down Broadway, looking at the sedately handsome houses and knowing that she wouldn't miss them when she left. The house that she had missed so acutely was much smaller, much simpler, with painted beige and white trim and bright flowers in the front garden in the spring. Almost as though her feet knew what her head was thinking, she found herself walking in that direction, until she turned the corner and saw that it was only a block away. She didn't really want to see it. Yet somehow she knew that she wanted to be there, to sense once again the love she had known there. She had said good-bye at last to the house she had known with John Henry, now it was as though she had to let go of the place where she had known Alex too. And maybe then she would be free to find another home, a place of her own this time, and maybe one day a man she could love, as she had loved Alex, and John Henry before that.

She felt almost invisible as she walked there, drawn by some powerful lure she couldn't really explain. It was as though she had waited all week to come here, to see it again, to acknowledge all it had meant to her, and to say good-bye, not to the people, but the place. The house was dark when she got there, and she knew that no one was inside. She wondered even if he were away, in New York maybe, and then she remembered that Mandy was in college. Perhaps she had gone home already for Christmas vacation, to Kay, or to Hawaii again, with Charlotte. All of those people seemed suddenly so far from Raphaella's life, and she stood there for a long time, looking up at the windows, remembering, feeling all that she had felt there, wishing Alex well, wherever he might be. What she did not see as she stood there was that the garage door had opened and the black Porsche had stopped at the corner, the tall dark-haired man at the wheel sitting and staring. He was almost certain that it was Raphaella standing across the street from the house, looking up at the windows, but he knew that it wasn't possible, that it was an illusion, a dream. The woman who stood there, dreamily staring, seemed taller and much thinner and she wore old khaki pants and a thick white sweater, with her hair tied in a familiar knot. The silhouette was much like Raphaella's, as was something about her expression, from what he could see at that distance, but he knew that Raphaella was in Spain, and according to his mother she had just about given up life. He had lost all hope of being able to reach her. She had never answered his letters, and from what his mother had said she was beyond hope. She had cut herself off from everything she had once cared about, given up dreaming and being and feeling. It had almost killed him for a year, but now he had made his peace with what was. Just as he had learned that he couldn't go on tormenting himself over Rachel, he had also learned that he couldn't hang on to Raphaella anymore. She didn't want him to. He had understood that much, and so, reluctantly, after a year of sorrow he had given up. But he would always remember . . . always. . . . He had never loved any woman as he had loved her.

And then, deciding that the woman outside his house wasn't Raphaella, he put the car back into gear and drove into the garage. Across the street the boy who so passionately loved the black Porsche came out and stood gazing at the car with his usual awe. He and Alex were friends now. One day Alex had even given him a ride down the block. But now it wasn't the boy who caught Alex's attention. It was the woman's face that he saw in his rearview mirror. It was she . . . it was. He got out of the low-slung Porsche as quickly as his long legs would allow and darted rapidly under the automatic door just before it closed. And then suddenly he stood there, barely moving, only watching her, as across the street she stood trembling, watching him. Her face was much thinner, her eyes larger, her shoulders seemed to sag a little in the clothes she had worn to pack boxes, and she looked tired. But it was Raphaella, the woman he had dreamed of for so long and had finally understood he would never see again. And now suddenly she was here, watching him, and he wasn't quite sure if she was laughing or crying. There was a small smile on her lips, but the streetlights caught the shimmer of a tear drifting slowly from her eye.

Alex said nothing, he only stood there, and then slowly she began to come toward him, carefully, as though she were fording a stream that ran between them. The tears began to run swiftly down her cheeks, but the smile widened, and now he smiled at her. He wasn't sure why she was there, if she had come to see him, or only to stand there and remember and dream.

But now that he had seen her, he wouldn't let her leave him. Not again, not this time. Suddenly he took the last steps toward her and pulled her into his arms. His lips were on hers and he could feel his heart pounding as he held her, and then hers as he pressed her still closer and kissed her again. They stood in the middle of the street, kissing, but there were no cars around them. There was only one small boy who had come to see the black Porsche and had wound up seeing them kissing instead. But it was the Porsche that filled him with wonder, not the two grown-ups clinging to each other in the middle of Vallejo, laughing softly as the man wiped the tears from the woman's eyes. They kissed one last time as they stood there, and then slowly, arm in arm, they walked into his garden and disappeared into the house as the boy shrugged his shoulders, glanced for a last time at the garage that housed his dream car, and went home.